INTO THE EMBRACE OF FIRE

Into The Embrace Of Fire

Farshad Torkashvand

Copyright © 2022 by Farshad Torkashvand.

Library of Congress Control Number:		2021925211
ISBN:	Hardcover	978-1-6698-0430-7
	Softcover	978-1-6698-0429-1
	eBook	978-1-6698-0428-4

All rights reserved. No part of this book may be reproduced or transmitted in any form or by any means, electronic or mechanical, including photocopying, recording, or by any information storage and retrieval system, without permission in writing from the copyright owner.

This is a work of fiction. Names, characters, places and incidents either are the product of the author's imagination or are used fictitiously, and any resemblance to any actual persons, living or dead, events, or locales is entirely coincidental.

Any people depicted in stock imagery provided by Getty Images are models, and such images are being used for illustrative purposes only. Certain stock imagery © Getty Images.

Print information available on the last page.

Rev. date: 12/14/2021

To order additional copies of this book, contact:
Xlibris
844-714-8691
www.Xlibris.com
Orders@Xlibris.com
747214

Contents

Chapter 1 1

Chapter 2 7

Chapter 3 26

Chapter 4 27

Chapter 5 33

Chapter 6 34

Chapter 7 38

Chapter 8 43

Chapter 9 46

Chapter 10 51

Chapter 11 62

Chapter 12 65

Chapter 13 83

Chapter 14 118

Chapter 15 130

Chapter 16 137

Chapter 17 154

Chapter 18 171

Chapter 19 211

Chapter 20 239

Chapter 21 319

Final Chapter 349

Chapter 1

Try to imagine a mathematician who has trained himself to think his whole life objectively. Now he wants to write his biography. He wants to tell the deranged story that he had, the things that changed him entirely to the last cell in his body.

How boring would it be?

What made me think I could do that was realizing that I had a common ground with other people. I have read novels, books, and magazines about human relationships and their suffering to the extent of madness and self-destruction. And in all, people tend to go to the same road. The road is called Love. People are still using it. Thousands of years have passed since we became *Homo sapiens*. We evolved as a being. We got smarter and taller and everything else about us—our belief, taste in food, affection, and even our choices of God. So did "Love." It is a touchy subject for everyone. Aren't we pursuing it every day of our lives? Is it our mistake or parental teaching that we never understood the meaning of it?

The common ground tells me that I can do this biography since I have feelings like anybody else. I get hurt when I get rejected. It becomes a joy of my life to see the laugh of the person I am attracted to, and I get sad when I find out that the feeling she had isn't the same way I had. These and many other things brought me to the conclusion that I am human like anybody else and capable of having feelings. I don't know what kind of reader is going to read this book, but I am sure that my story, like anybody else's, is going to be interesting. Since this is my story, I want to share it the way I like it.

But before that, let me tell you an old story about the moth's love and the candle.

In the nighttime, an eclipse of moths gathered together, desiring to find the mystery behind the candle's light. In unison, they said, "One of us should go find the secret behind what we are looking for."

One of the moths went afar, saw a candle in the castle, and observed how it shone through the darkness. He came back and told the others what he had seen as much as he could. But the wise moth, the leader of their assembly, perceived, "That is not the secret of the candle."

Another moth rose and visited the candle, and this time, he drew near it. He touched the flame by his wings. He whirled and twirled around it, but the heat of the candle drove him away.

The candle was victorious, and the moth was defeated.

He returned and told them his part of the story, but the sagacious moth said to him, "Your explanation is no better than your comrade."

A third moth rose, drunk and inebriated; he went and sat on the candle. Embracing the candle and its fire, he became one with the candle. His body became the same color as the light that it sought.

The knowledgeable moth saw the whole thing from afar. He saw how the candle identified itself with that moth, and then he said, "Only this moth knows the secret and no one else. Who could tell the mystery of the candle but he?"

The story usually starts with the childhood of the people, how they became the people who they are now. But I want to break the unwritten law and start writing the way I like. It is going to be chaotic, but it is going to be fun.

My story starts with believing in love. Should I believe in it? Or should I try to find the truth about it?

Well, let's see. Do I believe in it?

Many years ago, someone thought that I was the love of her life. She had this notion that if I were with her, she would be the happiest girl in the world—same old cliché. She didn't see what was coming; neither did I.

On the morning of my final exam, I finished my test and was waiting for my ride, then I saw a woman or, should I say, a mother. She had this motherly look all over her face, from wearing cheap dresses to not even trying to put so much effort into putting some makeup on her face. She didn't care at all about her appearance. If it weren't for her kid's embarrassment, I believe, she wouldn't put that effort either. It was interesting to look at her. It made me curious what she was thinking. Do all mothers do the same things? So I looked around, and I saw that most mothers had the same figures. It was like all of them came and went to the same lousy mall. They didn't care about their appearance. Still, I could see the beauty they had. Some of them colored their hair to golden blond, and some hid their white hair in black or red. Their bellies puffed from the experience they had from giving birth. I could see the dust of life was heavy on their faces, and it pulled down some faces with it.

I looked back to the woman who made my morning different. She was sitting on the chair and was looking far away. She wasn't looking at anything. It was obvious. Anyone with good observational eyes could tell you the same. She was instead thinking. I don't know what she was thinking. I wanted to give her at least this little privacy she got. She was drowning in her own thoughts. Maybe she was thinking about what she should do if her daughter or her son goes to college. Is it going to be okay? What's going to happen to her baby kid then? She invested too much to let it be a failure. She wanted the best things for her youngster. She always does, doesn't she? What would happen to her little one when she is GONE? Is it okay to leave them now? Are they going to be Okay? What if her kid met terrible people? Draw her teenage boy or girl to do the wrong things, to do drugs, to smoke, to be a parent without knowing it? What if her child became successful? Is it going to be okay then? What if people started abusing her baby? Someone marries her adolescent child since her youngster is a successful person, not because of how wonderful her young one is? Or people, because of their envies, put her sweet child in difficult situations? Her fine, loving tot must make long hours work to satisfy those people. Or because of the laziness of some people, her baby must endure all the responsibility? Oh, her sweet, loving child. The kid is too young to have that kind of hardship. She wished she could do something about it. Of course, still, her stripling is in need—in need of her guidance—so she had to be strong. As long as she lives, no soul can harm her sweet, loving child. She could still remember when she gave birth to this beautiful creature, and she is thankful to the universe for giving her this beautiful gift.

The moment she saw her toddler, she fell in love with it. There was something that clouded her vision at the moment that wouldn't let her see her child. Oh, that silly tears. What untimely moment it had to come. For God's sake, even her nose was running. Droplets blinded her, so she wiped it out. She didn't want to lose a second of not seeing her kiddie. She became deaf from hearing other voices. She only wanted to listen to her infant. A slight move to reach her child and a tremendous feeling of pain rushed to her body. She remembered the amount of pain she had to endure to give birth to this affectionate creature. In those moments, she made a commitment that she would never go through this again but look at her child. Her child was beautiful and perfect. She was aching to hold her babe. She moved again, and the rush of the pain immobilized her again. She was so disappointed in herself that she thought she was too weak to reach her adoring infant without other people's help. She helplessly held her hands up in the sign of a request to have her ardent babe. The nurse understandably handed in her kid. Even though she said this sentence more than a thousand times, but she still said it with a smile on her face.

"Your child is beautiful."

She looked up and understandably nodded. She was holding her adoring child. Her kid was so vulnerable and breakable. She was too afraid to move fast or do something stupid that would harm her minor. She could see the little face and the closed eyes and those little hands that were moving around aimlessly. Maybe those hands were trying to grab something, so she put her index finger slowly on one of those little hands.

And those fingers, with no waste of time, held her finger. She could feel the warmth of the skin of that little hand. That hand wouldn't let go of her. It just made her smile more to see how strong her kid was. She noticed the little head that was moving side by side.

Does it want something else?

Even though it hurt her feeling, she pulled out her finger from those little fingers to free her hand to pull out her breast. As soon as she did that, those little hands were wandering around to grab something.

How vulnerable.

She pulled out her breast successfully with one hand. Doing that made her proud of herself. She showed her motherhood skill to her child and made sure her youngster understood that THIS mother was skillful and reliable.

The kid's head was still wandering around from side to side, with the hands searching for something. Even those little feet were moving around.

How sweet and vulnerable the tot was.

She slowly turned the infant's head toward her breast, where her nipple was to let the little love have it. It was the one and only mission the child had to do. Million years of evolution taught the fond one just to do that, to survive. The baby started suckling with excitement. She put her hand on the baby's head kindly and traced back the line of hair. Those shaggy, wet from the womb, were a mess. This kid made a hell of an entrance into the world, and she whispered in the young one's ear.

"Welcome."

I could see all that in her eyes. I saw the pain, joy, disappointment, pride, laugh, hope, disgust, anger, kindness, passion, and delight. I didn't know what to do with this kind of self-revelation. Not two hours ago, I was mapping out how to take off so many panties from the girls and collect them as a badge of honor or trophies. I wanted to push out this strange feeling that I got from this woman. I didn't need that in my life. I just wanted to get laid. Pathetic? Maybe. But who cares for this kind of bullshit? Where was that selfishness when I needed it?

However, I was curious to see whose mother she was? At that time, my ride came, and I never found out who she was.

Chapter 2

"What is this heat?" I asked. My friend quietly walked beside me and didn't bother to answer.

"Are we in hell? What the hell did you do?" I asked again.

"Well, isn't summer supposed to be like this, you idiot? Maybe your farts made this greenhouse. Congratulations for making these phenomena," my friend told me.

"Well, I couldn't do it all by myself. I have to thank the sandwich I ate and the people who made it and the people who tirelessly worked so hard to make that shitty sausage, and let's not forget our good fellow government who allowed those people to work. I couldn't be here if it weren't for all those people," I told my friend with a grin on my face. "And my special thanks go to you who bought that fucking cheap sandwich."

"I didn't hear any complaints when you devoured like a snake the whole fucking thing," my friend said without looking at me.

"Well, when I didn't eat any shit all morning and add to that playing soccer, well, no surprises that it made me like a zombie," I told him and tried to walk a little faster.

"Is it my fault that your lazy ass can't wake up early and make a fucking breakfast?" he said it calmly. We were having fun, and we always enjoyed witty comeback conversations. We weren't arguing. Well, we were just best friends. What is a best friend good for?

"Don't give me that shit. Who came early in the morning and asked me, 'Get your ass to the field'?" I told him with ease.

"Well, how should I know that your lazy ass wants to sleep all day?" my friend answered.

"Look, for your information, it is summer break. I believe it is my very right to sleep whenever I want or wake up whenever I desire to. I had enough crab in school ti—" My glorious comeback got cut short because I saw heaven for a second. "Are you seeing what I am seeing?" I told my friend, and when I looked at him, I saw he was already drooling. He just nodded his head up and down. The bastard didn't want to lose a second looking at those beautiful girls.

"What the fuck?" my friend said loosely.

"Or should I say, where the fuck you bitches were in my whole life?" I responded.

"What should we do?" my friend asked me.

"How the fuck am I supposed to know?"

"Well?"

"What? Do you expect me to go there and say, 'Excuse me, which one of you wants to fuck on this beautiful summer day?'"

"I knew that you didn't have the balls for it."

"Okay, show me how it's done, Mr. Having Balls."

"Forget about it. I should've known you haven't had it in you."

"But seriously, look at them. Are those for real?"

"If only I could."

"Well, dreams are made for young people."

"Fuck you."

"Youuuu fuuuuucker."

After a moment of silence, I asked my friend, "Can you at least make a plan?"

"Here." He showed me his pocket, put his hand in it, and then pulled out his hand and showed me his middle finger.

I shook my head from side to side with a smile on my face. "At least go there and talk to them."

"Why don't you do it yourself?" he answered.

"What an idiot I am with," I said low enough as if I were talking to myself and loud enough to let him know about my disappointment.

There were three girls who were playing with boys. As it happened, they had the same taste of sport as us. They were playing soccer. One of the girls had light-blond hair, and her height was almost 1.7 meters. She had a perfect butt by the eyes of humans and mathematics. If you are wondering if you—I mean, the girls and women (because this formula only works for women)—have a perfect butt, punch in the numbers, and voila, now you know that you have a perfect butt or not. The best part is that you don't have to listen to your friends or plastic surgeon to know the answer. I'll stop the suspense and give you that fantastic formula:

$(S + C) \times (B + F) / T - V.$

S is for shape, C is for spherical, B is for wobble or bounce, F is for firmness, V is for hip-to-waist Ratio, and T is for skin texture.

Before people start carrying pitchforks and a torch and put every mathematician in the crucifixion and put in a blaze to make sure there won't be any resurrection, I should point out it wasn't from a mathematician. It was from a psychologist named David Holmes.

It is fun, isn't it? Well, this happens when a member of the International Mathematical gold medal winner is too horny to think about other things. In the meantime, he put it in the concept of mathematics. My friend and I were two geeks, and everyone hated us for being too bright for our own good. I saw the world through the microscope of mathematics, and he liked to see things through the actual microscope. He was passionate about biology. We always had an argument about which field was more important. My opinion was that the language of nature is written in mathematics. Through those, we understand what nature is trying to say. My friend argued that it was horseshit talk because biology IS nature. I fired back to him that it is thanks to mathematics that he could observe any shit through a microscope. We always had this kind of argument.

The first time my friend and I met was in the geek center where we were supposed to learn how to talk to important people, a bunch of political losers who didn't know which hand was right or left, so we could have the honor of accepting the gratitude of a nation for being passionate about something we loved.

"What a loser," I said when I saw what a big deal they were making of everything. I was talking to myself.

"Excuse me?" the guy right beside me said.

I looked at him. I saw an average-looking guy with black hair and eyes, and he had this round white face. He gave me a look, which was saying, *I dare you, say it again*.

"Which one is your father?" I responded.

"None."

"So what's your problem then?"

"I thought you were talking to me," he said.

"Don't take yourself so seriously. Seriously, no one does. Trust me on that," I told him without looking at him.

"Are you looking for trouble?" he answered furiously.

"I look for anything to get out of this shit show," I told him the way that showed him I didn't care and wasn't afraid of him.

"Me too," he responded with a smile on his face instead.

"Marshal," he said and stretched his hand for a handshake.

"Agustin," I said and accepted his handshake.

"I like you, Agustin," he said it casually.

"Thanks, but I like girls with big boobs," I responded.

He giggled and put his hand in front of his mouth to hide his laugh from other people. After a while, when he got a little bit of control of himself, he looked at me and, with a grin on his face, then told me that if he were gay, he would have fallen for my charm.

"What a waste of time. Isn't it, Agustin?" Marshal said.

"Holy shit, don't tell me you were actually listening to this moron? I went to a coma the second he opened his mouth, and all this time, I was calculating how I could kill him by throwing this pen or something else into his mouth," I responded.

"Shit, yeah, you are right. I should've done the same thing. You know what? I could've brought a virus that could only kill him, and no one else gets infected and saved us all this headache," he whispered.

"Look at us. They try to teach us the proper manner for those assholes, and now we are planning how to assassinate an idiot. For their safety, they should get rid of this shitty thing," I said.

"Is there something that you want to share, Mr. Adalbert?" the asshole who was talking for the last two hours was asking.

"No, sir, I was memorizing your speech, and I have this bad habit of repeating it to myself to remember it. I didn't notice I was too loud. Please continue," I said it the way that didn't sound like sarcasm, but my friend now pressed his hand on his mouth and tried not to laugh.

The other girl had midnight-black hair with a pixie-cut hairstyle, which showed her long and beautiful neck, and most importantly, she had this pointy breast that was huge for a girl of that age. She had long and beautiful legs, wearing casual black shorts for soccer, but it didn't stop her from being cute, and she was wearing a blue shirt. She was slim and had the fragile body of a girl who could break at any moment, making her more appealing and desirable. She was 1.87 in height, as I am. Coincidence? I don't think so; tell that to the universe. Her white and round face with blue eyes made her look like she was a doll in her past life.

The other one had medium cool-blonde hair with a Hime cut; she had two beautiful green eyes. She also had a long, slim leg, wearing the same shirt and shorts. She was 1.75 meters in height.

"I don't know what they are trying to show," I said to Marshal. Marshal gave me a look, as if to say, "Explain yourself, you idiot."

"Well, look at them. Are they trying to kill every fucking male on Earth? Who can look at them and not have a serious incident or death?" I explained myself. "Yeah, you are right. It made me wonder that if we came from the same ancestor, they are different species. I believe they are called *Homo pulcher*," he told me. I looked at him and gave him a puzzled look. "*Homo* what?" I asked him. There it was, the fucking smile on his fucking face. He usually enjoyed himself teaching me one or two things. There was always this competition between him and me. We were friends, but we always kept our swords sharp for each other. "*Homo pulcher*, it means 'beautiful men,'" he answered. I hated to admit it, but it was a good and proper one, so I gave him a thumbs-up. Then suddenly, something evolutionary happened inside me. Was it a thought? No. It was more like a plan. Now at least I had a plan to approach them and give them a geeky line.

"Hey, Marshal, I've got a plan. Follow my lead. At last, your fucking biology came in handy," I told him. He was happy about my acknowledgment, but he was also curious, so he asked, "What the fuck are you talking about? What plan?" "Just follow my lead," I answered and walked away. "Hey, pssst, wait a minute," he whispered and tried to catch my attention, but I showed him by my head that he should follow me.

"Hello there. May I have your attention?" I said it formally with a trembling voice. My friend arrived and tried hard not to laugh about what I had just said. The girls looked at ME, and at that moment, my brain went blank. I questioned myself at that moment, *What the fuck am I doing here?* My first impression went straight to the toilet. In mathematics, when you realize that you aren't using the right formula, you should stop the shit and you don't continue. Go over it, analyze it, and if needed, use another formula. So by saying that, it would be the most stupid thing to continue hitting on the girls, but they were waiting for me to say something.

"Aaaaaaa . . . Ummm . . . well . . ." I looked at my friend for help, but the son of bitch was busy trying not to laugh by putting his hand on his mouth, but I could hear his laughter through his fucking nostril. *Thank you, you piece of shit*, I thought.

Then I found courage. I accepted my loss in battle; I threw the towel and left the ring like a true gentleman. Meantime, the girls were trying hard not to laugh like my stupid friend. I think they were thinking about not making me more embarrassed by putting their delicate finger on their lips, but still, I could see their smiles.

"Well?" the girl with medium cool-blond hair asked me. My situation changed from shit to a position that was more like being in a shit pit trap. What the fuck was I thinking about coming here? And more importantly, what the fuck was I expecting?

"You see . . . I was . . . I mean, we were . . . Me and my friend . . ." I showed them the stupid person right beside me by pointing at him. "Well . . . you see . . . Uhmmm . . . me and him . . . ahhh . . ." By saying that, I just wanted to die. What was wrong with me? And that was the last straw. My friend burst into a laugh, and with him, the girls were shaking from chuckling. I got pissed off from the situation that everyone was laughing at me that I didn't care anymore. Also, I knew Marshal wouldn't let go of this for eternity. Yes, he is that kind of best friend. "You see, this is my wingman, and he was supposed to help me out, but instead of helping me out, he is busy pissing his pants from laughing." And by saying that, the girls started laughing too. Great, now all people were looking in our direction. I thought I could put some attention to Marshal, but the son of a bitch still kept laughing. I turned red from the shame and the anger. "Can you just stop it? I know, I was an idiot, okay? People are looking at us and wondering what is going on in here." I looked at my friend and asked him if we could leave. Now he was coughing from all those laughs. I could see the pain he had in his chest from all those laughs. I took his hand to lead him out of the scene while he was bent and had his other hand on his chest since it was in pain.

It hurt. It hurt so bad that I couldn't breathe either. I was ashamed and humiliated. I should've known better that I could do well in mathematics, but not in social life. In mathematics, when I make a mistake, no one laughs at me, and when I come with victory, it would feel like I got a YES from those girls. I had a plan. What happened to it? It was a good plan that made me believe I could win those girls over—such a waste.

"Hey, wait a second!" the girl with light-blond hair was shouting.

Great, I just needed that. What else do you want from me? I thought to myself. She caught up with us.

"Sorry for laughing like that. It wasn't our intention to do so, but you were cool and funny. Trust me, it was the bravest thing you did out there. Well, if we didn't have any boyfriends, we would definitely have accepted whatever you were trying to say out there," she said while she was biting her beautiful lower lips from laughing. I put my hand on the head the way that I could give my head a massage. I usually do that when I try to solve a problem. Let me think. Here are the facts. I humiliated myself for nothing. Nothing. A rookie mistake. In mathematics, you must first realize if the question is right and logical; if not, then the problem is unsolvable. I couldn't find any solution to the wrong question. No one can. Even the greatest mathematician can't do that. The problem has to be a logical one. I made a BIG mistake. Even with the most excellent plan, I couldn't win them over. That was cold. Of course, was my friend and I the only men on Earth? Every man with the right mind with sexual desire for the girls would've fallen for them. Marshal once explained to me what evolution means, not that I didn't know about it since I had science class too, but he read more books about it than me. There are so many things that derive the "Evolution"—natural selection, Sexual selection, Nature, and so many other things that make sure the gene survives. I couldn't understand the whole idea of evolution, and that was okay, according to Marshal. He quoted a scientist that said, "If you think that you know the Evolution theory, you know nothing of it." Anyway, I was calculating by which one I could win them over. In natural selection, I had to wait for all males to die to have a chance to be with them, which meant Marshal and I would have to develop a virus that would get rid of all males in the world without infecting us. Well, that would make us terrorists, and trust me, no one is going to say, "Ahhhhh, that was such a romantic gesture," but you gotta do what you could do to make sure those damn genes survive. Or we could go for sexual selection. Well, anybody who looked at us and compared us to a football player, they probably would go for the football player. Healthy and fucking strong genes they have. By my calculation, with all respect, even the quarterback in the shittiest high school had more chance than us. What a world we are living in! Even two gold medalists, me and my friend, don't have more opportunity than those brain-dead footballers. Ahhhh, the fucking footballers who are being designed to bully people in high school and then steal your crush in front of you. Just thinking about those assholes doing French kiss with girls makes me vomit. What is it with girls that they fall for those assholes? It becomes an absolute cliché. It would be such a big surprise that these girls weren't already with those assholes.

"Thank you," I managed to say. I looked at my friend. The idiot couldn't stop laughing. He made me more embarrassed, but he could manage to say thank you as well while he was laughing.

"My name is Bernadina, and it was nice meeting you," she said while holding her hand up for handshaking. I shook her hand, and at that time, I felt her soft and warm skin. How delicate her hand was. I didn't know what would happen if she were my girlfriend. The lucky bastard, whoever he was, he shouldn't let go of this hand. I was so excited that I didn't notice that I was holding her hand for too long. What was wrong with me today? It seemed whatever I did, it turned into dust. Against my wish, I let the hand go. I looked at my friend. He managed to get ahold of himself a little bit. He shook her hand, and I knew what that bastard was thinking at that moment. Probably the same thing I was thinking, or even worse. "My name is Marshal, and it was such a pleasure meeting you as well," he said. What the hell? When did he become such a gentleman that I didn't notice? Ooh, I see what he was doing. He tried to say, "I am different from this moron." *You know what? Fuck you,* I thought. I wished I could say it out loud. Then she turned back to me and looked at me. *Now what?* I thought. I just wanted to get out of this fucking place as soon as possible. She kept her smile on her face. Meanwhile, she was waiting for something. *What else do you want?* I thought. *When is this fucking nightmare going to end?* Then I heard my friend say with fucking smile on his face, "His name is Agustin, and he is the smartest idiot I ever met." *You are a dead man. Let's get out of here, and I know what I should do to you,* I thought. She giggled at Marshal's comment. Why shouldn't she? Now I am a clown in high school. Thanks to Marshal. To be honest, I was a little bit jealous of Marshal. He acted calm, which made Bernadina laugh. I wished I could do it. Bernadina. What a beautiful name she has. I was wondering what those other two girls' names were.

"Now that the cat is out of the bag and we know that you are taken, I don't see the reason why we shouldn't go to the coffee shop and have a civilized conversation. It would be a great honor for this idiot and me in here"—he pointed at me—"to get to know you. We were actually heading that way. Would you like to join us?" The girl was still smiling. *Marshal, you are going to die a virgin. You can't get away with this,* I thought. Bernadina looked back to her friends and then looked back to us again. "I don't know," she said. "Well, you know where we are if you want to join us," Marshal responded. "I don't know. I will talk to them. But thanks for the suggestion," she said. *Were we heading to the coffee shop? When did that happen?* I thought. Look at Marshal. When did he become an expert in hitting on the girls? I was proud of him, like a mother bear to her cub after three years, right before kicking him out of her life. Marshal started walking away, so I just followed him. After I ensured we were at a safe distance, I elbowed him and said, "What the hell, man? You just embarrassed me out there." "What?" he responded by looking surprised. "You were mocking me out there, in front of those girls." "You did it yourself. You didn't need my help for that," he answered. "You Fucker," I responded. "Aaa . . . bae . . . daaa . . . mmaaaaa . . .," he responded. I shook my head with a smile.

"When did you become so calm and cool? I lost my mind out there when I wanted to talk to them," I asked.

"Well, I thought that was your plan. You play like an idiot, and I become the knight." Now he started laughing again.

"You are hopeless. Seriously, if you were okay to talk to them, why didn't you?" I asked.

"I needed an idiot to shine," he responded. I told you so. He wouldn't let go of this.

"So why didn't you insist on coming now?" I asked.

He looked at me as if I were serious then said, "Are you kidding me? Don't you know that if you insist more, the chance they come would be lower? They don't need a needy person. As you know, they already got boyfriends, and if you were listening, I told them that we just want to hang out, and that would be all, so if I insisted more, she would have thought we had an ulterior motive," he answered.

"I don't know. I've never been good in social life, and I didn't care at all until now," I said.

"Well, there it is, your problem. Humans are built to be social like many other species that have a social life. In other social life species, if a member gets cast out, that member has a great chance to die. It isn't different for humans. If you put a human in a solitary cell or island, it doesn't matter how isolated the person was before. The life expectancy of that person goes down, and the insanity goes up," he said.

"Okay, okay, Mr. Knowledge. You don't need to rub it on my face, but I should say this. You were cool out there. I give you that."

"It is all thanks to you for being an idiot."

"You are not going to let go of this?"

"Not a chance."

"You know, when I was talking to Bernadina . . . Bernadina, what a sexy name she has, doesn't she?" I said, and he nodded. "Anyway, I was calculating the chance we had to be with them. Do you want to know what the result was? It was epsilon, ε. Unless we kill all other males on the planet, we don't have any chance of being with them, according to your beloved scientist, Charles Darwin, in natural selection. I checked other aspects too. It is not good. Do you think they are with a football player?"

He laughed and shook his head. "Do you know why there are tall people and small people in human society? Because in one point of life, women liked the small people for not consuming too much food where food was famine or just because they could hide better from a predator, so they could live long enough to mate. On the other hand, they also liked the big guys for protection or because they were good hunters. What I am trying to say is, we don't know what the future is holding for us. As you mentioned, some girls like big and bully guys like the football player, and there is a chance that the girls get disgusted with those idiots and looking for a smart guy like me."

While I was laughing, I said, "Like you? Fuck you. Anyway, as I said, I liked how you acted."

"The way you went for the girls, for a moment, I thought, *What a cool guy I am with*, until you screwed up," he said while laughing.

We arrived at the coffee shop. We went inside. I ordered a spicy Chai, and he ordered a black coffee.

"Do you think they will come?" I asked.

"What do you know about Komodo Dragon?" he asked.

"Not much. Why?"

"Because I just used the technique of Komodo dragon. This reptile has a poisonous bite, so when it bites, it makes other large animals bleed out or get weak. After that, the reptile doesn't do much but stalk the prey. It just waits until the animal is too weak to move then starts eating it. Well, guess what? My bite was poisoned too."

"You are sick."

"Wasn't it you that suggested killing all males?"

"No, I have a tender heart."

"So what was your plan that you rushed into them without thinking? Whatever it was, it was like a hyena cub rushed into the lion's pride."

"Stop it. I had a good pla—" I said when I saw him smiling while he was looking behind my back.

"What plan?" the girl with Pixie cut asked me while she was standing behind me. For the second time on the same day, I had been frozen.

"He was trying to explain to me how to open a conversation with girls. That you interrupted him," Marshal answered. Then he looked at me and gave a signal to continue.

"Nothing," I managed to say.

"Oh, come on, it's not like we haven't heard it before. It was more like, 'Am I dead? If not, why am I seeing angels?'" she said while she had a smile on her face.

"Or more like, 'Found it, finally found it, The God greatest art on Earth,'" Bernadina said. Now everyone was laughing but me.

"Well, I assume that those lines worked for you guys," I said while my head was down. They all laughed.

"Why don't you sit here?" Marshal suggested. The Pixie-cut hair, with Bernadina, the two of them added three more chairs to our table. The other one was busy ordering coffee for themselves.

"Now we really like to hear yours too," Bernadina said.

To add to your résumé? What a bitch you are, making other people embarrassed, I thought.

"Take it easy on him. He is a shy person, and he is going to die alone with it," Marshal said with a smile on his face, and the girl made such a noise that it was like they just found an orphaned kitty.

"I was going to say if you know anything about *Homo pulcher*?" I said it finally. Marshal burst into a laugh so suddenly that the other girls were wondering what just happened. However, they got curious, thanks to Marshal.

"What?" the girl with the pixie-cut hair asked. Although she had a smile on her face, she wanted to know what it was. What a beauty she was. Her blue eyes could hypnotize any man. Her long and delicate neck wasn't helping either—just more distraction. As for Marshal, it was fuel in a fire. He started laughing so hard that no one could stop him.

"Maybe he can explain it to you, girls," I responded. There were tears in Marshal's eyes because of those laughs. After a while, when he calmed down a little bit, he explained what a Homo *pulcher* meant.

"Ahhh, that's so sweet. I appreciate it. Are we that beautiful that you call us *Homo pocher?*" the girl with the pixie-cut hair said. The other girl who was on the counter joined our table with a tray of coffee and asked what was going on here. The girl with the Pixie-cut hair was so excited that she was the first to explain it to her before Marshal or I had a chance to explain it. Marshal and I were smiling when she explained it to her friend with her sweet voice while making a mistake pronouncing *pulcher* to *pocher*, but none of us dared to correct her. **Let her have her moment,** that was what I thought. Her sweet and innocent voice was enough to change anybody's mind about anything.

"That's new. Is it me, or does the pickup lines become so educational?" she said it with a mischievous smile on her face. "Anyway, you must be Agustin"—she pointed at me—"and you must be Marshal. You guys made life difficult for other students. Now every parent and the teachers want us to be like you guys. Do you realize what you have done?" the medium cool blonde said.

"It wasn't our intention to make life difficult for anybody as the football player try not to make our life miserable by bullying us," I said. I couldn't believe what I had just said. Was it me or my demon side? I don't know. Marshal turned his head and started scratching his head. Even he couldn't save me from that. However, the three goddesses started laughing.

"Oh, do they bully you?" Bernadina said. Before I could answer her, she continued, "Well, we never liked them either." I looked at Marshal and gave a look. **Can you believe her?** Marshal responded with a smile.

"I have never been bullied, but when I see other students are getting hurt, it bothers me," I told them. They nodded the way that they understood but didn't believe me. "I came. I mean, we came with a deal with them. We give them free tutoring as long as they don't bother us and give us the protection from others," I explained. They looked at one another and started laughing.

"Well, that is the smartest thing to do if you don't want to get hurt," Bernadina said.

"Did I say I was afraid of them? Or because of fear of getting hurt, we are doing it? It has been seven years that I have been attending Wing Chun classes besides other classes, so if anybody is going to get hurt, it wouldn't be me," I explained. Bernadina looked at her friends, and they smiled together. They still didn't believe me.

"Well, he is not lying. If you don't believe him, just go to one of those boring classes he goes to," Marshal said.

"Then why give them the free tutoring?" the girl with the pixie-cut hair asked.

"I forgot to ask your name. What's your name?" I asked.

"Calysta," the girl with the Pixie cut said. I looked at the other one and waited for her answer. "Aiko," the cool-blond girl answered.

"Look, Calysta, did I say it right?" I asked, and she nodded. "There are so many different people with so many different attitudes. I like puzzles, and people are like puzzles to me. I sometimes challenge myself to do something stupid, like negotiating with those brain-dead footballers. It is not because I am afraid of them. I think of myself as a person with social life. Even though it is awkward for me to be a social person, I try my best to learn from everybody, even from those idiots. It is because I know at some point in my life, maybe in the future, I will face them again, and I know that fighting isn't always the best solution."

"Wow, that was a good speech," Bernadina said.

"It wasn't mine. It was from my instructor on the first day of the training, except for the puzzle part," I replied.

"You are such a nice person. I wished all people were like you," Calysta said.

"Oh no, even having one of them is too boring. Having a world full of them would be disastrous," Marshal said with a smile on his face. All girls laughed at his comment about me.

"When did you become so cute and funny?" I asked him, annoyed.

"About two hours ago."

"Well, I am happy for you. At least one of us has a future as a clown in a circus," I replied.

"Well, I need someone to show and make fun of in order to make people laugh. Who is better than you? So don't worry about your future in a circus. We are going to be together in it," Marshal responded, and the girls laughed. I smiled too.

"You guys are too much. I had no idea hanging out with you would be this much fun," Aiko said while she was laughing.

"I hope it doesn't bother your boyfriends. You know, they don't like their girls laughing with a stranger," Marshal said.

"Or as you girls pointed out, the enemies," I said with a smile on my face.

"Well, once we explain to them how wonderful you guys are, they are going to be cool," Calysta said.

I looked at Marshal, and we both knew that wouldn't be possible. We were on them; they would be a fool if they thought that we didn't have any ulterior motive for them. I didn't know either. Maybe we actually could be friends, but they were too beautiful to think of them as a friend only. Hey, don't you dare to judge us! We are men, and we only want to make sure our genes are going to be passed onto the next generation. What is wrong with having that in mind?

Personally, I liked Calysta. Who was the lucky guy who spent his time with her? Each time I looked at her beautiful eyes, it was like someone was poking my chest with something sharp. Her sweet voice and her long and beautiful neck with short-cut hair was out of this world. She was my Aphrodite, the goddess of beauty and love. I could see every move she made, or better to say, I was memorizing her actions so that I could review them later—what it would feel like if a girl like that kissed me on the mouth. One could not simply survive from that. Her laugh was more painful. I loved her laugh the most. She was self-conscious about her beauty and her attraction. I could see that in her eyes. I think she understood my hopelessness for her beauty, and for that, she let me watch her beauty. Anyone could go under her spell with just one look. Simple, just like that.

"Well, you guys made big chaos in high school by scoring two gold medals. Everyone is talking about you guys, how smart you are, and the teachers, they don't have enough of it. They always exemplify you, and you guys are the models for any parents," Aiko said it with a wry smile on her face. "So if you could just help us out on our homework, we would appreciate it. What do you think?"

Did she think that we were that desperate to do her homework for her? Well, she wasn't that much wrong, but abusing us? Even if she were my girlfriend, I wouldn't do that for her.

"What exactly did you mean by saying that?" Marshal asked her politely before I could say something stupid.

"We just need help with our homework," Aiko said.

"She is right. I hate mathematics. It is too difficult to learn, and I didn't learn anything from it. It is torture for our souls," Calysta said with her angelic voice. Then she looked at me and bit her lips. I could see the smile on Marshal's face.

"I understand, but I can't do your homework for you. However, it would be a great opportunity for me to tutor you. I am tutoring those brain-dead. Why not you? Who happens to be my new friends," Marshal said with a smile on his face. I looked at him and gave him a look. ***Back off or die.***

"I couldn't agree more with Marshal. For once in his useless life, he said something beneficial," I said, and the girls laughed. "As you know, we don't have so many friends in here, and I am tired of seeing his face. So that way, we all benefit from it. And, Calysta, trust me, when I am through with you, you are going to love mathematics as much as I do. I promise you." While she was laughing, she looked at me with those sapphire-blue eyes, and without looking at her friends for confirmation, she nodded. I couldn't help myself but smile. I could see. Yes, I could see those beautiful eyes from now on, which was a victory in my dictionary.

Chapter 3

"Hello?" I answered the phone.

"Hello, is this Mr. Adalbert?" a female voice asked me on the phone.

"Yes?" I answered and was curious who she was.

"I am calling from the hospital, and I am afraid I have bad news for you."

"WHAT?" I shouted.

Chapter 4

"Which one did you pick?" Corwin asked me for the thousandth time now, I guess.

"Pick what?" I answered, even though I knew what he meant.

"The girls, which one did you pick?" he asked again.

"None," I answered.

"Seriously, I already chose five of them," he said with pride in his voice.

"What do you want to do with that number? Make an orgy movie?" I asked.

"No, but I let my options open, so if one of them said no, I go for the other one," he answered with a smile.

"So which one did you pick?" I asked. I was curious.

"I won't tell you until you tell me yours," Corwin said.

"Look at you. You are in university, and you behave like a high school kid who got his first kiss. Now tell me who they are, so in case, we won't have a conflict of interest," I said it casually.

"Nope, you first," he responded.

"For the thousandth time, I told you, I didn't pick any. Which part of 'they aren't my type' that you don't understand?" I told him. He irritated me. I wished I could punch him in the face, so it made him shut up. I was wondering what would happen to his bony face with that curly black hair. He thought that he was a guy who knew everything, and worse than that, he thought he was a player.

"So I won't tell you who they are," he responded. Childish, that was what he was.

"It is fine with me," I responded. I never thought about the girls that way since I saw that look from that woman. She was a mother. What would she feel about a guy like him who had only one thought about girls—that they were made for men's desire? I couldn't blame him. Not a while ago, I was like him. But the look of that woman changed my life. I couldn't bear the thought of playing with her dreams. She had plans for her sweet kids. How dare I challenge that after knowing that? A guy like him always became so blind and self-centered that he didn't care about anybody else.

"Seriously, you haven't chosen anybody?" Corwin asked again.

"My answer hasn't changed from two seconds ago," I answered.

"I don't know. Maybe it's been changed. Who would you choose if you wanted to pick one?" he asked with persistence.

"I don't know. I would choose anyone for now just to get rid of you," I answered.

"Okay then, choose one," he requested. Oh boy, I can't believe I'm saying this, but I missed Marshal.

"Okay, okay. Just promise me, after that, you leave me alone, okay?" I said.

"We'll see," he answered, and when I gave him a look that said "Either that or you go home without an answer," he said okay.

"Let me see," I said while scanning the classroom for the girl whom I wanted to pick up. I don't know why I went through that length of trouble to find a suitable candidate for my choice. I should've chosen the first one I saw. After a while, with so much effort and scanning, I decided on a tall girl with dark-brown hair with pure hazel eyes. She was nicely dressed up. She was wearing a long black dress, which matched her hair. She seemed to be simple enough, but not losing the edge.

"That girl who just walked by," I said to Corwin.

"She was one of them, but I'll let you have her," Corwin said.

What the hell he thinks he is? Is he a celeb or the prince of some country? What a crazy guy I am dealing with, I thought.

"Thank you. You are so generous. I'll remember that," I said.

Next Day

"Here comes your crush," Corwin said in front of some other classmates. I just wanted to remove him from the earth.

"It's not what you think. I just told him that to get rid of him. Yesterday, he went nuts," I said and hoped they would believe me. Not a chance. Now they had something to play with or, better to say, tease with.

"She I'nt tat bad. Ai laik ho she woks," David said.

"Got the message. It's Dave's. Hands off," I said and hoped they would let go of this.

"Not a chance, mate. She's oll yo's," David responded.

"What is wrong with you guys? I don't know her name, and you guys think I have a serious crush on her?"

"Her name is Marina. What other excuse do you have?" Corwin said.

"When the fuck did you find out?" I asked. We started walking toward the coffee shop to have lunch. It was a good day if I wasn't with them.

"Yesterday," he answered.

I had nothing to say. They were all laughing, and I knew they were playing with me, which **means** being social. Fuck you, Marshal. They were all talking, but I blocked them out. I was enjoying the sunrays on my face. It was my second semester in Pure Mathematics. I hoped that someday I would become a mathematician who could solve any problem. Not speaking highly of myself, I was doing fine in university. All teachers and professors relied too much on me. I think they were abusing me because they asked me to go to their class and teach math each time they wanted to take a day off or anything else. To be honest, I enjoyed teaching math. I didn't care who was learning and who wasn't. If they don't want to hear the beauty of nature's language, it is their loss. Almost all students in university knew me and asked me to tutor them, but I had to refuse, not because I was too proud to do it but because I was too busy doing other projects with other professors. I was solving problems for the computer, chemistry, biology, and other cool stuff. As soon as I finished one, another one was replacing it. I was way ahead of all my classmates and grad students, even though I was a freshman. I had the teachers' respect, and they took my work seriously, so if any students ran into a problem, they usually referred them to me. Also, I was a member of art classes. I continued doing the things that I had done since high school. I was passionate about music, painting, and theatre. I was doing those kinds of staff because I was lonely and had too much time in my hand in high school before I met Marshal. With all those works that I had, I didn't have time to eat lunch peacefully. I didn't mind that since I was learning everything from every field so fast. Next time, if I see Marshal, he is going to be fucked. How can he compete with a guy like that?

I felt someone was elbowing me, so I looked and found that gaunt face of Corwin. **What now?** I thought.

"Look, there she is. Your crush is following you. I think she likes you," Corwin said.

I didn't respond. It would be a waste of time. I just gave him a look that he should stop it or else.

At the time I came to the university, Corwin was sitting beside me as my good fortune. That was what he told me all the time. He introduced himself, and after that, he forced himself into my life. Since then, I never saw peace. He was a dynamic fellow. He would be a good friend if I had more time to spend with him.

"Now dat am loking, she lok tasty. Gud job, Agustin," David said, and with it, he started laughing with Corwin and Winn. I liked Winn. He was an intelligent guy and didn't talk too much. He just wanted to be with others, but he didn't force himself to others as Corwin did. Winn was studying Theoretical Physics. He had a scholarship for it. He also had this bony face with light-brown skin. His hair was short. I could see that every girl could fall for him quickly. He was handsome and neat. We became friends when his teacher introduced us together to help him in mathematics about Quantum Physics. He received my respect. He was brilliant, and above all, he was the opposite of Corwin in talking. He always had this kind of manner in his talk. He couldn't swear. He couldn't raise his voice to anyone. It was like he wanted to be invisible. Oh boy, who knows what happened to him when he was in high school. Understanding that, I felt sympathy for him, but I never pitied him.

"Why don't you go there and talk to her?" Corwin asked.

"I thought she was in your list if I remember correctly. Since I want you to have a full life without regret, I'll let you do the honor. Now go there before Dave does," I answered.

"Wat do you theink of me? If ai had a chance, ai wod do it without a second thought," David responded.

"See, you have the blessing of Dave. Now go there," I persisted.

"She is your girl. I wouldn't do that to you," he responded with a smile.

"What do you think of her? Do you think she is going to be your girlfriend just like that? Just look at her. Her shape, the way she walks, her manner. She is going to be a great challenge, even for Winn. She isn't an easy thing. It's a tough one. As all of you know, I don't have time to go to the toilet, and hitting on her takes time. Until she knows who I am, what the fuck I am doing in this university, and what kind of person I am, I'll get old enough to be the daddy of all students in here. Between the three of us, we all know that Corwin would be the best. You are one of those sneaky sons of bitches. I know you like her, so don't play with your food and go there like a man and see what you can do, okay?" I said it while I was putting my lunch on a tray.

"Are you setting me up?" Corwin asked.

"No. I told you the truth," I said. Winn and David agreed as well.

I saw the girl sitting with her friend; they had been together since morning. To be honest, she was terrific. Her smile reminded me of Calysta. Her smile was beautiful. Marina, what a lovely name she had. Still, I couldn't bring myself to be THE GUY who just wanted to have sex with her. After seeing those eyes of a mother on that dreadful day, it was almost impossible for me to be that man.

"To be clear, you won't get mad at me if I go there and be with her?" Corwin asked.

We didn't smile. We just shook our heads to let him know it was an okay from us. He then told us that at a suitable time, he would ask her out. I was glad that now he had another hobby to play with, even though it would be harsh on the poor girl. Now he was her problem.

Chapter 5

She rested her head on my chest. I could feel her warm breath on my chest. She was sitting on my lap. It brought tears to my eyes to see her in that state. She sounded sleepy, but now and then, she was coughing. Her head moved a little bit; her head fell back a little bit the way that her lips were angled toward my neck. Now I could feel her breath on my neck. My left hand was like a support for her back, and with another hand, I was stroking her hair slowly with such care that it didn't wake her up. She liked it. She always did. She told me that it helped her with her headache. Now her lips were touching my collarbone. I could hear her heavy breathing on my neck. With each breath, there was a whistling sound coming out of her. I was sitting on the bed and sitting back to the wall, having her on my lap. She cuddled herself in me. She was like a bird that was shaking from the cold. Her skin turned to a ghostlike white. I was sitting on the bed and not even able to see her. My tears blocked my view. *I have to be strong. I have to be strong for her. I can't let her see my tears. She had enough of that*, I thought. I stroked her hair to distract myself so I could stop crying. I tucked myself a little so that I could pamper her more. Then with a lot of care, without waking her up, I put my right hand under her knees. That way, I could lay down her feet on the bed, and while she had her head on my shoulder, I lay down with her carefully by having my arm as a pillow for her. She didn't wake up. Now her forehead was toward my neck, and she was breathing to my chest. I knew the time was coming. I wanted to cry, but the cry was locked in my throat. I wanted to scream, but I didn't have the breath for it. I was hopelessly lying down and watching her. I could hear the heavy breath she was taking. I kissed her forehead and felt how hot her head was.

Chapter 6

I didn't know what to do. The most beautiful girl was sitting right across the table. Even during thinking, she didn't lose her cuteness. She was shadowing herself on the notebook in a way that it was like she was hugging the notebook. That black hair was like a beautiful waterfall that had been frozen in action, and it was there to be watched forever. Her white skin was such a contrast that it made me think that nature must have gone through lots of trouble just to paint her. As Marshal pointed out, we must thank her ancestor for choosing the right people at the right time to pass on these beautiful genes, and now a horny teenager had only been thinking how to kiss her. I didn't know mathematics could be cute by having her in it. Her lips were moving and were whispering something that only she could hear. It seemed to me that she was battling logic with herself. I couldn't focus on anything by having her by my side. I was a teenager, a virgin, and horny. They were not a good combination. It was like dropping Potassium in water—explosive. I was explosive and ready to explode.

What was wrong with me? Why was I so restless? There were also Bernadina and Aiko, but I didn't care about them anymore. I was fixated on only one person and only one person, and she was sitting right across from me. At that moment, I understood the meaning of basic instinct. I just wanted to rip off her dress and make her naked so that we could have sex right there. I didn't know what I was supposed to do if the opportunity presented itself. What was the procedure? What do I have to do first? Unfortunately, I Had never been introduced to the world of porn, so consequently, I was clueless about sex. I was too proud to ask Marshal about it, but who cares? I wasn't going to be the lucky guy. I was just the guy who gave tutors to others.

I could see the frustration in her eyes. She tried her best to learn mathematics, but she wasn't born to do it, so I tried to make it enjoyable for her. The method I used was simple—reward and punishment. If she got the right answers from those practices I chose for her, those answers would coordinate her to a location where I hid something for her. In the beginning, it was a difficult task. I had to teach her coordination then figure out on what difficulty level she could solve the problems. Knowing what level she was, was the most challenging one for me since the easiest problems for me were difficult for her. In the beginning, I thought it would be an impossible mission, but look at her now; she was all in. Now she had the attitude of a real mathematician, and the only difference was, she received two rewards instead of one: solving the problems, which gave her tremendous joy, and finding the treasure. She had improved a lot just in a few months. After that, Bernadina and Aiko asked me to teach them math as well. I agreed on one condition—Calysta had to teach them both, and I only observed her teaching. Her look was priceless when I suggested that. She was so happy that she gave me a hug and a kiss on both cheeks. Ohh, what a wonderful feeling it was, her lips on my face. That was the first time she kissed me. After that, the number of her kissing increased to the level that she kissed me whenever she saw me. Who could have imagined that? When I looked up to see what she was doing, I saw her busy solving the problems. She was enjoying doing it, and that was all I wanted to see. She was more comfortable around me since the time we met. Maybe too comfortable that it made me wonder if she were sending a signal for me to do something, but I never wanted to lose her, so I acted cool around her. Donkey Greedy, the Donkey gets punched. I didn't want that for sure. Even though she broke up with her boyfriend two months ago, I couldn't bring myself to ask her out. What if she said no? How could I forgive myself for what I did? Also, it wasn't too long ago she gave me the news. She was recovering from that breakup.

Her boyfriend wasn't so happy about it. If it weren't for the bullies I was tutoring, he would've done too many stupid things. Only once, he and his buddies found me alone in a place. He confronted me. I tried reasoning with him, but he didn't want to hear anything. He was one of those idiots, so I put my years of training in Wing Chun in action. My mentor once told us that learning the techniques was easy, but when and how you use them were the challenge of masters, so you have to have a balance between being smart and being powerful. I avoided physical fighting for many years and never used it in street fights, but I learned how powerful I was on that day. I calculated everything they wanted to do fast, and I knew where I should punch them, which would stop them but didn't leave too much damage. The result was almost what I expected. The four of them were lying on the ground and having lots of pain. I didn't get even one scratch. It was like one of those crappy Hollywood movies but in real life. I felt sorry for the guy. I gave him some advice and told him that her girlfriend hadn't left him for me because I wasn't her boyfriend yet. I don't know whether he listened or not because he stopped harassing me and left me in peace after that.

I was happy being with her, so instead of going home and reading advanced mathematics, I brought the books there and read them with her. Marshal did the same. We all enjoyed studying. Calysta's mother liked me too. At least, that was what I thought. Whenever she saw me, she welcomed me into her home with open arms. She was beautiful as well. Calysta got her beautiful eyes from her, and as her mother explained, Calysta inherited more beauty from her grandmother. In the beginning, her dad wasn't so happy having me around, but when her marks in mathematics, physics, chemistry, and many other subjects improved, he started liking me. He enjoyed my company even more when I beat him in chess whenever he challenged me. It hurt me more when he asked me to take care of her daughter like a brother. Calysta was an only child and didn't have any siblings. I didn't want to be her brother. Even if I wanted it, it would be a difficult task. When I looked at her, anything would come to my mind but being a brother. My thoughts were too dirty to be her brother. On the one hand, I didn't want to disappoint the MAN. Such a drama I was in. On the other hand, every cell was aching to have sex with her. I didn't want to disappoint those people who were nice to me. I asked Marshal once what to do, and in response, he told me he had the same trouble with Aiko. We were doomed. Those fucking sperms weren't going to go to the place that I wanted them to go.

If I looked into it as a scientist, it would be logical. In the future, our kids are going to be smart and beautiful. What was wrong with having that in mind? Nothing. But in reality, having those nice people around and the chance that Calysta wasn't in the same wave as I was made me realize that I was screwed.

I looked at her again and watched her doing the math. At that moment, she looked up. Our eyes locked, and before I knew it, I was under her spell. Her sapphire-blue eyes made my heart pound really fast. My reaction was more like a thief who had been captured in action. I was ashamed and afraid, but then I saw her biting her lips from laughing, making it more like a smile. She shied away from my look. I looked down. I knew at that moment that I WAS IN BIG TROUBLE.

Chapter 7

"Marina! Excuse me," I said. ***Now or never,*** I thought. She was with a friend walking away from the coffee shop she came from. I decided to do it at that moment. I knew if I didn't do it then, I couldn't do it after. The sun was burning up there. My shade glasses weren't helping me either from the sun. Its rays were in my eyes. I was there for almost half an hour. It was scalding, but I was too determined to do it or, better to say, too stupid to let it go. After months of noticing her, now it was time to take action. Corwin took the first hit. He asked her out, but she refused. Not that I cared, but it made me curious about her, and it was enough to get me hooked. The more I looked at her, the more I liked her. I don't know what happened to that feeling I had before—the guilty feeling that I had when I saw that mother.

I liked her laugh. She reminded me of Calysta. Her long dark-brown hair was a beauty that came with pure hazel eyes. She was tall and had good shape. I don't know, but it seemed to me that everyone was hitting on her, and no one came out without a scar. I don't know what I was thinking at that moment that I thought I was different.

"Excuse me, Marina!" I said again. She turned back. She had this beautiful smile on her face.

"Yes?" she answered.

"Can I talk to you in private?"

"Is it something to do with class?" she asked, still having a smile on her face. It was unexpected. I didn't know what the correct answer was for her question. *Should I tell her yes? Or should I tell her the truth? The girls always like honesty. What if she doesn't want to talk to me? Who cares? I waited here for almost an hour. Anyway, let's get on with it. I want to rip off the bandage once and for all. Today I know for sure that she wants to be with me, or not?* I thought.

"No, it is not," I answered.

"Well, I'm sorry. I can't," she responded.

"Are you sure? Can't you give me at least five minutes? It won't take too long," I almost begged. Her friend was watching. I really wanted to tell her how I felt about her. Tell her that these past three months were nightmares for me. I tried to tell her everything, and maybe she took pity on me. I didn't ask her out because she reminded me of Calysta; I asked her out since she was beautiful and had a unique character.

"No, I'm sorry," she responded, and before I could respond, she left with her friend. I was frozen right where I was. I was speechless. I didn't foresee that outcome. I expected at least she would listen to me. The sun above me didn't stop torturing me. It was burning me alive. *What could I have done differently so that I could get a different result?* I thought. Shocked, rejected, and agonized, I was watching her walk away. Did I say something that I shouldn't have? She was getting far away, and my eyes were following her. There was a smile on my lips not because I was happy; it was out of sadness in my heart because it hurt. The taste of the rejection was horrible.

I couldn't think clearly. I couldn't move. I was in the same spot. Did I expect her to turn around and talk to me? I didn't know. I walked away from the place. I wanted to get away from that hell-hole, but I couldn't walk far enough, so I had to find a chair and sit there. When I found nothing, I sat on the grass. I was breathing hard. It felt like something superheavy was on my chest. There were tears in my eyes. It hurt. It hurt too much. People were passing by. I hid my face. I tried to stand up, but like a drunk man, it became a difficult task. I was angry at myself. I should've done it differently. I heard laughter from the people who were passing by. I hated them. Why were they so happy while I was so miserable?

I tried again to stand up. I stood up with difficulty. I looked back to where I talked to her and then looked where she headed. She was out of my sight. I don't know how long the process was to get over that situation, but I controlled myself and started walking again. I needed to get away from that place as soon as possible. *She doesn't deserve me. Whoever she wants, let it be him. I don't want to have a relationship with a person who is rude and inconsiderable about other's feelings. What was wrong with her? What did I do to her that she didn't want to hear what I wanted to say? Asking about class? Did she think she was more intelligent than me? No one talked to me like that, and she felt she could do it to me. Let it be. Time shows who was right. I hope she was right, because if she changes her mind, I won't give her the time of day. That was it. It was only one shot, and it was her loss. I feel sorry for her because she lost the opportunity to be with me, but she lost everything with one wrong move and only one wrong move,* I thought. I was trying to convince myself to reduce the pain and get rid of that strange pain. It helped a little bit, but my heart was bleeding, and I needed to stop it.

"Mr. Adalbert . . . Mr. Adalbert." I heard someone calling me. When I turned around, I saw Professor Oswald coming toward me. He was a Theoretical Physics teacher. Mr. Oswald was a respected teacher and well-known in his field. He was a skinny guy with a mustache on his mouth, dark hair, and tall. He was almost running toward me.

"Thank God I found you. Can you do me a favor?" he asked, and before I answered, he continued. "I need you to teach my class if it isn't too much for you. There is an emergency that I need to leave. I asked other teachers, but they don't have time for it, so it would be a huge favor if you taught the class for me. I won't forget that," he requested. I needed a distraction, so I accepted.

"Thank you. Thank you so much. You are my savior. I won't forget that," he said while he headed in the other direction.

I inhaled a deep breath and then exhaled it. I was still confused from that horrible moment I had, but thanks to the universe, I had a distraction. I loved teaching classes on different subjects. I even forgot to ask him where his assistant was. Anyway, it was a good opportunity for me to get away from those thoughts.

I headed to his classroom. The classroom was almost complete. I asked the first student about the subject that was going to be taught by Professor Oswald. After he indicated the book page and lecture, I opened the book and the lecture to review it. When I thought that I was ready, I closed them both.

"Hello, everyone. My name is Agustin Adalbert, your substitute teacher for today. There was an emergency for Professor Oswald, and as you can see, his assistant wasn't available for other reasons too, so you're stuck with me." I looked at the faces, and they weren't happy. "And add to that, I am suffering a PTSD now for what just happened to me not ten minutes ago." Everyone laughed at what I just said.

"Do you mind telling us what happened to you?" a female voice asked from the crowd.

"Well, not that it's your business, but I'll let you know some wisdom that I learned today. Never ask a girl out on a hot day, because if you get rejected, you will feel nausea, confusion, breathing problem, and worse than that, you can't tell if it is tears coming down or sweat. So you think that it is a heartbreak symptom, but it could be a heatstroke." And with that, the whole class laughed, and it continued for almost two minutes, and then they started chatting.

"Okay, okay, that's enough. The professor didn't send me here to do stand-up comedy for you guys, but I'm glad my misery is your amusement. I don't know most of you guys or, better to tell, none of you, so let's continue this lecture and get on with it and finish it fast," I said.

"Who was it?" one student asked.

"It was a beautiful girl with a great smile. I can't tell you what her name is because she is real and she is studying in this university, and I don't wanna draw too much unwanted attention to her, so let's move on," I answered.

"But it's not fair. I want to try my luck," a male voice protested, and by that, other students started laughing.

"It is not a sword in the stone that you want to try," I said, and the whole class started laughing again. "She is a human being and has feelings. As I said, I don't wanna draw too much attention to her. The reason I brought her up was to break the ice in the class. Now that you guys are more comfortable, let's finish this class." And by saying that, I started the lecture. It was in the middle of the lecture that I noticed a girl not too far away. Yes, it was her—Marina. She was sitting with her friend whom I saw earlier. When she looked up from her notebook, she saw that I was staring at her. She smiled, looked away, and pretended that she didn't notice me, but it was too late, and we both knew it. I didn't smile back; I don't know why. Maybe I was shocked, or probably, I wanted to show her she was nothing to me, which wasn't true. I knew deep down that I cared, but did she know? With lots of trouble, I finished the lecture and tried hard not to look in her direction. After the lecture, some students stayed to ask me some questions, and during that, I saw Marina getting out of class with her friend. That was the second time in one day that I was watching her walk away.

Chapter 8

"What are you talking about?" Aiko asked.

"Well, it means what it means. He is not answering anything. Not the phone, email, messages, text messages. The son of a bitch cut off everything and everyone," Marshal told her.

"But it doesn't make any sense," Aiko asked, confused.

"Well, don't look at me that I know every answer. Since Agustin and Calysta broke up, he put distance between himself and everyone related to her until he left the country to study in Cambridge. He was despondent that he drowned himself in mathematics all the time. It sounded like he was looking for answers in there. After a while, he didn't even talk to me either," Marshal said.

"Then why did he quit from Cambridge as well? Is he crazy or what?" Aiko asked.

"During the time he was in Cambridge, he didn't talk so much. His excuse was, there were too many things that he had to do for other professors, and he was happy about it. I don't know what happened there that he quit Cambridge and left for Geneva. He told his parents that he wanted to work in CERN as soon as possible. He got recommendations from all his professor that he could do great over there. Since then, I have tried calling him, but he didn't answer any of them. Not even a single message," Marshal answered, sounding concerned.

"Now you make me more worried about him than Calysta. I didn't know that he took it that hard. The thing that I can't grasp is, it was a mutual decision to break up, but not long after that, as you told me about Agustin, they both went crazy. Even though Calysta is at MIT and everyone is happy for her, she is really sad. Her roommate once told me that she cries every night. In the beginning, her roommate thought that maybe she was homesick, but Calysta didn't stop crying. Even one day, she fainted in the classroom," Aiko said.

"What is wrong with them? Are they planning to kill each other? If they like each other that much, why they broke up in the first place?" Marshal said. He was pissed off. He wanted to punch something or even someone. He was angry. He was furious. He has never been that much upset about anything, not even once. But he could see his two best friends were miserable. If he weren't so busy in University, he would have taken a trip to see both of them and punched them both in the face. He paced back and forth. He shook his head. He didn't know what to do. He was so surprised that their parents were so blind to see that their children were dying right in front of them. Both families were happy that their children were accepted into good universities, which might cause them the illusion that their children were delighted.

"I hope Calysta doesn't find out that Agustin quit college. It is the last thing she needs. It will kill her. She probably blames herself for that. I know her," Aiko said, sounding concerned.

"WHAT DO YOU WANT ME TO DO, HUH?" Marshal snapped and shouted. "THAT ASSHOLE DIDN'T GIVE A FUCK WHEN I WAS WITH HIM, AND NOW HE IS A MAJOR PAIN IN THE ASS FOR EVERYONE. FUCK. FUCKKK. FUUUUUUUUUUCKK!" he yelled furiously and didn't hold back. "WHEN CAN I GET A BREAK FROM THESE TWO FUCKERS? JUST TELL ME, WHEEEEEEEEEN?" Marshal asked furiously.

"DON'T YOU FUCKING RAISE YOUR FUCKING VOICE OVER ME, YOU FUCKER. HOW THE FUCK SHOULD I KNOW?" Aiko yelled back at him, and it worked. It calmed him down a bit. Now he was calmer and ashamed. He thought he should've yelled at those people who made him like that in the first place. He apologized. Aiko reminded him of the time he was with Agustin, so it made him laugh. Then he remembered Agustin and Calysta, both in trouble and ruining their lives, so it made him cry. When Aiko saw that Marshal was laughing and crying simultaneously, she thought that he lost it at last. She had no idea that Marshal was like that, but then she understood that he built up all those anger, and like a bomb, it exploded in a second. It was scary for her. Nobody yelled at her like that, and the last thing she wanted to do was judge Marshal when he was in the worst moment of his life. She actually liked it, to see how passionate her boyfriend was, but God forbid, he shouldn't find out about it, or she would get yelled at now and then.

She put her hand on his head, then slowly, she let her delicate fingers go through those black hair. Marshal turned his head around and looked into Aiko's eyes. Both of them had tears in their eyes. Marshal kissed the hand that was on his head. Then he bent close to kiss her forehead.

"Have I ever told you how lucky I am? Anybody else would have left me," he whispered into her ear. She nodded. She loved him. She loved him so much that she forgave him the second he calmed down. While having tears in her eyes, she returned the favor and kissed him on the forehead. She knew how sweet and kind Marshal was, and for that, she's never taken any grudge against him.

"He could have come to Harvard and be with me. Keeping that in mind, he didn't want to stay in the same COUNTRY that Calysta was in. He is that stupid," Marshal observed. They both chuckled, but in a matter of seconds, it died off. Then suddenly, Aiko looked at Marshal in the eyes. Marshal saw fear and excitement.

"What is it?" Marshal asked, and now he got excited.

"Do you think there is a chance that Agustin fell in love again and then he broke up again, and for that, he left Cambridge?" Aiko asked. Marshal looked at her eyes in disbelief. Was she serious? he thought, but then they were talking about Agustin. He shook his head and made a sad smile. Then he looked into Aiko's eyes—they were wet from the earlier tears—and then said,

"Fuck."

Chapter 9

She had her mom's look—sweet and lovely. The Oxygen tube was on her face and the small Oxygen capsule in her backpack. She was sitting on my lap and watching her TV program. Her witch's hat was right on my face. She wore all black, and add to that, she had pointy shoes as well. He was sitting beside me with an Oxygen tube on his face and carrying the Oxygen capsule in his backpack. He was wearing the knight's helmet with the knight's armor. His boots were a little bit big for him, but those were the only boots that were left on that dreadful day. The day we went shopping, it was like the actual medieval age and we were in the middle of a battlefield. People were pushing one another to get what they wanted. It was a dreadful day to remember. The witch and the witch-hunter were watching TV peacefully with oxygen tubes on their faces. It was peaceful sitting there with them. I put my arm around his shoulder and pressed him closer to my chest. He didn't resist.

"I didn't know that the stars die," she said . "Why is it happening?"

"Do you want me to spoil the program for you?" I teased her.

"No, but I want to know," she responded.

"Do you want the short answer or the long one?" I asked.

"The short one," she requested.

"Nothing lasts forever," I answered.

"And the long one?" she asked, which means she wasn't satisfied with the answer.

"Ran out of fuel, like your capsule," I responded and pointed out that she had to change the capsule. She laughed at my answer.

"It's not fair," she protested.

"I believe you are right, young lady. I shouldn't have given both answers. It wasn't fair for me," I responded. She giggled.

"I meant, you should have given me the long answer, but you didn't. You lied," she said and gave me a frowny face.

"Well, we should argue about that since the second answer had three more words than the first one. In dictionary and mathematics, it is defined as the longer one. See, I didn't lie," I responded. She was holding back her smile and tried hard to keep her frowny face. I was smiling the whole time.

"Can you give me at least a little bit more explanation?" she requested.

"Run out of fuel, like your capsule, get bigger, get shrank, and then they die," I answered with a smile on my face. Now her frown got meaner, still holding back her smile.

"Aren't you satisfied with the answers?" I asked.

"No," she responded quickly.

"Well, you and miiiiiiiillions of other scientists are sharing the same feeling. They are not satisfied with anything either, and they want to know more, so they try to find the answers by themselves, which is great. Sometimes, that dissatisfaction answers and the pursuit to find them, let them find the mistakes in the answers that nobody saw or find a new or better way to explain it. What I am trying to say is, you should always find the answers that make you satisfy. The real scientist doesn't care about who said what or how reliable the source is. They always try to find their answers," I replied.

"Do you think that I could be a scientist someday?" she asked.

"Do you wanna know the ingredient to become a scientist?" I responded.

"Uhuum," she responded.

"Well, the ingredients are questions, suspicious answers, trying to find the answers without being biased. If you combine them with orders, you make a good scientist. Right now, I see a witch who has a question, and she is not satisfied by the answers I gave her. Good. Is the witch going to find the answer that makes her satisfied?" I asked her.

"Uhuum," she responded and nodded her head as well to emphasize the answer.

"Well, we have a little witch scientist. It is odd, but welcome to the community," I responded. Her frowny face was gone. She smiled. She put her little lips on my cheek and gave me a quick kiss. After that, she lay back on my chest. Her little head was right below my chin. Now her pointy hat was on the other side of my face.

"Meleta! Valerio! You guys ready?" their mom asked from the bedroom. We all ignored her. Then she came to the hall. "You guys ready?" she asked again. Before anyone could answer, Meleta turned around and put her knees on my lap, so I had to close my two legs and make them tighter so she wouldn't slide through my legs. She nodded her head as a positive answer, then she removed her oxygen tubes with her right hand while holding herself steady with her other hand around my neck. I put my hand around her slim and light body and held her steady from the back. I didn't want her to fall back.

"Mommy, guess what? I am a scientist," Meleta said it with lots of excitement. Her mom moved closer to the couch where I was sitting.

"Then why do I only see a witch with a hat? Have you compelled me?" her mom responded.

"No, no, Mommy. Agustin told me that I am a scientist. He said it himself," she said.

"Maybe you compelled him to say that," her mom answered with a smile.

"Should I kill the witch?" Valerio asked with a smile on his little round face.

"Then you will get half the chocolate from the neighbors. It is not economical," I answered.

"Then I will burn her after we get our treats," Valerio said with excitement.

"That's the spirit of a knight. It is how it's been done since ancient time," I responded with a smile. His mom laughed at both of us. Valerio smiled as well.

"But, Moooooooooom! I am the reeeeal scientist," Meleta insisted. "Agustin said that I have all the ingredients for it."

"To make what? A potion?" Her mom was still teasing her.

"No, no! Agustin, you tell her," she asked me.

"She is a scientist," I responded.

"Not like that, the way you explained it to me," Meleta requested.

"Well, it was you who claimed to be a scientist to your mom, not me. A scientist always defends her claim by herself, not let someone else do that for her. By keeping that in mind, defend yourself by telling her the whole story," I responded. She got a little annoyed, but she did what I asked her to do. After that, she was breathing hard a little bit, so she put back on the Oxygen tube.

"Now I am convinced that you are a good scientist, and I couldn't agree more," her mom said while coddling her daughter's head. Then she kissed me on top of my head as a thank you.

"Let's change the capsules, and then we go out. We don't want to be late. Other kids might get your treats," she said.

I picked up Meleta with my left hand. She giggled. She liked it. She always liked it. Then I noticed her mom's face. She was beautiful. She was my Princess Fiona, and I was her Shrek. I saw her smiling and moving her lips without making any noise to say to me, "THANK YOU."

Chapter 10

Her room was so girlish. There were so many happy colors, such as pink and blue, on the wall and the furniture. Her blanket had a picture of one of those Disney movies. I believe it was Sleeping Beauty. Her father had a taste of humor when he chose that blanket. She also kept all kinds of dolls in her room. From Barbie to Bambie, there were all kinds of dolls in her room. Her desk was neat and organized. The room smelled fresh. Everything was in place. My interest was to look at her drawer, but I was too afraid to look into it. She went out to bring some tea for me, and it had been like ten minutes since she left, so she could come back at any time now. She had a big bookshelf. There were so many novels, which most of them were romantic ones. I wanted to try her bed. I wanted to see how she felt when she went to the same bed every night, so I lay down there. I opened my arms and spread them on the bed. The blanket was soft, and the mattress was a little bit hard. I noticed her bed didn't have those suspensions under it; however, it was comfortable enough. Her bed smelled sweet vanilla. The Panda was sitting right on top of the bed. He gave the look of "Be careful, bastard" to me with the frozen smile on him, and I give him back the look of "***Watch who you are talking to***." I looked at her window. The frame was pink in color. The window had a view of those tall buildings close to her apartment. Any pervert could watch her sleeping. It was a good view for the people who wanted to watch the city at night, but I wanted to see the stars and the trees. I wasn't really a fan of tall buildings or skyscrapers.

Even though they were the art of architects and mathematics, they weren't beautiful to me. I looked back to the bookshelf. I saw some mathematics books on the shelf, which made me smile. I was proud of her. She was my protégé. She changed. She changed a lot since we met. I don't know if it was because of mathematics or hanging out with Marshal and me that she changed a lot. She became more mature. The Money that her parents gave her for spending in school, she spent for other classes. She liked to paint, so she signed up for it. Now and then, she went to cooking class.

I even remember the day we were talking about food. I told her that nowadays, women are getting too feminists that they are losing sight of the best art—the art of cooking. Today's women lost the reason why cooking happened in the first place. Wasn't it to make healthy food for yourself and the family and pass it on to the next generation? Today secret sauce is using too much oil or using store-bought dressing. What happened to the passion they had once? The girls were talking about persona, and they had no idea what it really meant. They are too afraid to hold a book and read it because other girls mock them as geeks or losers. If they want to learn how to sew a worn dress, they are considered as cheap people who don't want to spend more money. People in the past knew how to fix things, so when the relationship problem came around, they tried to fix it together instead of being surprised by it. Now look at the society we are living in. The kids are growing up without either fathers or mothers. Why? Because their parents couldn't solve the problem. They found an easy way out, and they took it. It was sad to talk about it. She told me about the women who got abused by their husbands, and in return, I answered that I wasn't talking about those people. There were even some problems in mathematics that were not logical and didn't make any sense. No one would blame the person who couldn't find any solution for it, but because of some illogical problem, can we say let's forget about the whole math? Let's not solve any of them because there were some irrational problems in it, or even worse, let's just find the easy problems and not do the difficult ones. We talked, and we learned a lot from each other. I learned to like her the way she was. I told her once that her outer beauty was a bonus for her inside beauty.

"What are you doing?" Calysta asked. She caught me on her bed. She had the tray in her hand.

"I am sleeping with Princess Aurora. Do you think she wakes up if I kiss her?" I responded. She laughed.

"What if my father found you like this?" she asked while she was smiling.

"I would say that it's not what he thinks it is. I wasn't cheating on you with Princess Aurora on your bed," I answered. She laughed.

"Then you know what will happen after you said that," she said.

"He would laugh while stabbing me in the heart," I responded. She smiled but gave me the face that she didn't want anything bad to ever happen to me.

"I think he just gets disappointed and, of course, sad. He likes you too much to hurt you," she said with a proud smile on her face.

"I like your father too. I was wondering that I should start calling him father too," I said while having a smile on my face. She turned red while having the most innocent smile on her face.

"Now you sound like a player," she said while her head was down.

I smiled. That was the only thing that I could do. I stood up and took the tray and then put it on the desk. I kissed her forehead.

"I don't play with other people's feelings," I said. I took the cup and sipped the tea. It was hot, just the way I like it.

"Thanks for the tea," I said.

"You're welcome," she said while she was biting her lip. She sat beside me. I looked at her while she was looking down. I felt relieved. She trusted me enough that I would not do anything stupid, and I wasn't going to do it anyway. However, it wasn't an easy thing. Having my dream girl sitting on the bed right beside me, it was almost close to impossible to not have a dirty thought. She held the other cup between her hands, and I was jealous of that cup at that moment. There was this awkward silence between us. None of us knew how to get out of it, so we were silent for a while. I didn't want to stand up first from the bed. What would she think if I stood up? And fearing that thought made me sit still.

"Did you mean it?" Calysta asked. I knew exactly what she meant by saying that. I didn't know what to answer.

"I am not sure," I said honestly. She looked into my eyes. Those sapphire-blue eyes looked inside my heart. I knew from the eyes that she was hurt, and before it got too late, I continued.

"Do you know the story of a flower that fell in love with a beautiful girl?" I asked.

"No," she answered, but still, I could feel the hurt in her voice.

"There was this little flower who happened to fall in love with humans. As unusual as it was for the flower, every other flower told the little flower that falling in love with humans was crazy, but the little flower didn't listen.

"One day that little flower fell in love with a little girl who came every day and passed by it without noticing the little flower. Days and nights passed, but the little girl overlooked the love of that specific flower. The flower bloomed before any other flowers, which was really risky, hoping that the little girl would notice the flower, but nothing happened.

"Time passed, and the little girl became a beautiful young girl, and the little flower lost its natural color because it got weaker and weaker. It was dying. The little flower selflessly gave away whatever it had to make the girl happy and make her come back to the place where it was, so it traded its nectar to the moth to come at a specific time so the girl could see a creature that made her happy. It was painful for the flower to see that no matter what the flower did for the girl, she didn't notice its devotion and love.

"One day the flower got really weak that it could die at any moment. It tried its best to give its last nectar to the moth, but the nectar wasn't ready, so the giant moth flew off to other flowers.

"The little flower was really sad. Not because it was dying, no. It wanted to see that girl's smile for the last time.

"Sad and brokenhearted, waiting for its death. Suddenly, a hand came and picked it up. It was a young man who picked it up. The moment the flower thought that all hopes were lost, it saw the girl come with a big smile on her face. The young man handed in the flower to her. The flower died in her hand, and it gave away the best odor that is known between the flowers. She loved the smell of the flower, and somehow, it brought tears to her eyes.

"The girl kept the flower in a safe place from that day on. The name of the flower was Ghost Orchid."

"Why ghost?" she asked while she had tears in her eyes.

"I don't know for sure. It is said that the root of this flower is so blended into a tree that it seems it is flying like a ghost. You should ask Marshal about it. He knows a lot about it," I answered.

"It is sad," she said.

"Which part? Dying in the hand of the person it loved so much?"

"No, yeah. I don't know. All of it. Why did it have to die? Did she find out that the flower loved her? Why it had to be sad?"

"I thought it was a happy ending for the flower. It finally rested in a place that it wanted to be and be remembered by the one whom it loved the most," I answered.

"You are so cruel," Calysta said. Now she was wiping her tears. I reached for her head with both my hands. After I kissed her forehead, I asked her why she said it, but she didn't answer me.

"Do you know a lot of people consider this story as a love story?" I asked her.

"I know," she answered. Her head was pressed to my chest. I wished I could hold her like that forever.

"I am not cruel, but love is. It hurts. It makes people cry and makes them do unthinkable things. When I talked about love to your father and my father, they both laughed at me. I know why. It's because they believed I had no idea what I was talking about, and I think it is true. I'll be another stupid kid if I think I know more than them and not use their wisdom. I could see in your father's eyes how much he loves you and your mother. He'll do anything for you to keep that smile on your face, so he knows what he is talking about. When he advised me to wait until I grew up and learn it by myself, I thought I should wait and respect his advice. That was why I said 'I am not sure,' because I do not know the answer or have the wisdom for it. The last thing I want to do is hurt you just by not knowing," I said it calmly.

She put her hand on my chest and lifted her head from my chest. It was hurtful for me to let her do that, but what could I have done? I could still see the tears in her eyes, but there was a smile on her lips. Her eyes moved from my eyes to my lips. She then leaned over, and before I knew it, our lips touched. I could feel the fantastic heat from her breath on my lips and the soft tissue of her lips against mine. My heart raced. I could feel that my body temperature was rising. She parted her lips from mine, and I was aching to have those lips back where they were. I held her face between my hands and tried to reach her lips again. She didn't resist, so our lips touched again for the second time. I was in heaven. I didn't know what to do. *Can I bite them? Can I eat it? Does she mind if I do that? What the hell am I supposed to do now? Swallow your goddamn saliva. Where the fuck did I get this much saliva? Calm down, you idiot. Do as she does. There you go. She is sucking your lips, then it is okay for you to suck hers. See, it is easy. It's a piece of cake. Try not to do anything that turns her off,* I thought.

She parted her lips again. She was smiling and biting her lips by her teeth.

"What is wrong? Did I do something wrong?" I asked anxiously.

"No, you did well," she responded.

"Then why did you stop?" I asked. I saw her smiling.

"Oh, it's nothing. Don't worry about it, okay?" she responded. I didn't buy it.

"You know what? It is unfair. I am teaching you lots of things, but you are not teaching me anything. It's going to stop now. You have to teach me how to kiss. Deal?" I asked. She laughed hard. When she got her control back a little bit, she said with a mischievous smile,

"I don't know why you made such a big deal out of it. You didn't do anything wrong. I was afraid if I continued kissing you, I wouldn't be able to control myself not to go further. Are you getting what I am trying to say?"

I turned red from embarrassment when I thought about it, so I looked down. Now I wasn't sure what I would do if I looked at her again. She laughed at my reaction. Even the voice of her laughter was arousing me. She gave me some gratulation, which I had never felt before. I wanted it to happen again, but I didn't want to push it.

"What are you gonna do tomorrow?" she asked.

"I'll go to the site," I answered. Still, my head was down. I knew she wanted to change the subject. She would be Panglossian if she thought that I would get over it that fast. However, I played along.

"Again?" she asked and seemed annoyed.

"It seems like you are going to work there, not me," I responded with a smile.

"You are working too much, Agustin. Haven't you learned all the trades in this world yet? Marshal told me that you learned other trades even before you met him. It is great, but when do you have time to be young and stupid?" she said with a frangible voice. I knew what she meant was having more time around her, but the thing was, I wasn't learning those trades for my own sake. It was beneficial for anybody that I was with, mostly my father.

"Do you wanna know how I got to this mess?" I asked her sincerely.

"Uhuum," she responded.

"Those days that I was alone and I had no friends, I remember one day that my father brought a plumber to our house. I was ten at that time. The guy started working with pipes, and he did nothing special. He opened a pipe and decluttered it and then put it back, and for just doing that, he received a lot of money. It was a lot of money for me when I was a kid. One day I asked my father what he would do if I did the same thing in the house. First, he laughed at me. Then he saw that I was serious. He changed his attitude and asked me if I wanted to be a plumber. I answered him that the job was too boring, but if he gave me a good amount of money, I would consider just learning how to do the job for our house and business. He laughed and made a deal. So from that day on, I worked for free as an apprentice in many different trades but charged my father for each one I used in our house. How do you feel that your boyfriend built up and modified everything in his car, computer, furniture, and so many other things? And now his car is the coolest thing that any man can dream of. Anyone can go and buy a new sports car, but building a sports car out of scraps is an art that not many people can do," I said it proudly.

"I know. I like it. When I need a handyperson for anything, I don't need to look far. He is right here, and he is my boyfriend, but I need you as a boyfriend as well. When do you have time to be my boyfriend?" she said with a smile.

"Handyman? No disrespect to the handyman, but handyman? Why is it everyone else sees it as an art and calls me an artist, but my beautiful girlfriend calls me a handyman?" I said with a disappointed look.

She smiled and gave me a quick kiss on the cheek.

"I'm sorry. You know that my vocabulary for this kind of thing is penurious," she explained herself with a witty comeback. It worked. It made me laugh.

"Why do you have to be so cute and smart?" I said it, and without a second thought, I pinched her smiley cheek with care and love.

"Agusttttttiiiin? Are you trying to distract me? Still, you have to explain to me why my handsome and ARTISTIC boyfriend doesn't have time for me," she asked.

"I think I gave you time, and the evidence for it is, right now, I am here with you. But if you mean to be available 24/7, well, welcome to the club, and you should go to the line where my parents are waiting too," I explained happily, and I thought I was magnanimous, but she didn't like the sound of it. She was angry about it, so we didn't talk for a few seconds until her cuteness won me over, and I gave in by chuckling.

"I'm sorry. I should have asked first what you meant by asking me to have more time," I pleaded.

"Well, I don't have anything to say to you," she responded with disgust. It just made me love her more. Not that I like her being in that state. No, it just showed how innocent and fragile she was, and I had to take care of her carefully like anything precious in this world. I reached for her head with my hand. She resisted a little bit and tried to be playful, but when I reached for her, I put her head right where I loved the most—on my chest.

"I wish there was a taste for the feelings—the actual taste. For example, chocolate is for forgiveness and a rotten taste for grudge and hate. Ice cream is for being happy, and outdated milk taste for being sad, and so on . . .," I said it sadly, but it brought a smile to her face finally.

"What can I do to you now, huh? You come and say something like that to me, and it makes me feel like a bad person if I stay angry at you. I wish you weren't this much good, so I didn't have to be this much sad when you aren't around," she said with a smile but with a sad voice.

"Scheduling is everyone's nightmare. People don't realize how little time we have in this world and how much work needs to be done. I'm not talking about making a better future or those kinds of crap that magazines or motivational speakers are trying to sell. I am talking about all the passion and love I have, and I have to make time for all of them. I love painting, and I love to spend my whole life just doing it, but I also love composing music, and I want to do the same for it. You know how much I love mathematics. You know that I have to put the alarm on when I do the mathematics, I lose track of time, and It takes me to another wonderland. You know what I am talking about. You got interested in math too. Then there is the cool stuff I reaaally, really want to learn, such as different trades. I want to open things up like a surgeon and revive them. The joy of it is unimaginable. I love cooking, sleeping, learning new techniques in Wing Chun, hanging out with friends, being with family and you, traveling, and who knows where the list ends? However, I've got twenty-four hours, and it is not even enough for just one of those passions I love," I said it with a sad tone.

"So the time is cruel, not you. I got it. But do you know the reason why I attend so many other classes?" she asked me.

"I believe you like those classes and the skills," I answered.

"True, but the reason is, the main reason is, when I look at myself and you, I see that I've got nothing. I am not smart like you. I can't paint like you. For heaven's sake, I can't even cook better than you. So it is more like a pretty face for you, and I hate that. I'm embarrassed. I see how you like to learn new things. You actually dive into it, but I have to be forced to do anything at all. I'm not too fond of this feeling—the feeling that I am not good enough for you," she said.

Well, that was unexpected. What was I supposed to tell her now? ***"Don't worry. Everything is fine, and I like you the way that you are"?*** One wrong statement and I was out. She would think that I am not serious enough for her or, even worse, I don't care about her. What was I supposed to tell her? I didn't know, and it was scary. I didn't want to be alone again. Now that she was with me, I knew that I couldn't be alone again.

"I have a different perspective than you about my skills. I see loneliness. I see that when I wanted to play with other kids, they didn't let me in their teams. I see they wanted to hurt me because I was smarter than them. I was an outcast from anything that meant teamwork. I see the nights that I was crying in bed because I didn't want to let my family know how weak I was. I see a brokenhearted girl in front of me who is sad that why she is not like me? It is more like people see a warrior. They see how big and skillful they are with swords, but they don't see scars or how many people have lost their lives for that skill. They don't know the nights those faces haunted him. I have changed a lot. A year ago, I wouldn't care if I was alone, but not having you in my life would be another sad moment in my life. In the beginning, yes, you are right. You were a pretty face for me. But know that I got to know you, trust me when I tell you that you aren't just a pretty face for me anymore. You are precious and beautiful like a diamond, mature like Mother Teresa, and smart like Madam Marie Curie than any girls I know in our school. Don't beat yourself up because you are unique. I see your uniqueness, and I love it. I don't see and feel that I am better than you. It is the other way around. Do you want to know how many people hate me just because you are my girlfriend? I hear them say, 'Look at that bastard, how he got so lucky to be with Calysta. She is smart and beautiful, and look at him. He is another sorry ass who got so lucky,'" I said with my head down. She laughed and then smiled. She looked at me with her beautiful blue eyes, which I would never get used to, and then kissed me again on the lips. I lost track of time for the kissing. When we came to ourselves, it was her mom that was calling us for dinner.

Chapter 11

"They accepted it," I told Corwin.

"What the fuck," he responded.

"I'm doing research and study at the same time over there. Can you believe it?" I said happily.

"What the fuck? You don't even have a bachelor of science, let alone a PhD, and they want you over there?"

"I said STUDY and research at the same time. I've got so many recommendations and signatures from my teachers and other professors. They helped a lot. I can't believe it. I can go there and start working over there."

"Fuck. You deserve it. I don't see why they won't accept you there without any recommendations. But fuck. Should I go and be a teacher's pet like you? So maybe I'd get a chance to be there too."

"CERN doesn't accept dummies, you fucker."

"You are leaving as a virgin. Goodbye, virgin."

I smiled. "I am not a virgin," I responded.

"I didn't see you fucking any girls in Cambridge," Corwin said.

David and Winn arrived as well. They joined in our conversation after Corwin told them about the news. They congratulated me the way they knew best, by using my penetralia as their amusement.

"Anyway, you deserve it. Maybe you'll go there and change their pipes in the toilet now and then," Winn said with a smile.

"Or th'ir fart sit?" David joined in.

"What the fuck does that even mean? Fart sit?" I asked with a smile.

"It's a somth'ng thet you are gong to invent fo gathering other scientists' farts as your collection," David said while he was laughing. Everybody joined in and laughed with him.

"It is going to be difficult for me to leave you guys in here. I just made friends in here, and now I have to leave," I said in a sad voice.

"Don't worry. We'll send you the used condoms in post express to wherever you go. That way, you never miss us," Corwin said, and David and Winn laughed.

"What? You wanna tell me that you are still lonely and watching porn? Is that the message you want to send?" I responded. David and Winn laughed.

"We'll see," Corwin said, with nothing better to say.

"Ohh, here she comes. Your crush is approaching. Look," Corwin said with excitement. I turned around in the direction he was looking. I saw her coming with her friend. She was coming toward us. It was Marina.

Whenever I saw her in the last few weeks, I pretended that I wasn't into her anymore, that she wasn't important. However, my heart was beating so fast that it made me sweat whenever I saw her. I would be worried if I didn't see her for a day. I hated myself for having this kind of feeling for her. I wasn't important to her anyway. I was another boy who wanted to get to her pants. That was how she thought of me. True enough, because she was beautiful and attractive; it was also false because that was the last thing I wanted from her.

"Hello," she said with a happy face. She was looking at everyone for a response.

"Hello, how do you do?" Corwin said formally. I tried hard not to laugh. Then he took her hand to shake it.

"H'ello, Love," David said. She nodded as an acknowledgment.

"Hello," Winn said with his shy character.

"Hi," I said it like a whisper. I could barely hear my own voice. I believe I was still pretending that I wasn't into her, but to make sure she saw my response, I said it while I was nodding my head.

After greeting, she turned to Corwin, and I believe she asked him about his notes in one of our teacher's lectures. I am not sure what they said, but I knew that I wanted to be with them badly, so to save myself from myself, I told Corwin that I would meet him later that day. I left. My body moved away, but my thought and spirit were still there. I was frozen at the time when I heard her voice again. I was reviewing her slender and delicate body shape over and over again in my head. I wished I were the person who was talking to her. I watched her walk away from me only two times, and I was walking away from the place she was for thousands of times now.

What a day.

Chapter 12

"Cara, stop it. I am not interested in any of them. They are all the same. They all want to have sex with me," she said with frustration.

"But, Mary, isn't it the whole point? Going to school, getting a good job, so we could have anybody that we want or when we want?" Cara said with a smile.

"What the hell are you talking about? Are you here to get laid? Is that what you want? Then you could have gone to any university that you wanted to. Why go this distance to have sex?" Marina responded with a smile.

"True, but the seeds in here are better than anywhere else," Cara responded, and both started laughing.

"Marina, excuse me."

Marina stopped laughing and looked at her friend.

"Excuse me, Marina?"

Marina turned around and saw a tall, athlete-shape, inverted triangle cheekbone with long curly dark hair. He had shade glasses on, so she couldn't see his eyes, but so far, this guy looked like a movie star. Everything was suggesting that this guy must be a womanizer. With one look, any girl could fall for him, but not her. She didn't want to be a plain number for him. Who did he think he was? She bet that this guy made a bet with other guys to get her phone number. She couldn't believe she couldn't catch a break from these men. She thought she was free at last. She could at least focus on the subject she wanted to learn. To be honest, she was flattered that she got this much attention, but wasn't it too easy for her? Where was the romance she was looking for? She didn't like fairy-tale stories, but she wanted someone who was like a prince. Where was that hero? Anyway, she had to deal with this guy.

"Yes?" she answered.

"Can I talk to you in private?" the boy asked her.

"Is it something to do with class?" Marina asked, but the boy paused. She caught him off guard.

"No, it is not," the boy answered.

"Well, I'm sorry. I can't," she responded.

"Are you sure? Can't you give me at least five minutes? It won't take too long." The boy almost begged her, but she didn't want to hear anything about it, especially now that Cara was watching as well. She wouldn't hear the end of it. "What did he say? What did he want? Did he ask you out?" Or thousands of other questions she would probably ask.

"No, I'm sorry," Marina responded, and before the boy said something else, she took off. She walked fast. After she made sure she was at a safe distance, she slowed down.

"What the hell was that? I just want to know what the hell you were thinking. Are you crazy to blow him off like that? Did you even see how handsome he was? Oh my God, I hate you now. Couldn't you at least give him a chance to talk? Why it always has to be you?" Marina just walked and listened to her complaints and had a smile on her face. She thought it would be the end of it there, but it sounded like no matter which side of the knife she grabbed, it almost always cut her deep. Cara was still complaining. She thought she'd let her friend empty herself, and when she was done, then she could explain herself. The weather was hot. She felt like her brain was cooking inside her skull. She sped up again and was looking for a shelter or shade to hide from this torturing sun. She didn't wear so much makeup, so she wasn't worried about what would happen if it washed away. Cara was still complaining. Marina was thinking about the lecture of Professor Oswald. She had so many questions to ask him about the last class. Hopefully, he had a little bit of time to spare so that she could get some answers from him. She respected him. He knew what he was talking about.

Cara was still complaining. Marina thought that even the power of the sun couldn't make her friend shut up. Thank God she saw the department that she was heading to. Finally, there was a place to hide from this hellish heat. Cara sped up as Marina sped up again, but she didn't stop complaining. Marina didn't mind her friend's complaining. It was actually entertaining. Cara was precisely the opposite of her. Where she was shy, Cara wasn't, or at the time, Marina didn't want to talk a lot, and Cara would do precisely the opposite. They got into the building. The building wasn't cold either, but it was better than staying under the sun. They headed toward Professor Oswald's class. Now Cara got a little bit calmer. Maybe it was the heat that made her talk that much. That was what Marina thought. They went and sat on their usual seats.

"What if he was your love of life?" Cara asked, and this time, she waited for an answer.

"Well, poor me, I'll be miserable for the rest of my life. I will cry days and nights and then kill myself because I couldn't bear the thought he is not going to be with me," she responded with sarcasm. There was silence for a while. Cara didn't look at Marina for a time, and when she started talking, it was like she was talking to herself. She told her,

"Love isn't something to laugh about. It is hurtful. It is going to cause you so much pain that you've never had before. You think you will cry because of the pain, but you will actually cry to keep your sanity together. There won't be any drugs to heal you. There won't be any distractions to keep you distracted enough. When the time passes and it is all gone, you will look at yourself again, and the only thing you will see is an empty shell," Cara said with sadness in her voice.

"Ohh, Cara, I wasn't planning to mock you. I know I said something stupid. Please forgive me," Marina begged.

"You don't get it, do you?" Cara responded while trying not to cry.

"I wa—"

"Who is he?" a girl in front of them said. She was talking to her friend.

"I don't know. What is he doing in front of the professor's desk?" the other girl responded.

"Yeah, I heard he is a teacher's pet. Smart my ass, he doesn't know shit." The boys behind them were talking.

"Are you fucking jealous? He is smart, all right, or how else could he get in here? But the thing that pisses me off is, this fucker is everyone's nightmare. Look at that fucker. I bet every girl fell for him already," the other boy responded.

"But I didn't see him in any party," the boy said.

"Well, do you expect him to be like us? Going party to get noticed? If he wants a girl, he gets it. Simple like that," the other one responded.

Marina couldn't help herself from chuckling. They were probably right. She got the same vibe when she met him for the first time.

"Hello, everyone. My name is Agustin Adalbert, your substitute teacher for today. There was an emergency for Professor Oswald, and as you can see, his assistant wasn't available for other reasons too, so you're stuck with me." He looked at people in the front seats and then continued, "And add to that, I am suffering PTSD now for what just happened to me not ten minutes ago." Everyone laughed at what he just said. She turned red. She thought she had been discovered and he was going to embarrass her in front of the class. Now she was sweating. It wasn't because of the heat. Anything could happen now. The last thing she wanted now was lots of attention toward her. Why did it have to be him? Why today? Why this class?

"Do you mind telling us what happened to you?" a female voice asked from the crowd.

That's it. I am done, Marina thought.

"Well, not that it's your business, but I'll let you know some wisdom that I learned today. Never ask a girl out on a hot day, because if you get rejected, you are going to feel nausea, confusion, breathing problem, and worse than that, you can't tell if it is tears coming down or sweat. So you think that it is a heartbreak symptom, but it could be a heatstroke." And with that, the whole class laughed, and it continued for almost two minutes, and then they started chatting.

"I just want to punch his fucking face. He thinks he is funny now?" the boy behind her told his friend.

The other one chuckled. "Well, I'll give him that. He is a funny dude. I think you should take his advice, and don't do anything stupid because you can't tell you are bleeding out from the fight or you are sweating. I doubt that you can handle him."

"Perfect, now you are quoting him?" The other one was pissed off.

"Okay, okay, that's enough. The professor didn't send me here to do stand-up comedy for you guys, but I'm glad my misery is your amusement. I don't know most of you guys or, better to say, none of you, so let's continue this lecture and get on with it and finish it fast," Agustin said.

"Who was it?" one student asked.

"It was a beautiful girl with a great smile. I can't tell you what her name is because she is real and she is studying in this university, and I don't wanna draw too much unwanted attention to her, so let's move on," he answered. *Does he know that I am in his class now? What if he doesn't know and when he finds out, he tells everyone? What am I supposed to do, huh? Why it had to be him? I should have talked to him. At least let him hang dry. Tell him I will think about it. How the fuck was I supposed to know that it would be him,* Marina thought.

"Ahhhh, he is soooooooooooo nice. Even after what she did to him, he considered her well-being. If it were any other guy, he would spell out the name earlier," the girl in front of Marina said.

"I can't believe he got rejected. Who could possibly do that? She must be either a princess or insane or blind, and I know for a fact that we don't have any princess in this university," the other girl in front of Cara said.

Marina, for the first time, looked at her friend. Her friend was trying not to laugh too loud by putting her hand in front of her mouth, but her body was shaking from laughing.

"But it's not fair. I want to try my luck," a male voice protested, and by that, another student started laughing.

"It is not a sword in the stone that you want to try," Agustin said, and the whole class started laughing again. "She is a human being and has feelings. As I said, I don't wanna draw too much attention to her. The reason I brought her up was to break the ice in the class. Now that you guys are more comfortable, let's finish this class." He started his lecture.

"That was close," Cara whispered to her friend. "I didn't know that karma answers you this fast," she said while trying to hold back her laugh.

"Shhhhhhhhhhhh, please be quiet. I don't want him to notice us. Please, please," Marina begged.

Cara smiled and shook her head as a disappointment. "I don't think he would embarrass you if he discovered you. I don't think he's that kind of guy."

"Well, I don't want to find out what kind of guy he is today, okay?" Marina responded with irritation.

Maybe Cara was right, maybe not. Who knows? The time wasn't right to find out who was right or not.

"How much do you know about mathematics?" Agustin asked the class.

"Well, it's a subject that no one likes, but they're doomed to it," one male student responded. Some students laughed.

"I am glad you said that because today's lecture isn't about what Professor Oswald was going to teach you. Today's lecture is going to be an amazing journey from mathematics to physics, but before I start, I want you to be familiar with the perspective I have for math," he said, and then he started writing a sentence on the board.

"To be, or not to be, that is the question."

And then he wrote:

$$\pm 1$$

He turned to the class and asked, "What do they have in common?"

"Aren't they the same?" one student responded.

Agustin smiled and nodded his head. "Exactly. Now tell me what the difference is."

Everyone started talking to one another. For the first time, Marina got distracted to find the answer. She was still worried; however, she wanted to find out the answer, though she wasn't planning on answering even if she found it.

"Anyone?" Agustin asked.

"One of them is Shakespeare's quote, and the other one is used in mathematics for the probability of more or less."

"Close enough. The problem is that there aren't many people that know who came up with ±1, but almost all people know that famous sentence is from Shakespeare. Even though both of them have the same meaning, same beauty, but the other one practically has more function in real life than the line William Shakespeare said," Agustin said. He let the class absorb what he just said.

"It would be a happy story for the person who passed the finish line in Olympics one second less than the other one, or vice versa, it could be a sad story since the other guy tried hard, sacrificed everything, and that gold medal would change everything for him, but his body betrayed him.

"Or it could be a sad story of someone's life who lost his love of life because the medical emergency couldn't come one minute earlier to save her.

"Your imagination is the limit to make a happy or sad story with it," he said, and then he walked back to the board.

He drew a picture of a beautiful girl on the board. The boys started whistling and chatting. He let them talk. Then he turned around. Everyone got silenced and wondered what he wanted to say. The picture was drawn beautifully; the girls and boys both fell for the image.

"Now look at this person. And no, she is not real, but it could be anyone. What would you do if you met this girl?" he asked the class.

"I would dive in and ask her out," a guy from the crowd said. Some people laughed.

"Well, before you do that, how about the chance you have to take? Don't forget ±1. Would you still take that chance? By saying that, I mean, she could have an extra part or less. Would you still go out with her?" he asked the individual.

"It depends. If she has an extra part in toes or finger, I still will go out with her, but if she gets the extra part which each man, sorry, I mean, most men have, well, the answer will be no," he answered. Some of the class laughed.

"What if that person is everything you need, but she has the only problem you mentioned. Would you go out with her?" Agustin asked.

"It sounds so harsh. I wouldn't, but would you blame me for that? Would you go out with that person?" he responded.

"To answer your first question, I wouldn't judge you. Everyone has a different taste in life, and who am I to decide which one is good or bad? To answer the second part of your question, I don't know. Maybe or maybe not. To me, it is just a mutation that happens in her genes. It only describes what her body looks like, but it doesn't let you know who she really is. The mutation doesn't have time. It could happen anytime in life in any form. You are familiar with cancer. What do you think the cancer is? It is a mutation that could happen in any living cell in your body. That cell will grow and behave differently, and in the end, it will kill the host. You can say the same thing about bipolar, Coronaviruses which cause the common cold, HIV, Alzheimer's, Parkinson's, and the list continues. These are mutated at some point. What do you think HIV is? It is just another mutated virus. Some of the mutations died out because the host either couldn't find a mate or the host didn't live long enough to be mature. However, the mutation is still happening and taking place somewhere in this world or in our bodies. Ninety-five to ninety-seven percent of the mutation is eliminated through self-abortion during pregnancy. All of that is on the shoulder of one gene that does the correction. Self-abortion could happen at any time of labor. It could happen even before the mother noticed she was pregnant or after three weeks or a month or any time even before you are even born. The point is, you are always struggling with ±1 in everyday life, and it doesn't matter if it is +1 or −1 because it is going to affect your life anyway," he answered. The class was silenced. Everyone was looking at him and paying attention to what he wanted to say next. He smiled and then continued,

"And this is how I see mathematics. It could be a poem or a sad story that makes you cry even harder than Shakespeare's play. It all depends on how you look at the numbers. I know for a fact that I am only a number in this university. Most people have no idea who I am, but they know the number of people who got accepted into this university last year, and I was one of them. I don't know your taste. If you like art, see the number as art and try to find its beauty. If you like stories, as I showed, you could make a story with any of them. The numbers could be an alphabet, a word, a sentence, or even a story, and this is the language of nature. Learn and use it, and you'll be amazed in this wonderland. And by saying that, I welcome all of you to the journey from mathematics to physics."

Marina smiled. It was the most beautiful introduction she ever had in the class, and by the face of other students, she knew she wasn't the only one who got affected by his speech. Handsome, intelligent, and mature. Did she make a mistake not hearing what he wanted to say earlier? Now she wondered. She looked at her friend Cara only to see her daydreaming about him already. No wonder why so many girls fell for him. He was the recipe for trouble.

He started his lecture, and the way he was teaching, it was so engaging and methodical that everyone was only listening and enjoying the beauty of the lesson. His beautiful voice was a bonus. It was like a lullaby. It would put you to sleep and take you to dreamland.

Whenever Agustin was writing something on the board, Marina was distracted, checking out his back muscles, his legs, his biceps while he was trying to write something over his head. This guy was a complete package. Everything about him was alluring.

She couldn't believe that she just blew off this guy not an hour ago without knowing who he was. She looked at her friend and found her still daydreaming about him. Was it too soon for Marina to admit that Cara was right? she wondered. Nothing about this guy was natural.

She looked at her notes; she couldn't believe that she had just written so many notes without even noticing that her hand was hurting. She shook her hand to let blood flow in there. Then she looked up.

She froze.

Agustin was looking at her or, better to say, staring at her in disbelief. The situation was just so bizarre that it made her smile, but she wanted to hide it from him, so she looked down at her notes again. She put her hand on her forehead like a baseball cap to hide her face. She wasn't afraid of him to expose her. She knew that Agustin wouldn't do that to her. It sounded like Cara was right again, and it was her, the stupid one.

Agustin resumed his lecture.

Thank God. She didn't know what to do if he continued watching her like that. Now she was afraid to look up. What if he was still watching her? So she spied on him by looking at him through her finger. She saw that Agustin was busy teaching the class. After a while, she noticed that Agustin was trying not to look in her direction. Was he mad at her? She didn't know, or maybe he was trying not to get distracted by not looking in her direction. She wondered.

Now the lecture seemed a lifetime to be finished.

Marina looked at her friend and saw her daydreaming as usual.

She was so distressed that it felt like a piece of lava was in her stomach.

Finally, the lecture was finished. As soon as Agustin finished the class, a swarm of girls went for him, and it was followed by a few males who had a different taste than the other males.

Marina, with force and begging, asked Cara to follow her. Cara followed her reluctantly.

"What is it? Why didn't you let me go there and talk to him?" Cara asked.

"Well, good luck with that. Did you see how many girls went for him? It was like the class just saw a megastar actor," Marina replied.

"So?" Cara asked.

"So what? There isn't a chance that you can even say Hi to him, let alone talk to him."

"What is your problem? Why do you care? I wanted to try my chance. You blew off yours. Even if there were a small chance to talk to him, I would take it."

"Wow, slow down, tigress. I didn't say don't try. I am saying let's do it another day. Find him alone and go for it. It doesn't seem like he is going anywhere anytime soon."

"You are crazy, you know? Anyhow, your face was priceless when he mentioned the meeting he had with you. Oh my God, you were so shocked that it was like... you just saw a ghost. I felt sorry for you, but you deserved it. 'Who would reject him? Either she is a princess or blind, and I know for a fact that we don't have a princess,'" Cara said while she was laughing at her friend.

"How would I know that he was a nice guy? He just came to me and asked me if I want to talk to him in private."

"Oh, I would do much more than talking in private."

Marina Laughed. "You are nasty."

"I would eat him alive. Hummmmmm, Hummm. I bet he is delicious," Cara responded with a smile.

"Eeeewwwwww! That's disgusting. I had no idea you were this much horny."

"Why? Don't you find him attractive?" Cara said while she had the biggest smile on her face.

"You are crazy, Cara," Marina said while she was laughing at her friend.

Two weeks later . . .

"Hey, Mary, look over there. He is here," Cara said to Marina. She didn't have to tell her who she meant.

Agustin and his friends were sitting in a bar with some girls. The bar was a little bit crowded. It had a dance floor. They were sitting at the table close to the dance floor. The music was deafening. It was such loud music that when a person wanted to talk to another person, they had to yell to hear what the other person was trying to say. The bar had a dim light, so there wasn't any chance Agustin could have noticed Marina unless he scanned everybody in the bar.

Marina wasn't willing to show herself either way, because whenever she did, she saw that Agustin went in the other direction. She thought he was still angry at her. This was the first time she tried the bar. Recently, she was distracted and mad at herself. She hated herself to be this weak.

The floor had some kind of alcoholic drink on it. It attached itself to every shoe that was walking on it. The DJ was playing awful music, and it seemed that no one wanted to dance to it.

There was also a piano on the far side of the bar. It was clean, but it seemed that no one played with it for a long time. It was sad. The piano was still in good shape.

The chairs close to the counter were full of people, and every one of them was holding huge glasses of a pint. The poor waitresses were running back and forth to get the order.

There was this terrible smell that was rising from this vast population. The ventilation couldn't get the smell out fast enough. The odorous mix of women's makeup and men's cologne and add to that the scent of beers and people's burp made Marina nauseous. She wondered how people could come to this kind of place knowing that this heat and smell was waiting for them.

Suppose it wasn't for Cara's sake, she wouldn't come to the place.

There were three huge bouncers on each side of the bar and were monitoring people. One of them was outside the door and asking for identification.

There were some pictures of footballers and rugby players attached to the wall. Marina had no idea who they were. Some pictures seemed to be really old, from the '70s or even '50s. She didn't care. She wasn't interested in any sports.

The music kept playing nonstop.

Boooom, boooom, boooom. That was all she heard from the music. The bar was horrible; she was wondering why people called this bar a good bar. Cara convinced her that she would have a perfect time, but it just brought her headache so far.

Girls were talking to boys. Either they were shouting at each other, or even better for the boys, they talked to them like whispering in their ears.

"**Why did you bring me in this hellhole?**" Marina shouted to her friend while she covered her ears with both hands.

"**Aren't you glad you came? Agustin is here!**" Cara shouted back.

"What are you talking about? We came here to have fun. You promised me that. I don't see anything close to it."

"Well, there are lots of boys in here. You want to have fun? Go there and talk to them."

"Are you kidding me? With this loud noise? And who said I want to socialize with them? If I wanted to do so, I would have done it in university."

"Mary, what is your problem? Can't you just relax for a second and enjoy yourself for a bit?"

"What? Joy? I only got a headache."

"**Whatever,**" Cara said and got back to her conversation with her other friend.

Marina was pissed off. She was furious at herself for coming to the bar to be reminded that she lost her chance to be with Agustin.

Suddenly, she saw that Agustin's friend dragged Agustin to the piano to the other side of the bar. They were all drunk, of course. She had no idea what they were planning. Agustin laughed with them and begged his friend to stop doing it, but they didn't listen. One of his friends ran to the DJ, and the others forced Agustin to sit there behind the piano. Agustin sat there hopelessly and waited. The music stopped. People turned around to see what was happening there.

"Hey, hey, don't worry. We are going to listen to real music for a second, and then we'll go back to whatever it was playing before, okay?" one of his friends shouted.

"You are drunk, asshole!" one person shouted back. Other people started laughing. The girls were laughing as well. Even Agustin was laughing.

"Okay, okay. Just one music, okay?" the same person said.

Some people turned their back to the bar or the table and did whatever they were doing before.

Agustin shook his head, disappointed by his friends' behavior.

He struck the first key. It was followed by other keys. It was unrhymed. It was like a drunk person was playing, but he had a serious face on. It was funny for Marina to see him like that, which brought a smile to her face. People were laughing and shaking their heads. What a disappointment. He was playing worse than the DJ.

The music started to have some rhyme now. In a matter of seconds, it turned from a child's play to a professional one.

Now people turned to see him again. Girls got interested too.

The music had a sad tone in it, but it was a nocturne. It was soothing, talking to people's hearts. It winkled out the memories of people who weren't there. Missing friends and family brought a tear to anyone who was listening. It was splendiferous music. It came with gratulation and, at the same time, sadness. The depth of the music was rising. Only a magnanimous musician with a big heart could pull up all those feelings in one piece and give them to the people. Sadness, happiness, loss, laughter, cry, love, hate, and missing were boiling up simultaneously. The music took out the heart from the chest and showed the beating heart. Breathing was difficult. No one dared to make a sound to disturb the rhyme. Finally, when it came to an end, people were like landlopers; they were lost in a world that had never been discovered, and it seemed that they were the lucky ones to be introduced to it, just like Christopher Columbus. People were still in disbelief and woe.

Everyone applauded the musician.

Agustin rose from the chair and thanked them by bowing in front of them.

He headed toward the door. His friends followed him outside as well.

Marina was shocked. She noticed she cried as well. She wiped her tears while having a smile on her face. She couldn't believe she had just witnessed the most beautiful moment in her life. The night wasn't that bad after all. She looked at her friend. Cara was lost in memories. Marina sympathized with her. Who could hear such music and not be affected? And above all, how come a young person could compose such highly skilled music? In what universe was Agustin living?

She shook off her friend. Cara looked at her while her eyes were wet with tears. Marina asked her to leave the bar as well. It somehow amused Cara, which brought her a smile. Marina smiled back. Cara didn't have to tell her what she was thinking.

"Oh, shut up," Marina responded, and after that, they both headed outside gleefully.

The street was wet from the earlier rain, reflecting the moonlight, raising the mood for the night. The deciduous trees were already shedding their leaves and gave out damp and moist air. Each step they took echoed through the silent night. There was this *shelp, shelp* voice that shoes made while walking on wet leaves on the street. The trees were rustling with winds. The smell of damp and dead leaves was delicious. The freshness of the air helped a little bit to remove the memory of heat and heavy smell in the bar. Marina inhaled deep to get in nutrition to her body and exhaled the toxin out of her system, and with that, she already forgot about the bar and that monstrous smell.

Agustin and his friend were in front of them. They were laughing. They seemed to have a good night. The colorful dead leaves were absorbing their shadows. They walked, and they were oblivious about who was following them.

Marina was dying to hear what they were talking about. What could a gifted man talk about? It seemed to her that Agustin didn't drink so much. He walked normally while the others were trembling. His friends were talking out loud, but it was incoherent and hard to comprehend what they were trying to say, and all that time, Agustin was laughing. What kind of sadness drove him to play that music? Who did he miss? Was it for his family? A friend? Or a girlfriend? Did he have a lover before he came here? Marina wondered.

Marina and her friend sauntered behind them. After fifteen minutes of walking, at last, they arrived at the campus. She wished the walk wouldn't end this soon.

The moment Agustin disappeared in front of her eyes, she noticed her heart was pounding fast, and it wasn't only that. Her eyes were clouded with tears.

When Cara saw her friend's state, without any words, she put her hand around her friend. She hugged her tightly. Marina hugged her back, and she buried her face on her friend's shoulder.

There was only the sound of the trees' rustling leaves and a girl who was sobbing on her friend's shoulder.

Chapter 13

I was making cream puffs, while Calysta and her mom were making pasta salad. Mr. Kenward was outside and was busy making the BBQ.

I was so busy that I didn't notice that Calysta and her mom were laughing at me. When I looked up, I saw them whispering to each other's ears and giggling. I went back to my work to finish my cream puffs. I was smiling. I really loved to see Calysta's laugh. It made me happy as well. Her laugh was cute and innocent, like a child. I didn't care what subject they were laughing. It just made my heart race. I wanted to stand up and hug her. I wanted to kiss her so much that it started hurting me.

I focused on the cream puffs. I loved cream puffs. The sweet taste of them made my mouth watery. The plan was to create enough cream puffs for a big family, but I wondered if anything would be left after I was done.

I was dipping in those cream puffs to a bowl full of melted chocolate one by one. Finally, my inner demon won. I put one of them in my mouth. I closed my eyes and let the sensational taste take its place. I didn't want any other senses to interrupt it, but when I heard the laughter burst from Calysta and her mom, curiosity made me open my eyes and look at them. The mother and the daughter were both laughing, but they tried to hide it behind their hands. I knew they were laughing at me, but I didn't want to stop their laughing by asking stupid questions, like "What are you laughing at?" If they felt like sharing, they would. However, it didn't stop me from smiling. I resumed my work.

"I'm sorry, Agustin. I didn't mean to laugh at you, but your face was priceless when you were eating," Mrs. Kenward explained.

"No worries. I know I make silly faces sometimes. Someone is always there to remind me of that," I said, and then I looked in Calysta's direction. Both of them laughed heartily.

The pasta salad was almost ready. It only needed a dressing, which was left for the last minutes. They used a different color of pasta. It looked delicious. I couldn't wait. I was really hungry or, better to say, starving. The smell of BBQ on one side, the pasta salad on another side, and on top of all, the cream puffs made me like a zombie.

The table I was using was big because when I dipped in the cream puffs in chocolate, it needed time to get its shape. The freezer didn't have enough space, so I used liquid nitrogen to cool them down. It was a dangerous task, but I was confident that I could handle it safely.

I looked outside of the window and saw Calysta's father was still busy making BBQ.

It was a lake house that they rented. The view was breathtaking. The clean blue lake was surrounded by evergreen trees, red maples, shadbush, sycamore, black cherry, balsam fir, and honey locust. On the far side, there were hills covered with trees and bushes. The reflection of the trees and bushes on the water was the most fantastic show. The mist in the morning and the sunset in the afternoon made me cry like a baby. The house itself was designed in a way to capture every precious second of the view. Every part of the house had a window to the outside. It was like the whole place was sitting on glass. It was a good thing. I could see the deep woods from the back and the lake in front. The inside of the lake house was another beauty itself. The house was two stories. Downstairs, there were two couches that had been connected in an L shape. They had the color of a smooth cream with sandy-brown stripes. The couches faced two armchairs with dark-brown color on the arms and sienna color on the side woods. The armchair seating's cloth had a beige color with bronze stripes. The couches had three sets of cushions. On each set, there was a matching color cushion to the sofa. The other one was midnight blue, and next to it was sangria with some pictures on it. In the middle of the couches and armchairs, there was a dark-brown table. On top of it, there were three baskets with stones in them and two vases; each of them had jasmine in it. They were all on top of a Persian carpet, almost the same color as the couches. The whole setting was facing the fireplace. It was a stone fireplace frame. The house was painted in two colors. From downstairs to the edge of upstairs, it had been colored with seashell color, and from upstairs to the ceiling, it was colored in Rosy Brown. The kitchen itself had a view to the outside. The house had three bedrooms on the upstairs, and in each room, there was a master bedroom, and each of them was facing the TV.

The mother and the daughter were still laughing, and I was dying to know what they were talking about.

Marshal, Aiko, Bernadina, and her boyfriend were planning to join us as well.

It was Calysta's birthday, so everyone had to show up. The best thing was, we were spending the weekend in the lake house. Calysta was happy about it, and I was thrilled to get out of the city. It was the best idea for someone's birthday. They hit two birds with one stone—a party and vacation.

My gift for Calysta was too obvious. It was a giant painting of her, so I didn't think she could pull off a surprised face for her gift, but somehow, she was excited about it. I had no idea what her parents prepared for her. I envied them. They knew how to give a gift. Not like me that a three-year-old child could guess what her gift is.

My cream puffs were almost ready. I looked up and saw that those two were still whispering and laughing, which brought me another smile. I headed outside to get some air. Mr. Kenward was still busy making BBQ. The man loved doing it. In the heat of summer and direct sunlight, he was doing the BBQ. He was the man, not me. I was sitting inside and baking some cream puffs, which most of them would be devoured by myself. Maybe those two were laughing at me because of how sassy I was to sit inside.

"Can I help you with something?" I asked him. ***Perfect, now I look like a woman. Just ask him if he likes to have some lemonade so that you can fetch him some. That way, you make it official***, I thought.

"Ah, Agustin. It's you. No, dear, I'm almost done here," he responded.

"It smells delicious. I can't wait to try it."

He laughed and said to me, "Well, you aren't that bad either. The poor Eda feels threatened whenever you are around and trying to cook." I joined him, and we both started laughing.

"How is the cake? Do you think Calysta made it well?" he asked.

"Does it matter? Either way, we have to show her our happy faces whether it tastes good or bad," I responded. He burst into laughter, and I accompanied him.

"That was . . . that was the right answer," he said after he managed to control himself, but he continued chuckling.

"Oh boy," he said while wiping his tears and trying to control his laughter, "it's good to have you around. You are a nice young man. I like you a lot. It is kind of weird since it is coming from a daughter's father, but you are different."

"Thank you. I appreciate that," I said while being embarrassed.

"Do you think your friends are coming now?" he asked.

"They better be, or they have to go to the wilderness to find food," I answered with a smile. He chuckled.

"What you two are doing here? What are you laughing at? The whole house is about to tear down with you two laughing," Calysta's mom asked. She was smiling.

"Oh, nothing, love. It was just men's talk," he answered and then gave me a wink, which made me smile.

"Anyway, the kids arrived. The food is ready?" she asked.

"Almost," he responded.

I saw through the glass that Calysta was greeting Marshal and Aiko by kissing them both on the cheeks. Then she hugged her dear friend Bernadina tightly. She was so happy to see her. Lastly, she gave a handshake to Bernadina's new boyfriend.

Marshal waved a hand to say hi to me. I waved back to him and signaled him to come to the balcony. After a while, he joined us. Calysta's mom went back inside.

"Hey, how you doing?" he asked.

"Good. What took you so long? You just showed up in the nick of time," I answered.

"The traffic was heavy."

"Come on, can't you come up with a better excuse? Haven't I taught you anything?"

"Well, we saw a unicorn on the road, and Aiko and Bernadina wanted to take a picture with it. How was that?" he answered while he was chuckling. Mr. Kenward laughed too.

"Well, let me tell you, me and Mr. Kenward wanted to put your surviving skill on test in the wilderness if you showed up late," I responded. He laughed, but Mr. Kenward just smiled.

"Then I would use you as bait for the wild animals," he answered. Mr. Kenward chuckled and shook his head.

"If you dare, say it in front of Calysta. She'll make you a target practice before feeding you to the lions."

"How noble of you."

Mr. Kenward was laughing all those time.

"I like the back-and-forth conversation between you two," Mr. Kenward commented. Then he continued, "The food is ready, so no need to kill each other."

We headed to the house. We helped Mr. Kenward take the food inside.

The food was delicious. Everyone enjoyed the steak and pasta salad. The irony was, the main course had leftovers, but all my cream puffs were gone. Marshal knew how much I liked them, but the bastard took two and three at a time. It was like he was eating sugar cubes. Besides that, he showed me his smug face. I just smiled and shook my head. We both knew that if we were alone, he wouldn't survive long enough to give me that smug face. Calysta and her mom were laughing too. I think they were laughing at me for watching all those cream puffs disappearing in front of me.

After the food, there was music. We all started dancing. We even forced Mr. and Mrs. Kenward to dance with us. The old couple was dancing happily. Bernadina and her new boyfriend were dancing cheek to cheek. Marshal was a good dancer. He danced like a pro with her girlfriend while I was dancing like a person getting drowned in the sea. My hands and feet didn't rhyme at all. Calysta was laughing at my dancing, and I didn't care about my dancing as long as it made her happy. I loved her laugh. She was having a good time, and that was all I wanted for her.

After we danced, we gave our gifts to Calysta. She received a beautiful necklace from her parents. The necklace had a picture of a mermaid sitting on the rock. She loved it. She received perfume from Marshal, a beautiful and delicate watch from Aiko, expensive-looking boots from Bernadina, and a T-shirt with a picture of Snow White and the seven dwarves from Bernadina's new boyfriend, which I guess it was suggested by Bernadina herself because he didn't know Calysta that well.

At last, it was my turn to give her the gift. I fought and insisted on opening it last. I wanted to know how much trouble I was in. She didn't like the sound of it, but she compromised. When she was tearing apart the gift paper, my heart was beating so fast that I thought that my heart would stop at any moment. I was embarrassed about my gift. I should have talked to Aiko or Bernadina about what to buy for her. The embarrassing moment would be that my gift was less impressive than the gift of Bernadina's new boyfriend. A thousand thoughts haunted me when she looked at her picture.

She opened the gift. *Here comes the moment of truth*, I thought.

The moment she looked at it, her jaw dropped. She wasn't alone. Everyone, except me, joined her and watched the painting. They all had the same reaction.

"Wow," everyone was saying. That wow was the worst thing that I ever heard. Wow because "It is ugly. How dare you? Why did you draw this shit?" Or wow because it was unexpected.

I was holding my breath. I wished there was a place that I could hide. I wanted the earth to open up and take me in.

Then I saw tears in Calysta's eyes. *I've done it. I screwed it up*, I thought.

She ran to me, and before I could say anything else, she kissed me in front of everyone, especially her parents. I didn't know what to make of it. I was the one who got surprised after all. She looked at me with her teary eyes and started laughing. *Did I miss something?* I thought.

"Your gift is the best," she said while having the most beautiful smile she ever had.

"Ahemmm, ahemmm." Her father was pretending to cough, which meant "Enough is enough."

"Ah, Dad, your gift was great too," she responded. *No, silly girl, he meant to stop doing what you are doing*, I thought but didn't have the audacity to say it out loud.

"How did you come up with this? I didn't know you were this much talented," her mom commented.

Calysta was still hugging me tightly. She rested her head on my shoulder, and I was feeling her warm breath on my chest, which was great and pleasant. I was living in a dream. Then I saw Marshal smile, which reminded me of something that I had forgotten.

"Ammm . . . well . . . how can I say it?" And with that, everyone burst into a laugh.

I could feel Calysta was chuckling on my chest too. **Great, are you stupid or what? Why can't you talk like a human being?** I thought.

"Well . . . I always see Calysta like that . . . I mean . . . I mean, she is pretty like the sunrise in the ocean . . . and . . . and . . . her heart is as big as an ocean . . .," I said and hoped that her father wouldn't punch me by saying that.

"Ahhhhhh, that's so romantic," Bernadina said first.

"Uhuuuum, I had no idea you were like that. Is all mathematician like that?" Aiko said. I just smiled, and it made me more embarrassed.

The way I painted Calysta, it was like she was sitting on a rock. Behind her was an ocean, and it ended where she sat. One end of her evening gown was the ocean itself, and the other was the typical ending of the evening gown that exposed one of her bare feet. The color of the dress was the same as the color of the ocean. The painting's purpose was to see those beautiful eyes—those eyes that compelled me the second I saw them. The sun was rising right behind her, and with that, she was like a goddess—the goddess of beauty and the ocean. I never knew what to expect from painting her like that. She was so picky for even taking her pictures. Every cute and beautiful picture she hated the most, I loved the most, especially those where she made faces. So when I saw the tears, I thought I disappointed her so much she would break up with me right there. It was perilous, even though I put so much time to paint it. It took me almost a year and a half.

"He always does that. The moment that I think he can't be more romantic, he pulls off something like this," Calysta answered instead of me. After that, she gave me two quick kisses on both cheeks and ran toward her painting. The canvas was thirty-six by sixty inches. It was huge. She looked at it again. Then she put one hand on her chest while studying it. She looked at the painting again and then from the paint to me. After that, she raised the same hand from her chest to her mouth. She was trying hard not to cry.

I had no idea what the painting would do to her. She seemed to be really happy about it, but I hated to see her tears. I had a mixed feeling of happiness and sadness. I felt like an asshole who made her girlfriend cry. I always wanted to see her beautiful and lively laugh.

They all gave me a compliment for the painting and asked me if I could paint them as well. While I was melting from those compliments, I told them that I would think about it.

The whole party was on hold for quite some time. They were all talking about the painting.

"Can I at least have some of the cake you made?" her father requested with a really kind face. He was pleased to see her daughter happy, and above all, he was proud of her that she could at least bake her own cake. She was the love of his life.

"Liam, couldn't you at least wait a little bit more?" Mrs. Kenward said with a smile.

"Ohh, Eda, love, the way I see it, there is no ending to it. Is it wrong to ask some piece of the cake that my own daughter made for her own birthday before I go to bed?" he responded. Everyone laughed at his comment, but it made Calysta blush. She ran like a child to her dad and gave him a kiss. Then without any other words, she ran to the kitchen to bring her cake.

When she came back, she brought a cheesecake that had been topped with chocolate, and the top of the cake was decorated with fruit cuts.

She sat behind the table, and then she blew her birthday candles.

"What did you wish for?" Aiko asked. Calysta blushed. Then she looked in my direction, and she shied away.

Everyone laughed at her reaction, except me. I was melting too.

She started cutting the cake, and she gave the first piece to her father.

"Does anyone want coffee or tea?" I offered. After getting the orders, I went to the kitchen and came back with some coffee and tea.

The cake tasted good. She even put some banana and walnuts in the middle layer of the cake, making the cake tastier. She was a natural.

Everyone complimented her cooking, and it only made her blush more. She was such a sweetie.

I was in the middle of eating the cake when her dad came and sat right beside me on the couch. He stretched his arm behind my head so that he could rest his arm on the sofa.

"You know what? I am glad that I didn't have to lie to her about her cooking," he said. I choked; a piece of the cake was trapped in my throat, and I started coughing for air. He patted me in the back to help me while he was smiling. He got his revenge for the earlier incident—what a smooth way to do it.

After I got rid of the piece, I started laughing through some coughs. I really liked him. I think he had the same feeling because I never got a bad vibe from him either.

"Are you okay?" he asked me with a cheerful voice. I was only able to nod while trying to cough out the rest of the piece.

"Thanks, by the way, for the painting. It is such beautiful work," he complimented me again.

"Oh, thanks," I said, and then I made a solid cough to clear out my throat and also get rid of the remaining piece. Then I continued, "I did nothing. She was beautiful herself."

"I know," he said and then looked in her daughter's direction. Her friends surrounded her. She was happy. She had the necklace on. She was so busy talking to her friends that she didn't notice both me and her father were watching her.

"Do you know Calysta almost died when she was baby?" he said and continued looking at her. It shocked me. If I had another piece of cake in my mouth, I would have choked on it again. Some invisible heavy force punched me on the chest. I never thought of a world without her in it. I looked back at her. She was still busy talking to her friends. Her friends were spoiling her with some compliments and other things that I couldn't catch.

"No," I managed to say.

"Yeah, she almost died in front of me. The moment I had her in my arm, I loved her and loved her ever since. One day a doctor notified us that she got infected by some kind of bacteria, but since she was an infant, she was in great danger. The news was a big slap on my face. I searched desperately for any doctor to have a solution for the problem. Each day, she was getting weaker and weaker. I hated myself for not being able to do anything for her. One day, outside of the hospital, when I was crying out of desperation, a young mother asked me if I was all right. I don't know why, but I told her the problem. She smiled and told me that I should calm down. Then she gave me the address of a doctor who treated her son with the same problem, and the rest is history."

I didn't know how to respond to his story, so I kept quiet.

"She became everything for me since then." he continued. He wiped out the tears that were coming from his eyes.

I never saw him crying. It felt strange. I didn't know what to make of it. Anybody could sense how much he loved her.

It would be more like mocking him to say that I feel the same way for her, so I kept quiet.

I looked back at Calysta. She was still talking to her friends, but this time, she noticed that I was looking at her, so she gave me her alluring smile. I smiled back, but it died on my lips the second she turned her attention to her friend.

"She likes you, you know. As a matter of fact, she likes you more than I can approve of, but I can't blame her either for it. I can't thank you enough for being a gentleman to my daughter. Not only that. You helped her a lot in her life and studies. Between us, my love for my daughter made me blind about her activity. I spoiled her with whatever I had and possessed, but I got lucky again by having you in her life. She grew up in these past two years. She became more mature. She decides accordingly. It is all because she wants to impress you," he said while chuckling. "As much as I want to, I can't take credit for what she is now." He was laughing, but I knew it was kind of a sad laugh. Also, I knew, in fact, he was proud of her no matter what.

"Thanks." I had nothing else to say. It made him laugh again for some other reasons that I couldn't figure out.

"You take care of her, okay?" he said while he was smiling.

"Okay," I said with a weak voice. I didn't know what to make of it. It was all new to me. He came like a hurricane to me and made my whole world upside down.

He chuckled and kissed me on top of my head and stood up to refill his cup. He asked me if I wanted to fill mine too. I thanked him and told him no need for that.

I was sitting there with the plate and the remaining cake in my hand. I was trying to digest the whole situation.

I remembered the day that I sat with my father. It refreshed those memories, the conversation that I had with my father. He told me how I was born.

"You were a little rascal. You worried us to death because you weren't a usual kid at all. Almost all children cried for being hungry, or they wet their diapers, but not you. You were quiet all the time. You laughed and played quietly, and because of that, we never knew when we should have changed your diapers or give you food. We visited so many doctors to find out what was wrong with you, but all of them told us that we shouldn't be worried. You were healthy but a little bit underweight. That was all to it. Whenever I played with you, your laughter was torture for me. I thought I wasn't a good father since I couldn't find what was wrong with you."

I laughed at what he told me, but then he continued.

"Don't laugh, you little bastard," he said while he was smiling.

"What happened next?" I asked him.

"Well, back then, it wasn't like today, being surrounded with technology to search for them on the internet. We had to go hospital by hospital, city to city. We even asked if we needed to go to the other country to see if we could find a doctor for you. They told us that we were overacting. Your hearing was good, you could see, you could respond to any action, and you could cry if you get hurt. After a while, we listened to the doctors and waited. When you were only one year old, you started talking. That was a relief for us that you weren't mentally challenged . . .," he was saying until he got interrupted by my laughing. He smiled and continued.

"Anyway, as I was saying, it was a relief that you were smart, but you were too smart for your own good. Then you wanted to learn to read and write. It was our mistake to show you how to read. Do you remember the time we told you that you can't play around with the TV and you asked why?"

"Yeah."

"We told you that you may be accidentally getting electrified or mess up the TV programs. The next thing we didn't expect was, you went and read the whole brochure in the house. The situation changed, and you were the one that told us how to use them correctly." He started laughing. I smiled. I remembered every detail of it.

"Or the time other kids bullied you?"

"Which one?" I asked because I was bullied a lot.

"The one that you made them expelled?" he asked. I laughed and nodded my head.

"You were in first grade when you shouldn't have been. Anyway, one day you came home with blood and bruises on your face. You told us what happened back then, but what could we do at that time? We reported to the principal, and it sounded like the situation got worse than better. Then one day I noticed that you were reading *The Art of Warfare*. I didn't realize why you were reading it that time since you were reading so much, but two days later, the office called us and asked us to come to the school. You took a cam recorder and gave it to another poor student that had been bullied and asked him to record those bullies in action. The next day, they got into the trap. You had evidence that these kids were bullying you, and you asked the poor principal to expel them." He laughed and shook his head. I smiled. Then he continued.

"The principal asked us to talk to you and make you change your mind. After a long conversation, we were convinced to give those kids a second chance. We did what they asked, but you came and showed us the video and asked us what we would do if such a thing happened to us. If I get beat up and your mom gets raped in front of me, then I go to the police and they tell me that everything is okay and I shouldn't be worried at all and let's give them a second chance?" We both laughed.

"I didn't know what rape was. I just read it someplace which told me it was the worst thing that could happen to women," I said while laughing.

"It is scary how you manipulated us at such age," he said.

"Well, I had to do what I got to do," I responded.

"Anyway, I was furious when I saw how you got beaten up, then with what you said, you just added fuel to the fire. I went inside, even though your mom was reluctant. I told them that either those guys were out or I took you out of school. Then you came in and told the principal that it would be such a good idea because after that, you were planning to go to the newspaper and release the video to the public. You little bastard with no mercy told them the title of the newspaper would be 'The Victim of a Bully Got Kicked Out of the School, but the Bullies Were under the Protection of the School.' I wanted to laugh when you said such a thing, but I kept my face straight just for your sake. The poor principal didn't know what to do with us or, better to say, to you. I even remember the last shot she tried. She asked you if there was any way you could forgive them. You told her if she could give you a guarantee it wouldn't happen again, you would give them a second chance. She was so happy that she didn't realize she just went into your trap, so the poor principal agreed. Then you asked her to give you a written paper to say she would resign from the job if those people bother you again. That would be your guarantee. The poor woman had nothing to say. I mean, everyone was shocked. Me included. How you planned out this whole thing and made us pawns in your hand. Then I remembered the book you read, you son of . . . something." We both laughed.

"When she paused, you attacked without mercy. You told her even she couldn't guarantee that because her neck was on the line to guarantee that, but it would be okay if someone else's neck was on the line. You continued by saying that the second she realized that she was included, she wouldn't want to guarantee it. I couldn't believe my eyes to witness such a thing. It was like a court fight, and you were the lawyer. Let me tell you, no matter what the outcome was, me and your mother was proud of you. When she told you that you shouldn't go that distance for a fight between classmates, you cried, which I didn't know to believe it or not. Such drama queen. It was like you were playing in a movie to get an academy award or something, then you told her why not? What would she do if her neighbor abused her? Would she feel safe to go home then? Would she call him neighbor again? Why do adults think that it is okay if kids are being bullied? But the second they put themselves in their shoes, they don't want to be involved? What was the difference? Wasn't both the same? Why do they think the kids are more forgiving than adults? When you asked her those questions, boy, I didn't know what to say, let alone the poor principal. When she tried to calm you down and talk some sense to you, I remember what you did. It is like it happened yesterday. You grabbed your bag and headed out of the office, and on the way out, you said to her, 'I wish you luck with your bully students. You deserve each other. And I promise you that the whole world will know what is going on in this school. People will realize that the bully in this school can get away with anything.'"

We both laughed for a while. Then he continued, "Oh boy, that aside, you played us so well. I mean, your mom and me, when we witnessed such a scene, your mom was so worked up that she shouted at them and she told them that they should be ashamed of themselves. Then she followed you outside. I was livid. I was so angry that no matter the outcome, I wanted to change your school. Anyway, you know what happened to those kids after that. They got expelled, and you became the champion of the little kids whom they had bullied." We both laughed. Then he looked at me with a sad look. It was like he just remembered something horrible from the past.

"When we thought that life is beautiful and everything was perfect, you got malaria. I don't know how you got it. It wasn't important either, but we got so close to losing you. You know what it was like? It was like the world gave us the biggest gift and was about to take it away. We got to know you. We loved you dearly, and then the crazy thing happened. I hope you never go through this because it was the end of the world for us, for your mom and me. Your mom went nuts. Days and nights, she was crying. I was emotionally broken. I even got so close to losing my job too. Not that I cared about my job, but the cost for your hospital was astronomical. The insurance was covering it, and it was the only thing that kept me going to the job. Anyway, you survived, and you are here now. Maybe you get a sense of what I told you, but you never understand until you go through it yourself."

A pat on my shoulder brought me back to the time where I was. I noticed it was Marshal. His round face with black eyes was looking at me. He was happy and proud. Then he hooked his arm around my neck to get me closer to his face. He wanted to whisper something in my ears or just do some horseplay. I was about to find out soon.

"I didn't know you were such an ass. I don't know what I am supposed to do now. Aiko is giving me a look that says, 'Why aren't you like that?'" he said.

"Took her so long to find out that you are useless," I responded with the biggest smile.

He laughed.

"But seriously, such a piece of work. I was like, 'Look at me. He is my best friend. I am so proud of him.' Then I remembered you are an ass."

It has always been like that between us. We gave each other a compliment by adding some insult to it. I think that was called being best friends.

"Poor Aiko, she had such high hopes for you. She saw me and thought you were like me just to find out you were the opposite of me. It is too late for her now. She is hopeless now. She has your name on her, and no one is going after her even if you break up with her," I said.

"Bastard."

I smiled. I won this round. Then I looked at Calysta.

"I was so worried she wouldn't like it," I said with concern in my voice. He knew who I was talking about.

"She had to be crazy if she didn't. I don't know so much about painting, but I know the work you put into it was a lot. If an amateur can say that, trust me that everybody else can say the same."

"So you think that she liked it because she realized how much work I put into it."

"Don't be stupid. Look at her. She is the happiest girl in the world now."

"You know how picky she is."

"So what?"

"Well, I think we have different tastes of beauty. Whatever seems to me to be beautiful, it is ugly for her."

"Don't be stupid. Even if you are right, you only needed one shot to get it right, and trust me, you got it right. She loves it. However, if she pretends to like it, just give me a signal, so I can let Aiko and Bernadina know about it. They know what to do with her."

I smiled.

"You know that you are not off the hook yet. You are going to pay for what you did earlier," I said.

"What do you mean?"

"The thing you did is going to be washed away with your blood only, you bastard. Do you know how much time I put there to make those cream puffs? Then you ate them all like a grizzly bear that just came out from hibernation."

He laughed, and I smiled.

"Hey, can I ask you a favor?" he asked.

"What?"

"I need to borrow some money."

It got me curious. "How much?"

"Well, enough to buy a nice car."

"What?"

"Don't go scrooge on me."

"First of all, fuck you, and second, did you tell anybody what I am up to?"

"No. Why?"

Three years ago, I put some money that would be only a thousand dollars on the market and played with it. It was a mathematical challenge for me, and I liked it only because of that. Betting against something was like reading a card. However, you won't be kicked out of a place like a casino because you know how to read the pattern. When I had enough information about the market and taught myself the terms, I invested a little money. It became a huge success. My thousand dollars changed to thirty thousand dollars just in a few months. After a while, I got really good at it that when people were losing money, I was getting more money. It was just calculation, which I was good at. I was practicing mathematics in real life. My thousand dollars became two hundred thousand dollars in a year.

When I told my dad about it, first, he freaked out, but since I wasn't playing with my savings, he let me continue to do it. He was kind of proud of me, but he never let me know about it just in case. He doesn't encourage me to do reckless things in my life. In the second year, I was betting cheap. I mean, I didn't do too much risk. The reward was huger, because when I was losing money, it was only a little, but the profit I got from it was huge. Those shares in the market that were about to go bust, I bought them. They were really cheap, so if I lost the money in it, it wouldn't be a huge deal, but if I won, the bet would go up to 13:1 or sometimes 30:1, which means enormous money. It sounded easy, but the catch was, I had to know which one I had to buy, so I had to go around studying those shares. I had to see the history, which meant data. I had to put a fixed time for it. By saying that, I spent only two hours a day on it. In my second year, I nearly made three million dollars. In my third year, I made roughly forty-four million dollars. Only my family and Marshal knew about it. I didn't want anybody else to know about it because I wanted to have an everyday life.

I could have gone to college at an early age. At thirteen or fourteen, I chose those boring classes only because I wanted to have a normal teenagehood. I was not particularly eager to draw too much attention to myself. However, when other kids were in trouble to do their homework, I was reading advanced books in college and university. I was a private person. I really liked my **me** time.

Marshal found out about it only by accident. When I was in my room and doing the market things, my mom let him in. I was so engaged in the market and the news that I didn't notice him behind me. Then he became curious about what kind of business I had to do with the market. After that, he became a pain in the ass to find out how much money I made out of it. That happened two years ago. Now he knew how much I made. It was only a number to me, but for him, it was so huge that he made a long whistle.

"Are you kidding me? I told you it is confidential. I don't want anybody to know about it. Did you tell Aiko?"

"No."

"Fuck you. You are lying."

"No, I am serious. Look, I am not stupid, and I know what confidential means. I won't betray your trust, and in return, you won't either. Plus, I am already in lots of shit by being your friend. I wasn't joking when I told you that Aiko compares me with you. She does that," he said.

I laughed.

"I am serious."

"First of all, don't sugarcoat it, and second, I don't give a fuck about money. I could even transfer enough money to your account that you won't need me for a lifetime. What you do with it makes me concerned. Let's say you go and buy a Ferrari with it. How do you want to explain that to Aiko, huh?"

"Ferrari would be nice, but I don't need it now. When I said a car, I meant a Toyota or Honda or something like that. Second, I could tell her that I inherited it from a dead member in our family," he said with a smile.

"Seriously, tell me how you want to tell your family and Aiko about how you got the car, then you have yourself a deal."

"Well, I'll tell them that I borrowed from you. I don't need to lie about it."

"You just told me that Aiko compares us."

"She does, but what can I do about it? If she wants you, she can have you. Plus, the car is for me, not to impress her. I need it to go to work."

He knew how much I loved Calysta, and he was using it against me. It was a kind of joke that he told me that I could have her girlfriend. He loved her, and we both knew that too.

"No deal."

"Oh, come on. You know I can't lie to her, but I won't tell her your secret, I promise."

"When did you become such a child?"

"What do you mean?"

"Well, you look like one of those spoiled children in the mall that cries to embarrass his parents to buy him the toy he wants."

"With all respect, fuck you, you fucker. Second of all, no one suspects you to have that much money to lend me. After all, you are working in trades."

"As a volunteer."

"Just forget about it. As I said, you are an ass."

"Well, if you just give up like that, I won't trust you to have a penny from me."

"Well, I'll tell her to ask you how you made the money."

"Now you are dumping your shit on me?"

"I don't understand you. Why aren't you telling Calysta the truth? It's not like you are a drug lord and doing money laundering."

"Are you seriously that dumb? How can I tell her? Hey, Calysta, you know, your boyfriend happened to be a millionaire, and he forgot to mention it in a year and a half. Oops."

"The problem isn't how you want to tell her. The problem is if you are willing to tell her."

"Sure, why not?"

"So give me the green light?"

"Green light of what?"

Before I knew it, he called Calysta to come over. I jumped over him to stop him while he was laughing. It was a stupid move. It just made Calysta more curious. She came over. I was trying to make him shut up by throwing my hand in front of his mouth while he was dodging it by moving his head, which was a mistake because it made her more curious. He just put it out there and told her that I had something to say to her. It was like mercy killing. The first thing that came to my mind was what a bastard Marshal was. Second, what should I do? Now I had a window to tell her.

In a matter of seconds, I was under her spell. Her beautiful eyes and smile put a spell on me that I had to tell the truth or I would get cursed for a lifetime, but how? My brain froze.

"Come with me," I said to her while I was heading toward the balcony. She followed me like a good girlfriend.

"What is it, Agustin?" she asked me while she was following me.

"I'll tell you when we are outside," I answered.

When we were outside, I took a deep breath. I was excited. It was like the time I asked her out. I had no idea how to do it. That time, I was lucky. We were both on the same page. She only needed me to find courage, but she had no idea what I was going to tell her this time.

When I looked inside the house, I noticed that everyone was watching us.

"You know that I have lots of hobbies, right?" I said.

She nodded.

"And you know about my skill in mathematics, right?"

She nodded again. This time, she narrowed her eyes and raised one of her eyebrows slightly up while she was smiling. She does that sometimes. I interpreted it as "Either you tell me now or you will see my dark side," which she never said to me in words. Usually, it happened when she was curious. If I want to scale it between one and ten, it would be an absolute ten. There wasn't any space for wiggling in it, so I had to come clean fast or wait to see my punishment.

"Well, one of the hobbies that I have is doing the market things. Three years ago, it wasn't such a big deal. I started with a thousand dollars. Fast-forward it to now, I have almost forty-four million dollars." There, I said it.

"What?" she responded with a huge surprised face. I raised my shoulder in a way that meant I didn't know what else to say with my stupid face.

"What do you mean you have forty-four million dollars?"

"I don't know why people make such a buzz about it. It is just a hobby that I have. It is money that I am playing with. In Wall Street, it isn't that much."

"Why didn't you tell me?"

Here comes the thing that I was afraid of the most, I thought.

"You know how private I am with things I do. I didn't want to draw too much attention toward myself. In the beginning, I was afraid that I would get more isolated, so I kept it to myself like many other things. Then Marshal found out about it by accident. Now the son of a bitch wants to borrow some money from me to go and buy a car, but in order to do that, he had to expose me." Here I thought that I had taken my revenge.

"I don't understand," she asked with confusion.

"Obviously, he doesn't have the money, so he had to borrow it from me. The thing is, if he gets the money, and as stupid as he is, he goes and buys the car, then Aiko would ask him where the hell he got the money. He has to come clean. I mean, he has to expose my secret."

"No, I mean, why didn't you tell me?"

"As I said, I don't talk about it like my other hobbies. I know, I am stupid, but can you forget about it and get back to the party?"

"Agustin? I don't care about the money. It isn't mine, but hiding it from me, it hurts."

"I could lose it all tomorrow. That is all the point. One day rich, another day poor. That's how it is to play in the market." Well, it was not true. I knew the rules, and I learned how to play. I was like a hacker who controls someone else's computer, and it didn't matter what the host does. That person was at the mercy of the hacker. She wasn't convinced with what I said either.

"I hate Marshal. He turned a good night into a complete nightmare," I said and hoped she would leave it alone, but she didn't budge. She just gave me a disappointed face. I looked at the lake. It was dark. The sound of frogs and other night creatures filled the silent night.

"I made a mistake by not telling you. I'm sorry. It won't happen again," I said it finally. I looked back at her and waited for her response. She gave me the silent treatment. I knew she was angry and disappointed at me for not telling her. She wasn't a money person either. She was just disappointed in a person she didn't expect to. Half an hour earlier, the same person gave her the best present she wanted in her life, and half an hour later, the same person kept a secret from her for almost their entire relationship. What could she do about it? I knew how hurtful it was.

"I don't know, Agustin. Maybe you are hiding another secret from me and not telling me. How can I trust you now?"

"To be honest, there is another one, but I have to die first to tell you that. It is the most embarrassing one."

"Agustin?" she said it with a low voice and anger that sounded like a shout.

"I can't tell you that. Sorry. I love you, but I have to keep this one for a while." I smiled.

"What is it?" She showed me her agitation. Now that I got her curiosity excited, I dropped the bomb.

"I am a virgin," I said while smiling and being embarrassed. Somehow, my stupid body responded to it too. I felt something aroused down in my body.

She tried to hold back her laugh, but she couldn't. First, she smiled. Second, she put her hand on her mouth to prevent herself from making any sound from her laughing. And finally, she just gave up and started laughing while she was avoiding having eye contact with me. It was an embarrassing moment for me, but I had no way out of that conversation.

After she had her laugh, we went inside. I had to come clean. There was no reason to keep it secret anymore, so I told everyone about my market business. The reaction was as I expected. Everyone was shocked, except the people who already knew. The eyes of Bernadina's new boyfriend popped out. Bernadina and Aiko were speechless. Then all at once, they started chatting with one another. After that, they bombarded me with lots of questions, which I answered patiently. They asked me the same questions that Calysta already asked me about. I became the center of attention again. Now some of them wanted to invest their money in the little company I made.

After lots of conversation and dancing, we decided to go to the bedroom. The three girls went into the same bedroom. They were so excited about it because it reminded them of the old times they were sleeping over each other houses. They also had a lot to talk about. Mr. And Mrs. Kenward went to a separate room, which left us in one room. Bernadina's new boyfriend was wondering what to do. It felt kind of weird to sleep with a guy whom I had just met, so I told him and Marshal that I would sleep on the couch. Marshal also had the same feelings, so he said he needed to talk to me and excused himself to go to the same room. It only became beneficial for the dude. He got to sleep alone in the room. No matter how bad we were in his eyes, he got the better end of the stick.

I lay down on the couch, watching the ceiling, and Marshal lay down on the other side of the sofa. Our position on the L-shaped couch was like our heads were close to each other and our feet far away.

"Why do I get to sleep with you?" I asked him.

"Do you think that I am happy to sleep with you?" he responded.

"Somehow, I felt claustrophobic when I realized that I was about to sleep with that dude," I said to Marshal. He smiled.

"Same here. Where do you think Bernadina found him?" he asked.

"How should I know? A dork shop maybe."

"What you guys are doing here?" Calysta asked. She was wearing her pajama. The pajama was silver silk with solid black lace and a short sleeve matching her silver silk trouser. She looked hot. It was like she just came out of a photo shoot for a magazine. It took my breath away. My brain, as usual, became useless. I never saw her in her pajama. My virgin body got excited too. My animal instincts—or that "basic instinct," as people called it—was worked up thoroughly. I wasn't alone. Marshal got excited too.

"Huh?" I swear that was the only noise that came out of my mouth. I didn't know what I would do if Marshal weren't beside me. My instinct was shouting at me and telling me, **Who gives a fuck? Just do it!** And my penis, like a foot soldier who had been shouted at by a high-ranking officer, didn't know what to do; it did the worst thing. In order to cover up the embarrassment, I sat up and acted cool. Marshal did the same. I couldn't blame the son of a bitch. We both were hopeless. Calysta was smiling. I didn't know if she found out or not, but I hoped for the best. My earlier confession to her about my virginity wasn't any help either.

"I said, what are you doing here? Why aren't you in the bedroom?" she asked again with her mysterious smile.

"I was awed by the beauty of the house and the lake, so I thought I should spend the night here and enjoy every second of it," I said and then threw the ball to Marshal. "What's your excuse?"

Calysta giggled. Marshal didn't expect me to backstab him, so he just gave in laughing and accompanied Calysta.

"Seriously, you guys are the worst. Do you do that to all your guests? What if he goes and complains about you to Bernadina, huh?" she asked while she had a smile on her face. She wasn't angry at us. She was just concerned.

"First of all, why should I care? Bernadina is your friend. She is your problem, like Marshal **is** to me. Second of all, that guy is dreaming, only the devil knows what, on that comfortable bed. If that brat goes complained about us to Bernadina, he is a dork AND spoiled," I answered. Calysta smiled while she was signaling us with her both hands to bring down our voices.

"Agustin, I had no idea that you were like that," she said and tried hard to sound disappointed, but I didn't buy it. Anyway, now I had more troubles and concerns than thinking about a guy I didn't care about. I was distracted by how beautiful and sexy she was. I just wanted to hold her. I wanted to kiss her so bad that I thought I would die if I didn't do it. I was wondering why Marshal was there on the couch. If Marshal wasn't there, I could be alone with her. Who knows? Maybe I would get lucky too.

Then she came and sat beside me on the couch. Her perfume made me more confused and hornier. I was about to lose it at any time—what a feeling. I felt so hopeless. Were all men like me? Or was I the only weird one? Anyway, who could judge me for having those kinds of thoughts? It was natural. I was meant to be like that—to be a horny teenager who was confused about what to do with this beautiful creature. I was curious what was under her pajama or, even better, in her trousers. I had a general image of what a breast and a vagina looked like. They were everywhere in science books, but I never saw the real one. The real one was sitting right beside me. I became impatient for that very reason.

"Agustin, are you all right?" Calysta asked. She was sincerely concerned. Marshal was looking away and smiling. The son of a bitch knew what feeling I had. If anyone looked at me with the face that I made, they would realize that they should stay far away from me or even run from me. I felt my head was burning from inside out. It wasn't that hot, but I knew I was sweating anyway. My mouth became dry. My hands were shaking from the excitement that I had. If she touched me, if I felt her soft skin on any part of my exposed skin, I knew nothing could stop me. Even an army of men. Nothing.

"Ye-ye-yeeeh," I managed to say. Then she put her hand on my head. The moment she did that, I felt a rush of blood in my vein. My heart started beating fast, and above all, the junior Agustin was rising and getting harder. Now I had difficulty breathing. I wanted to kiss her. I wanted to take her shirt off. I wanted to kiss her long, beautiful neck. I wanted to suck one of those nipples until she screamed from sucking it too hard. I wanted to kiss every part of her body from head to toe, and if I managed to not cum by that time, I wanted to introduce my junior to her junior.

I knew the moment I was inside her, I wouldn't be able to hold back my sperm. It was too much work for my virgin body. The heat was rushing from my head to my chest, which made my breathing more difficult. I was really close to losing it. I was afraid at the same time. I was worried that I would do something stupid and make her scared of me for the rest of my life. She never saw this side of me. I was scared of myself. I was on edge. I was close, really close to losing it all. I knew that nothing good would come from losing myself. The dilemma was getting harsher. My heart was beating faster than before, and the blood was rushing down to my penis. I couldn't hold back anymore. The feeling was like a person who has been thirsty for water for quite some time but never found any drop of it for days in the ocean, and out of desperation, he drinks the ocean's water.

"Can you bring him a glass of cold water? I'll keep an eye on him for you until you come back," Marshal said. I couldn't even breathe to say thank you. It was too much task on my hand. Calysta rushed to the kitchen to bring me some water.

"Hey, get ahold of yourself. Are you crazy?" he told me the second Calysta was out of sight.

"Thanks," I managed to say through my hard breathing. That was the only time that I thanked him sincerely and didn't insult him. I owed him my whole relationship. I was about to lose it all if it wasn't for him.

"Just keep her away from me. Can you do that?" I begged him. He understandably shook his head and came and sat right beside me. He put his arm around me and firmly held me tight to himself. I think that was the best strategic move he made. He put himself between her and me. Now I calmed down a little bit, but I was a far cry from settling down.

Calysta came back with water. Marshal took the glass and handed it to me, and he thanked her for me. The cold water gave my body a shock when I drank it, and it was soothing. I was getting back my control. I was looking down and tried not to look at her. I knew the moment I looked at her, I would lose it all over again. I loved her. I didn't want to do anything stupid to her. That was the first time I was close to losing control. I could have destroyed the whole day or any image that I made this entire year. I worked too hard for it to lose it.

Then Calysta came and sat on the other side of me. That sweet smell came back again. Now she was more concerned about me. Her blue eyes were locked on me. Her concerned face made me hornier. Was there any glimmer of hope left for me that she could turn off my beast mode? I wondered. Anything about her was enticing. Marshal was smiling at my bad luck. He couldn't tell Calysta to leave me alone because she was my girlfriend. I was glaring at my lap while putting my left hand on my forehead so I could block her from touching my head again. She had no insight into the situation. She worried about me, but it wasn't a perfect time for her to be. Out of the blue, she put her hand on my lap and started rubbing my lap.

Are you kidding me? I thought.

Marshal laughed, and Calysta glared at him for laughing at me. "Sweetheart, are you okay? What's wrong?" she asked me with lots of concern. I was looking up in my brain in search of an evasive answer for her. No luck. I stood up and excused myself to go outside. Maybe fresh air could help me clear my head. In the meantime, Marshal was laughing heartily. He was really close to wetting his pants, but it bugged Calysta more.

"What is it? Why don't you tell me what is going on? Did I do something?" she asked. Her voice was a knife in my heart. How could I ignore her? I wanted to answer her, but how could I?

It just made Marshal laugh harder. I was pissed off for his childish act, but I understood him. If I were in his shoes, I would do the same.

"Oh, It is nothing. I just need to go to the bathroom. I'll be back," I responded. I don't know why I said bathroom. At that moment, I thought it was less insulting to her. However, when I said the word *bathroom*, it made Marshal laugh so hard that I could see the pain he had to take in, to breathe, so instead of me, the bastard ran to the bathroom. Only devil knows what he thought of me when I said bathroom. In the bathroom, I could still hear him laughing. The situation was getting ridiculous by the minute. Calysta was confused by Marshal's actions and my odd behavior. His laugh in the bathroom was so loud that Aiko and Bernadina came down to see what was going on. I was getting more embarrassed. I noticed that Bernadina was wearing light-pink pajamas with a Japanese anime character on them. The anime character had a frozen wink on the right side of her chest where her tit was poking out of her shirt. I just needed to see that to make myself more miserable. I got hornier, and add to that, my dick thought it was an excellent time to get hard in my pants. I could see it. I had to sit down to hide it again. Aiko was wearing a Pajama and shorts. It was steel-blue satin silk with lace trims. It had a V neckline with a contrast lace trim. She was really sexy in it. I could see her tit crack. The situation was dire. I put both hands on my eyes to block all those forces of nature. I needed help, but there was no one to help me out.

Then I felt a delicate finger on my shoulder. I knew in a heartbeat that it was Calysta's. I didn't need to see her to realize it was her. She asked me with a concerned voice again if I was all right. That was the last straw; I couldn't hold it back anymore. I took her hand and forced her to follow me outside the house. Her warm hand in my hand made the matter worse. Once we were outside, I made sure no one was watching, and I sheepishly confessed to her by showing her my hard junior. I explained to her bit by bit what was happening to me the moment I saw her in her pajama. Her reaction was cute. She put her delicate hand on her mouth and started laughing while I was explaining to her with anger and frustration. Her body was shaking. Her beautiful eyes were closed, and like Marshal, she put her other hand on her abdomen to stop herself from the pain that was coming from the hard laughing she had. Her huge pointy tits were bouncing in her pajama. She was torturing me unknowingly. I told her that I needed to be alone for the very reason she knew now. She couldn't move an inch. Her laughter was priceless. I never saw her laughing like that. The situation was so ridiculous that it made me laugh too, but it wasn't like Marshal and Calysta. It was kind of a pissed-off laugh.

I looked at the horizon. Those beautiful and colorful trees in the daytime, now it was painted in black by the hand of the night. It was peaceful. It was the only thing that I really needed. I listened to the music of the darkness. I couldn't tell it was the house cricket or the tree cricket that was singing side by side with frogs. They were all desperately singing for their mates, I guess.

I walked away from her. I wanted to stay away from her as much as I could. I tried to find a quiet place to hide. Living among humans was difficult. These few years since I met Marshal became a kind of blessing and curse for me. I was happy to be part of the group. I never had friends, let alone have a beautiful girlfriend. Every action and response from them were mysteries for me to solve. I couldn't tell what people were thinking. Sometimes they laughed at my honest answer and found me a funny person. However, I found it amusing how my anger and rage made others laugh. Was I missing some lines? These kinds of thoughts made me wonder. That night was the same. I couldn't tell why Calysta found it so funny to laugh about my condition. Wasn't it weird? I just confessed to her about a perverted person, but it made her laugh more. I don't know how, but the darkness of the night became my companion. That darkness took in all my bitterness. I had a little time to review all those scenarios and still couldn't figure out those people's reactions.

A few minutes later, I was ready to go back to the house, and when I got there, I saw everyone looking in my direction. Calysta had a mischievous smile on. I couldn't complain about it. I was happy to see her like that. I wanted to hug her, and this time, it wasn't because I wanted to have sex with her. This time, I wanted to hug her because I needed her to embrace me, but I was too shy to do it in front of my friends. I went and sat on the couch right beside her. I took her hand and locked my fingers to hers. After that, I gave her a quick kiss on her cheek and then whispered how sorry I was about the whole situation in her ear. She just responded to me by kissing me back.

We all talked a little bit more that night, a few laughs here and there. We didn't bring up the subject again. After that, the three girls went back to their bedroom, and Marshal and I sat there on the couch. Marshal wanted to talk and tease me more, but I was drained and not in the mood, so I just ignored him and lay down on the couch. It was a big day for me. Too many things happened in a short amount of time for me to process—the stress I had when Calysta saw her portrait, the revelation of the fact about Calysta's past, my embarrassing confession to Calysta about my virginity to keep from her mind the secret I kept from her for almost our entire relationship, and then a few hours later, telling her how perverted I was. It was too much to process. I just wanted to sleep and put this stressful day behind me. I was too hyper to sleep. I was thinking too much. I was reviewing the whole scenario again and again in my head. What if I told her that instead of this? Or took different actions for those scenarios? Finally, my body gave up, and I slept.

Next Day

I woke up with a scream.

Then the second scream made me jump out of the couch. I almost turned over the whole table beside the sofa. Marshal woke up as well. He was confused too. His puffy eyes became wide. Our hearts raced. We were wondering what happened. We were looking at each other for an explanation. The time was still.

The third scream, which was longer, made me run toward it. I ran as fast as I could. I didn't check to see if Marshal was following me. The adrenaline was pumping in. The screams were coming from upstairs. I was taking two and three steps at a time. When I arrived upstairs, I noticed the room that Calysta was sleeping in was empty. Then I ran toward the other room. Bernadina's boyfriend was at the door of his bedroom. He was confused too. I passed him in the hallway heading toward the last bedroom.

Finally, I arrived at the source of the screams. In the last bedroom, in which Mr. And Mrs. Kenward were sleeping, I saw Calysta lying on the ground close to the door in the arms of Bernadina.

My whole world went black. I couldn't believe my own eyes. My feet were pinned down to the floor. I couldn't take one more step. Calysta's head fell loosely in the arms of Bernadina. I saw her closed eyes. Her arms were hanging lifelessly on the floor.

I was scared. I was wondering what happened to her. I just stood there, not daring to take one more step. I was about to cry at any time.

I sensed that someone was standing right beside me, but I couldn't turn my head around.

It was Marshal. He walked into the room. He looked down at Calysta and then in the other direction.

Then I heard a voice that was more like moaning. It was coming from the other side of the bedroom. A female voice was begging anyone who was listening to save **him**.

I couldn't articulate what she meant by saying "Him" until I heard his name.

"Liam... Honey... Open your eyes." She was sobbing while begging her husband. "Please... Please... Please open them... Liam... Liam."

I don't know what force made me walk again. I walked into the bedroom. The first thing that I noticed was Aiko beside the bed trying to make an emergency call. When she heard the voice of the operator, she started talking and explaining the whole situation. She couldn't speak clearly. She was half crying and half talking.

Marshal asked her to hand in the phone. He was more in control of his emotions.

I looked at the bed where Mr. Kenward was sleeping. His eyes were closed.

Mrs. Kenward was still shaking him and begging him to open his eyes.

Bernadina was holding Calysta while she was crying.

Marshal went to bed and put his two fingers on one of Mr. Kenward's wrists while talking to the phone. He was getting instructions over the phone on what to do before the ambulance arrived.

While he was doing the things that the operator asked him to do, everyone was watching him. The eyes were filled with tears.

I could see a dim light of hope in the eyes of Mrs. Kenward. She was crying while holding his other hand in hers. I could see the desperation in her eyes. She was begging silently to have her husband back.

Marshal was still holding Mr. Kenward's wrist. He was trying to find a pulse.

"I can't . . . I can't feel it," he said with a sad tone, and with that, the tears found a way to his eyes.

Chapter 14

I was walking down Trinity Street and enjoying another rainy day. I probably wouldn't miss these crazy days in here. I passed the Whistles shop. I was getting closer to the Michaelhouse Café and Center. I wanted to drink some tea. What I found interesting about myself was that I was an Englishman even before I came to Cambridge. My preferred beverage was tea. I arrived at the café and ordered a to-go spicy Chai. I didn't want to sit in there. I was more interested in the following store, which was The Cambridge Contemporary Art. The shop didn't have any breathtaking paintings or sculptures, but it was entertaining for me to watch new ideas.

I knew the skills and the idea behind them. I took my order and walked to the other shop. I was disappointed when I saw there weren't any new paintings and sculptures, which made me pass the shop faster than I thought. There was another gallery not too far in King's Parade street, the Lawson Gallery. I headed toward King's Parade street and thought about what would happen if I dropped everything and started painting. I wasn't bad at it. I liked to do it occasionally, but I never thought to do it professionally. What if I did it? I wasn't struggling to make any money. As far as I knew, I was one of the wealthiest kids in the University, so what stopped me from doing it?

Nothing.

But if I wanted to choose a career between being a mathematician or being an artist, I would always choose to be a mathematician. Mathematics has always been a good friend of mine. The world of mathematics was always fascinating. Some of the works were useless at the time, but maybe in the future, it would come in handy. So far, whatever I did wasn't meaningless—programming computer, working in physics and chemistry labs, even doing some works in biology. Who knew that one day I would end up helping biologists? Marshal would love that. I missed him. He was a good friend and my only friend. However, whenever I talked to him, he always reminded me of Calysta involuntarily. He reminded me of those happy times that I was with her, and deep down, I always wanted to ask him about her. I wanted to know about her status. Was she single or not? It wasn't my business anymore. She could do whatever she wanted to do, but the curiosity was driving me crazy. I never asked him about her when we were talking. He knew I wanted to know about her, but he never mentioned her to me.

After a while, before I knew it, the friendship gap between him and me became so huge that I needed to cut it before it became too late for me to get back. I could always apologize to him for being a dick, but the thought of losing my best friend was more painful. I needed time. I needed to get over Calysta.

Marshal was a good person. He was a good boyfriend to Aiko, and they were doing great. I was afraid to break him apart from her. I didn't want him to get in a fight with her in order to be on my side. I didn't know that would happen or not, but I didn't want to be part of it.

I arrived at the Lawson Gallery, but the gallery was closed. So was the Nomads. The stores were closing one by one.

My tea was about to be finished. Luckily, the Copper Kettle was open. I went inside and ordered another tea to go. My trip home was a long walk. After refilling my cup, I headed toward Trumpington Street.

People were passing by. All those bicycles that had been chained, now most of them were gone. Everyone was trying to get home.

It took me a while to arrive at Mill Park, where I rented an apartment.

The street was quiet. The birds were sleeping. The mosquito and moths were dancing around the streetlamps.

The mood was perfect for me to call it a day.

I went inside and turned on the lights.

"SURPRISE!" everyone cried in my apartment. My heart was about to jump out of my chest. I knew it was my birthday, but I never told anyone about it. I didn't expect any birthday party. How did they find out? I wondered.

I smiled; I turned off the lights and went outside again.

Then I heard them protesting. Some of them laughed.

I went inside and turned on the lights again. They cheered me again.

They really surprised me. I had never had a surprise party before. Corwin, David, and Winn were in the crowd. Some of the students from another department were in the crowd too, and most of the masses, I had no idea who they were.

Then they all started singing *"Happy birthday to you"* to me. I was pleasantly surprised and thanked them all for doing it.

The most surprising thing was to see Marina in the crowd. She came with her friend to my birthday. I couldn't believe my eyes. I was happy to see her. She was wearing a one-shoulder black Grecian dress with bead embellishment on one side. She looked really sexy in it. She smiled the moment she noticed I was looking at her. I smiled back. I didn't know why I smiled back; nevertheless, I did it. I think it was the right thing to do.

I was slightly embarrassed by having those clothes on, so I excused myself and went to my bedroom. I put on my long-sleeved black shirt, which was made in France, and black pants and a belt. I chose a red tie to put on. Still, I didn't feel comfortable wearing them. I was never prepared for this kind of thing. I used a little bit of Clive Christian cologne to get rid of any foul smell I brought home from that long walk. Finally, I was ready to face the world. I came out of the bedroom and greeted them one by one and thanked them for showing up for my birthday. When it was Marina's turn, I was addled. Forcefully, I put a smile on and thanked her for showing up. She smiled back, but I felt it wasn't sincere. I got the feeling that she came to my birthday with force. She raised her hand for handshaking; I had no other choice but to accept her hand. Her soft and warm skin gave me a shock. I didn't expect that much delicacy from her. I always imagined her to be rough and rigid; it was another mystery for me. The girl who turned me down in a heartbeat was fragile like a flower. Against my wishes, I let her hand go. After that, I turned my attention to her friend. I greeted her as well, but unlike her friend, Marina, she was more welcoming and happier to see me. She even kissed me on both cheeks, and my response to it was only a smile, and I thanked her for coming.

It took me a while to be a good host by thanking them all, but it all finished. I went to the kitchen to drink some water. I felt so thirty. It was too much unexpected excitement for me. I would never imagine that Marina would come to my birthday. I thought she didn't like me. I thought I was nobody to her, but here I am, and here she was. I was pleased to see her.

"Hey, birthday boy, what are you doing here?" the voice behind me said. I turned around. It was Corwin.

"Oh, nothing. What's up?"

"Not much. How do you like your party?" he asked. I saw the wry smile.

"All of this is because of you, isn't it?" I asked him.

"You can thank me later."

"Thank you, and because of that, I want to kill you with this glass of water."

"And this is what I get for being a good friend."

"Just be happy that I am not crucifying you right now, right here. How did you get in the apartment?"

"The'r you ar'. What ar' you do'ng here?" David asked when he came to the kitchen.

"Not much, Dave," I responded.

"Ar' you hiding he'r?

"No. Only thirsty."

"Well, Corwin, I ne'd you to do somting for me. I ne'd an ambassador," he said while having a big smile on.

We coined the word *Ambassador*. We used it in a sense that meant being a wingman. The "Ambassador" goes and talks to the targeted girl. He tries to excite another person by saying his status and capability and other good qualities. He tells her about the rumors he heard about another guy and sometimes shows some jealousy. He advertises him so much that the poor girl is going to be "curious." The word *Curious* in our language means being trapped and confused. After that, the "Dealer," whom I guess to be Winn, will seal the deal. He just goes there and shows he is pissed off for seeing the guy who is just being advertised.

"Okay, I gotta go," Corwin said. He always liked the game.

I smiled. Even on my birthday, they didn't lose a chance to score someone. I took a deep breath and went outside to talk to my guests. To my surprise, it was a really good party, and I was having fun. I danced a lot to the extent that I couldn't feel my feet, so I took a break and went outside to get some fresh air. The night was great, and I thought what a great night it would be if I danced with Marina.

"Hello, Mr. Adalbert," a woman's voice said behind me.

"Oh, Hi," I said while I was caught off guard again. I turned around and saw it was Marina. I smiled involuntarily again.

"Is it okay if I stay here too?" she asked me.

"Yeah, why not?" I said uncomfortably.

"The inside was too hot with all those people," she said.

"I know. I am here for the same reason. I hope you are enjoying the party though."

"Well, I do. Thanks."

"Don't thank me. I was surprised by seeing all those people in my apartment. Believe it or not, I don't know most of them," I said. She laughed at my comment, which made me smile again. There was silence after that.

"Mr. Adalbert, I don't know if it is the right time or not, but I have to say how sorry I am for my bad behavior in the past. I shouldn't have done that," she said while looking away and trying to avoid eye contact. I smiled, but I wasn't happy to hear those words. It was true; she hurt me, but I never blamed her for it. I always thought I wasn't good enough for her, and for that very reason, I was pissed off. I only wished she gave me the time of day to know me so I could convince her that I was good enough for her.

I put my hand on my head and let my fingers go through my long hair. I was trying to think of a way to answer her.

"I'm not really good at social life. Certainly, I am not an expert to say what you did was good or bad, but to be honest with you, I never blamed you. I believe it was only natural because a girl like you only chooses someone she believes she deserves best. The fun fact is, we aren't the only species who do that, and that is the lesson I learned from biology," I responded. She smiled at my response, making me happy because I thought I had given the correct answer.

"Thank you," she said while looking down, and then she looked up and gave me a glance, which made me nervous. "But it doesn't explain why you were avoiding me." I knew what she was talking about, and it would be stupid to insult her by saying "*I don't know what you mean by saying that.*" I had to come clean, but in a way that it wouldn't make the matter worse.

"Have you ever had a feeling that you want something but you can't have it?" I asked her and waited for her answer. She nodded.

"Well, it was the same for me. Not that I am comparing you with a car, but I felt like a person . . . who . . . couldn't afford to pay for an expensive car, and the best way he found was to fill the void by changing his route to his home. Do you understand what I am trying to say?" She giggled at my answer, but she nodded.

"I know . . . I am Stupid," I said. While she was laughing, she shook her head to show me she disagreed with me. The voice of her laugh was sweet, but it had a personality in it. I knew she was intelligent, and her behavior just confirmed what I thought of her, maybe because I was a weak person to think like that.

I felt a little bit chilly. I came out without a jacket, and I noticed that she didn't have a coat either. Then I saw she was hugging herself. I believed it was because she felt cold. If I had a jacket, I would have offered it to her. That was a gentleman's move. I don't know, but I believe the girls like that.

"Do you still want to stay outside?" I asked her.

"Yeah, why?" she asked me in response.

"Well, I'll be back," I said and went inside the apartment. I forgot to ask her where she put her jacket, so I went to my closet and took one of my jackets for her. I came back and handed her my coat. I gave her one of my slim black autumn jackets. It looked nice on her, but it was a little bit big for her size. I wore the other one, which was a brown leather jacket. She thanked me and put the coat on like a blanket.

"If you feel so cold, then why don't you go inside? Is it so bad you'd rather stay outside?" I observed.

"No, I just don't feel like it. I want to stay out a little bit more."

"Do you want some coffee or tea to torture yourself a little bit smoother? You know, I won't judge, or if you are a hard-core masochist, I could bring the tea and drink it in front of you while you are chilling in the cold," I said it as a joke. It worked; she laughed.

"If you bring me a cup of tea, I won't complain," she said.

Without any delay, I went inside and brought two cups of tea. She thanked me again. After that, there was a long awkward silence.

"I'm glad you are here," I said it finally while looking at the street. I didn't want to look at her because I was afraid of her reaction. I was worried she would reject me again. I got the feeling she was kind of unpredictable.

"Thanks, but why?"

I turned around and looked at her. She was smiling. She wasn't mad at me. I smiled back.

"You know, I reviewed the day I wanted to talk to you more than thousands of times in my head. What could I have said differently to make you take a walk with me and hear me out? That day became my dream and nightmare." I looked at the street and back to her again to see any negative signal. When I didn't see any, I continued by saying, "I felt I was different from others. I mean . . . other males. I just want to know what you were thinking about me. Did you . . . Did you hear any kind of rumors about me?"

"No," she answered.

"Then why? Why didn't you want to hear what I wanted to say?" I asked. I saw her looking down. She was trying to avoid any eye contact with me. I felt she wasn't proud of what she did, but she was too proud to confess her mistake. I didn't mind that. After all, I accepted her whole. I received her good and bad parts altogether, so I smiled instead of pressing on and putting her on the spot. I smiled at my bad fortune. I smiled at those bad memories that I had to carry with me to Switzerland.

I looked at the sky above me. "The sky is so black and dark, and it is waiting for an artist to paint on it. It is a beautiful canvas up there."

"Do you paint?" she said finally after a long silence.

I looked at her. She was looking at the sky as well. "I do sometimes." After that, I looked up at the sky again.

"The picture you drew on the board was beautiful. Was it someone that you knew?" she asked.

I tried hard not to laugh. Here I was trying to change the subject for her sake. "No, it was a picture of a girl that I saw on the cover of a fashion magazine."

"Do you like those kinds of beautiful girls?"

"Define *beautiful*," I asked curiously.

After a bit of pause, she answered me, "It is difficult to answer it. In my opinion, it is having some features that others don't, which is being called ugly." Then she looked at me to see my reaction. I think she checked on me to know If I was laughing. I didn't.

"In my definition, it is an illusion. There is not really a beautiful or ugly person. It only shows the different tastes. It only shows how much girls spend their time in the mirror to attract boys, which I understand. The boys are doing the same by going to the gym and buying expensive cars if they aren't using some other stupid things, like putting on makeups." She laughed at my response. She knew I was right, but I knew she would challenge me on that.

"What do you mean you understand?" she asked.

"I had a friend back in high school. He won a medal in biology, and his favorite subject was Evolution. Once, he told me about research that has been conducted on the Guppies in three different ponds. The first one had a predator, blue acara, *Aequidens pulcher*. The second one had a predator that wasn't so aggressive as the first one, and the last pond didn't have many predators. The result was astonishing. The male guppies, in order to mate with females, needed to have a brighter color, which makes them easier for the predator to spot them and eat them. The other pond with a less aggressive predator was the same as the pond with no predators. Both ponds had the male brighter color and bigger in size." I looked at her. She was excited to know where I was going by telling her this thing. "The pond that had an aggressive predator, *Aequidens pulcher*..." When I said **pulcher**, I just remembered the day I met Calysta and her mispronunciation. It made me sad. Still, I continued my story. "It could develop kinds of guppies that can blend in the environment and hide from the predator, but here is the fact. They become glumier than other two ponds, but they never perfected it. They kept themselves shiny enough to make sure they met the minimum requirement for the female to mate them, and if they didn't, I mean, they didn't become shiny enough and instead camouflaged themselves in the environment, they do live longer than any other males, but they never have a chance to mate any females, so their genes are doomed, and it is going to be last in line." I let it sink in.

"You mean we have to work hard for beauty?" she asked me. I wanted to laugh at her response, but I didn't.

"First of all, human selection is much more complex than guppies. We shouldn't mix them up. I brought it up because I wanted to illustrate the illusion of beauty. I tried to show you the meaning of attraction. The guppies don't know about beauty, can't paint, and don't whistle when they see a really colorful male guppy passing by them. However, they tend to be attracted to more colorful males, which means something triggered inside them. The funny thing is, our responses to the colorful guppy are going to be the same. To choose between a colorful guppy and a gloomy one, we tend to choose the brighter one. It isn't because we are attracted to them in order to mate with them, but because, I think, like a female guppy, we are simply attracted to a more colorful one," I said and hoped she would understand what I tried to say.

"So you mean there isn't such a thing as beautiful or ugly, and they are just illusion, but what we have is only attraction, am I right?"

She was close, but she didn't get what I tried to say. "Let's put this subject on rest, okay? As you mentioned earlier, it is a difficult subject to talk about, but to answer your question, My taste for beautiful girls, I don't see any beauty anymore. I mean, I only see a reflection of lights on the surface of the objects. I am more like a blind man who is in the darkness. The only difference between a blind man and me is, my darkness has more colors."

She laughed at my response. "You just made me more confused," she confessed.

"Do you want to know how I fell for you?" I saw a shock on her face. Before she could answer my question, I continued by telling her the story between Corwin and me, how he forced me to choose a girl in the class, and the events after that. It was a long story, but she showed some interest, and because of that, I told her everything. In some parts of the story that I was telling her, she laughed so hard that it made me stop a little bit so that she could catch a breath.

"The reason I told you the story was to show you that I didn't target you because you were beautiful. However, you are one of the most beautiful girls in our university. I found out about your beauty after I found out how many men got rejected by you. Some of them were so broken that they claimed getting accepted in Cambridge was much easier than being accepted by you." She giggled at what I told her.

I wanted to tell her the reason why I didn't see any girls beautiful anymore. It was because I only saw one beautiful girl, and her name was Calysta. After Calysta, the world stopped being beautiful to me.

"It's such a shame," I said while simpering, but deep down, I was sad. I was having a good time with her. She made me happy.

"What do you mean?" She was smiling, but she had a curious face on.

"I wish we had more time. The semester is going to be finished in a month, and I just found a good friend," I said it with a sad tone and tried to keep my happy face on.

"Well, we come back next semester." She was still smiling, and it died on her face when she saw me shaking my head sadly as a disagreement. I guess she expected an explanation for my odd behavior.

"I guess that's it for me. My next semester will be in Switzerland, where I also work too," I said, but her facial expression told me that she needed more explanation. She wasn't smiling anymore. She was deadly serious. "I am going to CERN."

"What?" She almost screamed at me.

Chapter 15

She just came out of The George Washington High School. Then she headed down to Thirty-Second Avenue. The trail of parked cars was everywhere. The clouded sky gave a gloomy light to the afternoon. After a few minutes' walk, she arrived at Baloba Street. She passed the intersection. There were beautiful houses on both sides of the Avenue, but she wasn't paying any attention to any of them. She got used to them. It had been a few years since she had come to this high school. It was in this high school that she met Agustin, a guy who had everything she could ask for, but he was humble and oblivious about it. His handsome face, which always made her uncomfortable to the bone, was a masterpiece of the human race, but he always seemed to be dismissive no matter how many times she told him the fact. She arrived at Cabrillo Street. She passed the street again and continued on Thirty-Second Avenue. She was getting closer to the place she planned to. She could already see the Golden Gate Park's tree. She continued her walk until she arrived at Fulton Street. She turned left, and after that, she walked into the main entrance of the park.

She was meeting Agustin.

She was despondent about the things that were about to happen. She thought a lot about it, and the conclusion was that it would be really unfair for Agustin to continue this relationship. Her father's death was a big blow. It changed everything. The poor Agustin was nothing but supportive.

She sat on the bench.

She felt that even the bench was cursing her for doing this to the poor guy. It made her uncomfortable to sit. This bench was special for both of them, and they had too many memories on it.

It didn't take too long; she felt a touch of lips on her cheek from behind. It wasn't part of her plan, but it made her smile.

"Hello, beautiful," Agustin said with a big smile.

"Oh, Hi," she responded. He handed in her favorite ice cream, Spumoni. She thanked him for the ice cream. She was holding it in her hands and looking down to her feet. She looked ashamed. She thought she knew what she was supposed to do, but now she was not so sure.

"Do you think it's gonna rain?" Agustin asked.

"I don't know. Why?" she answered.

"Because I want to adjust my eating speed. You know, I don't want to have soaked ice cream."

She smiled. She knew he was talking about her ice cream. He was indirectly telling her to start eating, but she had no stomach for it. Not ice cream, not anything else. Agustin was always like that. He was too nice to her to tell her what to do.

"You can have mine too if you really want it," she said. She showed her acknowledgment of his hidden message.

"I will, but not before you finish half of it. It's gonna be more romantic. People will say, 'Oh, look at them, how romantic. They are sharing ice cream together.' Those unfortunate people have no idea that I already ate my share and eating my girlfriend's as well."

It made her giggle. She knew he was trying his best to make her eat her ice cream. The situation was like one of those scenarios parents do for their children to make them eat their nutrition.

She took her first spoon, and with that, she broke into tears.

She started crying. Her tears were pouring down like a rainy day. It got people's attention to see what was happening to this young lady. She hated herself for doing that and making Agustin embarrassed in front of others. He never complained. These few months, she was nothing but an embarrassment to him, but she couldn't control herself either. No matter how hard she tried. The pain of losing her dad was too much to bear. Being around Agustin made the matter worse. His kindness, laugh, consideration, love, and attention made her miss her dad more. He was taking care of her as her dad did, and this made her cry more.

In the last few weeks, she had been battling with herself about what to do. Was it okay if she kept being selfish and made life miserable for Agustin? Or do the right thing and break up with him? She just lost her father not too long ago, and now she was about to lose the love of her life. She wasn't ready to lose him. Not now or anytime soon.

Agustin was sitting there, not a bit concerned about what other people were thinking about him. It wasn't necessary to him before, and it wouldn't be important to him anytime soon. Calysta knew this about him, and because of that, she was worried that she was abusing Agustin's kindness.

"Sorry," she said while crying.

"I'm sorry too," he responded.

"What for?" she said while sobbing.

"For the same reason you are saying sorry."

It cracked her up. It made her laugh while she was crying, and at that moment, she decided to do it.

"Agustin," she said while trying hard not to cry.

"Calysta," he said casually. He just kept making it more difficult for her to do the right thing.

"I know you are gonna hate this, but I want you to break up with me," she said it finally.

Agustin just sat there and said nothing. She didn't expect this. She expected him to protest or ask why, but he did nothing. He was just sitting there silently.

"You know, the first law of thermodynamics is as beautiful as Edgar Allan Poe's poems," he said it after his long silence, without looking at her, but he was smiling, and before she said something, he continued.

"I always wondered where the energy goes. I mean, I know that at any moment, I lose energy as heat or kinetic, but where that heat goes? I wonder. However, I feel I am part of a big picture in the universe. My heat travels through space and sees the planets and the stars that I always wanted to see. In some planets far, far away, in a really far future, in million or even billion years away from Earth, a world which happens to have an intelligent life that could see the heat of other intelligent life on another planet through their excellent tools and devices, they could see my heat. How exciting a moment is going to be for them to find out they are not alone, and I am going to be part of it and contribute to it as long as I live, and it continues carrying the good message through space. Even better, for each calorie that I lose to raise the temperature of one gram of water to one centigrade, I become part of the phenomenon to evaporate waters and then become clouds. That particular one gram of water, which is going to be rain, is going to be part of a beautiful flower or fruit. That flower is going to be the source of food for honeybees, butterflies, or other insects or even be a symbol of love from one person to another.

"Look at that flower right there. I wonder if my calorie was part of it. Anyhow, I'm glad it's there. It is lively and beautiful," he said.

She saw the tears in his eyes, but he didn't turn around to meet her eyes. She knew that he wasn't talking about himself. Instead, he was talking about her dad.

Understanding Agustin wasn't easy for her at the beginning of their relationship, but she got used to it after a while. He was as mysterious as his favorite hobby, mathematics.

For the first time, she saw how sad he was. She'd never seen him like that, and now she could see that all this time, he was hiding his sadness from her.

"Are you gonna be happy if I leave you?" he said it with tears in his eyes, still trying to avoid eye contact with her.

She got the message behind it. He was telling her that if she wanted to break up with him just for his sake, she shouldn't do it.

Every cell and fiber in her body was screaming to say, "No, I won't be," but she knew if she told him that, he wouldn't leave her. It sounded so stupid.

She put her hand on his hand, which was grabbing the bench tensely. She felt the tension and the anger. The anger was real and dangerous. She never felt in danger around him until now. Knowing the years he spent in martial arts class, she never realized how strong he was. The vein in his forearm was on display for stupid people to tell them to back off. Now she saw the other side of Agustin, the danger of being a beast.

Who knew that Agustin could be like that? It only showed another miscalculation on her part. What if he loses control and starts hurting her? She never thought of that either, but now she sensed she must take her next step carefully.

"Agustin . . . I'm sorry," she said it finally while holding his hand in her hand. She could still feel the tension, and she accepted whatever was coming after that. As a matter of fact, she thought she deserved it.

But to her surprise, the tense was gone.

"That night when you were handing in cakes to everyone"—she knew he was talking about her birthday party—"your father sat beside me." Now she saw the smile on his face, but the tears were there. "He told me how much he loved you, from birth to that very moment. He was proud of you, and he was showing off how good his daughter is by telling me about the cake." His smile became wider. "At the end of our conversation, he asked me to do a favor for him. Do you want to know what he asked me to do?" Her cry got worse than before.

Now every pedestrian was looking in their direction while passing by. Some of them showed sad faces, and others were smiling. A few of them passed by without even bothering to look. They were trying to say they were in the same position when they broke up with their loved ones—Not a big deal.

He was still looking at the flower across the park with teary eyes and waiting for her answer. When she didn't answer him, he took her silence as an affirmation to his question. "He asked me to take care of you."

She had nothing to say but to cry more. She pressed her hand against his after she put her head on his shoulder. The weeping continued. He turned his clenched fist and opened it so that she could hold his hand.

"Now the daughter of the same man is asking me to break up with her," he said with a broken heart. "I am disappointed at myself that I couldn't be someone you needed at a difficult time. Do you feel happy if I leave you?"

"Agustin . . . Please," she begged him to stop torturing her.

He turned with eyes filled with tears and kissed her on top of the head.

"Take care, Calysta," he said with a bawling voice.

He stood up, took his bag, and left.

She realized that she misjudged everything when he left. Now she didn't want to break up with him. She howled his name, but he was too far away. She cried with lots of agonies. Somehow, she hoped he would come back and tell her he wouldn't let go of her.

People gathered around her and asked her what had happened, but she couldn't speak. She just continued crying. The void of his presence was too much. Only one word was coming out of her mouth. *Agustin*. Time passed, but Agustin didn't come back, and all this time, she was crying and calling his name.

A hand came and grabbed her under her shoulder and forced her to stay on her foot. She looked at the person in the hope she would see Agustin, but she saw Marshal. He was alone. He grabbed her bag and started walking with her. She was walking unsteadily while continuing sniveling.

It didn't take long for her to realize that Agustin had sent him, which worsened the matter.

The bench was empty after they left, and no one sat there because the two melted ice cream painted the bench.

Chapter 16

The lights of the projectors were bothering me. I couldn't see any faces from the audience sitting there, and the cameraman was moving the massive camera from one side to the other side. The blood inside me was boiling . I could feel my sweat glands pumping sweat all over my body. I hoped that no one noticed it. The show host was introducing me to the audience and was talking about my work, which he had no clue what he was talking about.

"So, Mr. Adalbert, can you tell us how old you are?" the host asked.

"Please, call me Agustin. I'm thirty-one," I answered him.

"Are you single?"

"Yeah, why? Am I gonna meet my blind date?" The whole audience laughed.

"That's funny, but I'm afraid you came to the wrong show. That show you are looking for is called *The Bachelor.*" The audience started laughing again.

"Is it too late for me to go to that show instead?" The laughing continued.

"I see that you have some sense of humor. I like that about you."

"Thank you, but I wished it came from a girl." The audience laughed and clapped for my response. I thought that I was good at this. I was a natural.

"You are a funny man, Agustin." He was laughing too. I hoped that I didn't steal his show.

"Thanks again," I responded kindly. After that, he asked me about my work, how important my articles were, and their influence on the science world. Since I knew that none of the audience was a professional scientist, I answered them as I explained it to kids. "Just be yourself and make it fun for them." That was the dean's advice after he told me the news that I had to go to this show, so I took his advice—what we, the scientists, had to do to raise money for our projects in university. After a few back-and-forth with the host, he told the audience that the other guest who was a singer was coming to the stage.

I heard the crowds cheered. The people were hurrahing from the heart. I felt that I was meeting The President, so I stood up like everyone else. Then I saw a tall blond girl wearing a sleeveless red dress walking toward the stage. She was wearing high-heeled shoes, even though she was tall. The host eagerly went and greeted her by kissing her on the cheek. When it was my turn, I shook her hand. She had long and delicate fingers. Because of the projector lights, I couldn't tell if she had blue or green eyes, but I could say she was beautiful.

The host shouted out her name, Taylor Lively, and people were applauding and whistling for her. I kind of felt jealous. When I did something great in the scientific world, I never received such applause from the audience. Instead, I received thousands of questions. It almost took minutes for the audience to calm down and sit on their chairs.

"Hello, Taylor. Welcome to the show," the host said.

"Hello. Thank you. I'm glad to be here," Taylor said.

"You look beautiful as usual."

"Oh, thanks," she said it with a smile. I could tell she heard that sentence more than a thousand times. However, I couldn't tell her smile was sincere.

I don't know why, but I really wanted to pull a prank on her. The thing preventing me from doing it was an excellent sensibility that kept telling me to control myself, to not do anything stupid.

In my opinion, the host was doing a horrible job interviewing her. It sounded like he had no idea what to talk about. They were exchanging awful jokes that no one was laughing at but themselves. I really got bored until I heard him talk about her status. He asked her if she was seeing someone, and she answered no.

Then a silly thought came to me, and I thought I had to do it. What I did was, while I was sitting, I bent my elbow and placed it close to my kneecap and had my forehead resting on my fist. I had my other hand on my other kneecap. It was a pose. It was supposed to show a thinking man in an attractive way. It worked; the whole audience laughed, and with them, Taylor and the host.

"Hi. My name is Agustin," I said while I was trying not to laugh at my own silly pose. I stretched my hand for another handshaking. She was smiling, but I knew it wasn't sincere.

"Hi. Taylor," she said. She shook my hand for the second time.

"I believe you just told him that you are single. Am I right?" I asked, but she only nodded. At least she had a smile on.

I turned to the host. "I thought that I needed to go to *The Bachelor*. You lied to me." The whole audience started laughing again.

"Well, I never thought of that," the host responded.

I turned my attention to her. I tried really hard to show my mischievous smile. It worked; it made her laugh, and with her, the whole audience.

"I believe we never met before," she said.

"I believe so." And with another alluring smile, I continued, "Just in case you are wondering, I am trying really hard to impress you." I felt that the whole auditorium exploded with people's laughs.

"Thanks." She laughed.

"I didn't know that you were one of her fans," the host said.

"Well, I am now," I responded.

"What do you mean 'I am now'?" he asked.

"It means that I've never met her before," I said.

"Do you like her songs?" he asked. At that moment, I've found out how stupid a move I made. I've never known about her existence up to that moment, and now I looked ridiculous. I hid my face by covering my face with the palm of my hands. It was amusing for the audience, but not for me.

"Don't tell me that you don't know her songs," he asked. I just could shake my head and show my guilty face. This time, she laughed sincerely at me.

"How would I know that she was going to be your guest? So at least I could listen to her songs. To be honest, I didn't know she existed," I responded.

"She is everywhere, for Chrissake—Internet, news, Magazine. But you blame me for not knowing her songs? Here I thought I was talking to a genius," he said.

I got pissed off for his disrespect toward me. "So do I, but it doesn't seem to me that anyone in here knows me either." I meant that I owned three different art galleries, which included music and orchestra, in three different countries. People like her come to me and ask me to see if I could exhibit their arts. She laughed hard. The host laughed too. They all laughed at me, but they didn't know I was right. I was pretty much famous in my field. I was everywhere, like she was, but not renowned for everyday people, who cover most population.

"Hey, Taylor, it seems to me that the host is a party crasher or the guy who separates people. What do you think if we make a date in other places that he can't be there? For example, another talk show." She laughed with other people. The host had a nervous laugh though.

"Hey, hey, hold your horses." The laughing continued. "I brought you guys here, and you are telling me that I'm not invited to the party? That's just brutal," the host said.

"Well, what you did so far was . . . nothing. It is not my opinion. You could actually ask her too if you don't believe me." I was smiling. We both turned to her.

"I'm having the best time ever." That was her response. The whole auditorium laughed with her, even the cameraman.

I ignored everyone and tried my last shot. "As I told you, I haven't listened to your music, which I'm not proud of, but it only shows you my honesty. Could you please at least sing a song for me? I think I deserve it after I made a fool of myself in this show." I wanted to put her on the spot, so I turned to the audience for agreement. It worked. Everybody whistled and cheered and asked her to sing. It was joyful for her. She grinned. Why not? More advertisement for her. Even the host asked her to sing. After she showed a little bit of reluctance, she agreed to sing, so she turned to the band in the studio and asked them to compose the familiar song she did in the past. The audience couldn't be more cheerful. They applauded her.

The band played their favorite song. I didn't see any beautiful composing in there. I mean, that kind of music had a short life expectancy. It would be ancient fast, and no one would bother again to listen to it. Her song was about her breakup with her boyfriend, how she missed being with him, but the music was jolly. It made me confused. If she missed her boyfriend, then why compose a happy song?

All in all, I was happy that I hadn't listened to her music. It wasn't my type. It had too much contradiction for my taste.

After she finished her song, she waved a hand to the audience and thanked them for their support. They clapped and gave her a radiant cheer.

"How was it?" the host asked me.

"I'm honored and speechless," I said. I already made an enemy in the show. I didn't plan to make another one. I didn't lie either. Thinking about it, she didn't have to sing any songs for me, but she did, so I was honored. However, I regret that I destroyed the image I made of her for myself.

"Don't you regret that you missed this great talent?" he said. I saw she was in a good mood, so I didn't want to disturb that.

"I'm glad that I heard her music now," I said. **Because I don't have to listen to her song when I get home,** I thought. I tried to dodge the question as much as possible and to be truthful at the same time.

"Do you like music?" she asked me.

"I do. I like the classic ones, from Mozart, Beethoven, Bach, Chopin to The Doors, Pink Floyd, The Beatles, and Rolling Stones."

"Wow, you listen to those old songs? And nothing new?" she asked me. I didn't want to crush her with my honesty.

"When I listen to the *Moonlight Sonata* and the *Für Elise*, I don't feel that I'm listening to the old music. I have the same feeling that the same people had almost two hundred years ago." People clapped for me and my answer.

"I didn't mean any disrespect to those legends. What I meant was, why not listen to the new music?" she asked.

"I did, and each time I listen to the music that the radio plays on the way home in a taxi, I just want to jump out," I responded. It made people laugh.

"Wow, you hated it that much?" she asked.

"I just have a high standard," I said it respectfully and realized that she didn't know what other things I do. I saw that I was drowning myself in a stupidity act.

"Don't mind him. I bet he doesn't know anything about music," the host said. The Audience booed him, and Taylor smiled. When he said that, I wanted to see the surprised face of the people who actually knew me.

"Actually, I do. Besides composing, I studied a lot about it too. You'll be surprised to know what beautiful Mathematics is in the heart of music," I responded.

"Wait a minute, you said you compose too?" she asked me. It sounded like she just caught a thief.

"You heard right," I said.

"Can you play a song for us?" She read my reluctance on my face, and before I said something, she continued, "I believe it is a reasonable request after you asked me to do a song for you." She did the same trick I did; she turned to the audience and asked them if they agreed. They were curious as much as she was, so they clapped and cheered for me.

I smiled. I wasn't ready to do it, and I didn't play in front of the audience.

"Okay, okay, you won," I said, and they hurrahed.

I asked the host to lend me a Spanish guitar. He turned to the band and asked them to give me one. I took the guitar and started tuning it.

"Your song was about the breakup and your feeling after that. Can I sing the same theme?" I asked. She nodded in conformation.

I smiled and let my fingers feel the guitar's strings. It didn't have any rhyme at first; I just planned to adjust my fingers to that strange guitar. It felt different, so I just made some strokes. I noticed people were waiting for me to play. Some of them already cast the judgment and started laughing at me, but I ignored all of them. When I felt that I was ready, I closed my eyes. Then the vicissitude happened. The music started having some rhyme in it. The provenance of all my sadness came back to me. The desiderata that had been piled up all those years came back to me. I wanted to show my vociferous feeling about the moment I felt she was out of my life, and then I sang:

There were broken glasses on the floor

The shattered mirror on the wall

Even though she is not here

You can't see it, can you?

I scream every night, cry every time

And my life goes like this

And I'm singing

How are you doing? How are you doing? How are you doing? How are you doing?

You wanted this, Didn't you?

I don't need another proof

Your beautiful eyes shine like the sun

And they can make me fall for you

I'm sitting on the broken chair

A broken heart

Waiting for the death

She comes and says

How are you doing? How are you doing? How are you doing? How are you doing?

I've seen this before

I've tasted this before

Listen now

I've been lonely before I know you

Then I see it again in my dream

Waking up with a scream

And continue singing

How are you doing? How are you doing? How are you doing? How are you doing?

If there was a time you loved me

Please let me know

I want to know

But you don't want to tell me, do you?

I remember the time I was kissing you

The universe was happy too

I've kept singing

How are you doing? How are you doing? How
are you doing? How are you doing?

May I say about love

If anything I learned about love

How to forget about you

It's not your fault

I know that

You are not with me

I know that

But I keep thinking

How are you doing? How are you doing? How are you
doing? How are you doing? How are you doing? How are
you doing? How are you doing? How are you doing?

I felt the last string my finger touched, and with it, I opened my teary eyes. The projector's light was still in my eyes, so I couldn't see the people's reactions. There was silence in the auditorium. No one breathed. No sound was coming from them. There was a lamented silence in the air. Everyone was waiting for someone else to break the silence. The heat was bothering me, and the silence wasn't helping either. I wanted to break it, so with having a half smile on my face. I wiped my tears with my handkerchief and said, "How was it?"

"Wow," the host said while he was getting rid of the tears with his own handkerchief. The whole audience waiting for that moment joined in and started clapping and applauding so hard that it made me overwhelmed. Some of them whistled. I don't know who stood up first, but after him, the rest of the audience stood up with him, even the host and Taylor.

In response, I thanked them all by nodding and acknowledging their kindness. It took a while before the host could manage the audience again. After calming down the audience, making them sit, and asking them to be quiet, he continued his interview.

"Who was it?" Taylor asked me before the host could continue his interview.

"Someone in the past," I responded.

"Did you love her that much?" Taylor asked.

"Or him?" the host interrupted. Some audience laughed. I laughed with other listeners, but I was already planning revenge on him.

"I still do, even though it's been many years that I haven't seen her," I added that last sentence to emphasize that I am not stalking her. The crowd made a sympathetic noise.

"Are all scientists like you? Kind and romantic?" Taylor asked. I laughed, and with me, the whole audience. I laughed because it reminded me of the same thing Aiko and Bernadina told me a long time ago, but I think the spectators laughed because they thought she was funny.

"Well, if you omit the image that Hollywood made about the scientists, I mean, made them either evil or dorky, you'll end up with a group of people who are passionate in their professions, and like everybody else, they know how to show a good time to beautiful girls like you."

"Way to go, Dr. Adalbert. That was smooth," the host said. The house laughed at his comment.

"It is not a compliment if it is true," I said with a mischievous smile on. It made her laugh too.

"What other hobbies do you have? Besides science and music?" Taylor asked.

I looked at the audience and smiled. "Well, that is a discussion over a date-night dinner. Saturday night, at eight?" The congregation laughed with me, so did she.

"You are not backing down, are you?" the host asked.

I shook my head and said, "It's worth every bit of it." The audience roared with laughter. They were all having a good time.

"I think *The Playboy Magazine* should interview you for their next issue," the host said. I tittered.

"If you tell me one other hobby of yours, then I'll consider going out with you. Deal?" Taylor said. Obviously, she ignored the host's comment.

I looked at the audience and threw my hand up as a surrender, which was amusing for them, then continued, "You won. I also do painting."

"No way," the host said, and I thought what a dickhead I was dealing with that night. He was nothing but a complete douchebag.

"Why not?" I responded.

"I don't know. I guess you would say anything to have a date night with Taylor Lively. Even claiming that you are the president of the USA."

"First, the president already has the First Lady, and I don't think she is going to be happy to find out about a mistress. Second, I don't find any reasons to lie to her. What I am doing here is to convince her to have a date with me. That's it. And last, I just don't understand why it is so difficult for you to believe I have other hobbies too," I said, and the audience agreed with me. They booed and hissed at him.

"Okay, okay, I take back what I said." He raised his hands as a surrender. I felt pity for him. He was a tool.

"Can you paint me?" Taylor asked.

"Of course, I can. Just like Jack and Rose in *The Titanic?*" It cracked her up, and she was followed by the gang's laugh.

"The moment I thought it couldn't get any weirder," the host said.

"I couldn't agree more. Can I take it back?" I asked Taylor, but she was already dissolved into laughter. She couldn't talk. It took her a while to calm down and start talking.

"Can you paint me now?" she asked.

"Now?" I said. She took me off guard. In response, she only nodded her head.

"Well, I can't paint you right now if I wanted to. It takes lots of time. The thing I could do is just to draw your face with a pencil. Hence, I don't know if we have enough time for that either," I said politely. She turned to the host and looked at him. The host looked back at her and nodded. He said I had only five minutes to draw her, and I said It would be enough.

After that, they brought me a pencil and a piece of paper. I took them and started drawing her. I liked the challenge. I've never done it before, but it sounded amusing for me to do it in a short time. While the host was interviewing Taylor, I tried my best to draw her and not screw it up. I just needed one glance to remember her facial features. After that, I only used my imagination. The time passed, and it was the only time that night that I didn't notice how the time passed at such speed. The host asked me if the drawing was ready. I felt bad. There were so many features that I could add to the picture, but the time ran out.

"To be honest, I don't like it so much," I said it and knew it wasn't my best work, but I gave it in. The cameraman zoomed it in, and the whole audience went silent again for the second again. I heard some of them use the cursed word "Wow" again.

"Wow, I love it. Can I keep it?" Taylor asked me with excitement. She was actually exhilarated in the act too.

"I could do better if you give me more time. This isn't my best work. I'm kind of embarrassed about it."

"Oh . . . My . . . God, do you mean you could do better than this? I'm wondering what else you can do to make it better. To be honest, I'm looking forward to our date night," she said it while she gave me a wink as a bonus. She wasn't alone; the audience agreed with her, and I could see the surprise on their face too. They were talking to one another as if to say, **"Can you believe this guy?"**

I was happy that Taylor liked my drawing despite my best work.

The way I drew her, it was as if she were sitting on the bench and arching on both her hands. Her elbows were sitting on her lap while her hands were holding her face up. She was wearing a long dress, different from what she was wearing now. The bench was covered with a few flowers and tree branches on top. The tree's body was out of the picture. Her long hair was a good feature because it made me spend a little time on her face and fingers, so her golden hair covered both her fingers and face. Her eyes were the tricky part. All that could be destroyed by drawing her eyes badly. It took more time than necessary to draw them.

"I'm glad you like it. I only wanted to add some small animals too, like a rabbit, chital, and squirrel. I don't even know if you like animals. Do you?" I said.

Her reaction to my question was cute. She opened her mouth as a surprise and put both of her hands on the side of her face, just like the picture I drew, except the open-mouth part. She looked at me and then looked at the audience. The audience melted.

"I love it. I love it. Can you do that for me? Yes, I do, I do, I do. I do have a cat," she said. Before I could say anything, the host jumped in.

"Well, I hate to be the bad guy in here, but we are out of time in here. I thank Dr. Adalbert for coming to our show. It was a great honor meeting him. And I also thank Taylor Lively, whom her presence, once again, made our show great," he said to the cameraman.

However, Taylor was so excited that she couldn't wait for us to go out, and so she asked me again after the host announced that the show was over. People found her reaction cute. I found it as being impatient.

"I even have a better idea. How about I draw your cat instead?" I said, and somehow, she got more excited. I don't know if the camera was still rolling or not, but I saw her rising from her seat, coming to me, and kissing me on both cheeks.

That was delightful and surprising. I came out of the auditorium and headed outside. Somehow, she managed to turn me off. I just wanted to be out of her side while she was talking to her fans. I felt her impatience wasn't cute at all but relatively immature. I didn't want to have another drama in my life. I walked. I walked as fast as I could. If I got out of the place, maybe she would forget about all this. She didn't have my address, and I figured she wasn't that kind of person to pursue after me. To her, I was another male who tried to get to her pants, and I was too tired to prove all over again that I am not such a person at all. Maybe I was, or perhaps I wasn't.

I arrived at the door.

I stepped outside. I welcomed the fresh breath of air. I needed it to cool me down. The show was horrible, in my opinion.

The cloud was dressed in orange and yellow. The trace of the dark shadow of the birds on the horizon, dancing up and down, was beautiful. Some of the cars started using their headlights. The tall buildings became like shadows of the same structures in daylight. The city started turning the lights on. The asphalt absorbed the remaining light.

I inhaled the fresh air again and headed toward my car. I wanted to walk. I wished I didn't bring my car. I wanted to walk home. I rarely got an opportunity like that. The world was going too fast for my taste, and I wanted to push down the brakes. I wanted to be outside of the iron box. I wanted to hear the music of nature. The feeling of what kind of bird was singing was priceless. What happened to me all these years? Science became everything that I have now. Was it too much to ask for more? I saw the new brand and model of cars. I never got so excited or impressed with them. They were all the same for me. They were all shiny and excellent for people who lost the touch of nature and were looking for beauty elsewhere. I stood right beside my car. I knew standing in one place on Earth didn't really mean staying unmoved. The Earth was moving. I looked up at the sky again and took a mental picture. I unlocked my car.

I heard a car stop right behind me. I looked back. It was Taylor. She was riding a new Maserati.

"Are you hiding from me?" she asked kindly.

I smiled. She got me, and she got me right. "I was trying to hide from all those people. I don't know how you handle it. That heat, interviewing with those kinds of hosts, expectations from all those people. I believe one talk show was enough for my entire life." I didn't want to be rude by admitting to her. After all, I was hiding from her too.

"I hate it to be the person to give you the bad news. If you hate paparazzi and attention, you shouldn't have asked me out in front of the camera or be seen with me anywhere," she said.

The feeling of standing under a cold shower rushed to my body. I didn't know about that. I could tell that she wasn't joking either. Finally, my ignorance about the celebrity's life caught up with me. I was famous, but not that famous that every newspaper was knocking at my door or watching every move I made. **What have I done?**

"Are you okay?" she asked and looked concerned.

I gulped. Unable to answer her, I shook my head. I could tell she was laughing behind her beautiful smile. Deep down, I knew I deserved it.

"How long do you think it's gonna last?" I asked.

"I don't know. A week or a month. It depends on how fast another big news comes." She looked away for a few seconds and then looked back at me. "I believe you aren't going to finish that drawing for me anytime soon, are you?"

I looked at her. She was smiling, but behind that smile was bitterness. I could feel it. Sometimes I had the same smile. Hiding my sorrow and loneliness behind a happy face became part of me.

"I could do it now. It won't take too long," I said.

"Thanks, but I don't think it's such a good idea to do it here. The last thing you need is to be seen with me alone."

"Well, I'm a scientist, and I'll bore them to death by asking them to give a donation for a scientific research." It cheered her up and made her laugh.

"Thanks, but are you sure you wanna do it?" she asked.

I looked at her, and with one smile and a nod, I assured her of my decision.

"Okay then." She reached for her dashboard and took a piece of paper. She wrote something on it. It took her a while. Then she folded the paper and handed it to me.

"Thank you." she said, and before I could say anything, she took off.

I unfolded the paper and expected to see an address. Instead, I saw a message:

> You seem to be a great person. I had a great time with you, and I thank you for it. I know you will make someone very happy one day, and I'm not planning to ruin that for you. I wish you all the best of luck.

I looked in the direction she took off. Her car was out of sight. I felt horrible. My judgmental opinion took the best of me, and thanks to that, I just lost a good friendship.

"And to you too," I whispered.

Chapter 17

The tiny thing, which looked like a ping-pong ball with an odd shape, kept growing in my hands like a snowball. It was growing too fast. In a few seconds, it became so huge that it buried me alive. I couldn't hold it anymore. It was too big and heavy for me. After I was buried under it and died, I revived again to experience it all over again. No matter how many times it happened, it felt fresh, and the experience was as horrible as before.

I can't recall how many times that nightmare came to me, but I remember even after waking up from it, in consciousness, it kept happening to me. Teeth clenching and body shivering came after it too. I felt cold to my bones.

Even though the whole world was cycling around me like a carousel and made me imbalanced and dizzy, It didn't stop me from getting out of the room. I could still feel the weight in my hands. The imaginary odd-shaped ball was still there and kept growing and killing me over and over again.

I came out of the room. The light was on in the living room, and I saw my father was doing some paperwork. **Some luck at last,** I thought.

My throat was so dry that it felt like a piece of bone or fork was scraping it or someone was pouring hot metal into my mouth forcefully. I felt helpless. I headed downstairs, and by that, my father noticed me. He looked up from his papers and looked at me. He didn't like what he saw. He frowned out of concern.

"How are you doing?" he asked.

"Good," an alien voice, even for me, came out of my mouth. I felt like I was talking through the strangling hands of a murderer.

I headed straight to the kitchen. I opened the fridge, and there it was—the holy water. I topped the glass and drank it whole like a frantic person who hadn't had any for many days. My thirst wasn't satisfied. I poured another one and drank it as fast as I could. It soothed my throat. Then I noticed the sweat that was coming down my head. I felt the sweat on my eyebrows. I wiped it with my sleeve. I walked back to the living room. I liked the light because it forced me to stay awake, but I was too tired to stand up or stay awake, so I crawled to my father's side and lay down on the couch. I put my head on his lap; it felt strange and weird.

When I was a kid, I used to do that a lot when I had nightmares and fevers. Somehow, being on his side with his strong hand on my head, I felt comfortable and safe from the monsters in my head, but now I felt estranged. I felt I was too big doing that now, but I was too tired and defeated to let that strange feeling win.

He didn't resist me, and add to that, he put his hand on my head like he used to. It made me close my eyes for a second, but the odd-shaped ball reappeared. It started haunting me all over again. I opened my eyes; still, the shape was there. I felt so cold. I clenched my teeth and started shivering.

"Agustin, your fever hasn't gone yet?" he asked.

"I d-d-d-doo-n't . . . know," I answered through my chattering teeth.

"Do you want me to take you to a doctor?" he asked, concerned, but I could only shake my head to answer him.

"D-ddd-dad. Ca-ca-can I a-ask . . . y-you . . . sss-something?" I managed to say.

"Of course," he responded quickly.

"Ah . . . ahhh . . . I . . . w-w-w-want to . . . to . . . go to another school," I said and expected him not to ask me why, but he did, and he asked me about my friends and what would happen if I left the school all of a sudden. He also asked me if anything had happened between them and me. I couldn't answer. The moment Calysta came to my mind, my eyes started pouring out tears. I missed her. I missed her so much. Worst of all, her smiles and laughter were haunting me. I wanted nothing more than to be on her side. My body missed her warm and soft hands. I wanted her warm kisses. I wanted her to assure me that everything was going to be okay and this was all a nightmare that I would soon be awakened from.

I closed my eyes and felt the trace of tears going down the side of my eyes to my father's lap. He didn't ask me more questions. He sat there and rubbed his hand gently on my head.

The following day, I woke up with a headache. The sun's ray was on my eyes, and the thirst came back to me. I was still on the couch. I felt uncomfortable lying there, so I sat up, but an unknown force pulled me back to lie down. I was too weak to resist it. I wished I was born in the other animal kingdom; that way, a lion or hyena would end my miserable life way sooner. Let them feast on something unworthy. At least let others who wanted to live, live.

My thirst forced me to stand up and go to the kitchen. There, I noticed my mom was in the kitchen and preparing breakfast. I opened the fridge and looked for the water. The sound of the opening door of the fridge made my mom jump. I looked behind the door. I saw my mom put her hand on her chest and breathing fast like a scared bird. It brought a grin to my face.

"AGUSTIN, you scared me," she said.

"Sorry, love," I said to her, which made her smile too. I just copied my dad's phrase when he was in trouble and had nothing better to say.

"Are you hungry? Breakfast is almost ready," she said while she still had the smile on.

Thinking of eating anything turned my stomach inside out, so I told her no. Her smile vanished in a matter of seconds. She looked at me with a murderous look of a lioness who was about to kill her cub because it was too weak.

I poured the water into a glass, and on the way out, I kissed her forehead. She didn't budge; she still had that angry face on, which made me kiss her again.

"Mom, I can't eat anything. My head hurts, and thinking of eating anything makes me vomit," I said it with a sincere voice, but still, it didn't wash away her anger.

"Enough is enough, Agustin. You've been sick for a week. You don't eat properly, you don't talk, and you imprison yourself in your bedroom. What happened? Why don't you talk to me about it, huh? Are you planning to kill me?" she said it madly. I was livid at myself for doing that to her. I would rather see her hit or slap me on the face than see her like that. She was too nice to me, and she never once raised her hand on me.

"I never dream of it. Who wants to handle Dad? Me?" I said it casually, but deep down, I was cursing myself for doing that to my mom. It worked. She tried hard not to laugh, so she looked away. I could see her tears in a mixture of laugh and anger. When I saw that, I started hating myself more for being alive. I walked toward her and tried to hug her, but she pushed me back by her arm while hiding her face with her other hand, but I forced myself on her. I hugged her tightly.

"Do you wanna sit and talk?" I said, but she still refused to look at me. "Even if I promise you to tell you everything? Not even Dad knows." I tried to make it unique and to make her feel special. I don't know why, but somehow, when I was a kid and teenager, I felt there was a fierce competition between my dad and my mom to see whom I liked the most and from whom I inherited the most genes.

"Promise?" she asked.

"Promise," I responded and tried to put a smile on.

We headed toward the living room and sat there across from each other. She was still trying to get rid of the remaining tears. It made me sad, and I felt horrible. I waited until she was ready to talk.

When she looked at me and our eyes locked, I knew it was my cue to start talking. However, I didn't know how to start. I looked down and up again.

"Moma, was there anyone else besides Dad that you loved?" I asked, and I saw a shock on her face. "I mean, did you love anyone before Dad came along?" I thought I made a correction by asking her the correct version of the question, but she was still surprised by my question.

"Why are you asking that?" She looked puzzled.

"Moma, it is a two-way conversation. If you don't like it, we could stop it here, and there won't be any hard feelings. I don't like to sit here and be interrogated." I thought I made my argument clear, but it only made her eyes narrow.

"Why do you want to know that?" she asked me the same question with a different phrase.

I thought a little bit. If I were in her shoes, I would be curious too. "I am just trying to find common ground to talk to. Please, answer me honestly." She looked at me, and to me, she looked agitated. She moved her head side to side, not knowing what to do with me.

"What do you want to do with that kind of information?" Again, she asked the same question with a different phrase.

I could stand up and go back to my room to show her my agitation, but when I looked at her, I could tell she wasn't comfortable talking about her past, whatever it was.

I loved her too much to do that to her, so I gave in. "You and Dad seem to be happy and love each other. I am just wondering if Calysta is going to be the same. Is she going to be happy with another man? Will she ever remember that once I loved her dearly? Or she just moves on? What will happen to me? Am I going to meet a girl like Calysta? Will I love her the same way I loved Calysta?" Those feelings were important to me. I felt my heartbeat again, even by mentioning her name. I went through the nightmare I had last night. This time, someone cut off my head from my body with a cleaver.

"Did she break up with you?" my mom asked cautiously. I could only nod. Without saying another word, she came and sat beside me. My headache was getting worse, and my throat was hurting me again. She put her hand behind my back and rubbed it up and down. She tried to comfort me. I just wanted to lie down. I wanted to sleep to death and never wake up again, so I stood up to go to my bedroom.

"Agustin, don't you want to eat anything?" she asked me again. I could only shake my head for an answer, and I kissed her forehead again. I knew I couldn't eat anything even if I forced myself to do so. I headed back to my bedroom and dragged my body. I looked back in my mom's direction only to see her hunched and hid her face in her palms. I guess after seeing me like that for almost a week, I finally broke her down. I hated myself to see another woman I loved the most was hurting because of me. I went inside and closed the door. I found my bed. Lying down, I felt chilly, so I put the blanket on my shivering body. I closed my eyes to see the deserving nightmares again.

I woke up with a much more painful headache. The brain inside my skull was pushing out my eyes. For the first time in a week, the pain gave me a cathartic experience. That was the irony since only pain could heal my emotional pain. Putting both hands on my head, I tried to push back my brain to where it was. It was just wishful thinking. This agony made me cry and moan involuntary. My throat was dry again.

I attempted to stand up to go to the kitchen, but suddenly, the whole world was spinning around my head. It threw me back where I was. I started panting for air, but it didn't matter because I didn't get enough of it. I sat up and did not dare to stand up again. With both hands on my head, I rocked back and forth repeatedly to reduce the pain, but to no avail. The pain was getting worse in seconds. It brought me down to my knees on the floor, and it was followed by my hands on the floor. Now I looked like a beggar on the floor, asking for any kind of mercy. The hickory wood on the floor absorbed a little bit of coldness, and for some unknown reason, my body thought it was a good idea to have a little bit of it, so without any resistance, I laid down my face on the floor. Facedown on the floor, I was still panting for air. The pain eased up for a millisecond and came back with full force again. I moaned in agony. I stood up with all the energy that was left in my body and planned to take a shower. That way, I could give my body either cold or hot water. I was in too much pain to think clearly, and somehow, I felt that death was close by. I grabbed the navy-blue shelves two feet away from my bed to help me not to fall down again.

I couldn't lean on it because the shelf didn't have any wall support behind it, and add to that, some objects could fall and break, especially Calysta's gifts to me. Looking at her gift eased up my pain. The shelves acted like a separator from my bed to the rest of the room. On one side, there was my burlywood-colored bed, which was facing a forty-five-degree angled ceiling six feet away, and it was bordered by navy-blue shelves with the regular ceiling. In the middle of the angled ceiling, there was a painted picture of a galaxy (the name of the galaxy is NGC 6503 with dark blue and black color in the background), and on another side of the shelves, twelve feet away, there were other white bookshelves full of books, except on the top middle, which was holding my four stereos. In the middle of that shelves, there was an empty space that had enough room for a two-seater couch with the same color as my bed. On top of my sofa and below the top shelves, there was a big picture of Neptune on the horizon, and in front of the couch, there was a two-by-four blue web–colored carpet. Sitting on it was a white table. On the left side of the sofa, which would be close to the corner of the room, I had a white **L**-shaped desk. It had my computer on one side and other staff on the other side. A window was located on top of the desk, which I had a beautiful view of the east.

Calysta loved the work I had done to my room. Every piece of furniture was made by my own hands, and she was impressed by it. I wouldn't forget the face she made when she saw my room for the first time.

The pain in my head was a nonpareil. I have never felt it before and couldn't compare it to anything. ***If I am going to die, why does it have to be this painful?*** I thought.

Somehow, I managed to walk to the door. I tried to open the door, but I noticed that I had difficulty opening it—the same door that I opened more than a thousand times without any effort. I was worried that my mom would discover me in this tohubohu, and I knew what it would do to her. My encephalon failed me again. Anyhow, I headed toward the bathroom by having one hand on the wall for support. Finally, I arrived there.

I never thought that I would have a doleful life like this. So pathetic. I went inside and welcomed the confinement. While I was taking off my shirt and pants, I noticed a picture of a stranger in the mirror. Two eyes that turned bloody red were looking at me. The face was too pale for a living human. The cracked lips were begging for water. No wonder why Mom was so scared when she saw me like that.

I walked into the bathtub and turned on the tap water. The cold water kissed my skin. Chills ran through me.

Good.

It made me forget about the headache and other things. My sore and beaten body gave up to the gravity, and I sat in the bathtub.

The running water was music to my ears. Each drop made a merry dance on my skin. They were running like children in the field—carefree and happy, singing in harmony. It was so unearthly and beautiful. The water started getting warmer, and my skin welcomed the sensation. Deep down, I wished that my life would end at that moment, and with it, my headache and the memory I cherished for the little time that I had. Those sweet memories of Calysta that made me smile each time I thought about it, now they became my never-ending nightmares. I was too tired to have my eyes open for that long, so I closed them, hoping not to open them again.

A few minutes later, I heard someone knocking at the door and calling my name. It was my mom. I thought she was checking on me, so I responded, but she told me that Marshal was downstairs and waiting for me. Great, now I had to deal with him too. The world didn't want me to have a little break after all. The moment a sense of relief came to me, it put me right back to hell.

I stood up and noticed that the bathroom was so foggy that I could barely see my two steps ahead. *How long have I been here?* I thought. I guess I lost track of time. I stepped outside of the bathroom and started drying myself with a towel. Then another realization hit me when I saw my hand and foot skin had been wrinkled.

The pain of the earlier headache had been reduced but didn't go completely. It was better than nothing. The fogged-up mirror hid my face. It sounded like it wanted to warn me not to look at myself at all. Who cares? I wasn't curious to see my beaten face either.

I stepped outside of the bathroom and headed toward my room to put on something. I chose the red sweater and the sky-blue jeans. With a towel on my head trying to dry my hair, I headed downstairs.

Seeing him sitting on the couch and listening to my mom complain, I had to admit, it cracked me and made me laugh a little bit.

He looked up and noticed me. He tried to hide his concerned face behind a smile. I smiled back to hide my pain.

"Who let this guy in?" I asked my rhetorical question.

"Agustin!" my mom protested.

"I was talking to your mom. Guess what I found out? Did you know that you were adopted?" Marshal said it with a big smile on his face.

"Marshal!" My mom scolded him too. "You two better behave, or I'll let you know the feeling of being in hell."

"Mom, don't ask him an impossible mission," I responded. She laughed. She stood up and left us alone. That was her way of giving us a little bit of room. After she left, I sat across Marshal. I was happy to see him, but also sad because I didn't want him to see me like this.

The world was changing for me. The taste, the color was turning bitter and black. I could see that I was sailing into a stormy night at the ocean with no lifeboat on it. Those black waves were crashing every inch of the ship. The sound of twisted woods under those pounding waves was a warning that the ship was going to give up at any second.

"Hey, are you all right? I came here to see what happened to you. You didn't show up at school, but I know the reason now."

I looked at him blankly. I had nothing to say. What was there to say? Life wasn't as usual. Everything changed, and it was a sad moment in my life that I had to deal with. I was a tyro about this kind of thing. I never knew about being heartbroken or anything like it. My life was simple and logical. If I failed at anything, I knew exactly where I made a mistake, but now everything was chaos. I had to answer questions that I didn't understand. What was my mistake? Where did I fail Calysta? Why did she want to break up with me? She was probably thinking about it for a while. Did she consider what would happen to me if she left me like that? Was she that much cold and I was the only one oblivious about it? What should I do now?

The truth was that I wasn't a good companion to her. Somehow, I made her feel lonelier than ever and brought her to a conclusion: It is better to be alone than to be with this guy.

"We broke up," I said and tried to hide my sadness. I was trying to save my pride in front of him.

"Why did you break up?" he asked, but how could I answer a question that I didn't understand myself?

"We both came to the conclusion that it was time to part ways." I was still trying to stay calm so that he wouldn't worry about me.

"Bullshit. I didn't know you were that cold. Do you know what state she was in when I got there? Thank God, at least you had a little humanity left when you made that call, or I don't know what would happen to that poor girl," he said it angrily. I didn't know what happened to her after I left, but me being cold? What the fuck was he talking about? My mind was in a state of chaos when I left her. I still remember my body was shivering in the middle of a warm weather. When I was out of her sight, I started vomiting in the corner of the park. People were looking at me either with sympathy or disgust. It didn't take me long to go back to being myself, hating everyone. I wanted to be alone or be left alone. Even in that situation, I was considering her well-being. That was the reason I made a call to Marshal. I don't know what she was feeding him, but putting my best friend against me was a whole new level of being a bitch.

"What happened?" I asked him genuinely, but he looked at me with disgust.

"If it wasn't for your mom calling me to come here, I swear I wouldn't come. You know what? It makes me happy to see there is at least karma for what you did. The whole week, I was defending your actions to Aiko. Do you know how close I am to breaking up with her?" I could see the hatred in his eyes. He was looking for an answer as well. I was pissed off for the whole situation.

"What happened?" I asked him again, backing it up with little anger. However, he just looked at me and gave me a smirk. Our eyes were locked, and if we weren't home, there was a high chance that a fight would break out. I was tired and had no patience. The headache wasn't helping either.

"Do you wanna go out?" I asked him. He stood up as an answer. I didn't know what kind of argument would break out, but I didn't want my mom to know about it. She had been through enough.

"Okay, let's go," he said. I tried to stand up, but it was too demanding for my body. If a fight happened, I knew the result already. I was pissed off. The person whom I called my best friend had been brainwashed. How stupid he must be to think that I was the person who broke up with her. I was so pissed off at myself for liking that witch. Is humanity dead? Is there no limit to shame? Why would she do that to me? Wasn't it enough what she already did to me? Now she put my best friend against me? Anyway, whatever energy was left in me was spent to make myself stand up. I couldn't believe my own stupidity. I was in that state because of her.

"Mom, me and Marshal are gonna go out!" I yelled and hoped she wouldn't ask where, why, or any other follow-up questions, but as usual, the universe didn't give a shit about what I wanted. After explaining to her and convincing her that outdoor activity was good for me, I followed Marshal outside. I was strolling behind him. He was storming out; I, on the other hand, had to stop many times to catch my breath. Even being outside wasn't helping. My body was begging for air. When I reached outside, I felt like a champion. It was like I conquered the mighty Everest. I was too tired to take even one more step, so I gave up, and my body made me sit on the doorstep. I knew the world was unfair, but I never expected this much unfairness. Sometimes I wondered how the universe was for other people. It was probably a sherbet for ruthless ones, but for people like me, it was just poison.

"So what did you want to tell me?" Marshal asked. I didn't expect that. I thought a fight was about to break out.

"First, I need to know what she told you so that I can defend myself," I answered with bitterness.

"She told me nothing. Whenever I or anyone else asked her what happened, she just burst into tears. What did you do? Why did you do it?" he said it with anger behind his voice. I needed time to absorb the new intel. So she didn't tell them anything, and they assumed that I was the one who broke up with her. In the end, they didn't realize how important she was to me. It was sad. I never felt so lonely until that time. Even my best friend doubted my feelings toward her. I wanted to tell him everything. That way, at least I could salvage my friendship, but to what end? Anyhow, I decided to change school. What was the point of telling him everything other than making him take a side and end up like me? I owed him that much. Also, I didn't want Calysta to lose face. Maybe I would never find out the reason behind her breakup, but whatever it was, the thought of damaging her by telling a one-sided story wouldn't make me feel any better.

I was in a better situation. I had my parents, but she had just lost her father. She needed more support than me. After a long pause, I responded.

"The reason we broke up is something between Calysta and me. If she doesn't want to tell anyone, it's her choice. I am leaving the school anyway, so you guys shouldn't be worried about seeing me again," I said it, meanwhile being miserable from inside.

"What the Fuck is wrong with you? Are you retarded or what? I asked you a simple question, and you are trying to act like a hero," he said, agitated.

"What the fuck did you expect me to say? Do I have to tell you every detail of my life? I never asked you to take my side," I said it by being a little bit louder than him. I thought if I made him hate me, maybe he would take Calysta's side. I wanted that when Calysta started cursing me, instead of taking my side, he would curse me as well. I wanted to be hated. That was the last thing I could do before I cut off all my ties with her.

"You are an idiot. What is wrong with you? I don't need permission to defend my friend. If someone disrespects my friend, it is like they disrespect me, even though that friend could be an asshole," he said it with the same tone as before. He continued, "If I am asking what happened between you two, it is just because I want to help you out. Also, I want to know what kind of shit I am in."

At any time, I would have laughed at his comment, but the time wasn't right. He was angry, and I was tired. I wanted to end the conversation as soon as possible. I looked at the sky. The sun was calling it a day. On the horizon, the sun turned the sky into a fantastic canvas. The sky close to the sun was colored in orange, then Yellow, then light pink, and then dark-night blue. It was beautiful. It shouldn't be like that. I wanted a gloomy sky, just like my heart, but no matter what I desired, it turned to be something else. I decided to leave school. Maybe things would change for me over there. I don't know. There was no doubt that it was a radical decision. Changing schools for a girl was stupid. Add to that, washing my hands off a beautiful friendship was idiotic too. No one asked me to do any of that, and the reason I was willing to do it was unknown to me at the time.

Compathy is one of those beautiful words I came to love. Calysta and I shared the same pains. We both wanted to be left alone. At least that was what I thought.

I looked at Marshal and felt terrible to be a rebarbative friend. I caused him so many painful arguments with his girlfriend. I tried to stand up, but there wasn't any energy left in my body. I wanted to be a real man, a mensch, who shoulders his own responsibilities. I needed an ostensible reason for my breakup without revealing so much so he would leave me be; however, I, by being so pathetic and helpless, couldn't even convince him of anything, let alone a made-up story that I was about to tell him.

In chess, there is a move that is called **zugzwang**. It is a situation in which either the person loses a vital piece or gets into a dangerous situation. I put so many people in zugzwang but never thought of a day that I would end up in it too.

"Come and sit here," I asked him nicely. He looked at me, and I could tell there was displeasure on his face. I didn't wait for him to sit down, so I asked him a question, "Do you know the story of Orpheus's wife?"

"No, I don't," he told me with a little bit of temper. Then he continued, "I was never into this kind of thing."

I looked at him, and I couldn't help but smile at him. We were always in competition. Even then, he didn't want to admit he knew less than me, so he tried to make it sound less important than what it was.

It was his lucky day, I guess. That was because I wasn't in the mood for gloating.

"It's a Greek myth. When I was learning to play piano, my teacher told me about Orpheus's story. I remember that he told me that Orpheus was known for being a legendary musician and poet. Also, He was a prophet too. His music was so good that all living things and even stone were influenced and moved by it. My teacher told me that level of mastery should be my goal for playing music and song, and nothing else matters. No amount of money or fame can replace that sacred place. He told me that it should be a goal for all musicians. However, nowadays, people couldn't care less about that, and he asked me not to be like that. If a flower doesn't enjoy my music or an animal escapes from me when he hears my music, but I make tons of money just to make sloppy music, I shouldn't call myself a musician. He wanted me, as a pupil, to inherit this philosophy."

I looked at Marshal and saw indifference on his face. Then I looked at the other side of the street and saw some pedestrians passing by. I continued, "Later on, when I did a little bit of research about Orpheus's life, I found out how tragic his life was. He lost his wife, Eurydice, to an accident. The story is that she walked in tall grasses, and a serpent bit her on her ankle. She died on that spot. Later on, when Orpheus found out about the incident, he became so sorrowful that he played and sang a sorrowful song that made Gods and animals gloomy too. The Gods suggested that he go to the underworld and retrieve his wife, so he did. He went to the underworld with only the tool or weapon he had—his music. His music was so strong that it made Hades and Persephone kind enough to let him take his wife back on Earth. However, there was one condition. He must walk in front of his wife and never look back until both of them reach the upperworld. They started their journey to the upperworld. When Orpheus arrived at the top, he was too excited to see his wife that he forgot the condition and turned around to see her, and by doing that, his wife disappeared, but this time, forever." The sun was passing on its light to the moon, but between that, there was a twilight. The pink color deepened in the sky, and there was a shade of dark blue. These two colors above the city were giving a minatory feeling to the people underneath. The message was clear: The darkness is coming, and it is a long way till dawn.

Marshal didn't say a word. I think he was trying to understand the connection. Why would I tell him such a story? Was I trying to change the subject or give him a clue about what happened?

"Don't bother. I am not Orpheus. I am not a deity or great musician, but look at it this way. What if, for my own selfishness, I could cause Calysta to be lost forever? The decision we made to give our relationship a break was there only for our own good. Even Though it's a bitter pill to swallow, but it was a necessary thing to do for our relationship. I couldn't do that if you weren't there for her. I mean, it gives me a sense of relief to know that you are there to protect her. I know it makes me an asshole to ask you to do that for me, but I am asking you for the old sake of friendship we had in the past. You'll do this favor for me," I said it calmly.

"But why do you think you need to break up to save the relationship? This sounds like bullshit to me—bullshit that every asshole uses to justify their shitty acts. However, I am not gonna insist on it. She truly deserves a better person than you. The poor girl was crying and calling your name. It was really embarrassing in the middle of the park. I just can't comprehend what kind of monster leaves a girl just like that. She just lost her father, and instead of helping her to get her back on her feet, you broke them instead," he said it in vexation. I never indicated that it was my idea to break up, but somehow, he assumed it was my idea. I guess I couldn't blame him. If I were in his shoes, I would assume the same way. Also, there was a new revelation too.

I just found out that Calysta was calling my name after I left her in the park. Was she regretting the decision she made? Or was it a momentary regret? If it wasn't a momentary regret, then why didn't she call me or make any contact of any sort? I just convinced Marshal to take her side and take care of her for me. If my assumption about her repentance were wrong, which most likely was, the damage would be incomprehensible. Anyway, I had to put aside the notion she regretted the decision she made. It just would make her a total fool without saying. I concluded that if she had any regrets, it was just momentary. It would be unwise to go back and ask her about her resolution. It would only open up the old wounds again, if not open any new ones.

Was I successful in confusticating and confusing Marshal? Wasn't it what I wanted all along?

"I'm sorry to disappoint you. I think you came here to find a good reason why we broke up to defend me, but there isn't one. I'm sorry that I made you look bad in front of Aiko, but now that everything has become a little bit coherent, you should act accordingly. There isn't any sibylline and mystery to be found here. It just is, as it is." I couldn't believe the words that came out of my mouth, but they did. Whoever, with a right mind, listened to what I just said, the proper action would be to punch me and knock off my teeth.

"Fuck you," he said before he left me. His exasperation was reasonable and understandable.

Now I truly felt lonely. I thought back to where I was many years ago, but the big difference was that I had already tasted the apple. I had this knowledge that I didn't have before. Now I tasted the friendship, and I was afraid of losing it. Like a heroin addict who needs methadone to leave that bad habit, I needed something else to distract myself in order to survive. Finding new friends and moving on wasn't the correct answer for my case, but phasing out of it was, so I decided to call Marshal after a few days and reduce my communication from there. I admit that I wasn't considering Marshal's feelings, and using him for my own purpose was a despicable act, but at the time, I was convincing myself that it was suitable for Marshal too. It was because he could phase out the same. Was I mitigating? I couldn't tell at the time.

I tried to stand up, but the damn thing was too demanding. I felt I needed a superman strength for it. In the end, I stood up. I took a deep breath in and said goodbye to my old life.

Chapter 18

What the fuck have I done? That was stupid. I am an idiot. I was swearing at myself at Greenwich Street's stop. I was regretting using the car to get to my destination. I should have used a bus or a taxi. Fuck the pride or the class. I wasn't trying to impress anyone, so what was the reason that made me use the car? I passed Mason Street and stopped at another stop sign. Pedestrians were passing by slowly, but before doing that, they made sure to check out my car. The young ones were curious about the manufacturer's brand and were confused that they hadn't seen it before, and the rest were swearing at me or the car with their eyes. I could tell with the way they were looking at it. Was it jealousy? Who knows? A few of them took out their bulky-sized Nokia or BlackBerry to take some pictures without asking my permission. It wouldn't bother me if they stepped aside and let me drive. They stood on the pedestrian crosswalk and tried to get pictures. Who does that?

The traffic wasn't helping either. *Good luck finding a parking spot in this area.* I was reminding myself how stupid it was to bring my car. After some honking from the cars behind me, the pedestrians started clearing the pass.

I turned right and started driving at Columbus Avenue. The scenery was disheartening. All the way that my eyes could see, there were cars parked on parking spots, and there wasn't even an inch to let a cyclist park, let alone a car. I crossed my fingers, hoping there would be a parking spot for me when I arrived at the restaurant.

I don't know who I helped in the past that karma was so kind to me that it let me park exactly at the Cole Hardware store.

I got out of the car, took a deep breath, and enjoyed the fresh air. I looked up at the sky. It was sunny and clear. I went to the other side of my car, opened it, and took out my jacket and briefcase, and after that, I closed the door.

First, I put the jacket on. I looked at my reflection on my car's window. It made me smile. The natural color of my coat matched my Cadmium-blue shirt. If there was anything I learned in Europe, it was how to dress up appropriately. Then I hung the leather briefcase on my shoulder. It was a little bit heavy because I was carrying a laptop and a DSLR Camera, so no complaints about that.

After looking at the watch, I noticed I still had little time to spare, so I took out the camera and adjusted the lens zoom to 18 mm. I wanted to take a landscape shot from the intersection of Vallejo Street and Columbus Avenue. This picture would be a reminder that I should never take my car for an appointment. It was also inspiring. The light was good, and it made it easy for me to angle the camera up and take the picture. I took several photos to ensure that if one wasn't good enough, the other could replace it. After I took the picture, I reviewed them and cropped them as I desired. I knew better that I should check them later on the bigger screen. Then removing any noise in it. Maybe, later on, I could use the Adobe Photoshop software to enhance or manipulate the picture too. That part was my favorite.

It was time to go, but when I tried to put away the camera, I noticed some people were looking at me. It kind of made me shy. Why were they looking at me? I wondered. I put the shades on to have a little bit of privacy. Then I looked back, and I noticed that I was standing beside my car. Maybe they were looking at my car, not me, and wondering why I took pictures from the sky and building and not the vehicle. It gave me a sense of relief. I hated to be in the spotlight. However, there was a feeling that made me think they were actually looking at me, not the car. I looked at the watch again and noticed ten minutes passed just like that. I went to the parking meter in a hurry and paid as much as a lunch price for the parking spot.

I headed toward the Molinari Delicatessen. It was right in the corner, but before going there, I wanted to spy on them in the distance to see if they had arrived. It made me feel like a stalker, so with a creepy smile on, I looked at the tables. There they were, sitting and not noticing the creepy guy in the corner. It brought me joy and relief to see them there. It had been years not seeing them. I wanted to capture the moment, so I took out my camera again and noticed the lens that I put on earlier wasn't proper for the intended photo I was about to take. It wouldn't be a problem for the group photo, but I knew better that there were too many unwanted elements in the image if I took the shot, so I changed the lens. Using 80–300 mm, I stepped backward until I got my desired frame. I was smiling at my silly behavior. A few shots in and I noticed the facial expression of one of them changed from noticing to inquisitive, then to incredulity, and finally, to a burst of joy. I captured all of them. I couldn't be happier with the result.

After she exposed my location to the others, the rest of them turned around to look at me. I captured that moment as well.

"Hey, asshole, you are in my way." I looked up and saw a skinny white dude who dressed up as a punk was looking at me. I stood up and faced him. I knew he was looking for a problem, so I ignored his comment. I cleared his way and let him pass. I was walking toward my friends when he threw at me another comment.

"Hey, asshole, you didn't say that you're sorry."

The second he said that, I knew that I should have my hands free in case a fight broke out, so I put back the camera in the briefcase and faced him. "I'm sorry for not being careful. I hope you enjoy the remaining day." I was trying my best to de-escalate the situation. He already ruined my mood, and I didn't want to spoil others.

I kept walking toward my friends. When I got closer, Bernadina came around the table and ran the tiny space between us with open arms. She gave me a firm hug and started kissing both my cheeks, and with that, she lightened up my mood again.

"Oh my God, look at you. You became a man and all," she said while holding my arms and admiring me from head to toe with her look. She was the one who noticed me first.

"Hey, come here, you bastard," Marshal said while walking toward me to give me a hug. When I was free from Bernadina's, Marshal came and gave me a bear hug and started swinging me from left to right.

"Man, I missed you so much, which I shouldn't be. You don't call. You don't write," he said while having a smile on his face. I guess it didn't matter what answer I gave him. It sounded like he already forgave me.

"I miss you too, and to answer your question, the place I was, there was no telephone or internet, and the birds that I sent you have been eaten by eagles and hawks," I said with a smile on, which made him laugh.

"Can you believe this guy? He has no shame whatsoever," he said it happily. It didn't take us even a minute to get back where we were.

"I learned from the master," I said with a beam on my face. He answered me with more laughter.

"By the way, who was the guy that you were talking to?" he asked me, and before I could answer, I heard another voice who had been annoyed with our behaviors. It was Aiko, who impatiently was waiting for her turn.

"You guys never change, and God forbid if you do," she said while I could see the dimple on her face.

I looked at her apologetically and opened my arms for her. She came in without hesitation.

"Oh, I missed you, missed you, missed you so much," she said happily.

"I missed you too. Let me look at you." By that, I looked at her with admiration while holding her by the shoulder. "Look at you. So beautiful. How did you end up with this guy?" I said jokingly while pointing in Marshal's direction with my head.

She smiled. "We all make mistakes." We all laughed at her comment, except Marshal, who was shaking his head in disappointment.

"Come and sit. What took you so long?" Marshal said while inviting me to sit beside him.

"I brought Frigg," I answered. They became joyful by hearing her name. I took my seat right beside him.

"Where did you park it?" Marshal asked.

"Close to the Hardware store," I said.

"You came with style. Just look at you. You become more and more handsome every second I look at you," Bernadina observed and gave me a playful wink. We all laughed at her cute wink. "I missed Frigg. It was a good idea to bring her," she said gleefully.

"The traffic doesn't agree with you," I said with a bitter tone in it.

"Isn't it time to get a new one instead of that old hag?" Marshal said carelessly.

"Marshal!" both Bernadina and Aiko protested.

"When you build up a car from scratch and make it as fast as Koenigsegg and give it the beauty of Pagani or Ferrari, only then you have the right to criticize my Frigg," I said it arrogantly.

"All right, all right. Chill out, guys. I was just messing around," Marshal said defensively.

"Tell me again how this idiot became a neurosurgeon? How much they had to dumb it down so this guy can be one?" I said it with a tease. Aiko and Bernadina laughed at my comment. Poor Marshal had to laugh too, or we considered him a person who didn't have a sense of humor.

"What's up, man? When did you come back? Why didn't you call us that you are coming back? And who was that guy?" he asked me after the laughter died down. I looked at him with a smile and answered, "Aiko, I thought you left your children at home, but it sounds like you brought one in here." When I said that, she burst into laughter.

"Ha ha, you are too funny, but seriously," he persisted.

"That guy came and confessed his love to me, if that's what you are asking," I said jokingly. He shook his head in disappointment. "You haven't changed a bit," he said it with a low tone.

"But I think he changed a lot, if you ask me. He looks more serious even though he is joking around," Bernadina observed.

"Yeah, you're right," Aiko supported.

I just smiled in return. I didn't know that I had become so serious. Here I thought that I didn't change a bit.

"When did you come back?" This time around, it was Aiko who asked me. I was trying to avoid the question when Marshal asked me. The husband and wife were synchronized. I couldn't ignore the question anymore and had to give in.

"About three months," I answered honestly. However, they looked at me in disbelief.

"You are joking, right? You mean, if I didn't call you earlier this week, you wouldn't call us at all? Is that it?" he said. I could tell from his facial expression that he was pissed and disappointed. I couldn't blame him or any of them, but we weren't on good terms the last time we separated. Just calling him and writing some emails was the most that I could do. On the other hand, I didn't want to remind them of the past.

"You are right. I should've called. But my whole life's work is on the other side of the ocean. I wasn't sure that I would stay here this long." By saying that, a flood of sadness came into my heart. They didn't know about the secret that I was holding in. That secret was tearing me apart mercilessly.

"So Marshal was right. You didn't plan to call us," Aiko said it with a despairing voice.

"Oh, come on now. Aren't we the one who cut the friendship? Now you are blaming him shamelessly for what we did," Bernadina said it defensively.

"You girls did, but I didn't. Last time, if I remember correctly, it was him who stopped calling me or even answering my calls and emails," Marshal responded. We all knew he said it to defend his wife. He was protecting her from feeling guilty. I didn't mind that. It was a kind of bittersweet situation for me. Now I knew I was forgiven for the past. Bernadina was the evidence of that. However, the bitterness of the past was shadowing me around. Now that the elephant marched out of the room, I didn't fear bringing up the past or even using it to stop the quarrel. Before Bernadina could answer him back, I jumped in, "Hey, come on now. If I knew that there would be a cat-and-dog fight, I wouldn't answer that call either. Saying that, I thought you guys moved on and forgot about me, and before you guys jump to the conclusion again, I should point out that I didn't forget about you. I only tried to move on too."

There was deadly silence hovering over us. Even though I was prepared for this outcome, I didn't have any plan to come out of it. I looked at Aiko; she was still shaken by what Bernadina said, and Marshal was pissed and angry at everyone. I think he didn't expect this repercussion at all. Meanwhile, Bernadina was looking at everything to avoid eye contact with all of us. I took out the camera and aimed at them, and all of a sudden, I had their attention.

"Oh, come on now. I wanted to take that priceless picture of you. It was going to be my computer's wallpaper," I said it playfully.

"Wow, look at him. He came prepared," Marshal commented. He tried to give me a hand to get us out of that awkward silence.

"I always carry it around," I responded. We got their attention.

"Really? Since when?" he asked casually.

"Since I went to CERN. I had to carry out a camera all the time to take a picture of damage or proof of the work," I answered.

"What a show-off. You just had to bring up CERN. It sounds like no one else worked there but only you," he said it teasingly.

"If one day the theory of Higgs Boson is being proved and many others, then I want to take that picture of your face. Laugh as much as you want now, but the future belongs to us scientists. You are just too simple-minded and materialistic to understand the work we do," I teased him back.

"Holy cow, I am lucky that the Higgs Boson wasn't your theory, or I wouldn't hear the end of it. That aside, materialistic? Who? Me?" he retorted.

"As I said, you don't have any intellectuality to understand the papers I wrote for mathematics, which revolutionized the mathematics world. Also, yes, you, who ended up being a neurosurgeon," I countered, and here we go, back to where we were. He started laughing. He didn't mind it at all. He knew I was joking.

"What about you, Mr. Company Man?" He came back at me with that. He referred to the multiple companies that I founded in Europe and was a major shareholder of them. One of them was a software and chip maker for enterprise business and research and targeting those clients. The other one was backing up and building up start-up research or the idea and expanding from there, for example, cleaning the water or finding a solution for decreasing the cost of solar panels and batteries. The last company was making medical tools for hospitals. However, besides those projects, I invested money in making hotels in Europe as well. Of course, there were art galleries too. Damn the internet and the interview on that talk show that exposed all my life the days after.

"Well, it is all for the science," I retorted. They all laughed. "I didn't mean it to be sarcastic. I actually do it for the science, and that is the reason I am doing all these kinds of things," I defended my position.

"But how?" Aiko asked me and gave me a skeptical look.

"To simplify it, the big chunk of the profit I make is spent on the research and the experiments that may or may not be profitable in the future. For example, Doing research in biology or funding mathematicians who are not trying to find an algorithm for the company's benefit but trying to understand mathematics better or even answer the millennium problems. That is what I am doing," I said without holding back.

"Bravo, bravo. That's the Agustin that I know of," Marshal said with admiration.

"Wow, look at you. You have my respect. You had a dream, and you just chased after it," Bernadina said it with a voice that made me a little bit gleeful.

"Thanks," I said by lowering my voice, which hinted at the shyness for all those kind words. I often heard the same compliments from others, but none of those matched the ones that I received from my old friends.

"You sound so cool and, at the same time, elegant. No wonder why you are so popular," Marshal said it with an admiration that only a teacher gives to a student. It was like he was the person who brought me up, and now he sees the fruition of his work. It just made me smile nonetheless.

"What else do you do?" Aiko asked me. I thought that she was just curious, but her body language told me otherwise.

"Wasn't this enough? I mean running multiple companies and, on top of that, doing my own research and study. There wouldn't be enough time for doing any basic things like inhaling oxygen into my body," I responded jokingly. Marshal and Bernadina giggled, but Aiko smiled, and her smile was with closed lips. It means that she was faking it and holding back something. She wasn't satisfied with my answer. On the surface, she was laughing with everyone, but years of profiling and reading the body language of other people told me something else. The young Agustin was gone, and it had been replaced by another Agustin who had to read people's moods as if his life depended on it. The key to successful leadership was understanding the people who worked for me and what they needed. When a leader understands what it is that an employee or labor wants or even involves them in big corporate decisions and makes them speak up about their concerns, that is where you'll know if a corporation will succeed or not. The exceeding success from all the companies I was involved in was the evidence of the right pass that I took.

"Aiko, you didn't like my answer. Are you trying to ask me another question, but you are afraid it is not polite to do so?" I asked her cautiously. I took her off guard. She looked at me in disbelief. She wanted to deny the accusation immediately, but after a bit of pause, she looked at her husband and said, "How come he can read my mind, but you can't?" That was enough to make us laugh again. Poor Marshal became a tool for our laughing, and I felt sorry for him. "Well, I want you to have that little privacy," Marshal answered. We burst out laughing again at his response.

"Are you avoiding my question?" I asked her before we changed the subject.

"Okay, if you insist," she said and made it look like it was my idea to bring up the follow-up questions. "Tell us about your personal life. What did you do all these years? Have you met anyone when you were away? What stories do you have for us?"

"All right, all right, don't ask too many questions at the same time if you care about the answers. I am just giving you a tip about myself, okay?" I said and gave her a wink to give her approval for what she did. I sympathized with them. I knew that they were curious as much about me as I was to them. "I thought the media covered that part of my personal life when I tried to hit on that pop star, but here I give you an exclusive interview if that's what you want."

"Speaking of which, what happened between you two?" Aiko asked me impatiently and already forgot about all those questions she just asked me.

"Yeah, tell me about it," Bernadina sang the same song.

"I just couldn't believe what you did until Aiko showed me the clip. When did you become so confident and charming? Europe must be the cause," Marshal told me as a proud friend. Meanwhile, I was trying to remember the questions that Aiko had just asked me.

"As I said, don't ask me too many questions if you care about the answer. It is kind of difficult to talk to you if I don't remember the questions," I protested.

"Yeah, I forgot that you got old," Marshal said, and before I could respond to him, Aiko and Bernadina protested his untimely comment and asked me to continue. Poor Marshal couldn't take a break. It wasn't his day.

"Nothing happened between her and me. As soon as we got out, we went our separate ways. She wanted to sell her new album, and I wanted to raise a fund for the research for our university. The people wanted a show, so we gave them one," I said and tried to hide my embarrassing moment from them. I didn't want to tell them that I didn't like paparazzi spying around me and having no personal life, and I didn't get a really good impression from her either. Who would believe me that I had a taste?

"So it was staged?" Aiko asked. She tried to sound disappointed, but her body language betrayed her. Somehow, she was happy about it. It was the best way to escape from that awkward question, so I went with it and nodded.

"Oh, I really wanted to befriend one of those celebs," Bernadina said, but like Aiko, her body language was telling me that she was happy nonetheless.

"Damn it. I knew it was too good to be true," Marshal said, and only his body language agreed with what he said, which made me laugh. "I thought she really liked you. There was chemistry going on between you two. Are you sure that you didn't screw this up?" Marshal insisted on it.

"Well, reality sucks an—" I said, and before I could finish it, I noticed the girls looking behind me, and there was a voice inside me telling me who it could be before I turned around. I turned around, and there she was. She dressed up in red with high heels. Her long black hair was tied up to expose her long and delicate neck. She was wearing a one-piece red dress. She didn't use too much makeup, but her red lipstick was conspicuous. Her sapphire-blue eyes hypnotized me where I was. Her youthful look was gone and had been replaced by a mature one. Other than that, she looked the same way I always remembered her, beautiful and elegant. I stood up to greet her.

"Hello, Agustin," she said. When those words came out of her mouth, they became soothing, like a lullaby song. Those words came to life and started having their own existence. I knew those words would be burned in my memory and would start torturing me whenever I had time to think. I was aching to hear her voice again, and now I had no idea what to do. I played a scene like that in my head over a million times and still came out clueless about what to do if the opportunity presented itself.

The universe was cruel to put me through such a thing again. I had been tortured by the hands of this vicious woman who put me through misery and agony. My life became hell, and I lived in it because of her. She dismissed all the feelings I had for her and selfishly distanced herself from me. The unanswered questions were boiling up inside me. Those ravenous beasts woke up again, and they were up to no good. They wanted answers. They wanted to know why. Why did she left me? What did I do to deserve that kind of behavior and conduct? If she cried after I left her, why on earth didn't she call me? Why didn't she tell her friends the reason behind her breakup? These questions were savages back then, and they stayed brute. She didn't take even a small step to help me out and then withdrew herself from the problem she caused and left me alone to pull myself out of it. This enchantress was merciless, and so was the universe.

"Hello, Calysta," I said, accompanied with a fake smile. I knew that she would find me out, but I didn't care nonetheless. Damn these women who are like living lie detectors. If I had been reading people's body language for a few years, women were doing it most of their lives effortlessly, and for that, I knew she would notice my fake smile as I did hers. Her closed lips and the muscle close to her eyes gave her away. I didn't extend my hand for handshaking. I wasn't trying to be an asshole. Actually, the purpose of doing that was contrary. I didn't want to force or to put her on the spot for handshaking. I wasn't sure she was comfortable doing that. I even surprised myself for caring for her after all she had done for me. Then I noticed she was holding her right elbow with her left hand, and in her right hand, she was holding a small handbag. It was like half arm crossed; it would be complete if she weren't carrying the purse. Her body was telling me that she was defensive. I think I had a pretty good idea why. All these years were enough to make us strangers. Like I thought, she felt like an outsider toward me. It was another blow to my gut knowing that. It all happened really fast. After that, I heard Bernadina's voice, which was welcoming her by saying hi to her. As soon as Bernadina did that, Calysta let her arm go and opened herself for a hug. Bernadina didn't disappoint her and gave her a gentle hug while kissing her on the cheeks. It was followed by Aiko and Marshal. On top of that, I noticed that Bernadina heeded to another man who was staying close to Calysta, and the way Bernadina was looking at him was the same way Calysta looked at me. He was a stranger to them.

"Hello, my name is Novak." He offered his hand in the direction of Bernadina. Bernadina smiled and shook his hand and said hi to him as well. *Amateur.* That was what I thought of him. He didn't notice Bernadina didn't want to do a handshake. Aiko and Marshal did the same. When it was my turn to give a handshake, I saw he gave me his upper hand. *Are you fucking kidding me? Who is this asshole? And who does he think he is?* I thought to myself and felt about him. That handshake was telling me that he was above me and had more power. I wasn't submissive to anyone and wouldn't let anyone do that to me. However, I didn't want to cause a ruckus, so I gave him a handshake, but a counter one. When I took his hand, I took one step closer to him and invaded his personal space. It got him off guard. It gave me an opportunity to turn my hand up and make it look like we were in an equal position. I did that while I was giving him a fake smile. He shook my hand firmly and gave me a genuine smile.

Imbecile. That was what I thought of him. I have to admit that I was no different than him years ago.

He was tall and had black hair. He was wearing half-rimmed rectangular black glasses. His hair was short but spiky in front. He was wearing a business suit but without a tie. He let the shirt's collar be open so that it could give him a casual look, but I bet he used the same suit for business. I guess that was his selling point or advertisement to tell people "I am a businessman and have money." These people mostly came from the management department. All those years, I had dealt with them, and I knew what to do with them. However, they never saw any aggression from me until it was too late.

"Agustin. Nice to meet you," I said and invited him to sit at the table where we were sitting. The look Bernadina gave to Calysta didn't escape my perception. She was smiling when she was looking at her, but it was a look that was yelling at her and asking her, "What the hell are you doing, girl?" In return, she gave another fictitious smile. I could see it was awkward for her, but she tried to play it cool in front of Novak and me.

She succeeded against Marshal and Novak. They didn't notice the look these women exchanged, but I could hear it like a loud conversation.

"So how are you? I heard a great deal about you from Calysta," Novak commented and addressed it to all of us. He tried to break the ice and show himself as a stylish man. It was hard for me not to laugh at him, so I put a hand in front of my face in an attempt to not be rude, at least, and I laughed without making any noise. It was impossible to hide it from the watchful eyes of these women, so just to tell them I was not an ass, I looked away with my hand on my mouth and looked in a direction that no one was looking. I was avoiding their eye contact. It only took me a few seconds to get ahold of myself. However, I knew the smirk was there. While I was doing that, Bernadina and Aiko were covering for me by engaging him in conversation. I should take note of that and thank them later. Still having the slight smirk on my face, now I looked at Marshal, who was sitting across the table beside his wife and Bernadina. He noticed that I was looking at him, so he responded with a quick smile. During Bernadina and Aiko's conversation with Novak, I found out that he was a manager at one of the departments that Calysta was working for.

Novak was sitting between Calysta and me, and I had no complaint about it. He just made it much easier for me to be there. The last thing I wanted was to sit right beside Calysta, and it only made us uncomfortable and awkward. I found it so childish of her to bring her date to our reunion. Even Though I was a little sad when I didn't see her at the table when I arrived, I got over it. The reunion was going well before she showed up. For me, it was kind of surprising to feel so cold toward her. I never knew that a day would come for me to be like that. I could guess why she did it. She wanted to portray herself as a happy person or a person who moved on; however, she missed the mark as the only thing I wanted for her was to be happy. The reason I gave in to her request years ago was to make sure she would have a chance to be pleased with another person, not be like this. I didn't know the whole story.

What happened to her? What did her romance life look like? The picture I had in my head for her was something like Marshal and Aiko's life. I thought she deserved it, and I came to be at peace with it, despite the fact that it was killing me for years, but eventually, I moved on. I could guess the deep root of my exasperation and dejection was realizing that she wasted my sacrifice. When I departed her, I thought she knew what she wanted. Still, her action that day showed me two things: First, she wasn't married and didn't have the life I always wanted for her, and second, she tried to hurt me again by bringing this man or, even worse, pretending to be someone she wasn't and thinking I couldn't figure it out.

I looked across the table to engage myself in the conversation Bernadina had with Novak. I observed she was multitasking. She was talking to him by telling him about herself and what she does for a living and also talking to her friends with her eyes and telling her that she was going to have a serious conversation with her afterward. I almost felt sorry for Calysta. She was an extremely emotional person. Nevertheless, I had a bigger problem at hand than be worried about Calysta's feelings. I wanted to finish the meeting and go back to my life.

"So why did you choose this place for eating?" Novak asked, and it was directed to all of us.

"When we were students, we usually came in here and had sandwiches. Today was our reunion with an old friend whom we didn't see for a long time, and we tried to relive those moments," Bernadina responded, and the bitterness of her answer was also directed to Calysta. Even I got a chill in the bone by her response.

"I didn't mean to intrude, and I'm sorry for that, but who is this friend who came back after many years?" he asked, and I could see that he wasn't sorry at all. He came with a great expectation from someone, and he couldn't care less about the comfort of anyone at present. He came with one goal in mind, and I could see a mile away what it was.

"It would be me," I answered and tried to have a smile on my face.

"Oh, nice. How do you like coming back here? And where have you been, if you don't mind me asking that," he asked me casually. I figured he wouldn't really want to know the answer, and any response would be sufficient for him.

"It's so far so good, and no problem for asking that. I was in Europe for study and work, and before we continue this conversation, aren't you hungry? Should we order something?" I answered and asked everyone. Marshal was the first one to respond to it. He rose from the chair and was ready to order. I asked for the usual homemade chicken salad. Bernadina chose the same. Aiko asked for Renzo's special. Marshal said he was going for Joe's special. That was a bold and daring move to have garlic for lunch, but I guess he'd have a gum after that. Novak didn't know what to order, so he went after whatever Calysta ordered, Luciano Special.

"So how was it there? Being in Europe?" he asked me after Marshal disappeared into the store. He was ignorant about my past and Calysta's. It was a touchy subject to bring up. He wanted to know about what my life like was over there. Was I enjoying myself over there?

"If I want to describe it in one sentence, it would be 'It is good,'" I answered and tried my best to be polite and considerate.

"Come on, you can give me more than that, can't you?" he said and looked at Aiko and Bernadina for approval. They just responded with a forced smile, and both of them looked in Calysta's direction. Calysta was in big trouble. I could guess what they would tell her after this was over, especially Aiko, who was living with Marshal. She just ruined the reunion for everyone and made it awkward for everyone. Since I knew Aiko's character, she would defend her friend no matter what, but ruining her day with Marshal would be another story.

"It is beautiful and has a long history. I have been there for over a decade now and haven't finished all the sightseeing yet, even though I try my best to travel a lot. Lots of countries and different cultures always amazed me. I love the food, and what they do with it is staggering for me. I shouldn't forget to mention I get to see the live soccer matches. And last, living in stress is much lower than here," I responded and attempted to be considerate toward Calysta.

"Well, I am glad you are enjoying yourself. Are you planning to stay here?" he said. One look at him and I knew he wasn't happy for me at all. I'd never met him before, but he had this adversary look in his eyes that wanted me to suffer. What was wrong with him? He had the same look as a person who thought everything was handed to me, that I live in heaven; meanwhile, he lives in hell. It was a pity to see him like that. As a matter of fact, I didn't care so much what he was thinking of me. I wanted to hear Calysta's voice. In all this, I didn't hear a thing from her. She really screwed up. I looked at the table before answering his question.

"I didn't plan to stay at all, but many things happened that forced me to it, and I am planning to go back there as soon as possible," I responded, but it wasn't directed at him. I wanted to let Calysta know that I wasn't planning to stay for long. Those things that made me stay were personal, and I wasn't sure if I wanted to share it with Marshal, let alone this stranger.

"It's that good, isn't it?" he said it with the creepiest smirk that I've ever seen. I could guess what he was thinking, but he was too stupid to realize that I wasn't the only one who caught what he meant. Bernadina and Aiko smiled, not because it was funny but for being nervous and not knowing what to do with this creep.

"I've never lived like that," I countered and tried my best to keep my cool in check. I thought I should take the food and leave and try to find an excuse; however, I felt I didn't do anything wrong, so why should I go? I was enjoying the company of three wonderful people. Why should it be me to throw the towel?

"Excuse me." It was not him to say that. It was a voice of a stranger behind me that requested attention. I turned around and saw a beautiful girl with her friend. She looked like a teenager. She was wearing a slouchy pair of jeans with white shoes and a sleeveless Catalina-blue top and wearing a café noir–colored woolen knit hat. Her style matched her chestnut-colored hair.

On top of that, she was wearing sunglasses so that I couldn't determine her eye color. The friend who was accompanying her didn't look bad either. She was wearing an olive-green sweater that needed buttons to close it in front but didn't have one, so it exposed her white shirt. She was wearing a classic black hat that looked like a fedora. It had a long brim and a bond that matched her black pants. Her green eyes matched her sweater. I'd never met them before, and I wondered what they wanted from me.

"How can I help you?" I asked the girl with slouchy jeans.

"Are you, by any chance, Mr. Adalbert?" she asked me cautiously in case she was mistaken.

When she asked me that, I assumed she was one of those people who saw my interview with that pop star girl, and now she wanted to take a selfie with me or ask stupid questions about the relationship I had with that pop star. The fiend inside me was telling me to tell her a lie and get rid of her, but at the same time, another demon was telling me to tell her the truth and, by doing so, hurt back the feeling Calysta gave as her gift to me.

"Yes?" I answered and asked.

"Oh my God . . . Oh my God . . . Oh my God . . . I can't believe this," she said it so enthusiastically that I thought she found a treasure or a paragon, which, by the way, gave me great pleasure. A little bit of showing off in front of the person who intended to incapacitate me after all these years was next to nothing.

"I'm studying music at the university, and I'm familiar with your work. Right now, we are studying your Piano Sonata and your symphony. I can't believe I found you here. I always wanted to come to Italy to one of your Art centers In Europe, but here I am, and here you are. You have no idea how happy I am now," she said.

I thought she was a typical teenager, all right. They tend to make everything more significant than it is. The work she was referring to was what I was doing when I had a little bit of time. I never thought of it to be that big of a deal. However, I couldn't resist the shape of the smirk that was forming on my face. At the same time, this kind of behavior this devotee of mine made in front of my old friends made me proud and bashful. Finally, there was someone who knew who I was and the work I did. I was tired of people asking me about that pop star and dismissing that the young singers and artists worldwide were applying to the art centers that I made for education and display. Singers like Taylor Lively would never make it there. Those art centers were so selective and sophisticated that only a few hundred were accepted out of millions of applicants. It was for a good reason because a good portion of my own income was directed to those art centers, which was the only source of income for the art centers, and I made sure that the people who were getting in were worthy of it. In other words, I was the poorest billionaire on Earth who spent most of his personal money on research in science and art. In Europe, I didn't have a house. I was living in the hotels that I invested in. I always thought having a home was such a waste of money, and it only burned up time and resources.

On the other hand, investing in hotels made me more money, which meant more investment for other projects. It was a cycle of money for me. The more money I made, the more I spent on the other projects or the upgrading. I never let the money sit in a bank for too long. It was the total opposite of what I did when I was a teenager. As a matter of fact, it was the same money that I made those years that made me capable of funding or investing in those companies. Later on, I found it distasteful and prodigal to make money out of nothing and just let it sit in the bank, so instead of doing that, I did something that made me feel good. Despite people thinking it wasn't a charity act, it was actually a grasping act for my egocentric idea and lifestyle. I didn't even bother to dissimulate doing welfare. However, I didn't battle the image they portrayed from the companies that I was involved with.

"So you are a student at the university. Have you applied to study overseas? Or even try to get to one of those art centers?" I asked and was eager to know.

"That was my first choice. Three years ago, while my family and I were visiting Florence, the tour guide suggested that we should take a look at the modern art gallery. We took his suggestion and visited there. I couldn't be happier than that. I loved the atmosphere. Those arts that have been displayed on walls and the background music were so overwhelming for me that they brought tears to my eyes. That was nothing when I found out that all those displays were made by the students and the people who worked there. It just blew my mind. I just couldn't believe what I heard. also, I found out that they weren't for sale either. When we asked the reasons for it, the person who worked there told us that these are the founder's treasures. As we were confused and did not know the meaning of the founder's treasure, the representative explained that these paintings and music are loved by the person who built the art gallery and funded it. It just made us more curious about you, Mr. Adalbert, so we asked about you. The art gallery's guide took us to the place where your paintings were on display and the music you composed and played by other students, and there is no word in any dictionary to describe what I felt when I saw your work. The *Atsylac*, The *Cimasa*, The *Fur Dich*, the *Die Traurige Erinnerung*, the *Meilleur Printemps en Hiver*, the *Silenzio*, and the *Cache* were all breathtaking. I was in Florence, one of the most beautiful cities in the world with a long history, but even there, your art gallery was standing tall and adding more beauty and attractiveness to the city. Oh, Mr. Adalbert, you have no idea how happy I am now to see you here," she said and ended her long speech. However, when I heard her mentioning the *Atsylac*, my mind went blank, and I started sweating like a pig. *Atsylac* was a playful word for Calysta. That student had no idea the picture of the person I painted was sitting two seats away.

"And I'm grateful," I said it coolly. Then I continued, "I assume you couldn't get in, am I wrong?"

"No, I couldn't. The process was bigger than I could chew on," she said gloomily.

"I understand, and I wish I could do something about it, but I have limited income, so I can't support everyone," I said it in a way that made it look like it was my fault, not hers.

"No, no, I didn't mean to imply anything here. I just wished I could be one of those that have been chosen . . ."

"Well, I never liked that system for exactly this reason. The people that came with big hopes and dreams just to be turned around and believe they weren't good enough makes my heart wrench . . ." She was about to interrupt, but by holding up my index finger, I continued, "I can only say I'll work harder." I gave her a sad smile and a nod to let her know that I had finished my thought.

"It is only fair to say that I'll do the same. If I weren't accepted as a student, I'd try to be one of the faculty in the future. I'm not done with that dream yet," she said it with determination.

"I wish I could continue this conversation, but as you can see, I am with friends now. If you want, you can leave your phone number with me, and when I can find a time, I'll make a call," I said it apologetically and took out my cell phone.

"Sure, sure," she said it so enthusiastically that it made me a little bit worried.

After she finished giving me her phone number, I looked behind her and looked at her friend who was silent all that time. "And yours?"

"What? Me?" she said it in a way that looked like I just asked her to jump from Mt. Everest.

"Yes, you. You didn't talk at all, and I have a soft spot for those shy and diffident people. I was one of them once. Who knows? Maybe I'll enjoy your company more than your friend's," I said it so balmy and with indifference that I couldn't believe it myself. Meanwhile, her friend's eyebrow behind the sunglasses went up so much that it almost touched her hat.

"I don't know. Uhm, well, I don't know," she said and was biting her lips and looking at her friend and the people I was with.

"Sorry, I didn't mean to put you in the spot. I understand."

"No . . . no . . . I'm just surprised, that's all," she said and proceeded to give me hers.

After I received her phone number, I said goodbye to them and sat back, only to be welcomed by the startled look of Bernadina and Aiko.

"I never imagined. You of all people. What happened to you? I remember you were a sweet teenage boy, as you said, a little bit shy, but Agustin, what was that?" Bernadina said before Aiko could.

"I guess, I grew up like all of you, leaving behind something while doing so," I said with a smile and indifference.

"Oh my Gosh, but how? Is there someone that I should know?" Bernadina said it excitedly before Aiko again.

I laughed and told her no. Then I continued, "I just had to practice like anything else in life. One hour a day, talking to a total stranger, no matter who, beautiful, ugly, homeless, rich. You name it, and I probably did it. It was just to get rid of that nonsensical fear. After a while, I molded myself into the person that I am today. Sorry to burst your hope for a gossip."

"So you can do it anywhere and anytime?" she asked and made me wonder if she forgot that I just did it there and on that talk show as well. How many examples did she need?

"It would be kind of narcissistic to say yes. I just kind of hoped to catch up to you especially. You had it all and still have it, beauty and bravery. I dare say even more now. You seemed to know what you wanted and didn't care what other people thought about it. You know what I'm talking about," I replied.

"Oh, come on, I wasn't like that at all," she said bashfully.

"We all beg to differ, and we liked you the most for it." I paused a little bit for a dramatic moment before I continued. "Me, more than any of them," I said and drew a cycle in the air to emphasize the latter statement, which meant all of them. Then I saw her blush, and I smiled wryly.

"Oh, wow. Look at the master at work. I think Bernadina is over the moon by now," Aiko said with a big smile on her face. Bernadina, who just realized what I just did, pressed her lips firmly and gave me the eye of disappointment. "Come on, try it on me too. I feel like being left out in this flirting game," Aiko said without care for what she just did. I looked at Bernadina apologetically, and she pointed out that she wouldn't have none of it by shaking her head.

"Aiko, are you trying to ruin this reunion? After many years, I just saw my best friend. You don't want me to leave him in a bitter mood, do you? Don't tell me he takes you for granted. That bast—" I looked beside me and looked another way to say "We are in the companion of a stranger, and I don't want to badmouth Marshal in front of him." Then I continued, "That creature called dibs on you before I could open my mouth years ago," I said and shook my head in disappointment and looked down as if I were ashamed that I wasn't good or fast enough the time needed to be. I knew that statement would confuse all of them. Was I interested in Calysta last? Was I interested in Bernadina or Aiko at first? Whom did I really want to be with first? I could see the confusion on both Aiko and Bernadina. That was enough for me. I saw Aiko's eyebrow crease together to show her confusion at the matter. "You guys are shameless. You two treated us like a prize or as a thing . . ." When she saw my smug and wink, then it clicked.

Her mouth was open wide in disbelief. "You, you . . . you are a depraved and evil man. How did you do it?" I took it as a rhetorical question and just smiled.

"Wow, wow. Amazing. I just got pregnant with that flirtation," Bernadina said. We all laughed at her comment.

"You are good. You are so good. That is scary," Aiko continued. By bringing my arm to my chest, I bowed my head to show appreciation as a showman.

"Saying that, I don't like what you did to those girls. We know you were playful with us, and thank God you let us know that, but those young girls . . . I can't believe you changed so much that you forgot to consider others feelings," Aiko said. I knew it was a sisterly consideration, and I didn't mind it.

"Who said I played them? Like I said before, I am not shy or scared to talk to them and pick their brains and life ideas. Just a simple talk. Aiko, it's not always black and white." I held my hand up before she interrupted and continued, "Believe it or not, it happens a lot to me since I teach in a university, and I know how to handle them the way it doesn't hurt their feelings."

"Oh, come on, you just admitted in front of them that they should compete or even fight for your attention," she retorted.

"That's a separate issue altogether. What is that to do with what I think you thought?"

"Please enlighten me of what I thought since you know," Aiko said.

"Come on, Aiko, we all know you thought he was going to sleep with them," Calysta's new date said. Even though he was right, I felt kind of dirtier than before his clarifications.

"Or maybe I was trying to break their friendships. Am I wrong?" I asked her. I didn't want to be in the same boat as that bastard, even if it meant being food for the sharks. I gave her a slack so she doesn't lose face in front of this guy. If she was angry and saddened before, she was furious and inflamed then.

Who was this guy to meddle himself in other people's affairs? That was my thought, and without a doubt, that was what the others were thinking.

"It doesn't matter. If you call them, you make one sort of problem. If you don't, you just make another kind. You just doomed their relationship and gave that girl who has been rejected another blow. You were her hero," she said.

"Maybe a test in their relationship is all they need. Either they come victorious from one side or are better off from each other on the other side. I learned that lesson the hard way." I knew it was harsh of me to say that and threw shade at them for what they did years ago when no one was wiser than others, but that grudge, that stupid man sitting beside me were enough fuel for me to burn an entire world with it. After I said that, I didn't feel triumph and victorious. Even though that made me sad, I was glad to stand my ground and not be contrite for my own beliefs.

"And who's to decide what test is good for them?" she replied. She wasn't backing off.

"Does it matter if their relationship is not based on bias and is not one-sided?" I said it coolly. I wasn't trying to pick a fight with her. It was just that she should know what my thought was. After many years of staying away from each other, our union was turning sour. We were pointing fingers at each other for who was at fault, like children. However, what bothered me the most was, they didn't talk to my parents. I knew that because every year since I went to CERN, I sent my parents a two-hour video highlighting what I was doing there. It was another great thing that I picked up on. Learning new software and technical photography and many other things came with it. It was that habit that made me carry a camera with me all the time. My mom loved the idea, and according to my father, she played each one repeatedly, and she showed it to anyone who came into our home. If they talked to my parents now and then and asked them how they were doing, I wouldn't be that much sad. They would know me better. How was I doing? It was like we were all trying to erase the past and pretend that it didn't exist at all. Even though my parents were visiting me now and then, they had no idea how my friends were doing. After a while, I just stopped asking them about it.

"Agustin, Aiko," Bernadina said and continued, "you two should stop poking each other like children." Then she smiled. It was like she was the only grown-up in this gathering, which wasn't far from the truth.

"I was only trying to put some light on another side of the argument. It wasn't intended to offend someone," I said with some detachment.

"I think we'll continue on that another time," Aiko said. She wasn't happy about it, but she was willing to back off for the time being.

"I always enjoy a good and educated argument with smart people. It always helps me to be open-minded. Also, it doesn't hurt if that person happens to be as beautiful as you are," I said with some appeal to it and with the right amount of wink. She couldn't help it. Even though she was shaking her head for my absurdity, everyone could see her beautiful smile.

Marshal came back with drinks for everyone. "What did I miss?" With that, everyone burst to laughter. Then Bernadina started telling him her version of the events. Marshal, who was awestruck, was looking back and forth between Bernadina and me. After Bernadina finished telling him, he let us know how sad he was that he wasn't there to see it himself, which brought him a sour look from Aiko. After that, the food came, and we ate gleefully with some laugh now and then.

When the time came to say goodbye to one another, Bernadina asked me if I could drive her home. She told me that she missed Frigg and was wondering if I could let her drive it. Even though it was tearing me apart, I accepted. That wasn't the only thing that lacerated me. All that time, I learned nothing new from Calysta, besides the fact she was still willing to hurt me.

Once we got into the car, she drew a deep breath and looked at me. "Well, that went well, wasn't it?"

"I don't know, Berna. Everyone was on edge. I'm only glad we came out of this bizarre situation as friends without killing each other."

As soon as she started the car, a calming piano piece started to play. She looked at me in a way as if to tell me, **"What the hell, dude? Can't you find a better taste in music?"** Which made me laugh.

"Do you know what the music is called?" I asked.

"No. What is so funny about it?"

"Because it's called 'Just for You' by *Giovanni Marradi*," I continued laughing, which made her laugh as well. Just to annoy me, she pushed the forward button, and it jumped to another song called **"Enchantment"** by Chris Spheeris and Paul Voudouris. It made me laugh harder. She tried her pouting face but wasn't successful. She couldn't hide her grin.

"I see that you haven't changed at all. What if we get into an accident and this music was on loop? The police would blame us for impairment driving."

"Yeah, I should listen to your music, which has the side effect of losing hearing and sanity."

"You are hopeless," She said with a twinkle in her eyes.

I took out a cassette collection of Ocarina by Audin and Modena so that she could enjoy the ride as well. It wasn't even close to what she would be willing to listen to, but it had beat to it, so we both compromised. The way she tapped the wheel and moved her head, I knew I had made the right choice.

After driving for a while, she broke the stillness between us by a question.

"You are still thinking about what Aiko said?" she said.

"She was my friend, and I like to believe she still is. However . . ." I shook my head in disappointment and took a deep sigh. I didn't finish my thought and just looked outside. People were bustling about their daily lives. The Earth was orbiting around the sun, and my problems had me as their only companion.

"You know how Aiko is, lots of emotions and fewer thoughts. It's like taking a shower either in extremely cold or super hot, and there is no dial in between." She smiled, and it was one of those painful smiles when she was in a dilemma. However, it didn't stop me from chuckling, but then I remembered she only does that to a stranger. Aiko would be more considerate toward her friends' circle.

"I don't know why I came. That selfish part of me wanted to see you all and hoped we passed the trivial past, but the damn thing has been chained to us. It doesn't matter what kind of conversation we started. It could be religion, philosophy, political, or engineering. It wouldn't matter. It would end the same way. All the rivers end up either in the ocean or sea."

She shook her head and gave me another sad smile. "After all these years, you are still protecting Calysta."

That took me by surprise. I looked at her with a suspicious eye and tried to see where she was going with this. Was she fishing for something? What was her end game?

The sad leer was there when she looked at me again only to see my reaction. Then she looked back to the road and continued driving with the dejected smile still hanging. "I'll tell you all about it when we arrive."

I was too shocked to voice any objections. Now and then, I looked at her to see any changes in her facial expression, to find a clue. Why did she want to talk about it in her home? Oh, she knew how to keep me in suspense and torture me with it. Was it payback? Payback for what she knew that went on between Calysta and me? Maybe like me, she wanted to get it out of her chest. I couldn't blame her for that if that were the case. I looked outside, and it dawned on me that I didn't know where she lived or any of them. In fear of not bringing up the past, that old petrifying culprit, we didn't go into details about our lives, especially me being conservative on any subject related to my personal life.

It didn't take us too long before she stopped in front of her home. It was a townhouse, which was normal living in the city. She was doing fine if that was her house in that part of the city. It was not glamorous in the sense that it stood out from others, but not substandard to show negligence. It was the total opposite of what Bernadina was all about. She was a head turner wherever she went. Maybe this was her inner wish, to be like everyone else.

"What a nice place you've got here. I really like it." The beam in her eyes and lips was enough reply for me.

"Thanks. Who knew talking to a computer and bossing it around to do this or do that allows me to buy this." She smirked, and it was impossible for me not to smile back. "At least you found a company to pay you for being bossy. Now I feel bad that you did all of that for free for all of us," I added. It was enough to get her to bust a gut.

After she wiped the few tears on her cheeks from laughing, she led me to her living room. "Do you want a drink?"

"Just water." I knew she wanted to tell me if I wanted to drink wine or spirit.

"Is that all? Don't you want anything else with it?"

"If you are offering a dance while I drink my water, who am I to refuse that?"

"Ha ha, funny. Is there a reason you don't want a drink with me?"

"It's not what you think. I just don't want to drink and drive, especially when Frigg is with me. Also, saving you the headache of me dying in a car crash and you start feeling guilty for forcing me to drink."

She shook her head, but the chuckle was locked on her lips. She left to bring me a glass of water and a drink for herself. Meanwhile, I was absorbing the beauty of her house. Her rug wasn't a fancy rug from Iran, but it combined well with the interior design. The white cycle beside each other and the space between them was colored black. It was in a way to elevate different shades of colors like gray and milky white. Her three-seater sofa was gray, and two single armchairs were creamy. The three-seater sofa was facing the two single ones, which had been separated by an oval-shaped table. Between the single ones was another table with a night lamp sitting on it. On the right side of the armchairs and the left side of the three-seater sofa were two gray chairs. Facing all that and the fireplace was another purple two-seater sofa. On the fireplace wall, there were two paintings that were hanging. On the oval-shaped table, there was a vase that had some different-colored stones in it. There wasn't any TV set to be seen on that wall, which was a good thing. It brought the aura of Zen and tranquility with the modern touch to it. Maybe what she wanted was a place for discussion and no distraction at all. A convocation for her friends, perhaps? I could easily imagine the friends gathering, the conversation and gossip they brought with themselves, the nonsensical argument about this or that, the laughter for silly jokes or teases. Even thinking about it made me grin like a Cheshire cat.

"What are you smiling at?" Bernadina said with two glasses in her hands.

"I like your house and the way you set it up. I guess someone took it seriously when playing in the dollhouse with friends," I said while accepting my glass of water.

"It's really nice of you to say that," she said while sitting right beside me on the two-seater sofa, gathering one foot under the other. Her whole body was facing me. It made me a little shy, so I put one foot on the other, hoping it would give me more space.

"I'm serious, Berna. I really and truly like your house." This brought me another beautiful smile of hers.

"Thanks," she said and took a sip from her drink.

The glass of water in the palms of my hands was turning from cold to mellow. I was glad that I chose the water. The way Bernadina was behaving was making me really uncomfortable and anxious.

"You are still as shy as ever," she said while showing me her beautiful set of teeth. I knew she was goading me, and if I did accept her invitation, there wouldn't be an ounce of resistance. But for what? At what cost? There was a line that I didn't want to cross. Even my body was disappointed in me. The voices in my head were screaming at me and calling me names—stupid, moron, not a man, degenerate, deserving to be extinct, a waste of good genes, masochist, chicken, a dog shit, and the list continued on and on.

"Berna, you said something in the car. Do you want to continue?" I said instead, and I could see the hurt in her eyes.

"It's always about her, isn't it?" she said. I didn't know if she shamed and guilted me on purpose or unconsciously, but whatever the reason was, I didn't want to hurt her more. However, I didn't want to give her the wrong impression either. She made the situation impossible. What was I supposed to do?

"Talk to me. What is it in your mind?" I said and hoped what she wanted was a listener.

"It's just that it's always about Calysta. What should I do today to make the princess happy? What is going on with Her Majesty? Is she in distress or something? God forbid if she is depressed because it is the universe's job to make her happy," she complained. I stilled my laughter inside because that was my thoughts exactly and tried my best to be attentive to her complaints. She took another sip from her drink and looked up to see my reaction toward her badmouthing Calysta.

"Please continue," I said.

"She is a shameless creature. After all, she had done, after all she hadn't done, and after all the sacrifices we made for her, how did she repay us? She invites herself to our little gathering and brings that asshole with her. Like I care who she is dating," she said vehemently. She took a long sip with disgust. It was like she wanted to wash away that bitter memory with a more pungent drink. It made me wonder. Was that her true feeling toward Calysta? Or was it for my own sake? How could she repeat what was on my mind on that meeting right back to me? What kind of sorcery was she involved in? I was nodding without knowing I was doing it.

She drank the last bit and was ready to get up and pour herself another one.

"Here, I haven't touched it yet," I offered my glass of water.

"No, I think I'll have another one."

"It is for my sake. I don't like to see you drunk."

She laughed. "You don't trust me around the drink."

"Right now, no. You are too emotional to notice how many glasses you had before blacking out. I guess you were right to say I haven't changed much. I still care about you a lot."

"But not enough to be with me," she said with sadness that I had never seen before. There was silence between us, and I was afraid to say any word to her. She was emotionally unstable, and anything could be misinterpreted. I was thinking logically, and she was holding her soul in her hands—two things that don't mix well together, like water and oil. What could I say that wouldn't make me sound condescending? She was about to stand up when I said,

"Tell me about your feelings." I invited her to sit back and continue. My wording was with care and diligence. I was walking on thin rope. It wasn't the first time I talked to an unstable person, but the stake for a friend was much higher than some stranger in the street.

She sat back and looked into my eyes and searched for something. Sincerity? Curiosity? Whatever she was looking for, I didn't know I had it or not, so I prescribed her a smile. I smiled in the hope she would ignore other things and continue telling me about her feelings.

"Do you remember the first time we met?" she said with a wry smile.

"Do you hate me that much to make me remember that fiasco?" I said while having those memories revisited again.

"Why did you choose me between all three of us?" It took me by surprise. I never thought that there were actions on my part that made someone confused. I knew the feeling too well just to pass over it.

"Because you were the most beautiful one, and I remember that you looked down on me like 'What does this peasant want from me?'" It made her laugh.

"I'm serious. Tell me, Agustin, what made you talk to me first?"

I thought I was serious, but if she didn't take it seriously, it meant she had an inferiority complex or my explanation had holes in it.

"You ARE the most beautiful of the three."

"Then why did you choose Calysta, not me?" It was a question she had been asking for a long time. Really? I didn't even know or have a clue that she felt that way toward me until this moment. How could she hide it for so long without me noticing it? Well, the teenage me wouldn't surprise me, but what was my excuse for today?

After a lengthy consideration, I continued, "Because at that time, I was superficial and didn't know what I wanted from a girlfriend. I didn't know any of you, as a matter of fact. But with a little time, I got attracted to someone who was like me a bit. At that time, I wasn't ready for a challenging relationship. You were strong and brave, dishing boyfriends left and right. I was afraid to be cast out of the group because you casually didn't want me anymore. That was the case if we were in a relationship, let alone if the feeling was unacquired and made the situation more awkward."

"I was a stupid teenager too. I was hoping by showing my new boyfriends, I could make you jealous. You didn't like my personality then?"

"You make it sound like I had a chart for each of you and made a pro and con content in it. Because of my low esteem, I chose a safer option. It wasn't that Calysta had any lack in beauty, but she was more forthcoming about her feelings than yours by teasing me with her mischievous smile and the way she called my name that no one could repeat." It was harsh and firm, to say the least, but at least she would know where she stood now. There was no lack on her part for me choosing Calysta, but rather, something more ancient than me and her was involved.

"What about now? Is my approaching not enough for you yet?" she said with a tone of sadness in it. I felt the frustration she had, but someone between the two of us had to act at his or her age.

"Back then, I hurt you unknowingly. Today I can't hurt you knowing that it only benefits me, not you." I looked at her. The disappointment was screaming at me. I continued, "I can't compete with a dreamy image of me in your head. That Agustin is perfect, and I am not. That Agustin never breaks your heart as this Agustin does." There was a deadly silence between us.

Then She looked up and asked me, "What do you mean it only benefits you?"

"It means what it means. Knowing that this relationship wouldn't end anywhere, I'll use this vulnerability of yours for hurting someone's back, using your body and soul for my end. After all that, I'll discard you like anything else that's past their usefulness." She looked at me with disbelief. Maybe she was looking for an excuse to convince herself that I would never do that to her. After all, How much could she bet on me to not be truthful to her, or more importantly, did she ever care? With that much sentiment and passion, all that anger and vexation, A sane person would choose the most illogical approach.

"I think it is better for me to leave." I was about to stand up when she held my hand. My body threw a dictionary full of swears at me from *A* to *Z* for being an idiot, an incompetent, a contemptible, a fallacious being without any redemption on his thought and posture. My body was willing to do anything that meant having that moment of sweetness between a man and a woman, disregarding any philosophical ideas that could prevent it—an instinct of sort that was necessary for enduring all the hardships we put ourselves through. I thought I reined in this beast of mine, but contrary to my belief, it pretended to sleep to just jump on any opportunity. I don't know if the women ever understood the nature of this ogre and how difficult it was to control it.

Simply put, the brain and the whole body are fighting with simple logic that can be ignored totally. For every reason that we convince ourselves we shouldn't do it, our brain gives us thousands of counter reasons why we should do it. For example, after all that talk I had with Bernadina, now my brain was telling me that I did my job, that she was an independent grown woman who had the rights to make her own mistakes, that I was just simply hurting her feelings by not accepting her, that I shouldn't shelter her with something that I was not so sure if it was going to hurt her, that I should meet her halfway, maybe all that she needed, and the list of reasoning went on and on. The brain itself turns against us and makes us feel like horrible people if we don't reciprocate. That's where all the problems come from. When someone cheats, all the reasoning has been dismantled by the brain itself. How can someone fight with all those odds against them? It would be much more difficult if it isn't even cheating to anybody if we just give up and answer her needs without regarding the consequence. It is true what they say that it is easier said than done. Suppose someone wasn't through it and wasn't genuinely tempted on that level and had no idea what they were talking about. In that case, they should shove all those advices that they came up with additional salt and pepper in their asses, so maybe that way, they would shut up about whatever moral sense they came up with on that day. All this and some people gloss over it as if it's something to be expected from a gentleman and someone chivalrous. Not understanding that some people are frail and not trained for it at all, the expectations are always there. So when I say I sat and hoped that she didn't go further than that, it would definitely go over some people's heads, not grasping the gravity of the situation. The difference between being a good friend at a vulnerable time or just being simply human is a fine line.

I handed over my glass of water. She accepted it graciously and took a sip.

"It's a bit warm," she said and was confused if she gave me warm water instead. Meanwhile, I was wondering how the hell all that water didn't evaporate yet, with all the heat that I was sure was emanating.

She looked at me and wondered for a moment if she should take the next step or not.

"Berna, did she tell you the reason she broke up with me?"

She looked at me in disappointment.

"I hate Calysta." By saying that, she took another sip.

"You were supposed to be with me, not her. She never understood you. It doesn't matter what you tell me. You can't convince me otherwise," she said stubbornly.

I was sure she was emotional at this stage, and I didn't want to hurt her by insisting on something that I knew would hurt her.

"Maybe you never understand this, how important that piece of information is for me and how long I waited to know the answer, but I'll never trade it for anything that will make you sad and uncomfortable." I looked at her. There were tears in her eyes. "I wish you'd understand how important you are to me. Berna, look at me." She looked at me with teary eyes, still as beautiful as ever. "In a few days, I'll come back here and talk to you like old times, but at that time, we won't even try to talk about that question of mine again. It is going to be about you, what you were up to, and all the goodies and gossip you gathered all this time. On top of that, I'll bring pictures and videos and explain my part of seeing the world. How does that sound to you?" I looked at her and waited for her answer. One middle age was crying, and the other middle age was comforting her. Maybe it is true that we are children in our hearts and that only the games change.

There was a back-and-forth between us. Now she wanted to share the information, and I knew that if she did, it would be a kind of manipulation on my part, so I refused to hear about it. I also explained why I didn't want to listen to it. That look of gratification she gave me, the firm hug she shared, the trust I got from her were as good as they could be. When we said goodbye to each other and I was driving home, the thing that was in my mind wasn't the question. It was Bernadina's smile.

It took me a while to arrive home. I was tired from the day's events. The streetlamps were turned on, and they were glowing yellow on the dark asphalt. The pitch darkness from above was swallowing the rest of the light. It didn't stop people from working on that hours. I felt the sadness weighing on me. I just wanted to sit on that curb where I sat many years ago. The decision I made that day affected me more than a decade later. I felt I could cry now without somebody knowing. I sat on that curb and looked right and left. The tears were coming down. Now and then, there were cars that were passing by. I hid my face behind my hands and let my heart empty itself—for this unjust world, this never-ending pain that we carry all the time, for the departure of those dear to us, and the memories we have from the past. After a while, when I was ready to get up, I remembered to take my bag from the car.

I took it and walked to my parents' home. Carrying my bag and all those computer and camera with it, I walked inside, and I heard the TV was on. I could hear my own voice when I was narrating something for my parents. Probably they were watching one of those tapes that I sent here every year.

My dad was sitting in the wheelchair with oxygen tubes going around his ears to his nose. My mom was lying down on her bed with closed eyes. Her chest was rising up and down. My dad noticed me entering the room and shushed me to be quieter since my mom was sleeping. She wasn't getting much sleep these days. The number of pill bottles was a testament to how many parts of her body weren't working properly, besides her memory loss of me. And my dad had to deal with mutated cell in his blood that was spreading and adventuring everywhere it wanted to. Both of them were in a twisted race to see who went first and had no regard for their only son. I quietly went to my dad and kissed him on top of his head and quietly, as he requested, asked him if he had his supper. He nodded and, by waving his hand, asked me to go outside.

They didn't even tell me about their situation until it was out of hand. I was blissfully benighted of all the things they were dealing with. My mom was diagnosed first many months before my dad. She was losing her short memories with each passing day; meanwhile, her immune system was attacking another nerve system in her body. She couldn't stand up. She didn't recognize my aged face at all. Her son was talking to her through those videotapes. That was how my father kept her calm when she asked to see me.

My father, who knew me well and knew I would drop anything to come back there or force them to come to me, hid it all. He liked to be where he and my mom made their lives. That was his plan until the good doctor informed him that he wasn't doing well either. They suggested he live his remaining days at the hospital bed where he could have access to the nurses and doctors. They thought it was a good plan for him and my mom. What they missed was, what was the point of all those troubles they went through to have a roof above their heads? What was the point of making all those memories if they were going to be discarded so easily? On that spot where she made him smile while he was having a bad day at work. The silly dances she made while she was holding me to make me quiet. The guests and the friends they made through all these years. Their memories were still hanging around. The scenery they both made as they liked the house to be. Our friendly neighbor made a nest close to our home in trees, and they were coming and going for many generations. It was their dream, like the birds, to pass on their house to the next one in line. However, their only son and their investment was on the other side of the ocean, far from where they wanted him to be, far from any celebration they made, and he wasn't able to come.

Their celebration ended by seeing their son on TV. It was then when my father decided to tell me about the situation. After all those years, he never asked his son for anything; he simply asked his son to come for a visit, asking him as a favor for the old man's sake.

Then His son realized that everything wasn't okay. His heart was broken to see them like that. His mom would never know that his son came back for her in the end, showering her with kisses that she thought was coming from a stranger. He would read her a bedtime story, which she thought was done by someone who looked exactly like his son. He would sing for her while combing her hair. She would never know the world was nothing to that stranger without her in it.

I walked to the kitchen, then I noticed the young doctor sitting in one of the chairs and drinking a cup of coffee.

"Hi, sorry I didn't notice you were here," I said sheepishly.

"No worries. I was just taking a break. I sent the nurse home. I didn't know that you were going to be this late," she said nonchalantly.

"Thank you. It means a lot to me," I said admittedly.

"Well, good, let's see how you can repay me." By saying that, she gave me a mischievous smile.

She was a slender, tall, beautiful woman in her thirties—the type who never had a problem finding a partner if she wanted to, the kind who made my father whistle in front of her when he saw her for the first time.

However, I was tired of the day's events. I wanted to end the day as it was—no more drama. However, I couldn't be rude to someone who was treating the most valuable people in the world for me.

So even though I was tired, I played along. I looked at her beautiful brown eyes and said, "Nah, I'm going to sit here, and you are going to make a cup of tea for me." It took her by surprise; her eyes were bulging. She couldn't believe what she heard, so she said, "Excuse me, what did you say?"

And for her answer, I only smiled. She probably had never seen anyone talk to her that way. She had most certainly never been treated like that. To be challenged in a way that made her feel alive. After not hearing any response from me, she asked me with a smile, "Why did you say that?" I knew she was fishing for me to say "I'm sorry," but the truth was that she wanted to see if I was bluffing or not. If I double down on what I said, that would only make me a rude person, but if I continue standing my ground, it would mean a lot to her than saying sorry.

"I shouldn't have taken the car. It was a foolish decision I ever made. There wasn't a parking spot to park, but I got lucky at the end." She was baffled more when she realized that I wasn't even answering her questions. Saying something totally out of whack and nonsensical made me smile more and made her grin more as well. I continued talking to her like that for a while. The more she was looking to make sense of the situation, the more I made it much muddier until she forgot what the discussion was about. When I was sure I got her attention, then we talked about the events of her day. Casually, without her noticing, I prepared a supper for both of us and put the remaining in containers for her to take home or to work, telling her if she liked the supper, she could come back again in the hope that I was in the mood to make another one, with no promises.

With her gone, my day came to an end. The darkness of night had one more secret to keep in its dark heart and one more night for me to keep it there and not let my friends know about it.

Chapter 19

She looked at the tall mirror. The mirror was telling her that she grew tall after so many years. The color of her eyes and her hair hadn't changed yet. It seemed nothing had changed all these years but her height. Only one thing might have changed—a line close to the edge of her lips that hadn't been there for a long time. How long had it been? A year? Two? Three? Or perhaps more? It felt so strange to have it there. It felt like she was occupying someone else's skin. Now what did she feel like? Sad? Melancholy? Unfazed perhaps? So what if she didn't have that before? It wasn't like she broke any law. What was this face she had now? Doubtful? For what? Was she that big of a deal as she thought she was? So what if other boys asked her out except the one who never asked again? What would she say if he asked her out? This time, she would say yes in a heartbeat, or would she? Trust. She didn't know the meaning of it. To whom could she trust? Her mom? Involuntarily, she touched her hair and rubbed her arms. Meanwhile, her eyes stood out and glared. Her brother? She touched her forehead. She looked at her broken finger that had been healed for years now, but the phantom pain was still there. Her sister? Who betrayed her in so many ways? For what? To be the precious girl in that messed-up family? Or maybe to reduce the attention of others toward her? Her neighbor? All of a sudden, she felt sick. There was turmoil inside her. It was like her organs weren't that happy to be in that place anymore. They wanted to move around. Even her weight seemed unbearable. The big gulp she took in hope that it would help. Now the tears were coming down. She wiped it as if she could wipe the memory with it. However, it didn't stop them from coming down. She got angry, frustrated, scared; all the feelings, all the emotions were attacking her simultaneously. What was she frustrated for? Oh yes, for how long did she have to carry that burden around? Why was it shadowing her all the time? Where could she find solace and tranquility? By trusting someone else? How many times had her hand been burned from the same fire? Trust wasn't a good thing in her life. It tormented her. It left scars in her body to remind her over and over again of the price she had to pay for it. Maybe this time was different. Wasn't that what she told herself before getting into big trouble again? Now she saw her tall body was getting blurry. The solution was easy for that problem. If she didn't want to see her tears again, she shouldn't trust anyone. Was this a difficult lesson for her?

"Are you all right?" Cara asked her.

She is the problem. Before her, my path was clear. She was the one who gave me the habit of trusting. She was totally the opposite of my character. It is probably because she didn't have my life. She had the things that I only dreamed of, but was it her fault she wasn't traumatized like me? Maybe that's what I aimed to have. A simple life, a boring life like hers. In a dreamy world, being hurt means not having that specific person in her life, not the opposite way. What is it that I want from my life? A good companion who will help me raise a child or two? A Fanciful house I grew up imagining? The friends I choose to have? Was her life as difficult as mine? We never talked about our past. Why talk about the history when there were so many juicy boys walking around now? According to my memory, whenever I tried to know my friend's past, she showed disinterest. It wasn't like I was all for it when it was about my past too, she thought to herself.

"Marina, is everything okay?" she asked again and approached her like she was approaching a wild and scared animal. She only nodded to her friend in the hope that she would drop the subject. If anything, she learned from her life that she could never ask for anything in her life. Ask whom for it?

"Marina?" Cara said diligently. She could see the concern in her eyes, not that kind of concern to see how much damage she caused in her body and might cause her trouble. She could tell the difference. Her friend was a sweetheart and oblivious to the danger around her. That trusting nature of hers could be used against her. They would use it for mockery, calling her stupid for trusting. Trust in her world was a luxury, something to have to feel better about life. But it wasn't necessary for her life. What was the point of having it? But her friend was like a stupid chicken going through any den, let alone one where there could be a family of foxes living there, whose lunch or supper just walked in by its own feet. Even though she could never have her trusting nature for herself, she liked to be around her.

"What is it, Marina? Why do you look at me like that? Did something happen?" Her friend almost begged her.

"It is nothing."

"Yes, there is. Tell me, what is it?" Cara said like a good friend she was. "Is it about your dress? Are you nervous about your dress?"

With that, Marina started laughing and hugged her dear friend tightly.

"You are acting weird. You know that, right?" she said while she hugged back her friend.

"I hope you don't act like that in front of him. This time, you may lose him forever. It's not that it's that big of a deal, but as a good friend as I am, I can't see you again heartbroken. Probably he is going to be over the moon for his surprise party, and that is your chance to do whatever you want to do with him." She had a sly smile on when she said that. "Grab that stubborn bull by his horns." She showed by grabbing the imaginary horn. "And lead him wherever you want him to go. Give him one of those beautiful smiles of yours. Don't be so cringey around him. You know the drill. Make him feel like the king of the world, and once the dust settles, do whatever you want to do with him. There is . . .," she continued telling her friend the proper way to deal with these kinds of people. She was happy to be a great help to her friend in need. What would Marina do without her? She was hopeless like a puppy. Cara looked at her friend and liked what she saw.

Marina took a deep breath, and while looking at herself again in the mirror, just by having her friend on that picture, those strange lines appeared around her lips. She didn't know what her friend was talking about anymore, but she didn't want to interrupt her. That way, everything was going to be about Cara, not her. She didn't like to talk, and Cara would do that for her happily.

"Do you think he'll ignore me again?" Marina asked with a concerned voice. Cara, who wasn't happy that her dear friend didn't let her finish her thoughts and advice, forgave her this once because her beautiful friend was insecure about herself. Had she ever seen herself in a mirror to see how beautiful she looked? Who, aside from that guy, wouldn't want to be with her? Just look at her. It was solid evidence that God or the universe, whoever runs the show, was biased when making her friend, and he had the least attention when he was making her. Her friend didn't know what to do with that. If it were up to Cara, all the boys would be chasing her. The world wasn't fair at all in her eyes.

"I swear to God, if he pulls one of this kind of shit again, he won't survive the night, let alone to see his next birthday. What kind of upbringing did he have to act like that? Thinking the world revolves around him? I swear, if he pulls such a thing, I won't forgive him at all. Why? I'm serious. Why he does that? Does he want to prove a point? I don't know who he has been with before that put his head in the cloud. He thinks he is a big shot. A big shot? What do you think if we call him Mr. Big Shot in front of him? I just want to see his reaction . . .," her friend continued talking about him. It was an interesting thing that her friend forgot that it was her rudeness that made this situation. What's wrong if someone has dignity and wants to keep it? Is it wrong to have self-respect? What would she know about it? It wasn't like she had been brought up to it. Anything that she knew was superficial. There was no depth to it. It lacked all the wisdom. What could she do about that?

Her friend was still badmouthing the poor guy. **Whatever**, she thought. ***If I let her empty herself, maybe that way, she feels less about her insecurities.***

She looked around at her dorm. There was nothing special about it. It was a dorm like any other. It was small and dingy. They purposefully made them for students to study and sleep.

"I don't want to think about it, Cara. I get nervous even thinking about it," Marina said and hoped for the best.

"Everything is going to be all right. Don't you be worried about that. I have a feeling that everything is going to work out perfectly," Cara replied. Marina could only smile about it. It was the same feeling she had when her friend put herself out there, to tease and flirt with the guy only to find out that he wasn't interested in any other girls at the university.

His friends, on the other hand, were happy to gain a hand in the matter. They offered to be her boyfriend if she wanted to. It was such a flattery for her friend that she was going on about it for a week. She even teased Marina as well. However, what bothered Marina the most was the reason behind why he didn't acknowledge her feeling. How was that possible? A minute he was that sensitive guy every girl dreamed of, and another minute he changed his attitude around 180 degrees. Ignoring all people around him made her wonder if he was blind or simply thickheaded. What was the reason behind his behavior?

Whenever she went to talk about an assignment or a project that their professor gave them, she could see by her own eyes the indifferent look he gave back to her and how he was distancing himself from her. The way other girls threw themselves on him, all that smiling when they approached him, all the laughing for the things that weren't meant to be funny, all the touching of his biceps and chest, nothing seemed to faze him. He returned the favor with an unflattering smile. His friends, on the other hand, were all for it. Their new ploy was to invite as many girls as possible for the surprise party they planned for him. That poor guy didn't even know that they were using him for their purpose, or maybe it was her suspicious mind that wouldn't trust anyone. It was possible that his friends cared about him. Possibly, she had been harsh on them. Still and all, any doubts she had, it was gone the moment her friend came to the same conclusion. She pointed out how shameless they were. Cara, the most trusting girl and sweetheart, could tell, but that guy was so gullible that he couldn't tell. It could be that he was blind to all that, or perhaps he just didn't care. Why would he? It wasn't his business to tell people what to do. They were all the same age, more or less. But why? Why hang out with those people? Couldn't he find better and more befitting people to hang out with?

"What are you thinking now?" Cara Asked.

"Oh, nothing specific. I think we should keep moving if we want to arrive before the birthday boy."

"That's my girl. What do you think about my dress?"

"It's as beautiful as you are."

"Can you help me with my hair? How does my hair look like from behind?"

"Oh, it's perfect. I should change to another dress, don't you think? The one-piece one."

"Really, do you think I should change too? But I don't know to what," Cara said.

"Anyway, I don't think you need to. Half the people are watching your figure. The other half are imagining you naked," Cara said it as a matter of fact, but it made Marina split her sides laughing.

"You and your dirty mind."

"What? I'm telling you as it is."

"Okay, okay, we should keep moving."

"All right, all right, let's go."

They hurriedly went one after the other. In the street, they got a ride from a black cab. After giving the direction and address, they took a deep breath, like preparing themselves for a deep dive.

The sky was cloudy. A patch of rays was coming through from here and there. Some shops started turning on their neon lights. The traffic wasn't accommodating. They were afraid to arrive there late.

They arrived there late, almost thirty minutes late than they planned to. At the entrance, the guy looking out for the arrival of the birthday boy greeted them. The way he was looking at them was obnoxious, to say the least, but they masked their unpleasant feeling by smiling. Marina told herself that she wasn't there for him or the others. Her eyes were already looking for the one and only one she came for. There were so many girls at the party. Some of them had already started dancing and drinking.

The apartment itself was mint and beautiful. It was in a vibrant neighborhood. It looked like one typical rich kid who was brought up by a silver spoon. There was no reason to think otherwise. Still, she couldn't understand how he didn't get spoiled. Did he get whatever he wanted from his family? She couldn't argue that he was smart. To be propertied, astute, good-looking, sightly, empathic, kindhearted and altruistic, top drawer in music and drawing, sensitive, and modest are the qualities that every girl can only dream of. Be that as it may, he behaved like he didn't have any of it. He was always trying to be helpful rather than ordering people around. Always busy doing something, running from a department to another, and having books in one hand and a pile of paper on the other, he seemed to be tapped on an unlimited source of energy. What was his motive? Why does he work so hard?

There were so many questions that she wanted to ask him. If he would answer any of them was another matter. Was he that mysterious by nature, or was he just doing it to hide from something? All the seats were taken already. Some people, while holding glasses of drinks, were chitchatting with one another. The food, if they call it food, was half eaten—pizza slices in boxes and on one used plate. Chips and dips were on the table, which was accompanied by soft drinks. The table was small, so the party planner tried his best to put as much of everything as he could put on the table until there was no space for anything else.

"It's crazy and deranged," Cara observed.

"It is. I think we just made it in time," Marina responded.

"Yes, we didn't need to be that stressed. See, everything is fine," Cara said. It was as if she were comforting herself rather than explaining the situation. By understanding that, Marina just nodded her head for reassuring rather than conforming.

"Glad to see you here." It was from that guy with curly and funny hair. She remembered he also asked her out. She couldn't be much happier to say no to someone like him. After observing him from afar and how he was acting, she was sure she had made the right choice. Corwin. She didn't care much about him. He thought that he was a smooth talker or tried to portray himself that way. However, she didn't buy any of it.

"Really, thank you. I assume that he hasn't shown up yet?" Cara said enthusiastically.

"No, I am not sure where he is now, but he should be here anytime now," he responded. Marina felt perturbed with the way he grinned. She could guess what he was thinking, and it wasn't good.

"Thank you for inviting us. It has been ages that we saw anything that didn't look like our dorm," Cara explained nonchalantly.

"Sure, it was hectic all over the place. So many assignments, so many tests, so much to do that made everyone go bonkers, unless that person is Agustin. I swear, this guy is a masochist. I don't know how long he can keep up doing this." His remarks on subjects sounded more like bitterness rather than friendly concern. What was his angle for badmouthing his friend? More importantly, why does he use so much cologne? She didn't care. If she cared about little things in the world, in her belief, she wouldn't be able to live at all. The only reason that made her talk to him was to get close to Agustin. Even though he was obnoxious, she could endure it for his sake. Still, she wondered why a person like Agustin would even want to talk to such a person. It was the only fault she could find. How many shortcomings did he have? Was it plenty? Or was it as little as this one? Those disdainful and cold eyes. The way he always tried to put distance between himself and her. He wasn't even trying to hide the fact. It was like he was yelling in an amplifier to announce that he wasn't interested in her. Did he hate her that much? Did his pride get so bruised for what happened? She had so many questions to ask.

"He is here!" someone yelled. As if on cue, everyone got quiet. The light was turned off, and as any surprise party custom, people's expectation was high. For what? She didn't know. Would he be happy to see any of them? Did he like to be surprised? What if he didn't like parties and surprises at all? The matter would be worse for her. She was already on his wrong side and didn't want to make the matter worse. She asked herself why she was thinking so much about him. When did this happen? Since when did she care about what a man thinks? Was it a good thing? Or was she going to regret it again? Whatever her thoughts of men weren't wrong up to now. Was she going to be proven right again?

The noise of turning the key at the lock made everyone quite dead. The door opened, and the light from the street shone through. The tall and dark postures at the doorway stood out from the background light. He turned on the light.

"Surprise!" everyone cried except the overwhelmed Marina.

The light was turned off again. The door and the shadow disappeared in the darkness. Some started protesting by making unsatisfied noises. It didn't take too long before the tenebrous figure reappeared and turned on the light again. This time, everyone cheered.

"That's one way to respond," Cara said. Marina just inclined. She was more curious about whether she and her friend were welcomed there, and as a habit of hers, she began overthinking the whole situation.

So far, he was smiling and greeting. She wondered if he did the same for her. Her answer came shortly when he noticed her. His eyes locked to hers. It was like she was thrown to another dimension where passing time was different than where they were. For the outsider, it would be a few seconds, but for her, it was an eternity. Those curious and beautiful eyes made her shiver. She felt he could see her naked soul and take in whatever happened to her in the past. She felt so little in front of those heavy eyes. She smiled to show her surrender, and he smiled back to show his acceptance of her concede.

Not much time passed that he disappeared to his room. Marina was about to scream for this unfairness. Why did he do that to her? He acted like a twisted, sadistic person who enjoyed seeing people in pain. What did he want from her? Wasn't her humiliation enough for him? What else did he want from her?

She was almost ready to burst into tears when she saw him coming out of his room. She was so embarrassed for what she thought. Those were the thoughts of a lunatic, not hers. The answer to her question was easy. He just went inside to change clothes. But why all black?

She observed him when he started thanking people for coming to his birthday. She turned her attention to something else. She didn't want him to freak out and think he had been under her observation. She looked at the wall, but her thoughts were what he was doing now. It was so difficult not to look in his direction. This game of cat and mouse, all of it, was unfair in her eyes.

Then she noticed the paintings on the walls. Those beautiful paintings were breathtaking. Who painted them? She wouldn't be surprised to find out it was his painting. She didn't know much about painting, but she noticed the different styles on display.

There was a painting that she couldn't make head or tail of, but she couldn't look away from it. It was an accumulation of different-colored animals. Every space had been used to paint a sort of animal in it. It was so chaotic but prepossessing. As difficult as it was to look away from that painting, she noticed calligraphic writing in the bottom, which blended into the painting. It was the name of the artist, Agustin.

She couldn't breathe. What the hell was this guy? How much talent did he have? She knew he could draw, but this was on a different level of mastery. Like that night when he started playing the piano, she just got bamboozled. She looked back in his direction before going back to the painting again. What a beautiful combination of colors. It was so dreamy. Then she reviewed other paintings and noticed they were all painted by him. Her heart throbbed as she discovered different styles of his paintings.

"Hey, what are you doing?" Cara asked.

"Nothing, I'm just looking at these paintings," she replied.

"Are you crazy? He is so close to us, and you are watching some painting?"

Marina was about to protest the unfairness her friend was accusing her, but then she noticed that Agustin was really close to them, and a few people were left before it was their turn to receive his welcome. She was glad that she had a friend named Cara.

Then it was their turn. However, the suspense for Marina was unbearable. The reaction he would have for her being there made her a little bit uncomfortable.

"Hello," he said.

One word after so many months of not acknowledging her existence. He came and spoke to her. She heard that word more than a thousand times, but this time, it had a different meaning. Exoneration and forgiveness, a new commence and start, and aspiration and hope could be the new meaning of it.

"Hello," she said shyly. However, she extended her hand for a handshake. Like anything else about him, his touch was different for her. It was so paradoxical. It was firm but dexterous, soft but rough, masculine but gentle, dangerous but safe. It was the same hand that played that piece of music; it was the same hand that painted these paintings. However, where was that roughness coming from? Was he doing some labor job? He just added more mystery to his already mysterious character. The curious look he had, in a way, was amusing. It made her smile. Then she saw he smiled back. After a while, he let go of her hand and turned his attention toward her friend.

"Hello," he said again.

"Hi," Cara said and threw herself at him and kissed him on both cheeks. It was funny for Marina, but she didn't dare to laugh. The stupefied look he gave Cara was priceless. Marina didn't expect that from her friend, nor did Agustin. However, he continued his courteous approach and thanked her for coming to his birthday. He continued welcoming his guests. Meanwhile, Marina and Cara were talking to each other and giggling for the stupid things they believed they did.

There was a dance, and Cara, without any care, went and danced. Marina, on the other hand, couldn't dance. She didn't have enough buzz in her blood to make her careless about what people thought about her dance. There were a few who offered their hands, but she refused. She wasn't about to make herself silly. They responded to her coldness by throwing up their shoulders to show her that they didn't care either. If she knew any dance move, she would do it to have some amount of Agustin's attention. In the middle of the dance circle, there was Agustin, who was dancing with everyone. Boys, girls, it just didn't matter to him. He wasn't that good of a dancer, but he was having fun. It sounded like he didn't care what people thought of him, and for that, he was happy. It was different for Marina. She cared too much, and she was too conscious about any move she made. She wasn't looking for attention. What she wanted was to get by, to survive. The lesson from the past made sure she stayed on course.

There was always a repercussion for her each time she forgot. The way she looked at Agustin was with envy and jealousy. He looked like an eagle born to ride on winds, and she was grounded on Earth. There he was showing off by flying to where no one else could do. It was so majestic, so beautiful to watch him. How foolish of her to think she had any chance with him. She felt so ashamed of herself for being naive. If she were honest to herself by any case, she would realize that she had nothing to offer him. What was there for her to show? He seemed to be rich, so there goes wealth. Art and music? He had them at a crazy level. Seduce him with intelligence and intellect? He seemed to have them too.

The more she thought about what she could offer him or anybody, the more she got depressed. It was an impossible situation for her or anybody else, and here she thought why he didn't acknowledge her existence. Meanwhile, the answer was in front of her all the time. How did she dare defy him? The nerve she had to think to come out of it unscathed. It must feel good to be an idiot. She felt hot; she wanted to throw up. She needed fresh air. She had no idea how long she was in that state. However, she needed fresh air, and she headed toward the balcony. She didn't check where Cara or Agustin was. To prevent more embarrassment, she went out. She took a deep breath and inhaled in some fresh air and a familiar smell. She looked around and saw that beautiful statue of a human being. He didn't notice her. Why would he? He just looked to the dark sky and gazed toward the moon. It was so beautiful and breathtaking. The moon was beautiful, and the person who was looking at it was too. Then she remembered the smell of cologne. It was the same cologne his friend used excessively. After that distraction, she turned her attention to him and realized how rude she had been to intrude on his privacy. Even though it tore her apart to lose that moment, she called his name. He turned in her direction. There they were. Those heavy and curious eyes were looking at her again. The uncomfortable feeling was renewed for the second time for her that night. That evening, she felt like a prowler, so she had to ask him if it was okay for her to stay there with him. He had a pleasing smile on his lips when he answered and assured her that he was fine with it. She didn't know why, but she thought she had to explain herself by being there, and he, as gracious as he was, showed sympathy toward her. He asked her if she enjoyed the party, which she responded by affirmation and thanked him for enduring her existence. He simply brushed off by saying he had nothing to do with it and threw a joke to ease the tension. She took her friend's advice and laughed at his joke. However, it brought awkwardness. There was a deadly silence between them. Her intuition told her to confess her wrongdoing, and to her surprise, it didn't make him happy. It made her more puzzled. Putting his hand to his hair to pull them out as frustration of her stupidity made her more ashamed. She felt she couldn't do anything right. She got frustrated at herself, and yet she wasn't willing to leave his side. The cold weather was bypassing her skin altogether. She started feeling it in her bones, but she endured it. Who knows how long it would take for him to take leave of the sky and land himself again? He looked at her again to address the issue she brought up. When he answered her, he tried his best not to offend her, and what she perceived was that she should take responsibility for her actions. He was giving her the throne, and she was throwing tantrums and sat in mud. The back-and-forth conversation between them was comical. One tries his best to prove her worth, and the other one is overwhelmed by self-doubt. Even when he confessed his feeling, telling her the story of how he saw her, half of what she heard was that he tried to be nice to her. The other half, she was too happy to listen to anything he was saying, so when he told her he didn't blame her for her actions, what she heard was that "I forgave you," and she was too happy to understand the simple meaning of that statement. Agustin, having a different mindset, and Marina, being in awe and aspiration, continued their conversation through the night.

There were good moments as well, like Agustin bringing her his jacket and a cup of tea, but even those sweet moments couldn't save them for the inevitable.

When he pointed out that he wouldn't be coming back for the next semester, she crash-landed to reality. It was like someone shook her to wake her up from that dreamy conversation just to see the whole house was on fire.

"What?" she pleaded. She didn't want to hear the answer. What was there to hear? More excuses? She wanted to shout, to cry, or even to beg. This was a nightmare.

She just wanted to go to her dorm and sleep. Maybe when she woke up, she would see that it was just a nightmare.

There was a longhorn from a car that was screaming for her attention. The driver was asking her to clean the road as if the horn weren't enough indication. She shouted back in frustration. She yelled. She took a deep breath and screamed from the top of her lungs. The scream came from years of pain. It was always there, and it needed a little bit more to overflow. The pain that fostered itself in years came out as a scream. However, the cars on the roads didn't care. They honked, and they wanted her to clear the road. Her problems weren't theirs.

A firm hand lifted her up, and without looking, she started throwing punches. She wanted to gauge out the eyes of the person who dared to touch her. Her eyes were closed when she began slapping and scratching that individual. The thing that brought her back was the familiar smell she had smelled before, that familiar cologne. Now she didn't want to open her eyes to see who she was hitting all this time. She was mad at the world. This world was too unfair to her. She knew who was carrying her, but she didn't dare to open her eyes to confirm it. Being embarrassed for what she did, she looped her arms around his neck and buried her shameful face on his chest. She started sobbing, and the flow of her tears didn't stop.

"I'm going to put you on this bench," he said so calmly and without hurry. The bench was cold on her skin, but it made her calmer. The hand supporting her back and the other one under her knees were removed ever so gently.

There was silence between her and him. Still, she didn't dare open her eyes. Then a torrent of questions hit her. It was as if she blacked out or was sleepwalking this whole time. Didn't she have any sense of how she got there? How did she end up in the middle of the street? Why did she start screaming like a lunatic?

Her night was getting worse by the second. Then she noticed she was still carrying his jacket. She wished she was never born. What was the point of her being alive? she wondered. She could still smell him. He was still sitting there and staying quiet. He didn't utter a word. Was he angry at her? Who could blame him for it? She couldn't do worse if she planned to, but here he was, and here she was.

Sooner or later, she had to deal with what she did. Slowly she opened her eyes. It was worse than what she thought; his face was covered in blood. The trace of her nails was a horror show.

She felt so horrible. There wasn't any word in any dictionary to describe her shame. What could she say or do to undo what she did? Here was his birthday gift from her to him. She looked at him again, and it didn't get better. She got angry at her tears. Those tears were soothing her, not him. She couldn't hate herself more than that. He was still sitting there quietly. He didn't waste even a word on her.

"I'm sorry . . . I'm terribly sorry." She ended her statement with more sobbing.

"It's all right," he said as he patted her back gently. "I'll be fine. Don't worry," he said calmly for her sake.

"Please, let us go to a pharmacy or a doctor to look at you." Then she grabbed the gravity of what she did. If he pressed charges, if they went to the police, her life would be over. Was it adrenaline? Was it stupidity? She just didn't care anymore. She was ready to meet her doom.

"If it makes you comfortable," he responded. He tried to smile to reassure her, but it made his face scarier, and her guilty conscience was even more burdensome.

They headed toward a hospital, and during that walk, they said nothing to each other.

"Oh, my dear, are you all right?" an old lady asked when she saw Agustin's bloody face.

"Yeah, it was a cat that did this. It's not that serious. I still have my eyes though," he lied before she could answer.

She felt even more guilty. She wanted Agustin to yell at her or punish her for what she did; that way, she could feel less guilty. However, he answered her by kindness, which was more unbearable. He just made her feel worse about herself. In a moment of clarity, it dawned on her, the mental image she had earlier—him soaring to the sky like an eagle and her only a grounded chicken. Without any shame, what she asked him or wanted him to do was for him to stoop down to her level. For that, she felt more guilty, and it seemed an endless loop she couldn't get out of. Here she was dreaming about what life could be with him, and she thought to herself that it would be nightmarish. The constant feeling of being in the wrong, mortification, not being good enough would drive her crazier.

For the time being, he was just walking silently beside her, and he had no idea what she was thinking about. They continued their silent walk to the hospital, and there, he was treated by nurses and doctors.

The good news was, it wouldn't leave a scar. The bad news was, he had to endure it for a while and keep lying about the feral cat.

The doctor was more curious about that cat, and when he was asking about it, he would often look in Marina's direction. She knew that he knew, and for that, she was more guilt-ridden. The good doctor also asked her if she was unharmed, in which she said she was fine. Then the doctor asked her if she wanted to call the animal control, and he was watching her closely when he said it, but she refused. She didn't know to be angry at him for all those insinuations or to be relieved that at last someone acknowledged how bad she was.

"Do you want to talk to her privately?" Agustin suggested. What was he thinking? Then it clicked. The good doctor and the nurse thought that he forced himself on her. She got offended for not even being acknowledged that she was the problem, not him. What was it with this guy that tormented her nonstop, even though it wasn't him doing it?

This whole sad macabre seemed to be unfair.

"Do you want us to go to another room?" the nurse suggested. To shut down any bad rumors, she agreed to it. In an instant, they were in the other room; the nurse turned to her with concern.

"Are you okay?" she asked.

"Yes," she replied.

"Are you sure? Don't you want me to check you out?" she asked politely.

"If it puts your mind at ease," she replied. She was angry at them for being stupid. How the hell did they turn the table around? She was the culprit and at fault, and what they came out with was, he was trying to rape her. Not only that, but she had also been that dense that she just walked in with him like a stupid girl in love. They associated her with one of those tragic girls who didn't want to get out of an abusive relationship.

"Who did this to you?" the nurse asked. Marina just wanted the Earth to open its mouth and swallow her up. She totally forgot about her old scars, the scars that her mom left on her, and now they think he did it to her.

"My mom did it, not him, and for your information, it was me who clawed him like that while he was trying to remove me from the middle of the street safely. Any more questions?" she blurted out.

"I'm sorry. I didn't mean any offense," she apologized.

"It's not me who you should say sorry," Marina responded. The nurse just nodded.

"It was his birthday today, and my gift to him was this," she said to no one and showed her bloody fingernails.

"Ask me why," Marina demanded it. The poor nurse had to comply.

"Because he wants to study somewhere else. We weren't even in any relationship. He never talked to me until tonight, and this is how I repay him. He gave me this jacket so that I wouldn't feel cold, and what did I do? I tried to take out his eyes." She burst into tears. "If that wasn't bad enough, I just made him look suspicious."

"How could you?" she accused the hapless nurse. The nurse's eyes were bulging out.

"It's all right. Don't worry." The nurse tried to be sympathetic; however, that simple sentence couldn't be said in a worse time or place. It set her off. Marina, who felt so guilty already and was under tremendous pressure, started screaming while holding her hands on her ears. She was screaming at the unjust world. She was wailing at the ineptitude of humanity. She bellowed at the punishment her mom did to her. She yelled to tell the world that she had had enough. She cried out for her guilty conscience. She screamed because she was at the end of her rope.

When she opened her eyes, she saw many anxious eyes looking back at her. The nurse was far away from her with her frightened eyes. The doctor and Agustin were in the room. The security staff was watching her closely. She couldn't be more embarrassed. In a momentary madness, she thought dying wasn't a bad option.

Agustin came close to her slowly. He put his hands on her shoulder.

"I'm ready to go if you are," he said it with such calmness and care that her worries and uncertainties evaporated. She just nodded her head, and he took her out while she was in his embrace. She hid her head on his chest. He led them outside the hospital.

Still, he didn't talk. He just walked as she walked. There was no rush. There were no dragging feet. He just walked at her speed. All this craziness and he didn't even ask the reason behind it.

"I'm sorry," she said with lots of shame. Then she felt he pressed her arm gently to acknowledge her sadness.

"Please, say something," she begged.

After a long silence and consideration, he said, "You didn't know that it was me who tried to help you. Your eyes were closed. I just couldn't wait for you to open your eyes. I had to do something. I hope you understand," he said calmly. Did he feel guilty for helping her? She was baffled.

"You didn't do anything wrong. It wasn't your fault," she protested.

"Thank you," he replied. Did he give up, or did he just not care? Which one was it? She couldn't decide which one was worse.

He didn't talk, and she was deep in thought. What kind of game was he playing?

"Why did you say thank you?" she insisted on it.

"I hope you don't take that in the wrong way. I only said it because I felt you cared about me and what I think," he responded. Was he serious? She was perplexed. Anyone with the right mind would run away. How crazy was he?

"I see my answer wasn't that good. What I tried to say was thank you for choosing me as your friend," he said at last. She couldn't believe her ears.

He was thanking her for being his friend. She looked at him in incredulity. It made her wonder who the crazy one was in here.

Over and over again, she was asking herself, What did she do? Why did he still want to be her friend?

"Do you know any restaurants?" he asked politely.

"No, I am sorry," she answered. She thought to herself that maybe he was high on drugs. She saw that too many times, and she didn't like it. Even though it was her fault to begin with, yet she didn't want to see him high.

"Did they drug you?" she had to ask.

"No. They didn't need to," he answered simply. He continued sauntering side by side. The sound of shoes was echoing through the night. She bundled herself with that black jacket he had given her earlier. She let herself be closer to him; however, her head was still down. She was grateful for his generosity and his craziness. Nothing about him was normal.

"Don't you want to know why I did it?" she asked.

He looked at her, and she looked at him. "My father taught me that I should rein in my curiosity when it comes to people," he explained simply.

"And you always listen to your father?" she asked.

He smiled and answered, "Me being here and studying in this university means not always. However, he doesn't tell me what to do all the time, only when his wisdom and age is needed." His answer was simple but enough for her. She got a little bit envious of him. She wondered how her life would be if she had a father. She noticed again that he didn't ask about her father or her family. Even though earlier he explained to her about his curiosity, she was bothered by it. She wanted him to ask about her life, and she would tell him everything. She wouldn't skip a tiny little thing. Nevertheless, he never asked, and she didn't speak. In her eyes, it wasn't something to brag about.

People passing by them were stealing a look or two just to see if they could understand what happened. Marina noticed that Agustin was ignoring all those looks. He just kept moving forward with certainty.

"I'm a bit tired. Can we go someplace and talk?" Marina asked.

"Sure, let's get something to eat, and we can go someplace to talk. I think going to the park would be a good idea," he responded.

She wasn't sure what he meant by eating something. She worried he would take them to a restaurant or someplace crowded. She wanted to object but kept her tongue to herself. That feeling that she was responsible for all the bad things that happened that night was still looming over her head.

To her surprise, he went to the convenience store, bought some mixed nuts, a few soft drinks, and water.

"I forgot to ask if you have any allergies. Sorry," he said gently.

"It's fine. I don't have any allergy," she explained.

"I didn't like the other stuff. They were either too sugary or too fatty," he said innocently.

"No problem there. Thank you for your consideration," she responded. She wasn't thinking about her diet. She just wanted to get through the night, yet she wanted to be with him. She was afraid that in the morning, there wouldn't be any friendship. The whole night was unreal.

They found a bench in the park. He took out his jacket and laid it down on the bench for her to sit on. She sat there not knowing what to say. He opened the jar and put it between himself and her. He also opened the bottle of water and put them on each side of the jar.

"Thank you," she thanked him.

"You're welcome," he obliged.

She didn't know how to start a conversation, and he wasn't any help either. He just sat there and watched the movement of trees.

"I'm not good at breaking the ice," she confessed.

"How do you do it?" she asked.

"Do what?" he countered.

"Doing this, like nothing happened," she explained.

"Can I think about your question and get back to you?" he asked. He looked deep in the sky and waited.

"Sure," she agreed. She looked at the sky as well.

"I wouldn't say that I'm indifferent. I just don't have enough information to act upon. One moment, we were talking . . ." He looked at her and asked for her permission to revisit that memory. She nodded. "And then I saw you running out of the door. It made me wonder if the news of me moving away had anything to do with it. How come it disturbed you? I came after you and called you many times, but you didn't hear me at all, I guess. Then I saw you in danger, and I tried to help you." He looked at her again as if to ask for another permission. She nodded again. She felt unsettled about what came after that. He just smiled to reassure her that he didn't take any of that personally. "When I was there, I just couldn't sit it out. I had to do something when I saw you like that. From there, I just hang around to see if you need more assistance. I'm glad that I was there when we were at the hospital. Again, I don't have information about what happened there. Over there, it was just another instinct that made me take you out. I thought you weren't happy being there." He looked at her again. She felt worse. Was he babysitting her? She didn't dare to say that out loud after all he had done. It would just show how ungrateful she was.

"I'm sorry for all that," she divulged. She was getting tired of herself for saying that all night. She couldn't blame him for any of that. He looked at her and shook his head to protest the statement she made.

"You misunderstood me. I wasn't trying to make you feel bad. I just feel that I'm somehow connected to all of this, even though I don't understand my involvement," he said honestly.

She understood what he tried to say. Did she have any feelings for him? That was his question. He just asked her without asking her. What could she say? She couldn't just admit her feelings after what she had done. It would come out as pathetic and crazy, but she couldn't hang him dry either.

"I have to say that I'm sorry again. I just can't tell you tonight," she said apologetically. She saw the disappointment in his eyes. She was the perpetrator in here, but he was getting punished for it. She was the one who acted crazy and made a scene. She was the one who asked him about his inner thought. After all that, she just told him sorry as if it would solve anything or even tell how miserable she felt for all that. He didn't say anything.

There was a crunching sound of nuts under his teeth. He clapped his hands to clean the nuts' residue from his hands. Then with the back of his hand, he tried to remove the rest of the remnant from his shirt and pants.

To her eyes, this simple act was done handsomely. She just wanted to watch him all night, even if it meant watching him eat nuts. When he noticed that she was watching him, he smiled and looked away. She knew that he was waiting for her either to lend an ear for listening or take a taxi to send her back to her dorm. She wasn't ready to leave his side, so she waited.

"Are you all right? Don't you need one of these jackets?" she asked after a while.

"I'm fine. I'm just looking at the sky. I think I know what I want to paint now," he said like a wondrous soul.

"I saw your painting earlier. They are beautiful." She remembered. She also remembered that she didn't mention that earlier when he talked about the sky as a canvas. He looked at her and nodded.

"When I paint, I'm not looking to capture a moment. I'll look for the right feeling. In this color of the sky, I'm looking at a mysterious feeling. I don't know what it is," he commented. It was as if she knew what he was talking about, but she didn't. She knew he would answer her if she asked him, but she didn't. A feeling told her that she shouldn't.

"I had a different plan when I came to your party. I had so many questions to ask, but I think I ruined that as well," she said instead.

"Ask away. Tonight, I'm in the mood to answer any questions," he said while looking at the sky.

"Why did you choose this university?"

"Because my heart was broken, and I wanted to stay away from that place and people." He looked down and then looked at her eyes. He was looking for something, but she didn't know what. "I may have deceived you into thinking I'm brave, but I am not. I am a coward. I break easily," he admitted. She couldn't believe what she heard. He was telling her his secrets offhandedly. She was wondering if she should ask who it was, but she decided against it. She thought it would be fair if he asked her something private. Since he didn't, she didn't bother either.

"Earlier, you said that you wanted to be my friend. Do you still feel the same after what happened tonight?" she asked cautiously.

"The moment that I decided to get to know you, I accepted all the outcomes—your behavior in the past outweighs what you did tonight. I think you just had a bad night. You and everyone else are allowed to have that. I won't judge you or anyone else for that," he said simply. It was assuring and a threat at the same time. How the hell did he do that? She deciphered the meaning behind it, which was that he had scope for being patient; push him more than that, he wouldn't treat that person the same, and he would change his type of friendship the way he saw fit.

"Why did you say No to Cara?" she asked him.

"Your friend? If she wanted to be my only friend, I wouldn't have any objections, but she wanted something that I couldn't give her," he answered honestly. She was afraid to ask him the next question, but she had to.

"What do you feel about me? Do you want me to be in the same group as your other friends?" She pulled the bandage.

"What? What do you mean?" he asked, but the line between his eyebrows was telling her he wasn't happy about it.

She knew it was ungrateful of her to say such a thing, but if he was about honesty. Why shouldn't she come clean as well? "Your friends, I am talking about your friends. They do all sorts of things, and they aren't afraid to even use your name. Do you think anyone with the right mind wants to be close to them?" she asked and waited for a response.

"They just like to hang around me. I don't spend much time with them. However, you forced me to defend them because you are talking behind them. Do I see what they do? Yes. Am I going to do something about it? No," he answered firmly. She was astounded by the sudden anger in his voice.

"What do you mean? That you just don't care?" she asked. If he acted like that, it would be much easier for her to forget him. As she guessed, he was just like any other man.

"It means I don't preach, telling people what to do and what not to do. If they ask for help, I'll help them if I can. I think that we have enough judgmental people in this world. I just don't want to add myself to it," he answered patiently and firmly. She couldn't wrap her head around what he tried to tell her. It sounded more like an excuse to her.

On the one hand, he told her being with him was an honor, and on the other hand, he befriended these kinds of people. She thought about the hypocrisy this guy had but didn't tell him that. What she missed was that he disagreed with what they do.

She stood up and threw out the Jacket that was wrapped around her. "I wished that we never talked to each other. The image I had in my head was different than this. I wish you luck." She didn't expect any comeback from that. She thought she burned the bridge between them.

"I wish next time we see each other, you'll be more understanding of what I've said today," he responded.

She started walking away when she noticed that he was following her. She wanted to shout at him, but instead, with lots of self-control, she asked him what he wanted now.

"I'll just follow you safely to your cab," he said calmly.

"You think you are a good person by acting like that?"

"It is not an act. I care about your safety."

"Really? Why do I get the feeling it is for another reason?" What she meant was that he wanted to have sex with her. Agustin understood it clearly.

"I'll assure you it isn't that."

"Why do you care what happens to me then? I thought you didn't care."

"You simply misunderstood me. When I said I wouldn't propagate to anyone, it is that I don't see myself as wiser than everyone, which is true. I can't dictate to people how to live their lives. My way of understanding the world is different than yours and many others. I have my morals, but they are limited to myself. Maybe some people chose this path before, but it doesn't mean my path is the only right one," he said patiently.

"If your friends touched me, what would you do?" she asked.

"I'll stop them if it means to put my life in danger, but not before I know you need my help," he answered.

"What do you mean 'Not before I ask for help'? How do you know I need help?" she asked.

"By simply asking for help," he responded.

What kind of stupid or convoluted mind does he have? She thought. ***What if someone puts a hand in front of my mouth or if they knocked me unconscious, what then?*** She thought and asked him the same question.

"In that situation, I'll consider that a consent from your part for me to help you out," he answered.

"Is it that difficult for you to know right from wrong in one glance?" she asked.

"Assumption brought many countries to needless wars. Your assumption before this conversation was that I had no morals. How did you feel when you had that assumption? What do you feel after knowing about my morals and what I stand for?" he asked.

She knew it was a rhetorical question, so she ignored it. She was still angry at the earlier confrontation, so she walked toward the street to catch a cab. She was mad at herself. She was mad at him. It was as if she wanted to compromise the excellent image she had of him. That way, it would be easier to forget him.

The cold breeze on her skin made her chill. She was rubbing her hands to her arms. Then she noticed she didn't have her purse with her. Could she be more stupid? Then the calm feeling that Agustin was with her found a way into her heart. She hated herself for that. He was right. The assumption only brought troubles. Before all this, she assumed she would have a wonderful time with him, but now that she knew he wouldn't be in that university, she didn't know what to feel.

"I'm not like this all the time," she said innocently. She didn't know why she said it, but Marina felt she needed to defend her image.

"It is one of those nights that everything goes against you," he sympathized.

"Thank you for your understanding," she said calmly and shamefully.

"I wish my best friend had given me this understanding. Fortunately for you, I learned from that experience," he said while continuing to walk.

"Do you want to talk about it?" she asked.

"His name is Marshal. I bet you would have liked him. He is a nice guy," he said with a sad tone.

"I bet I would," she agreed. Then they continued walking.

The streetlight was shining on her. A few taxis passed them by, but she didn't raise her hand for any of them. She had no money, and she didn't dare to ask for it. She was hungrily looking at the black jacket that Agustin was carrying. He didn't offer his coat back. He just walked with it.

"You forgot the nuts," she said.

"Food for other animals at least," he said without looking in her direction.

"Are you angry at me?"

"I don't know," he answered and was still not looking.

For a few hours, she forgot how he ignored her all those times, and those memories hit her hard. Did she want him to ignore her like this? At least she wouldn't be heartbroken if he left.

There was a decision to make—either pretend that this night never happened or enjoy the little time that they have together.

"Agustin, please don't ignore me anymore," she said that and came closer to him. She took that extra jacket. She put the coat on and took one of his arms and put his arm around her shoulder. That way, she could snuggle herself into his space. "I'm angry at you too," she said at last.

Agustin chuckled and pressed her closer to himself.

Chapter 20

The last breath of winter was hanging around above the grasses. The trees' leaves with their branches were dancing continuously. The chirping sound the birds were making at that time of the day was such a resemblance to humans' open market or bazaar. Was there any difference? Weren't they making those noises to know where their partners were? Or calling their partners to hurry up and bring food for their younglings? Perhaps to change the babysitting duty? The smell of fresh grass, which had been watered recently, was wafting through all sorts of creatures' nostrils. For some, it was a bell ring for lunch. For many others, the mixture in that fresh smell showed the territory of some animals who left their marks. The sun's rays were peeking through the gaps of leaves. Like children that never get tired of doing the same game over and over again, each shaft did the game skillfully. It wasn't all game and play. The worker ants were carrying the little pieces of grass-blade or some part of dead insects. Some were doing it alone, and some had been helped by other members of the colony. Above them, the dragonflies, butterflies, bees, and other flying insects were jumping from one flower to another under the watchful eyes of their predators. The food for the newborn chicks was down there.

"We are all here to celebrate the life of a great husband and father . . .," the priest was saying to the little mass of people. The gilded casket with a smooth surface reflected the sun's rays, which made a miniature of its size. It was as if the story of Narcissus were happening there. The sun wanted to see its image on everything. The assembly around the coffin was all wearing black. It was an abominable image to have; whereas everything was moving forward and being lively, some wanted to stop and think about the past. A group of people who weren't in harmony with nature, as usual, was gathered to celebrate the beautiful life of a husband and a father. They all had a solemn face for a celebration.

The children were imitating their bigger size in the future. Did they think it would be them in the future?

Some wore shades to match their outfit for this commemoration. The tears that came down on their faces were wiped by different-colored handkerchiefs.

This black mass ruined the beautiful color in the surroundings. It was as if nature painted a beautiful picture arduously to be ruined by a naughty little boy. This black mass wasn't welcomed there. The living world wanted to correct the image by removing it.

A woman who didn't know why she was wearing black was sitting beside me. She wasn't sad or happy. She just repeated the custom she learned when she was a kid. Since when she practiced, that custom depended on nature's or her parents' whims. She was obviously practiced on that. She was doing her part perfectly, but as a stranger, nothing more.

"He must be a good man. Look at this gathering. He had lots of friends, but where is his family?" she whispered to my ears.

"He was a good man. Unfortunately, he didn't have the brightest son. His wife . . . his wife doesn't know that he is gone," I whispered back.

"Oh, the poor man, how is this possible?" she asked.

"Oh, it's possible. In this twisted world, everything is possible," I replied.

"That is sad," she commented. I just nodded my head to agree with her. She took my hand to hers and tapped on it with her aged skin and bony hand.

"I'm afraid I have the same fate as this man. My son is far away from here, and I don't know where my husband is right now," she said, then she looked at my eyes. "Do you know where my husband is? I asked everyone I saw, but it seemed no one knew where he was. He has never done this to me. If I find him, I'll box his ears out," she said with conviction.

"If I see him, I'll let him know how angry you are at him," I replied.

"No, don't. I want it to be a surprise," she shared her evil plan. There was a cute but sinister smile forming on her lips.

I lost track of what the priest was saying. He was reading from one copy of the same book that every priest was carrying around. I thought he should have memorized the whole thing by now. Maybe he didn't care or wasn't getting enough funerals. The cover of the book was the same color as our outfits. He looked around the crowd with practiced eyes, reading the crowd's emotion. The solemnness and firmness of his voice was anything but merciful. Here he stood and talked about a person who didn't share any qualities of his, talking about a gentle heart, which he himself didn't know of. In the depth of his pupil, where darkness made a home, he spoke of the kindness of a man. It was a rehearsed act. There was nothing new about what he said. It was only a repetition for him but a new experience for me. I never lost my father before, so being oblivious to that feeling was a given. The priest was talking about where my father was as if he could pinpoint the exact location. Did he believe anything that was coming out of his mouth? Maybe in the beginning he didn't, but he reiterated it religiously so much that he believed it now.

Where was my father? Was he where this priest said he was? Perhaps millennia of seeking knowledge could tell us. We die; we break down into particles, if not eaten, until nothing is left but our bones. All those soft touches, all that laughter that made his face handsome and lively, all that strength who lifted me from the ground, all those warm caresses that wiped the tears from my face were going to be broken down in nature and memory. His body was falling through way before his passing. That laughter was replaced by his coughs. Those good memories had already been replaced by horror shows. Those strong arms were almost thinned to the bones. There was nothing beautiful about having plastic tubes on his upper lips. His face hollowed out so much that his cheekbone and teeth were obvious to see. There wasn't enough breath in him for laughter. The accumulation of thousands of years of science was telling me that his body was going to come to nothing. The thousand years of science and experimental accomplishments to fight a rogue cell was by injecting more poison to the veins.

His existence was reduced to a polaroid series of an image on a film.

A frozen moment of his beautiful smile was looking back at me, which had been framed for all to see. In the book of memory lane, there were so many pictures of him and my mom that I wasn't included—the time before I was conceived or even after that.

A squirrel, which stood on its two legs and was busy stuffing its face, was watching the show.

"Does his son have anything to say?" the priest asked with a reading-through voice. I just shook my head. What was there to say and to whom? I looked around and saw a bunch of strangers. His wife was alien to him than anyone else in that gathering. My friends became outsiders the moment I wasn't involved in their lives. Should I say something to those little kids who only knew something terrible happened and that they weren't allowed to laugh and play? Should I say something for the sake of the priest who was already bored and wanted to move on to his next ceremony?

To whom?

Slowly they brought down the casket to a deep hole in the ground. The pulleys weren't making any noise. They were being oiled enough for that. What was that for? To not disturb sniffing noise some women made? OR to hear a man clear his throat? The casket kept going down. It was going to the place where we were so afraid to go. The notion of hell was coming from that, wasn't it? The ground was swallowing it up. The reflection of the sun was getting dimmer.

To me, it was as if the earth were hugging it and embracing it deeper. We were like children running around doing this or doing that, and when we were tired enough, the earth opened its arms to soothe us. It Sings a lullaby for better sleep. Now it was taking one of her children in. I could almost hear the voice that was calling his name. "Come, child, come. You ran enough." It was like when he embraced me when I was tired or scared. Now a more prominent being was doing the appeasing and lulling. Then slowly, without waking up her child, she closed her arms around my father as if to protect that precious, sleepy child from us. After a while, my father was embraced wholly by the earth.

"Good night, Dad. Sleep well," I murmured to myself while a trickle of tears was coming down my cheeks.

Marshal's hand was on my shoulder and tapping me there to make me calmer.

People started disappearing little by little. Some, as a routine, gave me their condolences, which I returned by thanking them. They gave me pitiful looks when they saw my mom beside me. I didn't feel the same way. I knew that in a few months, it would be my mom's turn to sleep peacefully, and I would get rid of these pitiful people.

Involuntarily, I rubbed her back. She didn't need my comfort. It was for me. This munificent and benignant woman in a wheelchair will stop playing the game of life and leave her son to continue it. I envied her for that. I wasn't sad about that; I was sad this game wouldn't be fun without my dad and my mom in it. I had to do it all alone until my time came to retire.

"Agustin," Marshal called me. He gave me the signal that it was time to go. I just followed him numbly. He was pushing the wheelchair for me. I just followed. Aiko and Bernadina looped their arms around mine and led me away. One of Aiko's children was marching in front of her mom in her black dress. The other one was helping his daddy push the wheelchair.

I looked back to the place where my dad was. He was still there, and the Earth promised me to take care of him for me. I was assured.

Bernadina and Aiko led me to our cars. Marshal, with the help of a nurse, put my mom in a car. My mom, who was happy to see outside again, wasn't happy to get to that confinement. However, she stayed quiet like always. She didn't ask much for herself before I was born and didn't ask for anything else after I was born. Nowadays, she only asked for her husband and her only child. I went and sat beside her. Bernadina went and sat in the passenger's seat. Aiko was going to follow us by her car and her two children. One of them wanted to have a ride with his dad. The poor thing was disciplined gently by her mom's words while he was pouting and hating every grown-up for not understanding his needs. In the end, he succumbed to his mother's request.

The ride wasn't that long. Since we didn't talk that much, it was a quiet ride. My mom was looking outside and watching the cars and the people in them. Maybe she was trying to find a familiar face in that dense traffic. I was watching her and holding her hand to mine. She didn't resist because my face was friendly for a short period of time before I became a stranger again. Marshal was watching the front car. If that car moved an inch, he would drive that inch. Bernadina was watching the sidewalk and rear mirror to see how my mom and I were doing.

She was the one who spilled the beans. One day, unexpectedly, she visited me. Since she knew I was living with my parents, she came to hit two birds by one stone, but to her surprise, she found out about my parents' situation. I saw her in shock. After that, I had to witness Marshal's tears and Aiko's cry in his arms. That was how they found out, and Marshal was angry and upset at me for keeping it a secret. The quarrel between him and that young doctor was comical. He just walked in and stole her patient. "Fuck the patriarchy" was written on her face, and I could read that a mile away. Since I wasn't trying to antagonize Marshal more than he was, I accepted him as their doctor. He was a surgeon. I don't know what he could do for a cancer patient and the other one who had her immune system attacking her with a cherry on top of forgetfulness.

One day he asked me what was with that doctor. I confessed that he just took away her personal chef. Nonetheless, I should give him credit. He went beyond to visit my parents daily after his work was done. He jokingly told me he was doing that for his sanity. He claimed the job was stressful, and at home, Aiko and his children wanted him to run a marathon.

My father loved to see him there. They were always joking with each other. They talked about life and children. My father always looked forward to seeing his children. There was joy in his eyes when he caressed their hair with care. I often caught him giving chocolate and candy to them without their parents knowing, and he made me his accessory to his crimes by giving me a wink. Sometimes they sat on his bony lap like I used to so he could read some stories. Sometimes he told them how their father was when he was younger.

I knew how difficult it was for Aiko, but she was as committed as her husband. She was working hard in her office and at home. Bernadina was there too, if she needed to be. She was there to hear the complaints or act as a sour aunt to discipline those little devils. My parents' house became a hub for gathering. Even though my mom didn't know what was going on, she was happy to be involved in something. The children made the house lively by chasing each other, crying, and pointing fingers at each other for anything that put them in trouble. One day I found one of them who began realizing her inner artistic spirit by working on the wall on the second floor. She drew her mom, her dad, herself, and my dad in a wheelchair. She was about to get in trouble, but I insisted that I liked her work and would tutor her personally. I drew the lines on the wall and told her to paint it in whatever color she wanted. Soon enough, my father was there to watch us doing the painting. He was happy to have a new hobby and wasn't bothered at all about what we were doing at his wall. Above her drawing was my drawing of the same people she tried to draw.

Then there was the other one who was playing with cars. Strangely, those cars and trucks seemed to crash into each other a lot. He also made the sound effects of those crashes, the skidding, and the explosion of those demised cars and trucks. In his worldview, most people were lawless and wild. I was following his storyline the way he jumped from one part to another. It was confusing why they were doing all those things. There was no motive, no goals. Simply for no reason, the cars were speeding up, skidding, and crashing into each other. Was our story written in the hands of a child? That could be the reason why nothing in life made sense.

Those children made me wonder if I was like them once. I asked my father, and he answered that it was my wishful thinking to have that kind of childhood. I was too predictable.

I learned those lessons. I crashed those little cars, and I made it more cinematic. Even better, I made a simulation of his work on the computer and asked him if it was close enough to his imagination. The look he gave me was something to frame for.

I got close to both, and their world became a sanctuary for me to escape reality. It was as if I were catching up to them. Marshal and Aiko were happy that their children found a playmate to play with. For them, I was the free babysitter, and for me, they were the wisest teacher and shrink.

It wasn't all good. Sometimes I had to teach a class full of serious students with a half-painted face from that artist prodigy. I would take a picture of my class with a half-painted face and share it with my dad and my mom. Her parents loved it so much that they framed it and put it in her bedroom. That little girl loved it so much that she could hardly contain herself.

I was getting closer to them each time they came for a visit. I couldn't be happier to see my father was all smiles when they arrived. He was getting weaker by the day, so at some point, all the games we were playing were in the room that he and my mom were in. Sometimes my mom would get impatient when we interrupted her while watching the movie I made. Occasionally, we watched it together, and they bombarded me with all sorts of questions that I found difficult to answer, like if I were friends with all of them, if I were getting married to any of them, and if not, why not? Or if I knew where they were now. If I said yes, I invited one sort of problem. If I said no, another gate of hell was getting opened wide.

Meanwhile, my father enjoyed seeing me in my misery. The noise he made, which was supposed to be laughter, wrenched my heart. When my father couldn't read stories for them, it fell to me to do it. I did it for his sake. The problem with reading stories was that sometimes I had to read them many times. It was vital that they liked it.

Those days passed in seconds.

One fateful evening, my father's heart gave up and never started again. It was just like that. He left and made a vast space in my heart. Isn't it better to say the huge hole was created in my life, not in my heart? I knew the expression started as old as the whole civilization. In the past, people believed there was nothing in a human's skull and all the work was done by the heart. They thought the thinking and feeling were done by the heart and the brain was useless. If that were true, the same heart stopped working.

We arrived at my parents' house. Bernadina took control of everything. She attended to guests while I was laying down my mom on her bed. Aiko was attending to her children to behave, going back and forth to help Bernadina. Marshal was doing my supposed job, thanking the guests for showing up.

I didn't care for that gathering, and the people I cared for were busy being polite to my father's friends or some of his coworkers and acquaintances.

These people were stuffing their mouths in memory of the person who left and drank the strong drinks to forget the same person.

Those children in black were looking miserable, so I went to them and told them to go and play. To one group that chose to draw, I sat with them and started drawing that comical gathering and people.

Let the grown-ups play their grown-up games. We drew to please our hearts, not anyone else's. We drew the people who were busy doing something else. The time didn't stop for us either.

I had to play like a grown-up as well. I had to thank the people who came to give me condolences.

Marshal was there beside me when I was courteous. He was a big help. He did what I wasn't willing to do. The whole thing was orchestrated by Bernadina and Aiko.

The time that all the guests left couldn't come faster.

We were sitting at a round table and taking breathers while listening to the TV that was turned on in the next room where my mom was. We all saw those memories that I made more than a dozen times. By now, we could tell which one she was watching on which part.

"Thank you. I truly don't know what I could do without you," I said sincerely. They answered me with their tired smiles.

"Don't mention it. I'm just happy everything went smoothly," Bernadina said while resting her sore back on the chair.

"Thanks again," I thanked them again. Now they gave me a sad smile. It was an understanding that they showed.

"Thank you for taking care of Nadine and Robert and the other kids. You made the job much easier," Aiko observed. I nodded my head with a smile.

"I don't think it's proper for me to ask you to stay here longer. All of you have a life to attend to," I said offhandedly. They shook their heads in unison to show their protest.

"Besides, Nadine and Robert are sleeping. They'll be grumpy all night if we wake them up now," Marshal said.

"What about your jobs though?" I asked.

"I already took a few days off," he responded immediately.

"Me too," Aiko said as well.

"I think I could manage not looking at a monitor all day for a few days," Bernadina said as if obligated to say something.

"Thank you. I truly don't know how to appreciate your kindness," I said and felt guilty and happy at the same time.

"Oh, don't worry. We'll think of something," Marshal said to ease the mood, but Aiko and Bernadina gave him a glaring look with a smile to tell him to shut up. I just chuckled, and they accompanied me with it.

After some chatting, I saw the tiredness in their eyes. I asked them to go and get some sleep. The children had already conquered one room—the room that we were drawing on its walls. They had some toys of their own in that room after so many visits. It was as good as any place for them. Another bedroom was taken by Aiko and Bernadina, like the time when they were teenagers. It was my childhood bedroom. Also, there was an office that I was working there, so it left Marshal and me to sleep in the basement, which had beds for guests.

Marshal went and took the best bed and had the audacity to show me his teeth. I took the other one while having a big smile on. We lay down and looked at the ceiling. We didn't talk and just looked at the top. We were too tired to speak. At least he was. I, on the other hand, was too hyper to sleep. The home felt less crowded without my dad in it. He was gone forever. I think the reality sank into me at that moment. I couldn't hold back the tears. They were just there. More images and memories of my dad came to me, and it sped up the flow of tears. I won't see his laughter anymore.

It was between reviewing on those moments that sleep came and took me to another place.

The few days that my friends stayed with me went by too fast. The day that they left me, the house became too quiet. There weren't any children running around. There were no more teases and jokes. It was me and my mom and a TV that was rewinding my different life.

Marshal Still came every evening to check on my mom. My mom felt much lonelier than before, now that my father was gone. It was evident from the complaints she made and her agitated behavior. Even though she didn't recognize her husband in his last remaining months, she noticed the change in the air of the house. Her eyes were looking for something that wasn't there. Sometimes her husband was on those videos where she went on holiday with. Those moments were short though. Those videos were all about her child, showing what he was doing and keeping himself busy; that was what it was all about.

When I took her to bathe or brushed her hair or fed her, I wondered about my childhood. Was I as easy as she was? Or more like a little beast whom she had to chase to feed? Every day I played piano, violin, guitar, or some other instrument to entertain her. She listened attentively. It was a way for me to talk to her, telling her with the universal language about my feelings.

I decided to take my job in her bedroom. I quit my university job. It just didn't feel right to work. The other jobs could be done behind the computer. Aiko and her children were always a welcome distraction for me, but I don't think she felt that way. She always thought she was adding more burden into my life by bringing them. It didn't matter what I said; she wouldn't listen.

Two months have passed since my father passed away.

One day I was reviewing a project on my computer when my cell phone rang.

"Hello," I answered.

"Hello, it's me, Agustin," a female voice said. I knew the voice. It had been implanted deep into my brain like any other painful memory.

"Calysta?" I blurted.

"Yes, it's me," she responded softer.

"How are you?" I said businesslike.

"I'm good. Thanks for asking," she still said it softly.

"It's good to hear your voice again," I said and tried to be courteous.

"Thanks," she said with the same tone. It had been months, like ten or eleven months, since that day. There was an awkward silence hovering for a few seconds.

"I'm sorry I couldn't attend your father's funeral. I felt that my presence wasn't a good idea."

She was probably right. I didn't want to see her like that. It was difficult enough for me to let my friends back into my life. I was angry at them for forgetting my parents and not knowing about their conditions, but it took me a while to realize that I, as their son, didn't know either. Hence, they repaid me tenfold when my dad passed. The thought of not having them there was unbearable and unbelievable. However, Calysta was a different story. Neither I nor the others talked about her in our conversation.

"You are probably right, but thanks for your consideration," I said. There was silence on the other side of the phone.

"Do you think it is a bad idea for this phone call too?" she asked.

My thoughts were somewhere else. I didn't think about it until that time, but I figured who had given my phone number. It wasn't that difficult to decipher who. Bernadina wasn't that friendly to her for many years. That was what I gathered. My approach to her was like walking on thin ice after the curveball she threw at me about her feelings. I tried to convince her that by my actions and words, we could only be friends. It didn't matter to her. She thought I needed more time convincing. However, when she found out about my parents, she took it easy on me.

Marshal? It was out of his character to sell me like that. He always carried a face full of guilt whenever he was around me. My house was his second home before we met any of them. There was another side argument; he could be the one since he would have thought it was the best thing for me.

The most probable was Aiko. She was still in a good relationship with her and wasn't far from her character.

She was waiting for my answer on the other side of the phone.

"I don't think it is. I'm glad to hear your voice." I tried to be nice. That was what I thought.

"Thank you. It is good to hear your voice as well," she responded. Her soft voice still held a spell on me. On the one hand, I tried to show her that I was over her. On the other hand, my ears were aching to hear more from her. However, we ran out of pleasantry. I had nothing more to say. She still felt like a stranger to me. One part of me told me to say something, and the other part told me that I didn't have to. I listened to the second part. I didn't know why she brought up the worst things about me. I felt guilty about it. I felt it wasn't right, but something deeper prevented me from being nice to her. I thought she killed the nice part of me by herself.

"Thanks again for talking to me," she told me after a long silence.

"No problem," I said with a dead tone.

"I guess that's it. I just called to hear how you are doing," she responded and was desperate to continue as long as she could.

"Thank you again," I said with the same tone.

"Oh, one more thing. Do you want to meet and talk sometime this week?" she asked as if it had just occurred to her.

"I don't know. I can't promise you. I have my hands full," I said coldly.

"Oh, don't worry about it. It was only for my sake. I understand," she said. I could hear the disappointment and sadness in her response.

"Goodbye . . ." She was about to end the call.

"Call me . . .," I said and overlapped her goodbye.

We paused for a moment. She waited for me to finish my speech.

"Call me in a few days. Let's see if I could find the time," I offered.

Deep down, I was swearing at myself for being weak again. I thought she didn't deserve any sympathy from me.

"Sure. Thank you," she said with a happier tone. She didn't like the result, but she compromised.

"All right then, I'll talk to you later," I said.

"Yeah. Sure. Talk to you later," she responded.

"Bye," I said with a defeated voice.

"Bye," she said in triumph.

That evening, I talked to Marshal about it, and he responded that we were two grown-ups. He thought that we should leave behind the past and move on.

"You think so? Is she working on you as well?" I was referring to his wife. He just laughed.

"You know how they are. They are like sisters. I'm the bad guy who wants to share their sisterhood with you," he said it sarcastically with a smile on.

"The generosity you have," I responded.

"Bernadina is going to kill me," I said with concern.

"Oh, that, Jesus, man. Sucks to be the popular bloke in the block," he responded casually.

I confided Bernadina's confession with him a few weeks before my father's passing. He was as surprised as me to find out about it. He promised me that it would stay between us only, but he was Marshal and would probably tell Aiko about it. Aiko didn't say anything to me, and I didn't see any body language from her to suggest otherwise.

"Did you tell Aiko about it?" I asked.

"No, should I?" Marshal responded. He scratched his head while saying it.

"Jesus, man, what were you thinking?" I asked him. When he saw the anger in my eyes, he thought better than to deny it.

"Oh, Calm down. She knew about it for a long time. Why do you think they broke the group?" he asked.

"I don't know. I wasn't there," I countered.

"Well, after your breakup with Calysta, a few years later, I don't remember if it was two or three years later, Bernadina had a huge fight with Calysta. When I asked Aiko what happened, she gave me a look as if it were all my fault. I didn't pursue it after that. It didn't affect us. We still saw both of them, but these two never talked. In the end, I put my foot down and asked them for reconciliation. Here, now you know as much as I do," he said with his casual voice.

"Now what? I don't want Berna to be angry at me," I said.

"Thanks for thinking about me. You forgot that I married the craziest one," he complained.

"It's probably her scheme all along," I protested.

"Do you think Aiko has that much time for planning with two kids running around?" he defended her.

"You are an idiot if you underestimate her that much. She could govern the whole world and still have enough time to come up with a game plan for both of us to chase our tails," I said. He wasn't sure to be proud of her or fear her.

"If you put it that way, it's possible," he said.

"What Calysta wants from me? What if I said no? Probably, I had to face Aiko's wrath again," I said with concern.

"You could always ask her if she is fine with polygamy," he said with a smile. It made me laugh, and with my laugh, he started laughing.

"Can't I just pass the ball to Aiko to talk to her and convince her otherwise?" I said desperately.

"You are still assuming that she knows. You have no idea what kind of hell she unleashed when Calysta pulled that stunt," he objected.

"So what? Sooner or later, she is going to find out, and if she finds out you knew about it and didn't tell her, then I hope your ass is comfortable to be on the couch," I replied.

"I just want to know how you feel putting me in this kind of situation." He tried to make me feel guilty.

"Your debt is being paid for sharing our conversation," I said calmly. He gave me a look that said, "Dude, that was brutal."

After that, we changed the subject. We talked about politics, religion, and the economy. We talked until it was time for him to go. As usual, I gave him that extra food in containers. It was for him to take home and share it with Aiko and his children.

Two days later, I got my answer. Aiko wouldn't do it. She called me personally to tell me that. I questioned the reason behind it, and she only answered that she didn't want to be part of this game. I didn't dare ask her if it was her plan all along.

A few days after that, Calysta called. I agreed to meet her on Thursday evening. I had to arrange with a nurse to look after my mom while I was gone.

That evening, I couldn't be more nervous.

I walked to her door and rang the bell. Only to my surprise, a teenage girl around fourteen or fifteen answered the door. I thought that I had made a mistake. I looked at the address that Calysta gave me.

"Are you Mr. Adalbert?" the girl asked.

"Yes." I looked at her, not understanding what was happening.

"Please come in. She left me a message to tell you that she got caught up in work, and she was sorry about that," she said that to me and opened the way for me to get in. There was another issue besides that that I couldn't get my head around. Why didn't she make a call to me on my cell phone that she couldn't make it?

I went in, and the first thing that I noticed were children's shoes on the ground and in the shoes rack. Then I saw two children come from the hallway and stood looking at me. The curious look they gave me made me curious as well. Whose were these children?

"Sorry, it wasn't your mom," she explained to them.

The whole world collapsed on me. I barely breathed. I took a long inhale for my starved body. How long was it that I forgot to breathe? I didn't remember. The sadness was crashing on my chest like waves after waves in a stormy sea. That strange feeling that I had been betrayed by my friends again resurfaced. Why didn't they tell me anything? How could they do this to me?

Those kids were disappointed to see me too.

A torrent of questions like water reservoir in a dam rushed out in my head and started turning some gear. When did that happen? Was she married before? There were so many other questions.

To be fair, I had no right to feel anything about what other people do with their lives, but my Hypothalamus was complaining about how to keep my blood pressure balanced and down after this revelation. My Amygdala was telling me to escape and wasn't listening to the dorsolateral prefrontal cortex, which was preaching to be reasonable. My Pineal Gland was checking to see if it made too much Melatonin for this hour of the day since it looked like I was having a nightmare.

I knew I was unreasonable. Indeed, she would meet someone else since there was nothing special about me.

"Do you want to come in?" that teenage girl asked. I was about to say no. I even opened my mouth to say it, but shame, pride, or stupidity—I couldn't decide which—didn't let me. She invited me into the hall area, where a chair and sofa were arranged for the guest. I was too annoyed to care about anything else. I didn't care how the house looked like. I was cursing myself for going to that place.

I watched the two kids march in front of me. They went to watch their program on the TV. I found a place to sit, then I noticed that I was carrying my usual shoulder bag. I didn't know that I had even brought it. I threw it on the sofa—the hell with its content.

"Do you want something to drink?" that young girl asked me.

"No. Don't worry about me. Just continue what you were doing," I answered. I needed a moment to digest what had just happened.

Those kids were watching their TV, and I was watching them. After a while, when I cooled down a bit, I realized that I couldn't blame any of my friends for any of this. First, we never talked about Calysta and what she was doing. Second, it could be that it was so typical for them now by being with Calysta and her children that it was as natural as breathing. Anyway, I wasn't angry at them anymore. I was mad at myself. What was I thinking? What was I hoping to gain by coming here? Perhaps a warm hug with lots of kisses and hoping to go further? Still and all, the whole world had a different plan for me. It made sure of it by throwing me back to reality.

That little girl looked back at me and smiled, and my heart dropped. She had her mom's eyes, hair, and feature. She even had her mom's smile. I didn't know when I started smiling, but it was there on my face. I think she took that as an invitation to come and talk to me. She came to me with those little feet of hers. She tilted her head to one side, and by doing so, she made her grin bigger and broader.

"I'm Meleta, and that's my brother, Valerio," she introduced herself and her brother.

"Nice to meet you, Meleta. I'm Agustin," I responded. She raised her little hand to give me a handshake. I raised mine to do so. She invited herself and sat beside me then looked at me. **What now?** I wondered.

"Do you know any games? Do you want to come with me and play with me?" she asked, and without waiting for my answer, she took me to her room, which she shared with her brother by the looks of it. There were all sorts of children's books, toys, and small dresses and clothes. As I was accustomed to the rules of children playing, which there isn't one, I sat down to be hosted by that little girl.

"Tea or Coffee?" she asked and raised a tiny kettle.

"Tea, please," I requested. She poured the imaginary tea in a little cup for me.

"Oh, thanks," I thanked her. I touched the teacup and removed it immediately.

"It's too hot," I explained. She had the cutest laugh.

"Sorry, I should have told you the tea was hot." She played along.

"No harm is done," I dismissed her wariness.

"Do you like to have cookies or cake with it?" she asked politely and showed me the plastic cookies and cake.

"I like my tea like this. No sweets for me. Thank you," I said. She looked at me in a way that I committed an unforgivable crime.

"You don't like cookies and cake?" she asked.

"I only like the homemade one," I explained myself.

"Oh, I made them myself this morning," she swore.

"In that case, I'll have the cookie," I requested. She put a plastic cookie on a tiny plate. That cookie was big enough to cover that tiny plate. I thanked her for her hospitality and kindness.

"Oh, wow, this tea has a coffee taste in it," I complained, which brought a huge smile to her face.

"Sorry about that. I guess my brother used this kettle for his coffee," she explained. If I had any actual thing in my mouth, I would have choked on it. It made me smile instead.

"Unforgivable!" I exclaimed.

"I know. I told him many times that he mustn't do that, but he doesn't listen. Look, he doesn't even clean after himself." She showed me her room to prove her point, but besides car toys and pants, I saw pink dresses and shoes as well.

I shook my head, and she nodded as if she agreed with me that she couldn't believe how undisciplined her brother was. She was too much for me. Her cuteness was overwhelming. I wanted to hug her and shower her with kisses, but I didn't know I was allowed to do it since her mom wasn't there to ask.

"There you are," a familiar voice said behind me. I turned back, and I saw the familiar face. She was still as beautiful as ever.

"Hi," I said, still drunk from the happiness that the little girl gave me.

"Hi, I see you already met Meleta," she said.

"Yes, she is a great host," I explained. The grin that little devil gave me could energize the whole world, let alone me.

"Sorry, I was caught up in my work, and my boss wants it to be done today," she explained.

"No worries. I understand," I said, still dazed with her mini version.

"I'll go and change fast," she said and dashed out of my sight.

I saw that the little girl was pouting. She looked like she was about to cry.

"Is there something wrong?" I asked that precious girl.

"She didn't say hi to me." She was close to crying after that confession.

"That would be weird," I confessed as well.

"What do you mean?" she looked puzzled.

"Oh, nothing. This whole time, I thought your mom had hosted me." She looked more confused. Good. That way, I wouldn't see her tears.

"Tell me. How many times do you say hi to a mirror?" I asked her. She got more muddled.

"I don't say. Why?" she asked.

"Because I think your mom thought she was looking at her image in the mirror, not Meleta. You exactly look like your mom. You even act like her," I said and added the last part so she would be proud of herself. She nodded, but she still wanted to cry.

"You know what? I'm going to cancel my night with her. We stay here and cook something to eat. I hope your cooking is as good as your baking. What do you think?" I asked her.

She was still looking petulant, but she came to me with her open arms and looped them around my neck. I smiled and hugged her back and lifted her to take her to the kitchen. She wasn't as small and lightweight as I assumed her to be.

"Do you want to show me where the kitchen is?" I asked her to take her mind out of that unfairness she felt. Her buried face on my shoulder was raised to see where we were. Then she directed me in the direction that I was headed already.

"Thank you," I said. She just nodded. In the hall, the boy was still watching his TV, and that teenage girl was on a different couch and reading some magazines. We passed them without them noticing us. I saw the kitchen and headed there. When I got there with that little girl, I looked around.

"I don't know this kitchen. Would you help me to navigate?" I asked her gently. She nodded in response. I put her down.

"First things first, what should we make?" I asked.

"I don't know," she said casually.

"What comes to your mind when I say food?" I asked again.

"Pizza," she said immediately.

"Sei il Mio prefer to," I blurted. She looked at me in puzzlement. I just smiled.

"Where do you keep the apron?" I asked her. She showed me a drawer. I went there and took it.

"Where is yours?" I asked her. She was bemused.

"Are you telling me you baked those cookies without an apron?" I asked her. She smiled back. There it was, what I was looking for.

"Do you have pizza bread?" I asked.

"I don't know," she replied.

"Wow, so you are saying we have to make the dough ourselves?" I asked. She only raised her shoulder, not knowing what to answer.

"What you two are doing?" I turned and saw it was Calysta. She was ready at last. She let her hair down on her shoulder. Her sleeveless dress was green and elegant.

"What looks like we are doing?" I asked her back.

"Are you cooking something? Wow," she asked and looked baffled.

"Yep, we are trying to make a pizza. My Sous-chef and I"—I pointed in the direction of the little girl—"we're talking about ingredients."

Calysta smiled. This was the first time I saw her genuine smile for a long time. "But we are going to be late if we stay longer." Her eyes and lips were smiling.

"Forget about that. She already prepared us desserts. I don't want to waste those freshly baked cookies and cakes." I looked at her mini version. She was all smiles like her mom.

"What were you making?" she asked offhandedly.

"Pizza," her mini version said before I could.

"Pizza?" she exclaimed. The other two came to see what this fuss was about.

"Yep." I stood my ground. I put on the apron and asked where they kept their wheat. Calysta saw that I was serious and got annoyed and, at the same time, happy. Soon, she went back to her room to change her clothing. I asked Meleta to mix the yeast with the wheat. We were in the middle of kneading the dough when Calysta finally came back to the kitchen and joined those two audiences. I was on one side of the dough, and Meleta was on the other side. Obviously, I was doing the heavy lifting and kneading, but I let her push down the dough with her tiny hands. It was just to let her make her hands dirty. She loved every part of it. After kneading, we allowed the dough to rest, and my sous-chef and I started attacking the vegetables. Calysta, watching us from the counter, got nervous and protested against letting a madman teach her daughter how to hold the knife and cut vegetables. It wasn't as if I'd let anything happen to that precious little girl. What I did was to show that her thumb must always stay behind four fingers. When it was time to show her how it was done, I put her little hand in my hand and held her hand firmly with my thumb so that it wouldn't move. I started cutting vegetables. In other words, my fingers were on the line of fire, and I only tried to involve her more in action.

Nonetheless, she was her daughter, and she had the right to set limits in danger exposure. I showed her how to cut onions and stay extra careful around onions. Those things were slippery. One moment, someone is cutting onions; before they know it, they see they are also cutting their fingers as well. Calysta didn't object when I showed her how to whisk. She delightfully whisked the sauce with some spices. The little angel wasn't so happy when her mom stopped the madman from mentoring her to cut vegetables. When we were busy whisking the sauce, I noticed that one of our audiences was gone. That teenager was gone.

My Sous chef and I started preparing the dessert. Making the dessert was messier than the pizza. While we were making the dessert, it gave the dough time to rise and kept us busy doing something. I knew my ideal dough would take longer to form, but I wanted to wrap up the cooking. I wanted to start a serious conversation with Calysta. I could have made a simple food and less time-consuming. Indeed, nothing about the daughter and her mother would be that simple. That whole time we were cooking, Calysta and I didn't talk much. She was just sitting there and only spoke when she needed to, as if she were watching a cooking show that starred her daughter and me. Finally, the dough was ready, and when I looked inside the fridge, we just found out that there wasn't enough cheese to cook with it. It was my fault that I didn't check the fridge to know if we had enough; however, it was an unforgivable crime in the eyes of that angel. Calysta suggested going and buying some or just ordering one pizza, but I insisted there was a way around it. We could have made the pizza pocket version of it. It wasn't as good, but it was a solution. Then we made it that way. The compromise made pizza better.

Meleta liked that a lot. Her fruit of hard work was admired by her mom and her archenemy, her brother. I took only a piece and let the kids have their fill. The dessert was delicious as a well, which, if they were allowed to, they would have finished it that night. I never asked the name of that teenage girl, and when I asked Calysta, she told me that she was their babysitter. I forgot what her name was again in here. That meal ended on a good note. The kids were happy, specially Meleta, who got to be involved in the making of it.

I was planning to say good night and go back home, but Calysta insisted that I should stay. She wanted to talk to me that night, but she couldn't do it in front of her kids. However, she was glad that her daughter and I bonded fast. Cooking with that kid was like a surreal dream, but it was time to wake up from that fantasy.

After the kids went to bed, I sat across her. The mood changed in a matter of seconds. It was all business. I wanted some answers, and the person who sat across from me had all the answers. She changed my path, but before that, I had to call home and see how my mom was doing and tell the nurse that I wasn't sure when I would be back. It wasn't supposed to go this way, but since when did everything go as it had always been planned?

It took me a while to talk to the nurse, and after thanking and apologizing to her, we ended the call.

I was ready to have a long and earnest conversation.

"How was your mom?" she asked softly.

"Same as this morning." The first shot was fired. She nodded and tried to keep herself calm. The way she looked down was an indication of her sorrow and anger. She was making her body smaller to protect herself.

"I'm sorry to hear that," she explained and still made herself smaller. I felt terrible doing this to her, but one part of me would never be the same.

"You wanted to talk," I said. I didn't put it in question. I just wanted to get over whatever she wanted to say.

"Do you want something to drink?" she asked.

"I'm driving," I explained. She nodded and didn't dare to look at my eyes directly.

"You are good with kids," she said, but to me, it sounded like she was convincing herself.

"What do you want, Calysta?" I asked impatiently.

"Nothing," she said. I saw her fingers pinching her dress.

I didn't say anything more. I just watched her. That was my way of saying that "I won't waste my breath on you." I guess she had a speech planned in her head, but it didn't go the way she wanted it to. The silence between us was inviting more silence.

"Why did you do it?" I asked and cut the chase before she could say something irrelevant.

"Do what?" she asked. I was getting furious. I didn't like what she was doing. I didn't like that version of myself. The playful boy inside me had to get quiet if he didn't want to get hurt like before. The one that hurt him was just sitting across from him. However, the hellhound inside me was without a leash.

I stood up to leave. I've had it with her. To hell with whatever her answer was. I thought I could live without knowing why.

"Agustin, please," she begged me to stay, but I was moving with determination.

"I'll tell you." She gave in. I went back but didn't sit. I just stood behind the sofa. There were tears in her eyes—those eyes that I adored for so long. She made me feel much worse. My blood was boiling. The more I saw the tears, the more I wanted to cave in the wall with my punch. She was still merciless with her tears. There was a part inside me that remembered the promise I made to her father.

"Could you leave me alone for a while?" I requested and tried not to yell at her. I don't know what I was thinking at that moment, but I knew if I left that night, I wouldn't be able to see her again. From there, it would just get worse.

"If you don't leave now, there won't be anyone in this world that can convince me to see you again," I said coldly to her, and that wasn't an empty threat. Somehow, I knew that I would have done it. There was no doubt.

She looked at me with tearful eyes. Those eyes were still potent enough to cure and poison a whole country. I looked away. I wasn't as strong as I thought.

She gracefully rose and left. The answer she would have given me wouldn't be enough. I just realized what a tremendous gift I gave her. She would never understand that simple act of asking her not to be there wasn't because I was about to hurt her physically. It was because there wasn't any answer in the world to satisfy me. I would have brushed it off quickly by an angry response, or worse, instead of listening to what she said, I would have compared it to my feeling.

I lay down on the sofa. I was tired of this stupid game. I was too old to care what a teenage Calysta thought about me. She was the same as any other girl. I closed my eyes to breathe and think. I was hurt, and my thought went to my mother. At that moment, I felt like a scared kid who wanted to be hugged. Maybe my dad knew what to do. I wished he had been there to help me. Now I was playing the grown-up games—being angry at every small thing, finishing first at the line being more important, not enjoying the game, and lots of silly things to add to that list.

I don't know how, but I slept on that sofa, and the only reason I woke up was that I felt uncomfortable lying there. I sat up, and my joints were protesting. I looked at the watch, and it was too late to drive home. Plus, if I left, who would lock the door behind me? I couldn't sleep on that couch, so I slowly went to Calysta's bedroom and knocked on her door. It took her a while to come to the door. She opened the door a little to see who it was. I thought she probably closed the door because of me; otherwise, there was no need to do so. She was wearing a nightgown with a robe. She bundled herself up in that robe.

"I can't sleep on that couch. Can I come in sleep there with you?" I asked. There was no sexual attraction motive, and I didn't want to leave before talking with her. However, my odd request woke her up completely. Her eyes, from being sleepy, turned to a surprised look.

"What?" she asked in a hissing voice.

"Don't worry. There is no intention behind it. I just want to talk to you before I leave, maybe in the morning. Can I?" I asked shamelessly. She didn't know what to do with this crazy guy. It was a Western movie stand-up between us in the middle of the night at her bedroom door—one who was spoiled to his comfortable sleep and the other for honor and dignity.

"I'll go and sleep on the couch," she said at last and opened the door for me.

"Is this how much you trust me? No surprise that you forgot how much my words carry," I said with a tone of bitterness, but I went inside and lay down on her bed. Memories from the past that had been ignored for my sanity rushed in. Involuntarily, a smile formed on my sour face. It was a different time and different people. She was still at the door and second-guessing her decision, not for the comfort though. She knew well enough that if I say something, I stand by it. That was one of the reasons why she loved me. She told me that herself. After some indecisiveness, she gave in and came to bed. She was still shy about it and didn't want to offend me any further. She lay down as far from me as she could.

"I'm still a virgin," I said casually. I turned my head to her to see her reaction. Her reaction was hilarious and heartbreaking. "However, I slept with many girls. It all started with a girl that I met at the university. Since I was leaving the city and that country, I found it unfair to abuse her like that. She was the sweetest and extremely fragile being that I had ever met. I won't tell you why she was like that. It is her story to tell if she wants to. After leaving her, I decided to be more outgoing and started talking to different kinds of people. Poor, rich, beautiful, or ugly, it didn't matter. I went and started talking to them. I wanted to get rid of that shyness and be more forward. Like anything I do in life, which you know . . . you know very well, I put aside a time for that practice. Sometimes I ended up talking to stunning girls and wondered if I could convince them to sleep with me. In the beginning, I couldn't, but then eventually, I succeeded but never went through with it. It wasn't as if I was putting anything on the pedestal. I just couldn't do it. They all reminded me of you and that girl." I looked in her direction, and I bet that she wondered who that girl was rather than listening to the story. "It made me question my feelings toward all this process. I was holding on to the innocent time I had. I was afraid of what would come after it—tedium and monotony of doing the same action over and over for the rest of my life. Since I wasn't preaching it to anyone and sometimes lied about my virginity to shut some people up, I was fine with it. It was the discipline I was looking for, like being an alcoholic, putting a glass of whiskey on my lips but never drinking it. Smelling the ice cream but never eating it. Sex was like that for me. However, I didn't like the loneliness that came with that kind of attitude. That would be the reason why I slept with so many girls but didn't go through with it," I finished. That whole time, I looked at the ceiling, not at her. I looked at her and saw I didn't put her to sleep. "Aiko thinks that I changed too much. She already cast judgment on me. She thinks that I don't have any moral ground. Bernadina either doesn't care or sees it as a compromise. Marshal, you know how he is. However, I never told them any of this. I don't know why I didn't. I found it kind of weird and unnatural. Maybe I was afraid of seeing the disappointment in the eyes of Marshal. Maybe I just didn't care about Berna or Aiko since they washed their hands and cast a judgment on me without knowing the whole truth. What do you think? Can you tell the reason behind my actions? I don't know. I'm not dependent on them like before, but I do know that I'm much happier than those years without them," I finished my thought. When I looked back at her, her eyes were full of tears. She turned her face when I looked at her and her teary eyes.

She imitated me and looked at the ceiling. I looked back to the ceiling as well.

"It was never my intention to put you through this. I thought that I was doing the right thing when I decided to break up with you. I was miserable after my father's passing, and there you were trying to help me, and I rewarded you back that way," she said and told me the whole story from the school to the park.

"I did regret it immediately after you left, but either you didn't hear me or just ignored me. After a while, I thought you had enough of me for all those crying. I thought it would be a good idea for you to have a break from me. Then I found out that you never told them that I was the one who broke up with you. I planned to talk to you about it in school, but you never showed up again. You were much smarter than me, so I thought you knew what you were doing, and I went with it. Months later, I found out why you didn't show up. Aiko told me about it, and I felt worse than ever. They didn't do it on malice. They thought that I wouldn't be able to do such a thing to someone like you. Maybe they were right. Maybe they weren't. But I was glad to have them by my side. They helped me a lot during those days. In the end, it wouldn't be possible without your actions. You took the heat and gossip while I was receiving all the sympathy. You have no idea how I felt for a long time. The heavy conscience of what I did to you was always there. I'm not just telling you this for the sake of saying it. I wasn't doing well in college. I thought I passed the sadness in my life, but wherever I went, the thought of you was always there. I dated many other boys, but I had to bring down my standard to be able to talk to them. Some treated me horribly. Some just wanted to use me. Some of them gave promises that had never been fulfilled. At one point, I felt so alone that it put me on edge. I wasn't doing well at all. Then my depression started. It made me do things that I never knew I was capable of. One night I partied too hard and blacked out. I don't know what happened that night, but something happened that changed my life and path. Meleta and Valerio were the results. Agustin, they saved me. They came at a time that I was in the worst moment in my life. Many times, the thought of abortion or putting them for adoption came to me. Likely, they would be born after my graduation. I'm glad that I didn't go through with it. They forced me to get my act together. Thinking about them, not myself, changed my path. I graduated, and a few weeks later, they were born. My mom and Aiko helped me a lot. I almost broke the group again. One day when the memories overwhelmed me, I told Bernadina what went down that day. Bernadina started a big fight and called me names. The worst part was when she confessed her feelings toward you." She looked at me, and I saw in the corner of my eyes that she was looking for something, but she couldn't find it. She continued, "I felt worse. I mean, I saw girls that were bragging about how they slept with their best friends' boyfriend, and here I was. Not only did I take away her chance to be with you, I also poisoned her mind to take my side. The slap she gave me, the spit she threw at me, I can still feel them on my face. For a long time, we didn't see eye to eye. I wanted to apologize to her, but she never wanted to be in the same place as I was. I think it was because of Aiko forcing her to talk to me again." She was saying it with her broken voice. She was sobbing the whole time when she was telling me that story. "Then one day, out of boredom, I turned on the TV, and there you were. You were talking to the host and that pop star." She stopped talking. She was trying to figure out how to proceed. After a while, she continued, "The look you had, the boyish charm, the way you were talking, the way you handled the host, it opened a closed door that has been shut for many years. It is not an exaggeration to say that I didn't know what to do." The whimper was in her voice as she was telling me the story. "How you became so different yet still stay the same. That flirtation with that pop star . . ." She didn't know how to say what she was thinking without offending me. To tell me how proud she was to find me so confident and, at the same time, angry that I was doing it with someone else. To tell me the lingering feeling she still had. She was concerned about the image she would have in my eyes. She thought she wasn't allowed to be jealous. She continued, "Then you sang that song." Her weeping continued. She told me she didn't know what she was supposed to do after that song. "You told the whole world that you still loved me." Her weeping continued, but she didn't say anything for a few minutes. When she didn't hear anything from me, she continued, "Now I realize you may be singing about the girl you met in college, not me . . ." She waited for the confirmation or denial, but I gave her none. *The torture continues*, I thought that was what she thought. "After that show, I didn't know what to think. The question that you like to hear my voice again? was haunting me every second. Then I realized that I had no way to contact you if I wanted to. Marshal, on the other hand, had a connection in university, so he called you first." She was arriving at the part that she didn't feel comfortable at all, but she continued, "Aiko told me that you are meeting with them, and there was no mention of me. They decided it would be best that I won't show up at first. The plan was to warm you up to the idea of seeing me again. The only thing was that I had to wait." She paused again to gather her thoughts. "They said they understand how I feel, but how could they? They weren't me. They didn't know what went down between you and me. I wondered if you held a grudge over me or not, even though it happened many years ago. Anyway, I agreed that I should stay away." Her tearful eyes were looking for sympathy that wasn't there. I was continuously looking at the ceiling. It was as if I found a beautiful painting up there while there was nothing at all. "I thought I could do it, but when the day was getting closer, I was beside myself. I couldn't do anything. Many times, I did many silly things that I didn't know I was doing. I misplaced my toothbrush in the fridge. I was making too many mistakes at work. There was that guy, Novak, the one you met, that insistently asked me out. I thought in order to think about something else or somebody else, I accepted his request. I put it in the same day you were meeting with the others. The thing is, I chose a restaurant close to the place you were meeting. I don't know what I was thinking that I thought it was a good idea to do that, but that desire to see you again, to hear your voice again made me do stupid things that I thought were smart. I was sitting outside with my date, and the only person I wasn't looking at was him. My eyes were watching across the street to where you were. Novak noticed this and wanted to know why I was looking there. First, I denied it, but after catching me looking across the street a few times, I told him that my friends were sitting there. Things got worse from there. Now he wanted to impress me by introducing himself to my friends, and you know the rest. Maybe I wanted him to do that and was happy he did it. After that fiasco, after everyone stopped yelling at me, only then did I realize how selfish I've been. I undermined their requests by that silly excuse. That it was Novak's fault, not mine. I couldn't feel worse than that. I spoke too soon for that. I discovered weeks later about your parents and what you were hiding all that time. I took away the chance to unburden yourself. Then another realization hit me, the reason I broke up with you years ago was that you made me feel bad about myself. Feeling inadequate to be with you was unbearable. The worse part was that I realized that and chose an easy way out instead of improving myself. My thoughts weren't about how to redeem myself. Instead, I wondered if I wanted to have that constant guilty feeling again. In the past, I was tired of feeling at fault all the time. Being with you, not being with you, I'll get punished for it," she said at last. She was looking for something to comfort her, but there was nothing.

What could I say or do to help her? Anyway, I did nothing. Now and then, I looked at Calysta and then looked back to the ceiling. "Your story is the same as those people who worked hard for nothing. There is one kind who plants something in the ground but never eats the result of what they did. There is the other kind who knows but not doing anything. What is the benefit of having knowledge and not using it? Wouldn't it be the same as the person who doesn't know at all? You realized your shortcoming, but what did you do about it? Just self-pity or blame everyone for what you are," I told her without any filter. It only broke her heart more. She wanted to leave the bed, but she came with the realization again that it only proved my points. Later, she admitted that she felt that she would lose me forever if she left the bed that night. I, on the other hand, lay back and stoned my heart to her cries. I slept a few minutes later. She slept after crying her eyes out in silence. The disheveled hair and the traces of tears on her face made her look like an innocent child who had been disciplined by her parents.

The night passed, and the day replaced it. When I woke up, the first thing that I saw was Calysta's face. Her hair was stuck to her face where there were tears from last night. I gently removed her hair from her face, and she showed me her protest by moving her head. Her eyes were still closed. I rose from the bed and made sure not to wake her up. I looked back to where she was lying down. Nothing in the world could soften my heart the way she did. All that animosity inside me melted away. I didn't want to leave her like that or at least wait to say goodbye to her. I decided on the latter. I went to her kitchen to prepare something for breakfast while waiting for her to wake up.

I looked at the fridge and saw the cereal box and cornflakes on top of it; inside of it were some eggs, sausage, butter, and milk. I sighed and began making breakfast. I found some biscuits and the location of the salt and pepper. I threw the sausage in a pan and started making a sizzling sound. Then I melted the butter in a different pan and stirred it with flour. I cooked the flour just enough to change the color. I whisked the milk, salt, and pepper. I continued doing so until I got my desired thickness.

Since I didn't know how they liked the eggs, I made them all the same. I thought that way there won't be any fighting. I put the biscuit on each plate. On top of it, I put the crumbled sausage and covered it with fried egg. The milk gravy went on top of the fried egg, and I sprinkled it with some cheese. Then to help my guilty conscience for all those fatty breakfasts, I served them with some sliced fruit. The coffee was getting ready, and the kettle was boiling as well. I saw the mini Calysta walk into the kitchen with her brother. While she was rubbing her eyes and yawning, she asked me what was happening and where her mom was. I couldn't help myself not to tease her.

"Your mom said that I'll be taking care of you until next year. She said she'll be back as soon as she can."

"What?" she asked and demanded an answer.

"Well, she wanted to tell you yesterday, but she couldn't. She told me to tell you first thing in the morning, and I promised her that I'd do it." I also acted like everything was fine. I stole a look from her and saw that she was about to cry. I was about to disclaim what I said when Calysta walked in and asked what was going on. The mini version jumped to the big version and showed me her tongue.

"You didn't have to go through all that trouble. They usually eat cereal for breakfast," she said. I couldn't decide whether it was her "Thank you" or she was implying that "This is my house and my rules. I feed them the way I like to." That was important for me. One would flatter my heart. The other one would boil my blood. To put my mind at ease, I asked her what she meant.

"Oh, I didn't mean any offense. I only meant that they would be fine with either," she explained. It sounded like last night's conversation was forgotten and never happened. Either she acted fine in front of her kids or she simply tried to forget that last night ever happened.

We sat down and started eating breakfast, except for the little boy who looked at me with hatred. I didn't have to be a body language expert to see he didn't like me. I didn't try to impress him or acknowledge his hatred until he knew what it meant, so what I did was ignore him. I knew that infuriated him and made him hate me more, but I didn't care.

"Mom, can I have the cereal?" he asked her mom. Calysta looked at me apologetically.

"Oh, don't worry. I'll take that home. I'll give it to my mom's nurse," I said calmly. "I'll just make for three in the future," I promised. The look he gave me was legendary. Calysta was speechless. She was happy to hear that I would continue seeing her, and she was sad that her son, unlike her daughter, didn't like me.

"Really?" she asked me nonetheless. The big smile on her face, the eyes that were made to see only happiness shone like a sun. My heart was too weak to say no to her, but it wasn't as reckless as before. I only nodded. I knew my voice would betray me, and because of that, I only nodded. Her smile got bigger, if that was possible.

"Can I come and visit your mom?" she asked immediately. She wasn't taking any prisoners. I smiled from inside but kept my stern face on.

"Do you really want to see her like that? She isn't like before. I don't think she even remembers you." I tried to change her mind or set her expectations low. However, she didn't budge, and she wanted to see her. I gave in.

After breakfast, I drove home. She followed me by her car.

After apologizing to the nurse for being late and not showing up last night, I offered the breakfast I made that morning. She was glad to have such breakfast and went to the kitchen to warm it up a bit. I went in to see how my mom was doing. The TV wasn't on, so I assumed she was still sleeping. I walked in, and I saw she was looking at the window.

"Do you want to go out?" I asked.

"Who are you?" she asked.

"A nurse," I replied. She looked at me and then looked at the window again. What was the point of telling her that I was her son when she couldn't tell? It would only add more stress to her for not remembering me. Her comfort eclipsed mine.

"Do you want me to read a story for you?" I asked. She shook her head.

"Are you hungry?" I asked. She shook her head again.

"Do you want me to play for you?" I asked again, but her answer was the same.

"Do you want me to brush your hair? It will make you feel better," I asked. Her answer was the same.

"Do you want me to massage your head?" I asked, and still, she refused.

"Do you want to watch a video from your son?" I asked. This time, her head turned around and nodded. I put on the VHS and turned on the TV and watched the movie with new eyes. Calysta walked in with her children and looked in my direction. She was looking for permission, which I denied. I didn't want to disrupt my mom when she was watching her TV. She didn't like anyone to disturb her when she watched her child on another side of the world, which was almost always. She nodded to show her understanding.

I kissed her forehead. Like always, she looked at me to see recognition, but when she couldn't, she turned her attention to the TV. I left her there and went to the other room.

"Is she all right?" Calysta asked.

"She is. She doesn't like anyone to disturb her when she is watching her TV," I explained.

"I understand," she empathized.

"Thank you," I said. "Do you want to see the rest of the house? Marshal's children made a renovation."

She agreed to come with me. I showed her the artistic room where drawing and painting were on the walls. I didn't go there much since my father wasn't there to watch me drawing on his wall. I showed her my old bedroom, which my parents left the same. I showed her my office where I ran my companies from this side of the ocean. I showed her the kitchen and the basement. Except for a few modifications since the last time she saw it, the house stayed the same. She didn't have to tell me how sad she was. I could see it in her eyes.

"Do you want to draw on the wall in that room?" I asked Meleta. She didn't need me to tell her twice. She ran to that room to leave her masterpiece. Calysta's son stood behind. He didn't like me to tell him to go and have fun. He stood behind to protect his mom from me. We went to the hall and sat.

"Now I know why you are angry at me," she said out of the blue. I was too tired to be angry. I could guess what she thought. She thought that I was mad at her because of my mom. Maybe it was partially true, but she missed the mark. All the trouble she made in the past and the things that I had to go through were missing in her logic. It was my choice to do that for her, but the price was too high. I think at that time, I missed the mark as well. The happiness I had in my mind for her was different than hers.

"I stole your time with your mom," she explained. It wasn't true. At one point in my life, I had to move on and have my own life, and the outcome could be the same. However, my feelings didn't care about logic. My emotions were looking for a person to blame for my inadequacy. She wanted me to deny it, but I didn't.

"I have to go and make some calls and review some projects. Make yourself at home." I stood up to leave.

"Do you want me to leave?" she asked.

I looked at her. Was it manipulation? Did she want me to tell her to go so that she could break free of her guilty feeling? She would get angry feelings toward me; therefore, whatever she did in the past, in her mind, would be justified.

"You could watch all the tapes that I made if you are interested," I said. I didn't want to tell her directly to stay, so I requested that way.

"You don't mind?" she asked, but the happiness was dancing in her eyes.

"Yeah. Everyone saw it. I don't see why you can't," I responded. I saw her happiness dimmed. If I just nodded, she would still be happy. That lingering and tortuous soul of mine was set out to see pain, and happiness and merriment were poison to its nature. After showing her where the tapes were, I went to the office room.

After a few phone calls and reviewing the process and cost of operation and the research development, I went down to check on my mom.

The movie she was watching ended, and like always, she didn't tell anyone to change it. She was looking at the window, watching birds and trees. I went to her, and as I have been trained by nurses and doctors, I started massaging her legs and arms. I readjusted her pillow and tried to put her in the wheelchair so that I could take her out for a walk.

"What is wrong with her?" the mini Calysta asked. Such an innocent question to ask, but what was the correct answer for it? Should I explain to her my mom's medical condition by those medical names? Or should I explain to her level of knowledge?

"There isn't anything wrong with her. We just changed our roles," I explained to her. I thought that was as good as any since she couldn't understand the full extent of it.

"Sorry, I don't know how she snuck away from me," the bigger Calysta said.

"Don't worry. I was explaining to her my mom's condition," I replied.

My mom wasn't listening to our conversation, so she missed the part I called her my mom. Her mind was somewhere else.

"But I don't understand," the mini Calysta protested.

"Come here," I asked her. She came with her tiny feet and taller attitude.

"When you were this size"—I demonstrated by my hand the diminutive size she was when she was born—"who took care of you?"

"Myself," she proudly declared with a smirk on top of it. It made me and her mom smile as well.

"Well, for me, it was different. When I was that size, my mom helped me to grow up. Now that she is at this age, I'm helping her to grow older and get more rest," I explained.

"Is my mom going to be like that?" she asked with worrying eyes. Her mom pulled her back to herself to protect her from my response.

I remembered a poem that my colleague told me once:

>   These two days of my life proceeded,
>
>   Like flowing water to the river and wind to a meadow.
>
>   I've never worried about these two days,
>
>   The day that hasn't come yet
>
>   And the day that is my past.

"It isn't time for you to worry about the future. Why don't you enjoy your time with your mom for now?" I replied.

"My mom won't be like that," she said stubbornly. I didn't take it personally, but Calysta shook her gently to make her quiet.

"I love her the same. It hasn't changed by her age or condition," I said gently.

I didn't convince her. She had a set of rules in her head. One of them was that her mom wouldn't get old or sick.

I pushed my mom's wheelchair, and it started moving. Even though I was as gentle as I tried to be, she held the wheelchair's armrest firmly, with one hand pushing her forward and another I put on her shoulder to reassure her that everything would be fine.

"We are going outside a bit. Do you want to come with us?" I asked her. She looked at her daughter and wondered if it was all right to bring her.

"You can bring your children. We are going to the nearby park," I suggested.

"Are you sure?" Calysta asked, but Meleta was already impatient to go there.

"I think someone is coming with us, and she doesn't care if you are coming or not," I responded. I smiled at the little devil. She smiled at her daughter as well.

"Let me see if Valerio is coming as well," she said and left us to ask him. She left the little devil with us.

"Do you want to help me?" I asked her and showed her if she was willing to push the wheelchair. She nodded her head.

"What a brave girl, don't you agree?" I asked my mom. She didn't know what was happening. She just went with whatever we did. That brave little kid came behind the wheelchair, and with my help, we pushed the wheelchair forward. Calysta and her son met us in the hall.

I talked to the nurse and thanked her for the troubles. She left the house with us. She went in another direction. The weather was nice and sunny. We wheeled my mom slowly on the sidewalk. The birds were chirping. Meleta was walking in front of me and pushing my mom. Calysta was on one side of me and her son on the other side. We walked down the street in unison. It didn't take us much to arrive at the nearby park. I parked the wheelchair close to the nearest bench. Meleta and Valerio ran off to the playground and started playing with other kids. My mom was in her wheelchair and watched them playing. She watched them in silence.

Calysta and I sat on a bench close to my mom. A street musician was playing some songs on his guitar. The parents were watching their kids closely. With their explosive energy, the kids were climbing everything, and the things they couldn't climb, they wrestled with.

"How do you feel?" Calysta asked me.

"It is much better than before. Thank you for asking," I replied.

"I hate sitting on a bench. I remembered it as if it happened yesterday," she said with deep sadness.

I looked at her. Now that I know the reason behind our breakup wasn't that grandiose and it was because of her insecurity and because she mistakenly thought it was for my benefit, I felt empty about the whole ordeal. All those pains were for nothing.

"I need to drink to oblivion. The naiveté of me who thought being in love was an easy thing never saw the big wave of problems that it brought with itself," I said to no one. It was just a reflection on myself. We were young and stupid. I couldn't judge her for what she did in the past with a middle-aged me. It wasn't fair for her, so I told her that.

"Thank you," she responded.

I just nodded. I looked at the children play. The thought of teaching them what love was, was a joke. I wasn't sure what I felt for Calysta was love. Perhaps it was just an attraction.

What was love? No one seemed to know the answer. I looked at my mother. She was watching the children play. Maybe she knew, but how could she tell me now? Where could I learn about love when there wasn't a teacher to teach me?

"Do you know what love is?" I asked Calysta. She looked at me in a way that only meant that she expected preaching from me.

"I truly do not know," I told her honestly. I looked at the playground. Maybe the children knew, but would their definition make sense to the grown-ups? Perhaps it was as easy as playing in that area. Like mathematics problems, the answer was often easy, but it depended on the understanding of the questions in the first place. If so, what part of the question was confusing for me?

"I don't know what you mean," she replied at last. Maybe it was evident to her. Was I blind to the answer?

"Have you experienced love?" I asked her again. She gave me a look as if to ask where I was going by that question. Was I about to tell her that she never loved me?

"Yes?" she said suspiciously.

"Can you tell me when and who if you can?" I asked her.

"I love my children, my parents, and my friends," she told me. I thought she didn't understand my question. Maybe the answer was that easy. Maybe I was overthinking it. However, something inside me told me that was not it. I should have solved it by now, but why do I feel like I didn't understand it? Did I love my mom? I looked at her in the wheelchair. I knew I would do anything for her, and it wasn't an exaggerated statement.

Nonetheless, I knew that wasn't the definition. Maybe Calysta thought that doing anything for a person that isn't herself would mean love. Was she wrong? Or was I wrong?

"Are you all right?" she asked me. I just nodded but was still deep in thought. Some questions seemed easy to answer, but the definition was complex.

For example, 1 + 1 = 2. Anyone who had basic mathematical training could answer that, but the problem starts when they ask them to define each part. A trained mathematician would explain each part by proving it. First, they would describe what those numbers are and what rules they should follow. For example, if 1 were defined as equal to 2, then that equation would be wrong. Since the definition of 1 has been changed to 2, the equation should be read as 1 + 1 = 4. After understanding what those numbers are and what set rules they must follow, another problem arises. What is that plus sign? What is that equal sign? Each one must get clear definitions. It took a lifetime for Bertrand Russell to define the basics of mathematics, yet he couldn't do it all. The more he went for the basic, the crazier it got.

It brings me to this point. I'm trying to define love. Would I be able to answer that question ever?

"What are you thinking? I see you are in deep thinking," Calysta said with concern. I looked at her and saw the damage I had inflicted on her for the first time. Now I could see what I couldn't before. The curtain was pulled away. She wasn't built to be stern at. Plant a red rose in the middle of winter, and it dies. Put an evergreen tree in the same place, and it passes the winter without any problem. Should a red rose be abashed for being a rose in winter and summer? Wouldn't it be the foolishness of the gardener who expects too much from that rose? I was the foolish one the whole time. I disregarded her delicacy. Now she second-guesses whatever I tell her; she would try her utmost to decipher every word that would come out of my mouth.

"It isn't about what you said. I already moved on and was thinking about something else," I clarified.

My father didn't give me much advice. I didn't understand the reason behind it at first, but later in life, I understood. He gave me a few pieces of advice so that I could treasure and remember them. One of his advice was to have generosity and clemency with friends and toleration and forbearance with the enemy.

Which one was Calysta to me? Was she a friend or an enemy? It didn't matter because I didn't follow my father's advice. He wasn't all talk. Even though my friends hurt his family, he had that much wisdom not to bear any grudge against them. He opened his arms to them and accepted them when they came back to my life again.

"Come here," I asked Calysta and showed her the place next to me.

"Why?" she asked with wary eyes. I smiled to show that there wasn't any malicious intention behind my invitation. She was still hesitant. Didn't I sleep with her last night without any incident? It was an invitation, not a threat. I didn't want to insist on it.

Instead of looking at her eyes, I looked away and watched the playground. My right arm, as a habit, was still stretched on the back of the bench. If she wanted to come closer to me, she could do it on her time. She was like a scared bird, and anyone with knowledge about birds knew that they shouldn't grab the bird and hold it forcefully. That way, the person loses the trust of the bird altogether. It was my responsibility to adjust to her timing, not the other way around.

I looked at the other parents. Some of them were watching the kids from afar. Some of them were more involved in their kids' play. Some were watching at the edge of the playground. The kids were experimenting with each piece of equipment. They used the seesaw. They played it for a while and moved on to the merry-go-round, then to the swing set, and finally, to the climber playset. From there, they went back to the seesaw and repeated the cycle. They played and burned that colossal energy inside of them. I looked at my mom. I was wondering what she was thinking at that moment. Then I felt Calysta on my right side. Her warmth and delicate body touched mine. After so many years of being separated from her, she finally came back to me. Maybe we broke up for nothing, but I learned a lot during that separation. I met a lot of people, aside from DNA and fingerprints, who also had different personalities. They all desired a friendship, a companion, or a listener to their stories. All in all, we needed each other, and I needed her the most.

I saw a drop of tears from my mom's eyes. She was still looking at the playground. I touched her hand gently to have her attention. She looked at me with teary eyes.

"Is everything all right?" I asked her. She looked at me and back to the playground.

"I wish he never met her. I wish he never fell in love with her. He isn't here because of that despicable and wretched girl," my mom said with a tremor in her voice.

"Who?" I asked, knowing deep down who she was talking about, but I held on to that little hope that she was talking about an old lover or someone else, not me.

"My son. My beautiful and kind baby. He was so happy before he met her. She broke his heart and almost killed him. He left us and never came back," she said with a tone of sadness that broke my heart all over again. My selfishness and immaturity hurt her deeply. I thought I did my diligence by just making some videos about my life, not knowing that by each one of them, I was agonizing and tormenting her.

On my right side, I noticed that Calysta was crying again. She was trembling under my arm. Instead of seeing my foolishness, she took it personally. I felt trapped between them. Which one to comfort first? I pressed Calysta closer to my side, and again, I touched my mom's hand. My mom looked at me with her tearful eyes.

"I know wherever your son is, his feelings for you never changed. He always thinks about you, and you have a special place in his heart. I hope you forgive his foolishness and naivety," I said with difficulty. I don't know how I held it together.

I kissed Calysta's top head. None of this would have happened if I didn't blow it out of proportion for a measly conflict. Weren't all of us wishing we were somehow wiser when we were younger?

"It goes the same for you too," I told Calysta as well. She hid her face behind her hands and rested it on my chest. She was shaking like a leaf.

We sat there and watched the joyful children play with sad and weepy eyes.

The time passed.

Meleta and Valerio came back with big smiles on their faces.

"I'm hungry," Meleta said. Calysta nodded her head in affirmation and looked back to me to get permission to feed her children.

"I think my mom is hungry as well," I told her, and we started heading back home to cook something. Meleta resumed her position in front of me and started pushing mom. Valerio walked beside her mom. We didn't go that far when Meleta protested that she was too tired to walk. She was looking at her mom for lifting.

"Do you want me to carry her?" I asked Calysta. She nodded. I picked her up and let Calysta push my mom's wheelchair. She was hesitant to touch the wheelchair of a broken heart mother, but she understood the situation. She wouldn't be able to carry her daughter far before she got tired too. She reluctantly took the handle and started pushing her. We didn't go much farther when Valerio wanted to be lifted as well. Since Meleta was in my hand and I was beginning to feel her weight, I couldn't give the same offer. Calysta's hands were full, so she couldn't do anything either.

"Honey, we are almost home. Can you walk a little bit more?" she was asking him like a coach asking her pupil to carry on a little bit more. It only brought more protest on his part. He insisted that he couldn't walk another step. There weren't any Taxis passing through either.

"Would you be so kind as to let him sit on your lap for a while? We are almost close to your home," I asked my mom. She looked at me and Meleta in my hand. She then looked at Valerio and nodded. Her mom helped him to sit on my mom's lap. My mom held him securely. After that, we started moving again. In the corner of my eyes, I saw that my mom was brushing Valerio's hair gently. She didn't know whose child it was; nonetheless, she cared for him as her own. There were traces of smiles on her face. We walked the rest of the way in silence.

As soon as we arrived home, Meleta wanted to be on the ground and asked her mom to take her to the bathroom. Valerio came down from my mom's lap and followed his mother and sister. I saw my mom stretched her hand to hold Valerio for a little longer. I held her hand to mine and kissed them both. She looked at me again without knowing me.

"Do you want anything? Water? Food? Anything?" I asked her. She looked at me and touched my face with a caress. She had done it sometimes, but she would forget about it the next hour or day.

"Can you help me a little bit? Put your arms around my neck so that I can lift you," I asked her with care. She nodded her head and put her arms around my neck.

"I'm going to put one of my hands in here"—I showed under her knees—"and the other one in here." I showed her back. She nodded to show me she understood. "All right, I'm going to lift you," I informed her. She didn't have much strength in her, but I felt a little tension she put around my neck. I lifted her gently. Her feathered weight felt like nothing on my hand.

"I'm going to take you to your bedroom to rest," I told her our destination, so if she had any other plan in her mind, she would be able to tell me.

"Could you please take me to my son's room?" she asked. Sometimes she asked for that, and I obliged. After taking her there and laying her down on the bed, I asked her if she wanted anything else. She shook her head and embraced my old blanket.

After kissing her forehead, I went down to make lunch for nine people.

I went to the kitchen and took a deep breath and started cooking. I mixed dried rosemary, garlic powder, pepper, and seasoned salt.

I rubbed that over the chicken. Then I placed it in an ungreased baking pan. I covered and baked it for one and a half hours. I put the timer on for that.

Calysta walked into the kitchen with her children. She looked so apologetic.

"I think it is time for us to leave," she said with a sad tone.

"I'm cooking for everyone. The lunch will be ready in a few hours," I said, hiding the sadness that was creeping in.

"I don't want to be more of a problem as it is," she said. The tight lips and her narrow eyes were telling me another story. She was telling me to convince her otherwise.

"My mom likes Valerio a lot, and I need my Sous-chef here," I said and pointed at Meleta. She smiled and looked at her mom to see if she could stay. She couldn't say no to those little eyes, as I couldn't say no to her.

"Are you sure we are not making a problem here?" she asked as a courtesy. I smiled and nodded. I couldn't speak more. I couldn't give a quick-witted answer to hide behind it.

While we waited for the chicken to get ready, I started cutting mushrooms, celery, carrots, onions, and pepper. I handed my Sous-chef a large bowl with flour and salt and told her to mix it up. After that, I showed her how to beat eggs and let her do the beating. She was a blessing at that moment in my life. She made me think about something else. To teach her something that I learned in my journey in life, to satisfy those always curious eyes. I told her to make a well inside that mix and then add the beaten eggs, milk, and oil into that well. She did it happily. I told her to stir that together to form a dough. The timer went off. I drained the chicken and put aside that skimmed fat for later. I let the chicken cool down. Meanwhile, I helped my Sous-chef to knead the dough. I poured that fat into a Dutch oven and let it boil.

After we finished the kneading, I added the vegetables to that broth and let it simmer for half an hour. The little angel and I started making the noodle and deboning the chicken. The amount of residue on her little nose made her cute and lovely. While we were doing this, her mom was watching me to not do something stupid again. Valerio was long gone and started watching TV in the hall.

"Do you want to cut the chicken?" I asked Calysta. She nodded and went to wash her hand to do that. When I saw the soup was boiling, I put half of it in another container and added the noodles to another half. When the noodles were tender enough, I added Calysta's cut chicken to it and left it there to get ready. The other portion was left for Marshal and his family. When he came, I would add the noodle and chicken to it.

I took a bowl for my mom to eat in my bedroom. I let it cool down before I started spoon-feeding her. Even though the food was easy to eat, she still had difficulty eating the soup. After each spoon, I had to clean the residue with a napkin. I had to show her the same amount of patience she showed me when I was a child. Slowly, at her own pace, she finished her lunch.

"Do you want anything else?" I asked her. She shook her head.

"Do you know where my husband is?" she asked me. Even when he was alive, she was still asking where he was in front of him. My father always told her that her husband would be back in the morning. That answer became my answer as well. She would meet him one day if that tale had any truth in it.

I left her there while she was snuggling the blanket. I went to the kitchen to have my own chicken noodle soup. Calysta was there and watching her children eating the soup. They were tired and hungry enough to eat anything in front of them, so they ate their fill. After that, they found enough space to eat cherry-filled cheesecake.

After they were done and had no more space, they went to watch something on TV.

Calysta and I started eating after they left us. She was sitting across from me at the table. Seeing her sitting there and eating with me strung a cord in my heart that made me feel happy. Even after so many years, she stood to be both the poison and antidote for me. I was at her mercy, and she wasn't shy to use that power on me. Her eyes found out that I was looking at her. She raised her head, which made me smile like a teenager.

"I'm glad that you are here," I shared some honesty with her. She just smiled back at my comment. It was a tight-lipped one. She didn't believe me. I stopped looking at her and started eating my soup. It came out, but not the way I wanted. It could be much better.

The evening came, and with it, the promise that Marshal would be there soon. Because it was a long weekend, maybe he would bring his family as well.

The bell rang, and there he was as usual. He also brought his family. The kids who saw their own size abandoned the big one who played with them for the last few months. They rushed into the house and started playing. Marshal and Aiko were in big surprise to find Calysta with her kids there. My reconciliation with Calysta brought them a joy that I hadn't seen for a long time. Calysta gave Aiko a long and sisterly hug, and Marshal was happy for this unexpected encounter. Aiko wasn't shy to ask how we made up, which brought silence on my part. Calysta smiled and led Aiko in. I stood behind to walk with Marshal.

"I'm glad to see you two are together again," Marshal commented.

"I've been an idiot this whole time, haven't I?" I asked him.

"I don't know about that part, but tell me, how did you end up together?" he said and opened his ears for good gossip. The girls had already started their own, but I didn't know what to tell him. While warming up the broth and adding chicken and noodles, I told him the whole story—the things that happened years ago, my decision to leave the country, telling him about Marina, and the people I met there, and why I was angry at Calysta when I met her. I told him her part of the story as well.

Everything.

After that, I felt much lighter. Now he knew as much I Knew.

"To answer your question, yes, you are an idiot," he said while attacking the soup I put in front of him.

"Slow down. Don't choke yourself," I said and sat across him.

"I mean, you were with lots of girls, and you didn't do anything. What is the point of what you do if you are trying to be nice all the time? And for who? I know that you don't believe in any supernatural things," he asked and challenged an answer.

"How many times have you eaten something delicious?" I asked him.

"Don't change the subject," he said. Aiko and Calysta walked in, and they saw Marshal was busy eating.

"No waiting, I guess, huh?" Aiko asked him.

"He told me to eat, or it won't taste the same," he lied.

"Help yourself as well, or do you want me to come and help you?" I offered.

"No, I would be fine," she said and called the children to come and eat.

"You didn't answer me," I asked Marshal. He tried to avoid the answer again, but I insisted on it.

"A few times. Why?" He looked at me suspiciously. He thought I was trying to make a problem for him in front of Calysta and Aiko.

"Did they taste the same after you tried it for the second time?" I asked.

"Yeah?" he said and wasn't sure where I was going with that. I understood he didn't grasp what I tried to tell him.

"I mean, did it feel the same? Did you have the same experience when you tried it for the first time? Did you have the same amount of joy when you discovered something new and delicious?" I asked him.

"No," he answered.

"Then you have your answer there. Maybe it doesn't make sense to you why I didn't do it. It was because I wanted to hold to that first-time experience. Perhaps I never experience it, or it becomes too awful to try it first and have the opposite process, like hating it first and loving it later, but I will hold on to that first experience if I can. Good or bad, make sense or not, that would be my first-time experience. I want to experience it the way I like to. I hope it doesn't sound like pontificate to you because it isn't," I said. As I was telling him, I felt stupid. How could he understand me if he wasn't me? Maybe I gave him a simulation of my thought process, but he would never understand it the way I did. If he hadn't experienced it or never put thought into it, it would be a mundane and boring explanation. It was as if to answer a mathematics problem, if he didn't think about it thoroughly and didn't come up with an answer by himself, how could he appreciate it if that answer was given to him.

As I expected, he just nodded his head and continued eating. Maybe he didn't want to challenge me more in front of his wife.

"What are you two talking about?" Aiko asked.

"Food. Love," he said. I smiled at how he cleverly told her the truth while hiding it at the same time.

"Food, food . . . do you think about anything else?" Aiko complained. She missed the second part of his statement, which was love. She thought he was addressing her. However, it made Calysta laugh.

"Oh, I think a lot. I think a lot about how to punish this naughty girl," Marshal responded. He gave me a dashing smile and a wink.

"Marshal!" Aiko said, but she couldn't hide her smile.

The children started eating as well and were oblivious to the grown-ups' talk. Meleta explained to her counter that she made the food and asked her mom to back her story, which she did. Then they jumped from one subject to another. The excitement they had when they were talking, the simple joy of meeting unexpected friends in a place that they never thought was possible resembled exactly like their grown-up's version who believed the same. Marshal and Aiko were happy to see their friends in unexpected places as well. Then they started on the desserts that I gave Calysta's children to Marshal and his family. Calysta's children wanted a piece of it again. After a bit of back-and-forth between Calysta and her children, she gave them permission to have a little more piece. When they finished, I packed the remaining for them to take for later.

"Do you think we should call Bernadina to come too? She won't be happy if she is not involved," I suggested to Marshal.

"I don't know. It's your call. Going to hell or heaven will be yours as well," Marshal responded.

"I don't know, man. Can you persuade me otherwise?" I almost begged, and his response was to throw up his shoulder.

"I do know what kind of hell I will get into if I call her, but I don't know what kind of hell will rise if I don't," I responded. Marshal looked at me and gave me the look of "It's your funeral" vibe.

I braved my cowardness and called her. One hour later, she was at my door. She embraced her friends, but the hurtful look she tried to hide broke my heart. After that day of her confession, we didn't bring up the subject again. There was no time for it. First, she was more curious about the videos and asked me all sorts of questions about them—the people in them, the places, and the memories I had from those times. Then she found out about my parents. Knowing her, I guessed she didn't see it appropriate to bring up that subject. I reminded myself that she wouldn't need my pity. It would be wrong to assume that she wasn't strong enough to handle her feelings. In our group, she had always been like that.

The gang was together again. This time, it wasn't as awkward as last time. We laughed at our memories of the past. Once again, I became the butt joke of Marshal. They laughed at my expense, but I never minded that. Calysta's laugh made a beautiful symphony in my heart. She was made to laugh, but the cruel world didn't care about that. The universe saw it as an abnormality that needed to be weeded out. That was what the world was asking me, and if I tried to interpret that to her, she wouldn't understand. Her use in this world wasn't that of being adapted to this world; it was to escape from it. I looked at her, and the problems I had wouldn't diminish. Instead, they were put aside to be solved later. The sound of her laughter would bring me to a euphoric state. She was the brake pedal in a speeding car that was about to crash. It took me years to understand her nature. That night, I understood. My way of lifestyle needed her. It craved for her. I had been with beautiful girls after her, but none could do the things she could do to me. She was my ticket to another dimension.

My mom was lying down on my bed and missing a son and a husband that she could never see again, and here I was just wanting more laughter from Calysta. The sad feeling about my mom was there, but Calysta gave me a breather just by being there. I felt like I was under the water this whole time and my body was screaming for oxygen. Calysta was just that. Her sapphire eyes were in harmony with the sound of her laughter. The way she could manipulate me and change my feelings and mood at her whims was so unfair. Nonetheless, what did I know about controlling the feeling? Shouldn't it be in the hands of someone else who knew when to use it?

Knowing all that, my body involuntary raised its guard. The road that I stepped in years ago was treacherous. She had control of my feelings before, and it didn't bode well for both of us. If I decided to be with her again, I should make sure that I do my part of the job. If she were looking at the sky and telling me about that, my job would be to look at the ground and be careful of the potholes or the pits. If she told me about the beauty above, I should tell her where the dangers were under her feet.

Marshal and I went upstairs to check on my mom. She was awake and singing my childhood lullaby. I felt so terrible to leave her like that, but that was what she wanted. She wanted a private time with her child's memories.

"Do you want to go to the bathroom?" I asked her as a courtesy. She didn't have any control over her body. With Marshal's help, I took her to the bathroom. While he was waiting outside, I cleaned her and replaced her diaper. When she was ready again, with the help of Marshal, I took her to her own bedroom. Like always, she didn't ask much but to see her child on a videotape.

The gang gathered in her room. Even though Marshal asked my mom many times, he asked her to tell him about her child in the video, and my mom, with different words, told us the same story. She was proud of me, and she wanted everyone to know about that. She sometimes told us about my misbehaving and how prideful and stubborn I was. She told us stories, until in the middle of it, she slept.

We left her there and went to the other room and continued our conversation until it was time for them to leave. Marshal and Aiko said goodbye first and then Bernadina. When they left, Calysta turned to me to say goodbye.

"I think you should stay here. Last night, I was at yours, and tonight is my turn," I said before she could say anything.

"I really like to, but I don't think that would be a good idea with Meleta and Valerio around," she explained.

"So you are saying I have to wait until they are eighteen?" I protested. She laughed at my jest.

"You know what I mean." She tried to get away with that explanation.

"Let me make it clear. Nothing will happen tonight as well, but if you are just insisting and resisting because you are not comfortable here, I won't stop you," I said with a serious face.

"I don't know what to say," she said.

"Don't you want to get used to being here?" I said, and I threw her off guard. Was I too forward for my request? Maybe. But I needed her. I saw the hesitation in her. "It's all right. I'll see you later," I said and went to give her my goodbye kiss. I kissed her on both cheeks. "Are you sure?" she asked with concern. I nodded. I saw Meleta was already rubbing her eyes. Valerio was yawning.

"Where do you plan to put them if I stay?" she asked.

"My old room. The bed is big enough for both," I responded.

"Do you want to sleep here?" she asked them. They shook their head in protest. She looked at me apologetically.

"What if I buy a video game console tomorrow?" I asked. That woke them up in joy. If she was going to play dirty with me, I showed her that I could also play dirty.

"I don't know if I agree to that," she protested. It brought resistance in her children like the rise of the people of Russia against the Tsar. Those two that saw the idea of a video game console that was about to be demolished in front of their eyes were begging their mom to stay.

"I should have added that your mother has to approve of that. If not, the whole deal is off," I explained. I didn't want to let those little demons turn a good night into a nightmare. However, they pressed the nuclear button by showing their puppy eyes and repeatedly saying, "Mommy."

In the end, Calysta, whose tooth and claw was pulled out, agreed to stay. The kids jumped for their victory, and I joined them in my thought. I showed them my room and led them where to sleep. They went and slept on the bed. After they settled down, I went to Calysta. She looked defeated.

"Thank you for staying," I said. It was a reconciliation. She gave me the look that said "I can't believe you did this." After we brushed our teeth, we went to bed. I lay down on the bed and was just so happy that she was there with me.

What a difference?

One night, cold and unattached, and the next night, being beside myself to have her there.

"What a day," I said offhandedly. She nodded in confirmation.

"Are you still angry at me?" she asked me with concern.

"Why?" I asked back.

"I don't know. Last night, you hated me, and tonight . . .," she said and bit her lips. "Tonight, you are different."

"Last night, I slept with my enemy. Tonight, I'm sleeping with Calysta," I responded. She nodded and came closer to me.

"I'm not going to give you this side of the bed. This side is mine," I said, and she looked puzzled.

"This is what I see in TV and Movies. The women take a big portion of the bed," I explained. She laughed at my stupidity and came closer to me. She put my arm under her head, and her hand was on my chest. That was how fast I lost that portion of the bed not knowing it.

"I promised you that tonight nothing will happen, and I will keep my promise. You can go to sleep now." I think I said that to myself to slow my heartbeat, but I heard a protesting noise from her. After so many seductions and trying to convince me otherwise, we both went to sleep.

The next day, as I promised, I bought them a video game console. We made lunch and supper. I took care of my mom. I was massaging her from her head to toe. I read her one of her books on the shelves. In the end, I put back the videotape as she requested. From there, I went and helped Calysta with housework. My day passed as fast as it came. I was happy to have her there. That evening, Marshal and Aiko came back again. They were delighted to see Calysta there again. They started their gossips, and Marshal and I started our own. In a blink of an eye, the night came to an end. Marshal and Aiko said goodbye and left. When It was Calysta's time to leave, I was divided to let her go or not, but I decided against my desire.

"Thank you for staying here last night," I said to her. I saw disappointment in her eyes.

"No problem. You can call me anytime," she said. The sadness in her voice was unmistakable.

"I really like you to stay, but I won't force you like last night," I said to her apologetically.

"Why not?" she asked.

"Because you are going to work the day after tomorrow, and I don't want you to get exhausted by working here as well," I explained to her.

"Oh, that. Thank you for thinking about my well-being," Calysta said, but this time, the sadness in her voice was almost gone.

This time, when she told her children that it was time to go, they were the ones who wanted to stay without any of my persuasions. She didn't know what to do.

"Do you like to stay?" I asked her after seeing her children insist on staying.

She looked at me. "Do you really want me to stay?" she asked. I smiled and nodded.

"Are you sure? I don't want you to worry about us while you are attending to your mom," she explained. Was she serious? I would move a mountain for her, so I told her that I wanted her to stay.

We went to bed again, and this time, she was at my side and made herself comfortable. I held her closer to myself.

"Do you still have the painting that I made for you?" I asked her.

"I do, but it's in my mom's house. I guess you know the reason why," she replied. I understood.

"I made another one, but it wasn't a portrait. It was a miniature painting. The back of a girl who was looking at the fogged and steamed mirror. Her picture would be only revealed in one of the droplets in a mirror. Unless someone used a magnifier glass, no one could see the picture of the girl." Then I continued, "I named it Atsylac. It was my companion for a long time. I was forgetting your face, Hence the steam on the mirror, and if I wanted to see you again, I had to use a magnifier," I explained.

"I'd really like to see it," she said with excitement.

"You could if you go to the Florence's Art Museum," I said coolly. She raised her head from my arm and looked at me in disbelief.

"You put my picture in the museum for everyone to see?" she said that and slapped me gently on my chest.

"Don't worry. No one knows that it's you. Do you remember that fan girl who interrupted our meeting? She saw the painting and didn't put together that it was you," I said calmly.

"By the way, what happened to that girl? Did you call her?" she asked. She quickly forgot about the painting.

"I did call her. I called her friend as well," I told her truthfully.

"What? Why?" she asked incredulously.

"I said that I would call them, so I did. I took them out for dinner, and that was it. I didn't see why I couldn't talk to them. They were fresh air for me. Everyone was curious about what happened between me and that pop star that they forgot I had another life as well," I explained to her.

"What happened between you and Taylor by the way?" She just jumped from that topic to another.

"What do you think happened? I already told you that I'm a virgin. What is all this fuss about?" I explained to her gently.

"Oh, nothing . . .," she said. Her smile was cute and mischievous. I smiled at her devilish smile.

She looked at me in the eye and stoned me just like Medusa. Her hot breath on my cheek and chest drove me to insanity. Then I felt her lips were touching mine. She was biting and suckling my lower lips. I returned the favor. She mounted herself on top of me, and like a lioness going for her kill, she kissed my neck and gave me a gentle bite there too. I was getting sweltering, and each part of me she was kissing was aching to be kissed again. She pulled my shirt up and started kissing me from my lower ribs to the upper. Just like that, she removed my shirt and came back up again. She looked at my eyes and saw I had no power at all and I was at her mercy. She smiled and locked her lips to mine. I just wanted to be closer to her, if that was possible, so I hugged her more tightly. She moaned while our lips were still locked. It was as if I did this more than a thousand times. I maneuvered her under myself. Now I was on top, and she was under. Her hot body underneath me drove me crazier. I started kissing her on the cheeks when I saw she exposed her neck to me. No words needed to be said. I went for her neck and her jugular. Her neck was made to be kissed. I moved from there to her collarbone. I tried to do the same and copied her move. I pulled her shirt up and started kissing her from the lower ribs to the upper. Her body arched under mine each time I kissed her on the chest. I removed her shirt, but there was another piece of clothing. Her bra was there. I continued kissing her instead of removing her bra. My hands cupped her breast, and I kissed around it. She moaned a bit more. My lips touched between her breast, where she arched up more. Then slowly I exposed her left-side breast; the already erected nipple popped out. I don't know how I knew, but I started to suck her nipple. She moaned at first, but then she jolted and held my head with her two hands. "Oh, oh . . . more gently, please." I did as she commanded. Good thing that I didn't bite. Something was urging me to do so, but how could I? If she was uncomfortable by sucking hard, how could I go for something more severe? My tongue found it pleasurable to play with her nipple. She liked the work of tongue more than sucking by letting her moans out. My other hand exposed the other side of her chest and instinctively went for that one too. Her body was arching up and going left and right as if to escape from a predator. That movement became rhythmic, and she was grinding her hips to mine. That felt much better, so I did the grinding on top of her. She held my head with her hands again, and I wondered what I did wrong this time. Those sapphire eyes held me like a prisoner. Somehow, she made her eyes look bigger and turned them back smaller in a matter of seconds. I don't know what kind of sorcery she was using at me, but whatever it was, it enchanted me fully. I was acting like a madman. That duration she held my head with her hands was close to milliseconds before she kissed me again. That moment for me was like an eternity. She locked her lips to mine again and expertly turned me to the side, and she came on top of me again. She started kissing from top to lower part. She kissed my cheeks, neck, chest, and abdomen. She continued kissing until she arrived at my pants. Just her touching that area made me crazier. The feeling of her fingers touching my belt made me sit up. She kissed me on the lips to cool down the beast inside me, but how was such a thing possible? The thing that started all was calming me down while she was dexterously undoing my belt and button. She smiled and turned up the heat again. Her hand went under and started kissing my abdomen. I just wanted to hold her there. Her hot breath and her hair touching my skin was a joy beyond anything that I imagined. By one hand, she pushed me down gently. It was like a command. She unzipped my pants and slid her delicate hand in there. She grabbed what she was looking for and started stroking it. My penis was already erect with all this excitement. Nonetheless, she stroked it. Then she pulled down my pants and underwear altogether with a little difficulty and little help from me. Now I was exposed to her physically and spiritually. I was truly and fully naked in front of her. After she pulled down my pants, she started stroking my penis again. This time, she brought her head close to my penis and her hot breath on it. It made me harder. The mischievous smile was shown again on her lips. She puffed on it on purpose to tease me more. I moaned and grabbed the sheets with full strength. To tease me more, she brought her mouth close to my penis and took it away. Like a snakebite, she kissed one part and pulled back. She knew exactly what she was doing to me. Those teasing were on purpose and on point. I moaned more. I was asking for mercy by moaning, and she, like a good torturer, enjoyed hearing my pleas. Then her tongue touched my penis and pulled back. She licked again, and this time, it was longer than the first time. Then to my surprise, she took the top of my penis in her mouth and pulled back. I was over the moon and didn't know what she was doing. Then she started stroking me by her mouth. She was sucking and licking at the same time. She was doing that continuously. I thought that a torrent inside me was coming up.

"I guess I'm coming," I said to her so that she could go easy on me. She looked up and looked at me directly. She smiled, and without remorse, she sucked and licked continuously. In felicity and elation, my body released itself from that torment. The merriment and gaiety that came afterward were beyond anything that I imagined or dreamed of.

I was panting after that much ecstasy and exultation. I was smiling like a big idiot. I looked at her and saw that she was wiping her mouth and coming up to kiss me, but I refused. I told her to go and wash her mouth. I wasn't trying to be insensitive, but I didn't like something as foul as that in my mouth. She looked hurt. It was like I was judging her, but it wasn't true. I didn't know what I was doing there and gave the lead to her. She knew what she was doing, and I didn't.

"Do you like it that way? I mean, being dirty?" I asked

"What do you mean?" She was offended more.

"I'm just trying to understand if you did it for my sake or you just like it that way," I asked with more clarification.

"What if I like it?" she said and stood up to go to the bathroom.

"Then I have to try it to see if I like it too," I said. She looked at me with suspicious eyes.

"I'm serious. Don't forget. This is the first time for me," I said to defend my lack of experience. She smiled. Somehow, she liked the sound of it. Now she was better at something that I wasn't.

"I'll be back," she said and went to the bathroom. I lay back and thought about what had just happened. After a few minutes, she came back. She kissed me on the lips, and I smelled the fresh smell of toothpaste in her mouth. I smiled back.

"Do you still want to continue?" she asked with concern.

"I didn't have the main course yet," I said in agreement. She laughed at my silly response, but then she came and kissed me. This time, I kissed back and locked our mouths together. I pulled her half-bent body to the bed, and in one move, slowly she was under me. Our mouths were still locked. I started kissing the top of her nose. Again, she exposed her neck and cheek to me. I brushed my lips against her soft skin. Pecking her cheek and neck, I moved to her earlobe. She liked it and moaned with pleasure. I worked on it more until her body told me to go down on the lower part. I moved down to her beautiful, long neck. The hotness that was emitting from her neck was dazing me. I pushed her face on the pillow to expose her neck more. The whiteness and the pleasant temperature were startlingly good. I just wanted to stay there forever and kiss her to my heart's content. However, by moving her head, she signaled me to move on, but I hung around to kiss her shoulder bone to her chest. I kissed the clavicle exposed to me by the gap in it made on her shoulder muscle. Then I moved to the manubrium and sternum. Even though they were bones that every human has, those were different for me. They were more pleasurable kisses. My head was between her tits. The softness and bounciness of them made me more playful. I used her own technique on her when she played around my penis. I huffed on her nipple. She whined deliciously. She arched up to offer either of them to me. I smiled and pulled back my head, but to my surprise, she pulled my head down to one of them. The softness and bounciness of her tit made me open my mouth involuntarily and have her nipple in my mouth. She cried in joy. The lesson I learned earlier, which I shouldn't suck too hard, I applied again. I did what she did down there, sucking and licking at the same time. Playing with the tips of her nipple with my tongue, I noticed she was moving her head right and left. I enjoyed seeing her like that. From one side, I moved to the other side of her chest and repeated the process all over again. Then I moved down underneath her tit and, from there, to the abdomen. She was shivering in pleasure. I moved slowly to her lower part until I arrived at her jeans. Just unbuttoning her jean was empowering for me. I continued kissing on the area above her jeans. After, I undid her jeans, unzipped it. Using the same technique she used, I slid my hand there and tried to find her private part. First, she moaned and then started laughing. She giggled sweetly. I smiled and kissed her soft skin, but it didn't stop her from laughing. I raised my head and watched her laughter. Then I moved on. I tried to pull down her tight jeans by grabbing it from both her hips. I tried to pull it down, but the damn jeans was glued to her skin and pulled down her whole body. It was a kind of pleasurable resistance in that piece of clothing. She raised her hips to make it easier for me to remove it. It came off easily after it passed her bottom. She was still laughing and was playful by moving her body around. She teased me by not making my job easy to take out her panty. With little help from her, I removed her panty as well. Now I saw her shaved vagina. I smiled at her silliness and playfulness. I put my hand on her vagina again. The soft and warm skin in that area was so intoxicating. Again, I used her technique to tease her, but her reproductive tool was different than mine, so I made an improvisation. I put one finger on her vagina and started rubbing it sideways and up and down and sideways. She moaned again, and I didn't notice when she stopped laughing. It was enjoyable to do things to her. When she was getting aroused, I was getting aroused as well. Her wailing and moaning made me more focused on the task. While I was playing with her Vagina's lips, I went up again and gave a quick kiss to her pointed nipple. I kissed it again and moved down from there to her groin. Then I inserted a finger inside her vagina, and I felt the wetness in there. It was sticky. I let my finger feel inside her vagina; with my thumb, I played with her clitoral hood and clitoris. The wailing continued. I wasn't sure that I wanted to do that, but I went for it. I went down and put my mouth on her vagina and started sucking and licking it. While I was there, I continuously pushed my finger in and out of her. The moaning and wailing got louder than before. She continuously arched her body and dropped it on the bed. I realized I was doing it right, so I continued until her body tried to get away from me. She put her hand on top of my head to keep me there. She closed her tight and locked my head there, yet I kept going until I felt something came out of her, and she slumped on the bed. She was breathing hard with laughter.

"Where did you learn that? You told me that you are a virgin. Did you lie to me?" she asked me like a marathoner who just reached the finish line. She was out of breath.

"No, I just did exactly what you did with a little modification," I said defensively.

I sat up and opened her legs. I brought my penis close to her vagina, but I saw that she convulsed as if she were in a seizure.

"Are you okay?" I asked with concern.

"I'm . . . I'm . . . I'm fine . . . just give me a second," she begged. Even though it was difficult for me, I pulled my back. Then I tried to touch her breast, but it was like she was electrocuted. She shook and tried to stay away from me, but my animal instinct was forcing me not to let her get away. The amount of will going against that instinct was unsurmountable, but her comfort was more important for me. It was the same instinct that told me to bite her tit off as if I could do that. I pulled back and let her have her break.

"You are amazing like always. Everything you do is amazing. Wow, I never felt this good," she complimented me. Maybe it was for my bruised pride and confidence. I didn't want to ruin her moment if there was a chance there was truth in it by accusatory questions.

"Thanks. I had a good teacher," I replied. She smiled at my compliment.

When her breathing got slower, she looked at me.

She nodded her head and said, "I'm ready."

Once again, I brought my hip to hers. She put her delicate fingers on my abdomen to stop me from doing something stupid. My body, like a trained dog, obeyed her.

"Just go easy on me," she requested. I nodded.

I rubbed my penis on her vagina. It was so pleasurable doing that. The heat from her groin was intoxicating. The tip of my penis was itching to get into her. I slowly slid my penis into her vagina, and I found a new kind of pleasure, a wholly unique experience, as if whatever I did before that moment was a massive misunderstanding about sex. That sensation, that feeling I had inside her took me to another place. All these years, I starved my body to that sensation. I was like a person who hadn't tasted salt or spice all his life. Now that person couldn't imagine his life without it—what war and blood were shed for having that taste again.

I pushed my hips more forward to let in more of my penis. She inhaled through her teeth. It was like a hissing sound. A moan followed that. She grabbed my hips to adjust the speed of my motion. That way, I wouldn't move my hips too fast or slow. My body, as she instructed, moved forward and backward. The heat inside her was gratifying and fun. It was just a body temperature; it couldn't exceed thirty-seven Celsius. Maybe it rose to thirty-seven and a half, yet it felt like a hundred. Inside her was hot and wet. Her legs looped around my waist. She pulled me toward herself. I went down and kissed her lips. She was panting and whining at the same time when she had time to take a breath from my kissing and thrusting hips. The more she whimpered and moaned, the more I added speed and thrust. She held my body closer to herself. She hugged me with her whole body by looping her hands around my neck and her legs on my waist. Her breast was pressed on mine. I lifted her entire body up with a push-up movement and brought her down on the bed slowly. She took a breath and started pecking my cheek, neck, shoulder, and biceps rapidly. She gave me a leeway to raise my hip again, and as I did, she started biting me gently. I thrust hard this time. I wanted the whole thing inside her. It made her arch back her neck and raise me by her body. That alluring neck of hers was exposed again, and it was an invite to kiss her there. I kissed her throat and chin. She dropped her body again.

"Go faster . . . Go faster," she begged me. I sped up more. By her moaning in that speed, in that body heat, I felt another torrent coming up.

"I'm coming," she said before me.

"I'm coming too," I confessed.

"No, don't come inside me," she begged.

I moved faster, and she started to bite me harder in the shoulder. She was trying not to scream in the middle of the night, and she took her revenge on me for that, but I was too excited to feel any pain. When she released me, I kept pounding her with more force in my hips. Then I slowed down.

"Faster, faster, faster . . .," she was saying, and by each word, I added more speed, and then she dropped and screamed inside my mouth. Then she released me from her grip and slumped herself on the bed. I was about to raise my hips again when she bit me and screamed in pain. After she stopped biting me and lay back to bed, she put her shaky hand on my chest and wanted to distance herself from me. The sadist inside me ignored that polite request, so I thrust again on her.

"No more, please, stop. No more . . .," she was begging, but that demon inside me was blind and deaf to any plea. I thrust one more time with more force behind it.

"Please, please, stop," she begged me again, but I was about to have my climax. That ogre inside me insisted on continuing, but I pulled it out. I sat on her abdomen and started stroking my penis on top of her. I looked at her beautiful breast and tried to touch it, but she shivered like before. It was like my hand was a Taser gun. That sudden move of her and irresistible eyes made me come on her abdomen and breast.

After that, I was exhausted even to sit. I had to lie down. I wanted to kiss her, but she put her hand in front of my mouth like I was a repulsive person, but I saw the smile.

"I can't take it anymore," she confessed and breathed heavily. I nodded and just lay back on the bed.

"So this is what I was missing all this time?" I asked no one in particular. She laughed her beautiful laugh. She was still catching her breath and gulping any moisture left in her mouth.

"You are good. Actually, you are too good," she said between her heavy breathing. "Truly, you make me wonder if you told me the truth about being a virgin," she said pleasantly.

"You were the one who was leading me, remember? You pushed my head wherever you wanted me to go, and then you showed me how to tease. All of that, it was your doing. I thought you realized it when you started laughing," I said defensively. She laughed at my response.

"I didn't realize that I was teaching you. I just wanted to let you do whatever you wanted to do because it was your first time," she explained diligently. That made me laugh, and with my laugh, she laughed as well. We lay down on the bed and stared at nothing.

"That was the last thing that I held on to. I think there won't be anything close to that can happen ever again. I won't have this first-time experience ever again," I said it offhandedly.

"What do you mean? Just let me catch my breath, and I'll make you eat your words," she protested.

"Another sex with you or anyone else won't bring back that first-time experience. I think that's the reason we do stupid things like cheating. We are starving for that experience. The experience of the first time trying out something enjoyable can't be replicated. After the first-time experience, we try to have that jolt of excitement again, but it won't come back. It's ferocious and very unfair. However, knowing that, we try again and again to see if that experience will be back, with the same person or another person, and the more we try to relive that moment, the more mundane it becomes," I said.

"Thank you for being a downer after having sex," she said. She tried to be funny, but the pain behind it was apparent to me.

"You didn't get it. I shared that experience with you. The most important moment in my life has been given to you. Please take care of it," I clarified it for her. She had a big smile on but a teary eye.

"I'm sorry. I couldn't give you the same thing," she said. I nodded.

"It was my choice to live like that. I don't expect anybody else to do the same. It won't be a gift if it is expected from everyone," I said calmly.

"You always give me the best gifts," she said in her tears. She leaned over and gave me a kiss.

"You do too, but you never realized it. You were the one that gave me those feelings. You were the one that became my first girlfriend. You were the one who gave me my first kiss. You were the one who made me think about someone else besides myself, and you are the one that let me experience this feeling for tonight. I had many chances with different people, but somehow, I was locked out and couldn't do it with them. Even though they were willing to do it, but somehow, I felt bad about it if I did it," I explained. She came on top of me, laid her body there, and listened from there while her head was resting on my chest.

"Do you really mean it?" she asked.

I played with her hair. I drove my fingers into it and started massaging her head. "I do. If it wasn't for you, I don't know if I ever would have that chance. It's been a while that I thought that I would have the same fate as Isaac Newton or Nicola Tesla, and I came to be at peace with it," I said honestly. She nodded on my chest, and her breath was alluring again. As much as I wanted to do it again, but the day's task took its toll. I was barely able to open my eye. I kept massaging her head to cool down my desire. She kissed my chest and put back her head in the same place. The sleepiness made my eyelid heavy. I thought to close it for a few seconds, but my body took me to dreamland.

I opened my eyes. My mom was standing right where we were sleeping. Her hair was messy and wild. Her eyes were deep inside her skull, which shadowed the eyeballs and added to her eerier appearance. The wrinkled face of hers with loose skin under her chin made her look more terrifying. The eye socket looked like they had been bruised. She was breathing heavily with a whizzing sound. The aroma of disease had already filled the whole room. She was looking at me with disappointment.

"Agustin," she said with difficulty. It was hard to hear any sound other than her whizzing sound.

"Agustin," she said again. She was looking for my response.

"Mom? What are you doing here? Are you all right?" I asked with concern.

"You couldn't even wait for me to die?" she asked. I could see her veins bulging in her neck. Her dehydrated lips had cracks in them. She was smacking them together to run a little bit of life to it. Maybe she was smacking them to get some moisture there. Her heavy breathing made me more concerned.

"Was I a bad mom to you? Is this my punishment?" she said with difficulty.

"Mom, what are you talking about?" I asked. Now I sat on the bed. I wanted to let her sit on the bed.

"Wasn't she the reason you left me?" she said and pointed at Calysta's naked body with her bony finger.

"It wasn't her fault. I'm to blame for all this. I was too weak. I shouldn't have left you or Dad, not for her and not for anyone else," I confessed.

She nodded. Blood streamed down from the corner of her eyes. The blood droplets on her dress made me more nervous. **What is going on?** I thought.

She smiled. Her smile on that bloody face was unnerving.

"My poor boy, you always had a gentle heart," she said with more difficulty.

I woke up with tears on my face. Then I noticed a movement on my right side. I turned my head to see empty eye sockets looking at me. A slashed face revealed the inner muscle and fat, which was covered by gory red blood. That naked body beside me was the cause of that movement. Someone behind her with a bloody knife was stabbing the lifeless body beside me. That individual was stabbing repeatedly, and with each pull, a trail of red blood was coming toward my face and my naked body. I touched my face and looked at my hand. The things that I thought were my tears turned out to be blood. That individual didn't stop stabbing. Even though I registered this whole scene late, my body was ready to fight. I rolled over and jumped out of bed. Then it dawned on me, the person who was getting stabbed was Calysta. A paralyzing sadness and anger came over me.

I didn't know what to do. By the looks of it, she was already dead, and her body was moving like a dead body. There was no life in it. That individual raised the knife, and down it came with a thumping sound. A pool of blood covered the bed and drenched everything in red in the moon's light. That individual didn't stop stabbing. Then I noticed the bony figure who was stabbing her. She was covered in the blood of her victim. That messy hair, which clung to each other because of the wet blood, was glued to her face. She continuously stabbed the dead body. Deep down, I knew who was stabbing. She was slashing and stabbing.

"Stop it!" I yelled. I felt the deep sadness in my voice. However, that individual didn't stop. She continued her stabbing as if nothing had happened. It was too painful to watch the body of a person I had strong feelings for being violated just like that.

In that moment of insanity, I didn't care what would happen to me. I just wanted to stop that act. Those movements were easy to predict. It had just one motion, up and down. I went and grabbed the wrist of the hand holding the knife. I held it firmly. However, that hand wanted to continue its momentum. I stopped the hand from going to any direction. I stopped one hand, but the other one raised as a fist. Now that individual wanted to pummel the lifeless body of Calysta. I grabbed the other hand and stopped it from hitting it. However, that individual didn't give up. That individual was about to attack with her teeth. By crisscrossing those arms, I pushed back her whole upper body. Now I could see the attacker's face, and for sure, I knew who she was. My mom, with berserk eyes, was looking back at me. What happened to her? Why was she doing this? She was struggling to free herself. I was in too much shock to understand anything. There was no logic inside me. The moment that I realized that my mom couldn't do any of that because of her condition, the spell was broken.

I woke up. I looked around. Calysta was sleeping peacefully on my side. There was no one else in the room. I checked again with more cautious eyes. No one besides Calysta was in the room. I took a deep breath, just like when I surfaced from a deep pool. I relaxed as soon as I realized the horrible nightmare was over. Calysta's closed eyes were toward me, and she was breathing so close to the right side of my chest. My mind was in a haze after all that. I wanted to hug Calysta tightly, but I decided against it.

It was difficult for me to leave Calysta's side, but after that nightmare, I was worried for my mom. I wanted to check on her. I tiptoed out of the room. The sun wasn't out yet, but the darker blue sky was transforming into a lighter one. I walked to my mom's room with excitement. I felt heavy in my heart. When I saw her lying in bed with closed eyes, it made me relax and anxious. I was worried that something might have happened to her, but when I saw her chest rising and falling under that blanket, it made me have a relaxed breath. I went close to her bed to look at her closely. She was sleeping peacefully. She looked much different than what she looked like in those nightmares.

"Mom, I'm sorry that I wasn't a good son to you," I said to her. Her eyes were still closed.

"Just wait a bit more for this foolish son of yours. I'm not ready to let you go. The world is mundane. Nothing has replaced those beautiful smiles of yours. I wish you could scold me for leaving you alone for this long. The world doesn't have any music to replace those lullabies of yours. Our garden flowers don't smell good without you walking in them. You were my best friend when no one wanted to be my friend. Your chest is full of my silly little secrets. Please, forgive me again for the thousandth time," I said to her in despair. It was hard not to kiss or brush her hair, but I didn't want to wake her up, so I left her there and went to the kitchen.

I started cutting the potatoes, onions, and bell pepper. A mixture of paprika, black pepper, salt, garlic, and dried rosemary was added to those chopped vegetables. Then I poured some olive oil into it and put it in the oven. Since I didn't know what kind of protein they wanted, I put aside their portions and fried an egg for myself. Then I made porridge for my mom. I minced some fruit in it as well.

The daylight was up now. A new day started for me. My breakfast was done before Calysta showed up in the kitchen.

"Hi, how are you today?" she asked me in a good mood.

"I'm good. Thanks for asking." The formality in my response was a surprise to me too. The smile on her lips dried like a drop of water in a hot Sahara.

"Agustin, is everything all right?" she asked with concern.

"I had a nightmare last night. I can't remember the detail, but it put me in a bad mood," I said to her and lied at the last part. I didn't want her to feel guilty for a silly nightmare or overthink about it. She nodded, but her smile didn't come back.

"What do you like with this? Eggs? Sausage? Bacon?" I asked her and showed her the breakfast that I had prepared.

The fragile spirit of hers was as stubborn as a mule. "I don't feel hungry," she said with distaste and sadness. Probably, she thought that she had done something to tick me off. That was what I thought.

"Do you want me to force you by kissing or by tickling?" I offered my solution to her foolishness. That childlike spirit of hers came back. She smiled in a way as if to say to me, "I dare you to do that."

I took a step closer to her, and she took a step back.

"I'll chase you, and if I catch you, I'll tickle you nonstop, even if you pass out," I threatened her, but she smiled in response and took another step back. I was a man of my word. Two grown-ups were running around the house. Her laughter lit up the whole world, and when I caught her, she was laughing and begging me to have mercy on her. I laid her down on the floor to make my job easier. She was continuously laughing her heart out. I started tickling her as I promised. She tried really hard not to make her laughter loud, but I was merciless. I tickled her from both sides, and she tried to free herself fruitlessly. In her pleas, while she was laughing, she called my name many times. I stopped a bit to give her a breather and let her collect herself. Even the threat of starting over made her laugh and beg. She was underneath me and at my mercy.

"What should I do now? Should I continue your punishment?" I asked her. She shook her head for no more punishment.

"Are you going to eat your breakfast, or do you need to burn more calories?" I asked her and showed my finger as a threat.

"All right, all right, I'll go and eat my breakfast," she promised.

"Are you sure? Because I want to continue this for a while," I threatened her again. She nodded as a sign of surrender.

"The terms of surrender follow this:

1. You'll kiss me after I release you.

2. You go and eat your breakfast.

3. You won't tell Aiko and Bernadina about last night.

4. You are going to stay in this house until further notice.

Do you agree to these terms?" I asked her playfully. She was still under me.

"What do you mean that I have to stay here?" she asked cautiously.

"Do you want to stay here? Do you think your children will be comfortable here?" I asked her back.

"Agustin," she said with a sad tone.

I just lay down beside her. I slid in one of my arms under her head and looked at the ceiling, looking at nothing in particular.

"Don't you think we stood apart for a long time? Wasn't that enough?" I asked her. I didn't want to see her response.

"Agustin." She put her head on my chest when she said my name. I played with her hair.

"Every day I have a reminder in that room to tell me how little time we have in this life. I thought I was making her proud, but she doesn't give a damn about that. She only wants her child to be with her," I said and tried not to break down in front of her.

"I don't know what to say," she said.

"Don't worry. You'll know when you know," I responded. She climbed up and kissed me on the cheek and lips. After that, she put her head on my chest again. I continued playing with her hair.

"What's going on?" a little voice asked. Calysta lifted her head to see her little angel.

"Nothing," she disclaimed. She was like a child caught red-handed in doing something that she shouldn't. I didn't even bother to look up. I just lay down. Calysta sat beside me.

"Are you hungry?" Calysta asked her.

"Good. Augustin already made breakfast," she said and looked at me, but I was looking at the ceiling. I was looking for an answer. If I couldn't find the answer down here, shouldn't the answer be up there?

"Mel, what do you want with it? Eggs or sausage?" she asked her the same question I had asked her earlier.

"I don't know," she responded.

"Let's go and see what you like," she said, with a gentle touch on my chest. She stood up and left me where I was. I didn't see if Meleta followed her or not, but I stayed the same and lay down.

"Why are you lying down on the floor?" she asked me with curiosity.

"Because it is fun to do that," I answered her.

"Really?" she asked me in disbelief.

"It is for me," I responded.

"Mel, are you coming?" Calysta asked her. She followed her mom to the kitchen. I stayed there for a little bit more before I went to check on my mom. She was still asleep. I sat beside her bed and looked at her peaceful face.

"I wished I could ask you some questions. I miss the time when I could tell you anything. I'm looking for guidance, but my friends don't have your wisdom. Momma, I feel so lonely even though I'm surrounded by friends," I said to her and watched her for a little bit more. It didn't take much before she opened her eyes.

"Good morning," I said with a smile on.

"Good morning, who are you?" she asked me with searching eyes. I wanted to tell her that it was me, her son, but I couldn't. I tried that before; it only made her more distressed. She didn't believe me in the end. From that day on, I introduced myself as her personal nurse. Maybe this was my punishment for breaking her heart, to see her every day and not be able to address her. It was just like what I did to her. She watched me on those videotapes, but she couldn't address me directly. I had to go through it to understand it, but it didn't matter if I learned my lesson or not. The torture continued.

"Are you hungry? We have some porridge with different fruits," I asked her patiently.

"Where is my husband? Have you seen him?" she asked me. Since she had no sense of time, I gave her an answer that wouldn't stress her out. I usually told her that her husband had gone back to work. She would only nod her head and go back to her shell.

"Do you want your breakfast here or in the kitchen?" I asked politely.

"Anywhere would be fine," she said indifferently.

"There are two kids and a young woman in your kitchen. Do you want to go and see them?" I asked with a lot of caution.

"Who are they?" she asked. I didn't know if I should answer her honestly or keep lying to her.

"She is a friend of mine with her kids. I hope they won't be any bother to you," I asked for her permission.

"She has kids?" my mom asked. I nodded to her question.

"I like to see them if it isn't any problem for you," she said so tenderly. This was how carefree and lovely she was. Even though she considered me a stranger in her house, she still welcomed my friends and relatives.

"Do you want to see them in here, or should I take you there?" I asked her.

"I don't want to bother them while they are eating. Could you take me there if it is possible for you?" she asked me nicely, like always.

"Sure," I responded. I put aside her blanket and lifted her into her wheelchair. I wheeled her to the kitchen and introduced the guest to her all over again. The only thing I didn't mention was Calysta to her. I just introduced her as the mother of those children. She loved seeing children and being with them, but she never asked any of them to come to her so she could touch them or play with them. She was the opposite of my father. She didn't like to put people on the spot for her needs, which was her philosophy in her entire life. I never learned where she picked that habit. Was it her nature, or did she nurture it? I spoon-fed her breakfast. She was watching the kids while chewing and swallowing her food. After her breakfast, I asked her if she wanted to hear any story read by me, which she didn't want. As always, she wanted to see me on TV.

As usual, I did what I had to do in the office, and after I was done there, I spent some time with Calysta and her kids.

Then I attended to my mom. If she needed changing, I did that. The time passed like crazy. The afternoon came, and I helped out Calysta to prepare for lunch. The afternoon time passed as it came, and in the evening, Marshal showed up alone. He was surprised to see Calysta there for the third time in a row. Even though we didn't have that man-to-man conversation, we both welcomed the new change. The time was in a race to finish the day. The time that Calysta was about to go came.

"I enjoyed your stay here," I said truthfully.

"It was enjoyable for me too," she said and tried to hide her smile.

"I did have fun too," I answered her shyness.

"I really like to stay, but my work dress and everything else are in my house," she said apologetically.

"I understand. Next time, come prepared," I said to her.

"Can we take the console with us?" Meleta asked.

"And give away the only reason you want to come here? Nice try," I told her. She showed me her protest by stomping her foot on the ground.

"Can't we just stay here?" she asked her mom. Calysta was shocked to hear that, but to salvage the situation, she gave the grown-up reasons why she couldn't, like "Mommy needs to go home and have to dress for work" or whatever they had back home. When she couldn't convince her that way, she threatened that they wouldn't be back if she continued that behavior. That threat calmed her down but didn't quench her anger. I promised her that the next time she came, I'd read her some books.

I looked at Calysta for the goodbye. She looked at me quizzically. What was my plan now? I could read it in her eyes.

"Come here," I said and offered my open arms. She came and gave me a hug. She gave me a quick kiss and left.

I went back home. I went to my mom and stayed there. I sat beside my mom and started thinking. I thought about life and anything in it. Looking at her peacefully sleeping, I thought about the past, the nights I couldn't sleep peacefully as a child. It was this place that gave me a haven—the place where my mom gave me soft assurances, which now turned to trepidation and restlessness. Everything became upside down. It was nature at its best work to turn something sweet to sour.

It was in one of these peaceful looks that she slept and continued her sleep. Maybe in that dream world, her son would understand her needs more than I did.

Chapter 21

The blinds were pulled down. The lights were turned off. People inside that room stopped talking. The expectation rose.

A beam of light from the opposite wall was projected to another one by a small device—a picture formed on the screen. A name was written and the topic. Then a young voice broke the silence.

"My name is Valerio," he said with confidence. There was no breaking in his voice.

"I'm afraid at this age, this is all I know," he said with a charming voice. Some chuckled at his joke. "However, it doesn't stop my teacher for asking me the difficult question of what I want to be when I grow up," he said with a sarcastic voice. It made people chuckle more. "The difficulty of the question isn't about my dreams. What is my dream job or life? The difficulty of the question comes as to how much I know about myself. What kind of experience I had outside the school made me a person? What do I have to help me on this road? What kind of tools do I need for it? What do I like or hate? Do I like to interact with people or not? How curious am I on different subjects?" he said like a storyteller. He was calm and collected. "To add more challenge, our teacher asked to write it in one page," he said sarcastically. People laughed at his joke, and in their memory, they had those same questions themselves.

Then the picture changed. It showed a handwritten sentence.

It was just one line. "I don't know."

There was a tick mark in a red pen and an F in a circle.

"This is what she gave me for all that hard work," he said charmingly. The audience burst into laughter.

After people got quiet, he said, "This wasn't the end. She pulled me aside and asked me the reason I wrote that. I gave her the same answer as I told you earlier," he continued.

"You see, to understand my answer, first you have to understand someone else," he said Calmly. Then he showed a picture of her sister and then her mom. "This is my sister and my mom. These people are the reason that allowed someone like him"—he showed a picture of me smiling—"to enter into my life," he said. And without a hitch, he continued, "I see some of you fell for his charming smile, as my mother did." Some audience laughed. "I will tell you the reason why I introduced him like that." He showed some pictures on that screen—a painting, a music note, some furniture, some mathematical problems. In a slide, there were multiple pictures of the front entrance of companies and museums, then in another one, it showed pictures of landscape animals, insects. Then he showed a car and, lastly, shelves full of books. "These pictures can only show you who did all these just a bit, but I left out many other things he can do, since all this presentation would be me showing what he does and is capable of and nothing more." The audience didn't get the joke. "After all that, even when he was younger than me, he tried everything that the world could offer, or at least tried to." He paused for the suspense. "I asked him the question that my teacher asked me. Do you want to know what he said?" He paused for pondering. "'Where is the fun in that if I knew the answer?' When I showed him the failing mark, he laughed and told me, 'You lost a battle, but you won a war.'" He stopped for effect. "He told me that if I'm that bright to understand that question this well, then I'm way ahead of my time. See, he has a bad effect on me. The thing is, when he came into my life, I didn't like him much. He didn't try to win me over either. He didn't try to convince me that he was a good person. He just lives his life the way he likes. If I were childish and didn't eat what he cooked, he wouldn't try to convince me to try it at least once. Instead, he made enough for those who wanted to eat and left me out of it. He never told me to do this or do that. Meanwhile, my sister enjoyed his skills in many different things. He would talk to her about science, which was taught to her that day. Much later, when I accepted him as a member of our family, the discussion about my subject went to another level. For example, If I agreed to any of the facts in a class that I was taught, he didn't care if it was true or false. He usually asked my sister or me why we agreed or disagreed with those facts. What was our approach to the problems? If we got it right, there was a reward for us. If we got it wrong, he would tease us for it. This kind of approach was time-consuming and brought down our marks in school. The best part was, he didn't care about marks. He said, and I'm quoting in here, 'The universities are overrated.' That was coming from someone who studied in Cambridge and left it to do many other things. Before anyone in here starts protesting and telling me that he was wrong, he also explained the reason behind it. Since he was a kid, he didn't feel that he needed to go to the prestigious school to study with other smart kids. He learned that either the answer is in a book in a library or he had to find or solve it himself. In his opinion, the university or school job was to lead every student to that conclusion, but unfortunately, too many of them failed the students. It could be for various reasons, like political interference, the religious bias toward some subjects that made authority in power to cherry-pick facts, or the lack of negligence toward the teacher and the list continues." He stopped for the people to absorb what he said. "The best part was, he was teaching my sister and me this way without us knowing what he was doing. I thought he was a strange individual for asking those questions. What was the point of all these questions? Why did he care so much about our approach to the problems? It took me a while to realize that he was training us to be critical thinkers or show me the joy to explore beyond what I was taught in school. For example, if I showed interest in video games, he would show me how to make my own video games, even though they weren't as good as those commercial ones. If I wanted to check my answer in math, he showed me how to do it in a spreadsheet software. If I wanted to take a picture with a camera, I had to read a whole book and have the usual discussion about the Camera and how to do it. The next thing I know, I got one of those professional cameras to take pictures without any promise that I would get it. Everything that I wanted had to be earned. I couldn't believe how little time I had for anything. The length he went for us to have a good education was unbelievable. He told us, 'What do you think about going to another country to study?' My concern was that he was trying to get rid of us, but he explained that if we, My sister and I, agreed to it, he would convince my mom to come with us as well. The best part of that country was that we didn't have much homework and we could do whatever we wanted to do after the classes. Based on that premise alone, we agreed. However, he and my mom had a huge fight over it. As much as they tried to hide it from us, we knew it, and it was obvious to us. I felt so bad and guilty for it for a long time. I was afraid that they would break up at some point because I didn't want to do some homework. Fortunately, they never got to that point. When we moved to another country, he went to a different country to attend his companies." He showed the entrance of those companies. "It was difficult for me, my sister, and my mom. We felt so betrayed that he took us from our home and friends, only to leave us alone in another country." He stopped for the dramatic effect. Then he continued, "One day, when he came for a visit, I confronted him in front of everyone. I asked him why he did that. In return, he said, 'I'm trying to live my life as well and do the things I like to do.' Then I asked him why he brought us to another side of the ocean if he wanted to live his life. He casually explained to us that it was the last intervention he would do. He put everything on the line for that, for my sister and me. The rest was up to us, what we wanted to do with our free time after school. He allowed us to shape our lives according to our liking, and he would be there just enough to guide us. Then my sister asked him how he will guide my sister and me if he isn't there to do it. He told us that he believes my sister and I were ready for the next stage, which is to learn by observation, and that is a skill we need for our future. However, our question didn't end there. We didn't forget our mother. We asked him why he left her there. He answered that he believed we were ready for the next step, but our mother wasn't. If she wanted to be with him, she could come with him. After the horror of what he suggested, when I thought about it, what he wanted for us was to be independent, and if we made a mistake, he would fix it through his guidance. That was doable before we get to an age that we think we are too old for that or we no longer need his guidance. Again, he tried to help us by showing us some firmness, and we should learn to navigate through life without him or my mom telling us what to do all the time. You see, it wouldn't be possible for me to understand his motive if he didn't teach me enough to see the big picture. I would be more like another kid that would think he had a personal grudge against my sister and me. He was right about being ready to take the next step." He stopped and showed another picture. "I wasn't interested in science, but I liked taking pictures, and that was the thing I focused on. When I said I wasn't interested in science, I meant that I wasn't interested in doing extensive research. Nonetheless, I enjoy reading about the different scientific subjects without worrying about writing a paper about my finding. It is like I don't have to paint something beautiful to enjoy a beautiful painting by someone else. How long do you think it took him to make us like that?" he asked the audience. When there was no answer, he continued, "It took him two years. In just two years, he turned my life upside down. I knew where I was headed, but I didn't know what I wanted. You see, earlier I mentioned that I like photography, but I didn't know what kind. Do I like to take pictures for leisure? Do I like to take pictures of wild animals? Do I like to take pictures of injustice and war? Or simply, do I chase celebrities and get them in their awkward situation? I also found out that I'm interested in computers, not to that extent to write software or design hardware but enough to enjoy various tools in it for my purpose. Understanding some tools and their functions would guarantee my career at some company. Yet there is so much software to learn. Some of them are useful for my photography skill. Some software I picked up by observing this man." He showed my picture again. "All that while I was ten years old." He stopped again. "Yes, he wanted me to be independent at age ten." He stopped again. "Some would think what an outrageous act he did. However, I want to defend his actions," he said. "You see, he didn't throw us in the world and forced us to go to work and study. We were financially supported. What he wanted from us was to make an independent decision early on about our future without his or my mom's influence. He showed us how to read a map, and where to go was up to us. He would follow us some part of the journey, but not the whole way. Saying this, sometimes I really needed grown-ups' help. For example, how to approach the girl I liked in my class." He stopped and showed a picture of a girl with black hair and green eyes. "That was the girl that stole my heart." The audience made an *Aww* sound for him. He continued, "The problem was, I didn't know how to talk to her. First, I thought I should ask my mom how to do it. She just told me to be myself and then go and talk to her. That answer made this man"—he showed my picture again—"laugh uncontrollably. When my mom asked him why he was laughing, he told her that she forgot how they met. It was like a joke between them because both of them were laughing now. After their laughter, he told me I went to the wrong person for advice, which my mom took personally. She told him who was the right one because she wasn't impressed by his approach when they met for the first time. He called her my homo something that made my mom laugh again. He said, 'I didn't mean you are bad at giving advice, but what you missed was that he was asking you for a skill in communication, and your advice wasn't that helpful.' He said to my mom. 'What is your advice?' my mom asked him in indignation. 'I won't tell him. I will show him,' he said to my mom." He showed all that conversation like a comic book story, which made it funny. "My mom asked him what he meant by that. He answered her the same. There was a back-and-forth between them, but at the end, my mom agreed to let him teach me how to talk to that girl." He stopped there. Then he continued his narration, "He took me to a park and pointed to a random person and told me to go and talk to that person. I had to go and start a long conversation with him. I didn't know that guy he pointed at, and I was timid to talk to that person, So I informed him about the task's difficulty. He said to me that he would be there if I needed his help. I was hesitant at first, but I went through with it. My first conversation went bad. Then he pointed me to another stranger and told me to go and talk to that one. It was bad, but not like the first one. We continued doing that for one hour every day. I had to go and talk to random people. Men, women, old people, and the list continued." He stopped. "I know what you think. Every parent is teaching their children that strangers are dangerous, and he was teaching the opposite. But here is the thing: I was allowed to do that under either his or my mom's supervision. Meanwhile, I was getting frustrated to see when he would allow me to talk to that girl I wanted. I talked to everyone but her. Every day for three months, I went and talked to strangers. He was in another country, but he kept encouraging me to continue doing what I was doing. The girl that I liked a lot was talking to her friends, and I envied them for that very reason every day. For me, I thought I was ready, but I was waiting for someone in another country to tell me that I was ready. One time, the girl that I was interested in noticed me. She smiled, and the whole world seemed to be good. I smiled back. Then I noticed someone behind me came and went to her. He was the popular guy in our class, and she became her girlfriend." He stopped and listened to the other people's sound of empathy. "I went home and cried my eyes out. I was angry at everyone. I shouted at my mom. I didn't want to talk to anyone, especially this guy."

He showed the same picture of me. "He was the reason that I wasn't with that girl, and you know what he did after finding out about my misery? He didn't call me anymore." He waited for the people to get outrageous or made them curious why I behaved like that. "When he showed up two weeks later, he still didn't talk to me. One day I had had enough. What was the reason he wasn't talking to me? I asked him, and he told me he wouldn't have anything to say until I made up with my mom. He made it sound like I was the one who messed up, not them. Was it firmness or stubbornness? I don't know the answer, but he stood his ground. Every day that I was going to school and seeing the one that I loved with another person made me more desperate. I cried a lot, but he didn't relent. One day I was tired of this injustice. I went to my mom and asked for her forgiveness. Remind you that my mom wasn't the issue. She talked to me. She sympathized with me. She was kind to me, and she didn't mind my outburst, but he was the one that didn't give in. I went to my mom and apologized to her for my bad behavior. I felt guilty for that. No credit goes to him. A few hours later, he came to me with a victorious smile then asked me the reason I was rude to my mom. I wanted to yell at him, but I was too sad to do that. I told him the reason behind my outrage, even though he knew about it. Do you know what he told me?" he asked the audience. "He said, 'It doesn't matter. You are going to get her.' He asked me if I continued my one hour a day of talking to strangers. As if it would solve anything. Anyway, I answered him honestly. I told him that I didn't, so that afternoon, he took me out and asked me to go and ask out a girl close to my age." He waited for the shock he thought he had given the audience. "Me too, I was really shocked, but I asked him why. He said he wanted to see how I would handle it. Anyway, I followed his advice and went to ask that girl out. Then I realized that I wasn't afraid to ask her out. I was confident, and a few times, I made her laugh. I couldn't believe what I was doing. The fear was still there, but it didn't make me freeze. I could talk to her easily, and in the end, she was happy to be my girlfriend. I was so confused that time to realize what I had done to that poor girl. I knew that I would never be his boyfriend. Nonetheless, I asked her out. I didn't feel bad until I became wiser than I was before. When I went back to him, he was all smiles and welcoming. I told him everything, and when I finished, I was out of breath and word. He then told me that I was ready to go and talk to the girl I liked." He stopped for the gasp the people made. "I asked him what he meant by that. And he answered me if I was fine with letting someone else be with that girl I liked. My answer was obvious. He then explained that I should go to her and convince her that I was the better choice, not the guy she was with. That time, I was too shocked, too happy, and too confused to question him. The next day, I went to her, and as usual, she was with her friends. It didn't stop me. I went and started talking to her. The fear inside me was tremendous, but somehow, I channeled that fear to something funny coming out of my mouth. I didn't mention that I wanted to be his boyfriend though. I waited for her to come to that conclusion. I went home and told the story to my mom and him." He showed my picture again. "He told me to capture her heart is easy, but if I wanted to be her boyfriend for a long time, I should keep the practice. Every day I had to spend that amount of time talking to a stranger for the rest of my life. He promised that when he was around, he would be the one to supervise me. The rest falls to my mom. My poor mom, for my happiness, agreed to let me do this until I grew enough to protect myself. Anyway, to fill that hour, I went and started talking to other students in my school. That way, my mom wouldn't have to take me out for practice. Unknowingly, that expedited the decision-making of the girl I like so much. I became as popular as that guy in school by just talking to other students. It was unbelievable what I had become. I became comfortable talking in front of a whole class, and yes, as you can see, I became comfortable talking to a whole auditorium of people without a drop of sweat. He"—he pointed at my picture again—"taught me all that not only to be with the girl that I loved, but he also made me popular in school." Then he stopped for a few seconds. Then he showed a picture of a certificate. "He became my father way before this certificate. He taught me a lot, and I'm still learning from him. I'm not his biological son, but he treated me like one." He changed the certificate's picture to my picture. "When he found out about the problem my whole family developed, he dropped everything to come to be with us. My sister and I developed cancer because some company near our old house dumped its poisonous material in the ground long ago. That company hasn't existed for decades now, but we became sick because of it. If we didn't move to another country, we would be sick much earlier. We came back here, but to his old house, so my mom could be close to her friends." He waited for the audience to breathe, some to wipe their eyes, and a few to clear their throats. "He doesn't pity us. He wanted us to continue what we were doing before we knew about the disease. He pushed us forward." He pointed at my picture again. "He wants us to live our lives fully." He stopped for a few seconds. He continued, "Now I'm going back to the earlier question. What do I want to be? I still believe that I don't know. Not because I have a short time to live but my dad never knew, and I, as his son, don't know either. I feel lucky to have him as my father. He supported us without asking anything in return." Then there was a tremor in his voice, which he tried to hide. "So that brings me to the end of my presentation. I hope someone learned something from this presentation and the little experience I had." He finished his presentation by showing an artistic painting of him, his sister, his mom, and me. There was a signature on the bottom from everyone, including me. A bold text appeared on top of it that said thank you. The lights were turned on. The people started cheering and clapping, and the camera started shaking.

The movie went black. I closed the camcorder and looked at my watch. It was eight minutes after one in the morning. The hallway was empty of people. The lights were toned down. The smell of sanitization and cleaning products was as sharp as ever. A nurse with a red uniform and running shoes passed by me; I guess she was done doing her routine checkup. It reminded me that I should also go and check them up.

They were lying down on separate beds. The ventilators were going up and down. They were rhythmically breathing with their patients. The vital monitors were doing the same. Calysta was resting her head on Meleta's bed. There was an empty chair beside Valerio's bed. I went and sat there. I was thinking about the past—the way he looked at me, thinking that I knew everything. Those eyes were closed now. The needle in his arm was taped by some small Band-Aid. A tube that was delivering medicine was dripping one by one. It still had some left in it before it ran out. The memories of the past were awake—the conversations we had, the joy in his eyes when he got the girl he wanted, the pictures he took and showed to me for my approval or critique. I remember the time we talked about many subjects, including love.

"How do you know that you love someone?" he asked me.

"You are asking the wrong person. I can't answer that question," I said honestly to him.

"Don't you love my mom?" he asked me in front of Calysta. I thought to myself what a little brat he was.

"When I don't know what it is, how can I say I have it or not?" I replied.

"Are you a psychopath?" Calysta asked me in response. The hurt and anger in her voice were obvious.

"That question isn't as easy as you think it is. What notion you have about love is the world of princesses and princes kissing each other and waking them up from poisoned apples or a long sleep or something close to the movies they show these days. They tainted the word for getting some money," I responded.

"If it isn't that, then what is it?" she asked me.

"Well, that is my question as well. What is love? Is it simply what these movies are showing? Is it limited to the human? There are too many unknown aspects to it to think that won't make the answer as simple as that," I answered with patience.

"Maybe it's just an excuse for not saying it," she said stubbornly.

"A mother sees her home is on fire. She rushes in, disregarding her life to save her children. Do you think that is love?" I asked her.

"Of course, it is love. What else is it?" she answered in disbelief. It was like she was talking to a crazy person.

"What do you say if a stranger rushes in to save them? Or when other animals show the same response? Are we going to call it love or bravery or insanity? Is it a trick done by our brain? The neuroscientist believes that some levels of Dopamine, Serotonin, and Oxytocin are responsible for that feeling. Is that it? All that feeling sums up in some chemical reaction in the body and dismisses all the poems or stories written in the name of love. So back to the question, what is love?" I asked all of them.

"Oh, that's so romantic. It is every girl's dream to hear this explanation rather than that simple sentence," she said sarcastically.

"Do you want to hear a story about true love?" I asked her.

"I thought you didn't know what it was?" she responded.

"I don't, but someone tried to tell it through a story. Do you want to hear it?" I asked again.

"Okay, let's hear it," she said at last.

"There was a caravan that started a long journey. In it, two families were traveling together. They didn't know each other, but they stayed close during the travel and set up a camp. One couple was mooning at each other. The husband was a good-looking man. Not only that but he was also really charming and well-spoken. He was attending to his wife's needs all the time, from massaging and washing her feet to cooking foods for her. He was treating her like a princess, he as her servant.

"Then there was another couple who were the opposite of their neighbor. The husband wasn't good-looking. He didn't talk much and did none of what his neighbor did. For him, it was the opposite. The woman was attending to him dearly and treated him like a king. That bizarre behavior of the neighbor made the wife of the handsome man curious. She asked her neighbor the reason behind it. The neighbor responded to her that her husband loves her dearly, and that is enough for her. However, the wife of the handsome man didn't get a satisfactory answer. Why was she putting up with a lazy and ugly person? The wife of the lovely husband thought that that woman was strange. If it were up to her, she wouldn't put up with it for a second. Why should she care? He wasn't her husband, and they deserve each other.

"They continued traveling together, and nothing about their lives changed. One night, when they camped in the open, a group of bandits attacked their caravan. The handsome husband was nowhere to be seen, and his wife was running in the camp while screaming for her life. Meanwhile, the ugly man stood tall and fended off anyone who tried to come close to his family by his sword. It didn't matter the number of bandits who tried their best to break his defense, but it was for nothing.

"After the carnage, when the bandits left, they found that the handsome guy was hiding in the animals' stall. Not too far away, his wife's dress was torn apart, and her throat was cut open. The family of that ugly man was among those few who survived that fateful night," I finished the story.

"What are you trying to say?" Calysta asked after a few seconds.

"That love isn't as simple as what you think it is. Often, the answer to that question is scary for me. I'm afraid I won't know the answer until it is too late. I fear to find to that question ends with some kind of tragedy," I replied and went deep in thinking. Calysta didn't ask any other questions.

I remember the first time he called me dad, the joy and mountain of responsibility he dropped on my shoulder by saying that little word.

I remember the time when we found out about their condition, the fear in his eyes. He was looking at me as if I knew what to do or how to solve it. My shirt was damp with his tears. I remember his concern for his mom and his sister, such a Valiant character at such an age. He went to learn first aid in order to be ready when the time came so he could help his mom and sister.

His skin was too pale even in the semidarkness.

I touched his cold skin. The disease made this teenage boy lifeless.

He opened his eyes. When he saw me at his bedside, he smiled.

"Dad . . .," he said with difficulty. He held my hand with all the power he had. He was looking for assurance. It was like one of those moments when someone woke up from a nightmare and clung to the person he knew or trusted could calm him down.

I pressed his little hand gently. He smiled again.

"Dad, you can go and get some sleep," he said while struggling for air.

"I already did," I lied. He nodded his head. He turned his head to look at his mom and his sister. Then he looked back at me.

"I know you don't believe in the afterlife . . .," he said with great labor, "but can you tell me something more assuring than just dying?"

"Do you hate sleep?" I asked him. He smiled. He looked at his sister and mom to see if they woke up.

"You don't want to answer me?" he said and sounded hurt.

"You didn't answer," I persisted.

"No, I don't hate sleeping," he responded.

"Then do you have a problem getting more sleep than before? What is wrong with going to sleep and knowing that you don't have to wake up again? Would you miss those moments in the morning that you have to wake up and go to school? You have done it more than a thousand times. What makes that one special?" I asked him kindly.

"Do you think it will be like that?" he asked with a bit of surprise. It was difficult for me to say it out loud, so I only nodded.

"If it is like that, why are people so afraid of it?" he asked me with great curiosity.

"The problem doesn't come from those who died. The problem comes from the people who they left behind. The people left behind miss those moments they had together. Those memories will be there until they go to sleep as well. Anything that made us so angry at that time will be so trivial and insignificant, and the good memories live longer that way, making us miss them more. We cling to anything to see that person again. Even a made-up fantasy world would make much more sense than the alternative for some people," I said and held back my tears. I didn't know how much of that I believed myself. It was an observation from my own experience when I lost my parents. Their memories were as fresh as the time I lost them.

"Will you be sad?" he asked me with concern.

"I know that I will miss you a lot. You were the dearest friend that I ever had. Do you remember the time when you said goodbye to your best friend? It would be the same for me, but a little harder," I said with a broken heart. How could I tell him about the sense of loss when he never lost anyone? How could I talk about death and not cry my eyes out? What could I say to show or hide my pain? He was just a teenager and saw nothing of this world.

"You . . .," he tried to say. "You are the best, Dad," he said with a lot of effort. He pressed my hand again. The tears were welling up in his eyes. I tapped his hand gently. I tried to comfort him, but I think it was him who was comforting me.

A screeching beep rose from a monitor. I looked up. It was coming from Meleta's. I pressed the assistance button for the nurse and the doctor to arrive. I let go of Valerio's hand and went to Meleta's bedside. The electronic vital sign monitor was screaming for attention. Her heart rate was below average and was dropping fast. The beeping changed to something else. The urgency of the beep became more painful in the ears. Calysta, who woke up by all those sounds, looked at me for an answer. I anxiously watched the front door and counted the seconds for the nurse or doctor to show up, then the beeping became a flat and constant screech.

I didn't wait for anyone anymore. I just started doing the CPR. I pressed her delicate chest down in the hope she would come back. No change. I pushed again, and her lifeless body refused to come back. Her closed eyes were still closed. I was trying to save those memories. I wanted to make more of it. I pressed down again. Those moments of her sweet laughter filled my ears. I didn't hear anything else. I was in a trance. I pushed down and lost count of how many it was. I wasn't ready to lose that sweet face of hers. I didn't want her only in my memory. I wanted to see her grow old. I wanted to see the things she wanted to be. At that moment, I didn't care what but just wanted more time with her.

Then I felt some people trying to pull me away from her. I wanted to continue doing that no matter for how long. For the rest of my life? I didn't care. I wanted to do it. They took me away. They pleaded that I stay away. I went and sat beside Valerio's bedside. I felt so defeated. I took the small hand of Valerio for my own comfort.

A continuous beep started from Valerio's monitor as well.

Calysta's condition got much worse after that day. I couldn't tell it was days or months after that awful night. What could I say? The cries she made was like a rainy day that would've softened rocks and stone. Those who went through it know how it is. They know that it doesn't matter how much I write about the departed people; it wouldn't be enough. The magnitude of sadness or hole the departed made can only be understood by those same fate-driven people.

She kept herself devoid of everything. She would feel guilty if a smile came to her lips. All the foods became poisonous to her, add to that she did not eat. However, if it were the actual poison, she would take it in a heartbeat. The amount she took in by the constant begging from me and everyone else, her body wouldn't accept that betrayal and vomit it out. She didn't have much before she became so sick. During that ordeal, even when she tried to stay strong for her children, she lost much and became hollow of what she was. After her children's departure, she became the definition of a walking corpse. All the nutrition she was getting was only through the serum. She was walking with a stand that held that serum all the time. Her life became like a broken record, a continuous loop of doing the same thing all day, every day.

When she woke up, she was disappointed that she was still alive. She wouldn't come out of her bed. She only moved out of her bed to go to the bathroom or to be with me in another room. More often, when she came to me, it was only to continue her sleep in my arms. She would sit on my lap and rest her head on my chest, and there, she would dream of not waking up again. I don't know which one was the brutal one, the disease or her. Why wouldn't she fight for me even a bit? Just enough to give me a little hope she would defeat it. I witnessed how her eyes became lifeless. Those eyes that had me under her spell for so long were empty of life and happiness. The smile became a stranger to her lips. A ghoulish voice replaced her soft and delicate voice when she tried to speak. Her body was either too hot or too cold when I touched her skin.

She rested her head on my chest. I could feel her warm breath on my chest. She was sitting on my lap. It brought tears to my eyes to see her in that state. She sounded sleepy, but now and then, she was coughing. Her head moved a little bit; her head fell back a little bit the way that her lips were angled toward my neck. Now I felt her breath on my neck. My left hand was like a supporter for her back, and with another hand, I was stroking her hair slowly with such care to not wake her up. She liked it. She always did. She told me that it helped her with her headache. Now her lips were touching my collarbone. I could hear her heavy breathing on my neck. With each breath, there was a whistling sound coming out of her. I was sitting on the bed and sitting back to the wall with her on my lap. She cuddled herself in me. She was like a bird that was shaking from the cold. Her skin turned to a ghostlike white. I was sitting on the bed and not even able to see her. My tears blocked my view. ***I have to be strong. I have to be strong for her. I can't let her see my tears. She had had enough of that,*** I thought. I stroked her hair to distract myself so I could stop crying. I tucked myself a little so that I could pamper her more. Then with a lot of care, without waking her up, I put my right hand under her knees. That way, I could lay down her feet on the bed while she had her head on my shoulder. I lay down with her carefully by having my arm as her pillow. She didn't wake up. Now her forehead was toward my neck, and she was breathing to my chest. I knew the time was coming. I wanted to cry, but the cry was locked in my throat. I wanted to scream, but I didn't have the breath for it. I was hopelessly lying down and watching her. I could hear the heavy breath she was taking. I kissed her forehead and felt how hot her head was.

One second, I was watching Calysta sleeping, and another second, my eyes went black.

I was woken up by the cell phone ring.

"Hello?" I answered the phone.

"Hello, is this Mr. Adalbert?" a female voice asked me on the phone.

"Yes?" I answered and was curious who she was.

"I am calling from the hospital, and I am afraid I have bad news for you."

"WHAT?" I shouted.

Calysta opened her eyes to see what had happened. Her eyes were tired, even though she just woke up from sleep.

I sat on the bed, and my ears were in complete focus.

"Do you know Mar . . ." My ears blocked the rest of the sentence. My brain was racing to full speed.

I was dazed by the news, like a boxer who got knocked out and didn't know where the up was or where the down was; everything was cycling around my head.

"Hello? Hello? Are you all right?" she asked. What kind of stupid question was that?

Was it adrenaline or curiosity? I don't know, but it made me stand up and leave the room. I left Calysta in her bed. I went to another room and closed the door to muffle any noise.

"All right, tell me, how can I help?" I asked.

"We need you to come here," she said. She then proceeded to tell me which hospital they were in.

After I hung up the phone, I called Bernadina and told her to meet me there.

I went back to Calysta and didn't know what to do. There was not much life in her. Any bad news or stress would speed up her end. When I walked into her room, she looked at me with curiosity. It had been such a long time that I saw anything at all in those eyes.

"Is . . ." She coughed. "Is . . ." She continued coughing. I went and lay down beside her. I started caressing her head and back to relax her. In the middle of coughing, she still tried to tell me something.

"I know. I know. I'm here. I know what you are trying to ask me. As soon as I know it myself, I'll let you know as well," I promised her. I didn't know what to do. The news was bad enough to make me sick; it would end her.

The decision itself was like one of those paradoxical questions that philosophers were trying to solve in centuries, such as, Can God create something so heavy he can't lift it? If he does or doesn't, it wouldn't matter. His absolution would be questioned.

Now I was facing such a question as well. Should I tell her or not? If I put the question out there in the world, it will divide the world into two groups: those who wanted to share that news with her for many reasons, including the important one, that it was her right, and those who wouldn't like to share for the apparent reason that it would make her much sadder than she was. It wasn't right to do that to someone who was at her end as well.

In the end, it was my decision to make. She didn't have much left in this world. I believe the only thing she had left was her trust. Was it the selfish or kind part of me that didn't want to share the news? I don't know, but I didn't want to take away the only thing she had in life, her trust.

"Do you like to stay here until I come back? Or do you want to come with me?" I asked her gently. I still didn't tell her what had happened. I hoped she would find out by herself.

"Come . . ." She coughed. "I'm coming . . .," she said through all those coughs. I nodded my head and started patting and massaging her back.

It took us a while to change her into new clothing. I used a wheelchair to take her to my car. I put her in the front seat and tucked her wheelchair in the trunk. I hooked her serum to the hook in the car's doorframe.

"What . . ." She started coughing again. I put my hand on her shoulder to reassure her and nodded my head to show I understood what she tried to ask.

"I prefer not telling you. I just want you to find out yourself," I said with a sad tone. She was still coughing but nodded her head to tell me she agreed or understood me. I patted her back a little more. When her cough eased, I drove to the hospital.

She put her hand on mine while it was on the manual gear shift. Even though it would be logical that she would be the one on the receiving end of the comfort and empathy, she was the one giving it.

I shook the tears out of my eyes' side, those that didn't know the right time to show themselves.

We arrived at the hospital. I untucked the wheelchair and installed the stand behind it so that it could hold the serum. I wheeled her toward the hospital entrance. Using the special ramp for the wheelchair, we went inside. At the reception, I didn't know what to do. If I said the names, she would know what happened to who.

However, I made my choice.

I looked back at Calysta. My heart broke for what was about to happen.

"I'm looking for Marshal and Aiko. They are here for the accident," I told the receptionist. She directed me to another section of the hospital. I looked back to Calysta to see her in tears. Her coughs became more severe. I went on my knees so I could be at her level.

"Please, I know it isn't easy, but control yourself. We don't know what happened and how they are. You don't need to be worried now," I begged her. Her coughing and tears didn't stop. I knew it was a mistake; I knew how she would react to the news, yet my punishment continued. I turned to the receptionist and asked her to call a doctor or a nurse. The disgusted look she gave me for bringing a sick person like that in a hospital to share that kind of news stayed in my mind to this day.

A doctor came and gave her a sedative to calm her down. The doctor made sure to point out how stupid I was to share that news.

When they took her away from me to lay her down on the bed, I went with them to the room. They laid her down and transferred the serum from the wheelchair stand to the bedside stand.

I felt miserable.

After staying beside her bed for a few minutes, I went to the section where the receptionist had directed me earlier. There, I didn't need to look for Bernadina. She ran to me and started crying in my arms. She hugged me tightly and didn't lift her head from my chest.

"They . . . they are all gone," she managed to say. Whole new tears and cries came to her. My eyes didn't need any cue from me. We forgot that we were grown up. We were crying like two children who fell on the ground and, for the first time, saw blood. We were crying and cursing this unfair world. We cried because there was nothing else to do. This unjust world let the guy who drank his fill and disregarded the safety of others and caused a chain accident, which sandwiched Marshal's car, to walk out of it but killed Marshal and his family and many others.

This is the kind of world we are living in.

We sat on a bench. I lent my shoulder to her head. After all that crying, the reality set in.

We became lonelier than before. Our group reduced or would be reduced to two.

"How is Calysta?" she asked. She still refused to raise her head from my shoulder.

"She is here," I answered her. She raised her head and looked at me in disbelief. She knew Calysta didn't want to stay in the hospital. She wanted to come home with me. Even worse, she refused to go through chemo.

"What is she doing here?" she asked me, and the worry in her eyes told me that maybe her condition had gotten worse. She didn't suspect that I was that much stupid to bring her here for the news.

"She is in one of those rooms. Do you want to go there?" I said and gave up thinking altogether.

"Don't you want to see them for the last time?" she asked me curiously.

"This universe turned every good memory of mine to sour. I don't want to tarnish theirs," I responded.

I was pulverized and crushed in every way. I gave up. It didn't matter what I did; the universe showed me that it could hurt me more. It was such a messed-up game the world likes to play. On the other hand, I thought it was absurd to believe that the whole universe revolved around me or humankind, but how could I not take it personally? It seemed to me that it set out to torture me personally. No wonder there are so many religions around the world. Even the most isolated tribe in Africa or Amazon found themselves believing in something. How can we see such brutality and callousness and not blame anyone for it?

I gave her the room number where Calysta was and left her there to say goodbye to her friends for the last time.

I went back to Calysta and took a seat close to her bed. She was sleeping peacefully, but now and then, she coughed in her sleep.

I took her hand in mine and put my head on it. I needed someone to comfort me, to let me be a human. I felt the weight of the world on my shoulders.

I don't know how long I was like that, but then I heard the footsteps behind me. I knew who it was, so I didn't rush to lift my head. I felt her hand on my shoulder.

"Is she okay?" Bernadina asked. I lifted my head and kissed Calysta's hand.

"I don't know. I don't think she will survive this news," I said with great pain.

"Are you going to tell her?" she whispered in anger and surprise. It was more like yelling.

I came clean to her and told her how she insisted on being involved. I didn't care about the look of disappointment she gave me. How could a beggar be more humiliated than he was?

I ignored her questions and her anger. "Come and sit here. She would be happy to see someone else than me," I said to her.

"Are you going somewhere?" she asked. I noticed her eyes were full of tears.

"No, I'm just staying here," I said and went to the window.

"You didn't answer me. Are you going to tell her?" she asked persistently.

"Until then, I don't know. I hope she figures it out by herself or not at all. Until that time, I don't know," I responded.

She looked at me with revulsion. "How could you be such a heartless and an ass? When did you become like this?" she asked. She was angry at me. She needed to be mad at someone; why not me? She felt alone, and for that, she cried. For me, I was giving up on everything. How could I taste happiness and know that it would be crushed to dust? How could I just cry it out like Bernadina when I knew it wouldn't solve anything? It wouldn't bring back my parents. It wouldn't get back those children full of lives—Meleta, Valerio, and now Nadine and Albert. Those tears only trick me into thinking that one day a smile would replace it. How could I be like Bernadina and, at the same time, envy her for handling the problem better than me? I didn't want her to be like me.

I went to her and kissed her on top of the head.

"Just be more patient with me. Right now, I don't know if I'm making the right decisions. You were close friends to each other. What do you think Calysta wants now? Does she want us to deceive her in the last moment of her life or to be honest with her?" I asked her in a way that didn't sound condescending.

"I don't know. It won't change anything if she finds out but bring more distress to her. I don't want to see her crying when . . . when . . ." Her sobbing was obvious what she tried to say.

"Just like a soldier in a battle that is dying and looking for someone to tell him that he will be all right, isn't it?" I agreed with her. She nodded.

I kissed her on top of her head to thank her and went back to the window. It had a depressing view. All those lights from the darkness of night were indicating that many people stood awake. How many of them were staying awake for their loved ones, like me? How many of them were staying awake to comfort a child from the nightmares they had? How many of them were staying awake to be wasted on working? What was the benefit of me working so hard just to make the departure of a loved one easy? How many of them were staying awake because they couldn't sleep when they were thinking about or awoke from the hunted memories of dear ones?

How many?

"Berna, you are here?" She started coughing again.

"Don't, just don't," Bernadina begged her not to stress herself out. Maybe she was telling that to herself out loud.

"Marsha . . ." She coughed. "Ai . . ." She coughed more severely.

"They are all all right. It was just a minor accident. You know Aiko. She will kill you herself if she finds out that you are stressing yourself out like this," she lied beautifully and naturally. Calysta's cough didn't stop though. I think she was trying to laugh.

When did her coughs become like a Morse code to me?

She turned and looked at me while coughing, but it became milder. When her eyes locked on me, it became accusatory. She dared me to lie to her. I would rather die and lie to her now.

"She is accusing you of lying," I said to Bernadina. Her look changed to a person who had just been betrayed by the most trusting person she knew.

"You dare that. I never thought you had it in you," Bernadina said as if she had been hurt for the accusation, but she went and kissed her dying friend's cheek. The watery eyes of hers started a new set of tears.

"Berna . . ." Her cough continued.

"I know. I know," she said while crying her eyes out. Sometimes she looked away to hide her tears from Calysta, but she looked back again to see her friend and make sure she was okay. Calysta put her hand on her friend to comfort her.

"Marshal would say that this is hot," I commented. Bernadina was laughing and crying at the same time. Calysta had a smile on her face while coughing, which became her laughter now. Bernadina looked at me with eyes full of tears to thank me. I only nodded.

A few minutes later, the doctor came to give her another dose, but Calysta shook her head and then looked at me.

"She wants to go home, and she doesn't want another one," I said to the doctor like a translator.

"Are you sure?" The doctor tried again. She nodded her head for confirmation.

"All right," he said and looked at me as if I had something to do with that decision, then he left.

I brought the wheelchair with its stand to take Calysta home.

"Do you want to come with us?" I asked Bernadina.

"No, I don't," she said apologetically.

"Are you sure? I'll let you two sleep in my old bedroom," I asked. I thought maybe she felt that she was intruding on us by being there. Calysta laughed with her cough, and Bernadina smiled. After all the crying, she had a genuine smile, but it turned sour. I guess Bernadina felt guilty for having that smile. She looked at her friend and then at me.

"Are you sure?" she asked me.

"Are we sure?" I asked Calysta. Her coughing laugh and nodding were our answers.

I drove us home and left behind our friends. It was a quiet drive. I let Bernadina make the call to our friends' close relatives at an appropriate time. I didn't have the heart to talk to them. If I did, Calysta would know something was up if she already didn't guess. We arrived at our destination. I handled Calysta, who was featherweight, and lifted her and put her in the wheelchair. It felt like I was lifting bones rather than a human. Bernadina followed us and opened the door for us. I wheeled her to our home.

Then as I promised, I lifted her to take her to my room. She looped her hands around my neck. She rested her tired head on my chest and coughed softly. Bernadina was following us by holding up the serum. I laid her down on the bed behind that shelf. She looked at me appreciatively. I just nodded and left those two friends together.

Later that night, I went to check up on her. I saw both of them hugging each other like sisters. Bernadina had a trace of tears on her face, while Calysta was coughing smoothly and had a smile on her lips. Her eyes were still closed.

It was an unintentional good thing that Bernadina came with us. She smuggled out my black suit.

As I predicted, Bernadina handled their relatives. She helped them organize the funeral, and as usual, the close relatives to the deceased left the grave with a heavy heart, and the rest were there for courtesy. Marshal's and Aiko's relatives each found my embrace to cry on. They were old. They were ready to leave this world with a big smile knowing that their children would be fine, and now they were leaving with a broken heart. They were going to be tortured by their memories longer than my Calysta.

"Do you know why I chose the name Aiko for my daughter?" Aiko's father asked me.

"No, but it was a beautiful and fitting name for her," I answered.

"The irony is that it actually fits her now. Before I met Aiko's mother, I met a young girl in another country. I was a young ship captain back then. We fell in love, and I had a thousand dreams. We dreamed, and we planned. One of those plans was, in the next trip back to her, we would go and get married. When I came back, I found out that she had died in a car accident. Her Name was Aiko. Every time I called her name, my good memories from the past would rise from the ashes. Even though she had the look and temper of my wife, but that name was the only link that I had to the past. I was selfish to think that her name would outlive me, but now . . .," he said to me and broke down. I only could offer my sympathy. I don't know why he shared that with me. Maybe because someone close to me was dying as well.

It was true when someone said, "The whole life is two days: the day that passed and the day that hasn't come yet." We are living in the memories of the past, and we waste today for fear of tomorrow. Is this it? Is this what being a human means?

I couldn't spend more time with them. They understood why. I had to get back to Calysta.

I borrowed Bernadina's home key and went there to change into regular clothing before going home.

She imprisoned herself in the room and couldn't see me in black, but I didn't want to risk it. I would leave the key under the vase for Bernadina.

I went back to Calysta and dismissed the nurse after thanking her for taking care of the most precious person in the world for me.

I went to Calysta and lay down beside her. I didn't care what tomorrow would bring; I wanted that moment to be with Calysta. I thought I was smart, but it took me a long time to learn that lesson. I wanted to treasure every moment with her. She breathed heavily and sounded asleep.

It was in those precious moments of the day and night that I was hugging her, and it was in those moments that I didn't hear her suffering for breathing any longer.

Her eyes were closed when she left me.

I became too familiar with this place where those dear people close to my heart left me behind. I came back again with the black suit. The girl who stole my heart and broke it to pieces, she came back and gave me a short moment of euphoria, only to tarnish it to nothingness again. I looked at the Casket that was holding her in.

The priest who was only different in facial feature was reciting from that black book. I had Calysta's mom on my left side, and on my right, Bernadina was sitting.

"Is there anyone who wants to tell us about this wonderful mother and daughter?" the priest said and ignored the history I had with her. I took out a piece of paper and went there to replace the priest. The priest gave himself a self-acclamation and gave the spot to me.

"We had a tradition for our celebration. Instead of buying a gift for any occasion, we had to do something else. Grow a flower from its seeds to its blossom and give that flower as a gift than buying a neckless. I bought her jewelry, of course, but it wouldn't be for our anniversary or birthday. My excuse to buy anything for her was because I saw it and she came to my mind and I had to buy it. That way, our gifts had more meaning to them. I don't want to bore you with details of the past. This piece of paper that I'm holding is one of those gifts that I first gave to her on our anniversary, then she had the audacity to gift it back to me on my birthday," I said to the crowd. It wasn't for them though. I just wanted to recall that moment in her memory. Some of them laughed though. "She also told me that I topped my gifts by giving her this one. She also said there wouldn't be any gift in this world that could be an answer for this present. She begged me to exchange this gift for each other for the rest of our anniversary or our celebration. As usual, she would get what she wanted." I stopped so people could grasp what I just said.

"Now a little background about this gift. I had a colleague in university who teaches the Persian language. One day, when he was trying to tell one of his students the author's intent was different from what it seems to be on the surface, it made me curious about that conversation. For example, when the author talked about love, he was referring to his love for God or nature, but earthly love could be there too. The beauty of that kind of poem is like a painting. In its original language, it had rhythm in it like music, and inside of those beautiful words, there are many references and meaning," I said with a calm voice.

"He had me in painting. It made me curious enough to ask the name of the author and which poem he was referring to," I said and smiled at those memories. "This was my gift for her. I had to learn a different language to understand that poem and translate it for our anniversary. It wasn't easy, but it was worth every bit of it. You may not understand what I'm reading, but this is the best I could do to capture the meaning and the rhyme. I guess you all should have that journey yourself to understand it all." Then I cleared my throat and started reading it:

One night when I couldn't get a bit of shut-eye,

I heard the conversation between a candle and butterfly.

"That if I burn, I am the lover, and that is meet,

Into The Embrace Of Fire

but why do you weep and greet?"

The candle said, "O', my poor marra,[1]

I lost my sweet gabba.[2]

Since Shirin abandoned me,

Like Farhad, grief's flames scorched me."[3]

As the candle said with a flood of soreness,

Her pain was coming down on her yellowish face.

"You aren't a lover

since you can't give yourself over.

You 'scaped from a tiny ardor.[4]

I stood to burn my whole body to the core.

If love put your wings into ignite,

look at me, from my feet to head is on light."

All night, it was this conversation.

Till dawn, it made a congregation.

---

1 *Marra* means "friend."
2 *Gabba* means "Companion."
3 There is a pun and double meaning here. Shirin is a name, and it means "sweet," which implies the fact that a candle loses sweetness or beeswax when it burns, but it also implies the name of a heroine in old Persian Stories. When Farhad loses the heroine of the story, in sorrow and misery, he jumped to his death.
4 *Ardor* means "fire." In here, I changed the pronunciation from /ärdər/ to /ärdôr/ for the rhyme.

Not much left from the darkness,

That a Pari[5] face killed her eagerness.

As she was saying and dying, a smoke on her head was retiring.

"Young man, this is the end of my yearning.

You'll learn that the time when you are caring.

Don't shed tears on the grave of an admirer, be smiling.

That this has been accepted by that darling.

If you are infected by the love, don't cure it.

Like Sa'adi,[6] give up on it.

A true lover isn't afraid of his goals.

He accepts a storm of rocks and arrows.

Don't go to the ocean, be warned.

If you do, giving up to storm is owned."

Slowly I closed the paper and went down on my knees to get a fist of dirt. Then carefully, I went forward and put that paper on the casket and poured the earth on top of the paper and the coffin.

"I guess you'll be the one to receive this gift after all. You always had it your way." The tears were there. "Goodbye, my *Homo pulcher.*"

---

5   The *Pari*, in Persian mythology, is a description of fairy beings but malevolent. They fell from the grace of heaven and are banished until they redeem themselves for what they did.
6   Sa'adi is the name of the person who wrote the poem.

Final Chapter

The world is a place that either makes someone laugh for its absurdity or causes that person to be sad, dejected, and sorrowful.

A man walks down the street half or fully naked. Someone could laugh at his free spirituality, or that person could get sad to see another human being in that situation. This life and universe with all that folly and incongruity work like a magician or an alchemist. It turns and transforms anything into something else. Some people who were rich all their lives become poor and a vagabond. It turns a sad thing like a death of a star into something as beautiful as a Nebula.

A man like me who is sitting in the park and painting to just visit his past, either it makes me look like a pervert or creepy in the eyes of some families or an inspiring model for the young one. I already painted two of three paintings of the exact location. During the painting of those, I was approached by many people. Some of them came to see a man at work and enjoyed the process, something they usually see in many other places. Be it in a museum, an art gallery, or shops/stores, they only saw the finished ones. They didn't witness how an artist combines different colors to create another color or shadow something to make it realistic—all those tricks and tools to deceive the eyes, all that for the realistic painting. For surrealism, which could show the convoluted mind of an artist, another set of tricks needed to be applied. First, I tried to paint a realistic picture of the same place that I visited often. Some families got anxious when they saw a resemblance of themselves in that painting. They asked me why I was painting them and their children. My answer was that in that moment and place, that was the thing I was observing. I talked to those annoying people while I was painting. I didn't mind talking to them. That would fulfill my daily practice of talking to strangers. I hit two birds with one stone.

The second painting of the same place was more abstract. Even though it was in the middle of summer, I started painting it like it was in the middle of winter. The snow was falling, and the park was empty of people. This time, it attracted another type of people. They were curious to know why I was painting snow and not the people, and my answer was that I tried that and people didn't like it. However, I finished that painting. Still, it hurt me to see so much distrust from people. I also explained to them the reason behind painting the park in the snow was so people could leave me alone in peace. It didn't matter; they came and talked to me. Again, I didn't mind that; it was just wishful thinking anyway.

The third painting I was working on was a more apocalyptic and dystopian version of the park. The trees and grasses were burnt. The equipment in the park was either broken or rusted. Some benches were melted. That kind of creativity invited another type— the curious and anxious ones. They wanted to know why I was painting such a horrific picture. My answer to them was that I felt and wanted to do it that way. This time, they involved the police. The police came and asked me why I was painting such a thing, and my answer to them was the same. However, it didn't stop people from coming to me and asking me the same question over and over again. A logical person would think if a person doesn't want to be bothered with anyone, why not take a picture and do his painting in his home or other places that people can't bother him?

My answer to those people would be that I learned my lesson from the past that life seems logical, but most of the time, it isn't. When we start thinking that the whole universe is in order and runs by logic, we find a phenomenon that questions everything we know. Back to the question, why not take a picture instead of a brush on canvas? Because it would still attract those people who were suspicious. To their eyes, I would be creepier. I took pictures of many landscapes and parks; still, many concerned people sent their "Man" to handle me or see what I was up to. As if I were anything close to what they thought of me to be, I would confess.

"Hello," a female with a Londoner accent said.

Great, now I have to talk to a concerned mother, I thought.

"Hi." I didn't even try to look at her.

"Wow, that is depressing and sad. Why would you paint such a thing?" she asked me.

"For my amusement, my imagination, and my entertainment are good reasons for me," I answered. Then I felt a drop of weight on the bench. Her perfume attacked my nose. I still didn't look at her. It would only encourage them to make the conversation longer.

"I hope you didn't mind that I sat here," she said unapologetically. I just threw up my shoulder to show that I didn't care. I continued painting.

"If I remember, your other paintings were more . . . what is the word that I'm looking for?" she said to herself. I ignored her comment. There were some who actually saw my other two paintings, and they commented about those as well. She was one of them perhaps.

"Am I bothering you?" she asked.

"Not more than others," I replied. I heard her chuckle.

"That painting was full of different animals and combined in a different color. It was dreamy," she said. That made me pause a moment. She probably recognized me for my other works. I did receive those compliments a lot, but I was in different locations. It just surprised me to hear that after so many years of finding a hiding place from another type of pesky people. Those were the worst. They would go on forever to explain their feelings, the amusement, and the good memories they carried when they came across those paintings. That was a good case. There was another one who wouldn't leave my side. They wanted to follow me anyplace I was going, even in the bathroom, if I let them. There was another one who just wanted to have an experience with famous people. They would go to the extreme. It was a sad thing to see.

Anyway, which group of fans she was, I didn't know. Also, I knew that my time in this was getting shorter before every fan of mine came and gawked at me while I was painting. There it goes, another place that is going to be on my blacklist.

"I guess lots of people are bothering you as I do now, isn't it?" she asked. I could've been rude and shown my annoyance, but to what end? She won't be sorry for what she did in the sense that she did something wrong. She'd be sorry for herself that she wasted her time with someone like me.

"Tell me, what do you see in this painting?" I asked her so we could change the subject.

"I see you painted this park, but it has been burnt and abandoned," she said.

"Why?" I asked her. I could sense her smile.

"I don't know. Maybe there was a fire or an incident. Is that right?" she asked.

"There is no wrong answer or right answer in painting," I educated her.

"Oh, that's right," she said to show me she knew all along. She wanted to keep her pride intact.

There was silence for a moment, and I enjoyed that moment.

"What is your answer though?" she asked.

"I don't understand your question," I responded.

"What is your perspective in this painting? What do you see?" she asked.

"I don't think my answer would be that satisfactory."

"Try me," she challenged me.

"This is my hell," I said, and it made her laugh. Again, I didn't look at her. That would invite another approach from her. I continued painting.

"Why don't you look at the person you are talking to?" she asked me. **Because I still have a brain**, I thought.

"This painting needs my full attention. I don't want any distraction," I said politely.

"Oh, so I'm a distraction now, aren't I?" she asked. I just showed her my disinterest by raising my shoulder up and down.

"How do you know if it's a friend or a foe you are talking to?" she asked.

"Right now, I don't care about either of them. However, I know that my friends wouldn't bother me when I'm focusing on doing something," I responded.

"Oh," she said with a sad tone. Nonetheless, I didn't care about some stranger. I tried my best not to be rude to her, but she forced me to do it.

"Maybe another time then," she said at last. The excitement in her voice was gone. I didn't answer her. I hoped that would be our last meeting.

"Agustin, I told you not to ignore me," she said with a firm voice. That phrase sounded familiar to me. Then it came to me. I looked at her. There she was. She was wearing a sleeveless summer dress. Her long dark-brown hair was gathered on one side of her shoulder. I knew two angry hazel eyes were behind those sunglasses. The hat on her head just added more beauty to her.

"Marina?" I asked. I smiled. I was in total disbelief. She wasn't amazed by that.

"I thought you didn't like to see a friend at this time, IF I am one of them," she said. I ignored her silly comment. I knew that she was my friend, and she knew that too.

"Come and sit here. You have no idea how glad I'm to see you," I responded.

"Are you sure? I thought you didn't want to be bothered," she said. Even though I knew she was being unreasonable, I didn't take any of it to heart.

"Is this your concern?" I pointed at the painting. She didn't answer. I kicked the stand, and there it went, the artwork. It fell to its doom. I looked back at her and saw her mouth was wide open in disbelief. The way she looked at me, it was as if I had lost all my faculties.

She went to the painting and tried to pick it up. While she was doing that, she told me that I was crazy and asked me the reason behind it.

"You wouldn't believe me if I just told you," I accused her. She pouted to hide her smile.

After putting back the painting on the stand, she came and sat beside me, much closer than before.

"You didn't have to do that," she said. This time, she couldn't hide her smile.

"That painting is ruined now, but I like it this way. This ruined painting will be more treasure to me now. It will remind me of the day and moment that I met you again," I told her honestly. She attacked me with a hug and kissed me on both cheeks.

"I see. You still have that old charm of yours," she said. I laughed at her comment, and she laughed with me. It had been such a long time that I had this much fun.

A few years passed from that meeting.

Now she is resting her chin on my shoulder and watching me type the last words of my story.

Now she is biting me gently on my shoulder and telling me to stop reporting what she is doing. She doesn't understand that moments like these are treasures to me. I always remember them wherever I am or whenever I think of her. Even though my lesson from the past was brutal and harsh, but I learned from it.

CPSIA information can be obtained
at www.ICGtesting.com
Printed in the USA
BVHW091020190222
629447BV00001B/1